OUT OF SIGHT

CHERRY ADAIR

RANDOM HOUSE
LARGE PRINT

*The Library of Congress has established a
Cataloging-in-Publication record for this title*

0-375-43259-0

www.randomlargeprint.com

FIRST LARGE PRINT EDITION

10   9   8   7   6   5   4   3   2   1

This Large Print edition published in accord
with the standards of the N.A.V.H.

This one is for my brother,
Ric Noyle.
You were my very first hero, Ric-a-boy.
Ek het jou lief my klein broertjie.

A special thanks to

The Annie Sullivans.
We'll always have A.S.P.E.N.

T.J. and L.W. Stay safe over there, guys.

The warm and generous people of Cairo, for your help,
and great bits and pieces of interest. *Shukran!*

And as always, for David, with love.

CHAPTER ONE

WEDNESDAY, APRIL 3RD

She might be every man's wet dream, but right now Kane Wright wanted to nail AJ Cooper's beautiful ass to the wall.

A bullet slammed into the ruined wall behind him. Shards of ricocheted limestone stung his face, missing his eye by a blink. He didn't flinch. Hell, barely noticed it in the chaos around them.

"Cooper." He didn't raise his voice despite the volume of firepower lighting up the early-evening sky. The lip mic would transmit the sound of a gnat fart. Exchanged bullets kicked up sand and stone in a cacophony of noise and brilliant white light. "Get your ass back here!"

In lead position, AJ lay flat on her stomach fifty feet ahead of him on a cantilevered rock peninsula high above Raazaq's camp. She was in the ready position, but frozen like a deer in headlights, sniper rifle silent, and *useless*, in her hands.

"N-no," she whispered. Her voice shook on the single word, but she dug her toes into the sand and hunched over the weapon she held with a white-fisted grip.

Hell.

"Not a request. An order." Damn it. Another bullet pockmarked the building beside him and a new shower of rock and plaster rained down on him. The only reason the bullets hadn't struck any of his team was because the terrorist's camp was several hundred feet downhill in the shallow, palm-groved valley below them. The minute Raazaq's men got their hands on something more powerful than rifles, the odds would even up. This was the tangos' terrain; they had the home team advantage.

The element of surprise was shot. Kane and his team were screwed if they didn't wrangle their way out of this mess. Fast.

AJ's swallow sounded loud in his ear. "I can still get him."

"No," he said calmly. "You cannot." *Sharpshooter First Class, my ass.* She'd missed her target.

Hell. *The* target.

A clear shot, and she'd *missed!*

She'd been chosen for her uncanny marksmanship ability, and hurriedly pulled out of boot camp for this op, but clearly she wasn't ready for fieldwork. A little late in the fucking day to find this out. Sniping was a painstaking discipline, and she didn't have the cajônes for the job.

In the space of minutes, Cooper had gone from being Kane's best asset to his biggest liability.

Three separate cylinders of yard-long white flame arced over their heads. A line of tracers sprang from each muzzle flash, allowing the tangos to shoot without a metal sight on their weapons. AJ's slender shoulders went rigid as the ammo impacted close by.

"*Hit the limo,*" Kane ordered Struben and Escobar, as Raazaq's stretch did a wobbly rooster tail in the sand, then sped into the desert. One of his men managed to hit the left back tire. It swerved, but kept going. Shit.

"Hold them off until I get her clear," he told the two men. "Cooper? Take it slowly and ease back, we've got you covered."

Click.

"Did you just turn off your mi—Goddamn it, woman!" Nailing her ass to a fucking wall was just the beginning.

Kane started crawling toward her. Getting on her case right now wouldn't accomplish anything. She was scared. Fear did strange things to people. He recognized the signs.

Beneath the backward black ball cap she wore, her face was a pale oval, sheened with perspiration. Her soft lips, set and grim. The sniper rifle was tucked against her shoulder, her hands in position. But those hands were clenched, and no doubt sweating to beat the band. Kane had seen the same look from other rookies over the years.

Paralyzed with terror.

Rendered useless.

On some training op, that would be no big deal.

Tonight, she'd fucked it up for all of them.

Great. Just fucking great. This was all he needed.

In a training situation he'd have felt compassion and talked the rookie through it. God only knew, been there, done that. But this op was too critical, too time sensitive to mollycoddle anyone. She had to get her shit together. And she had to do it now.

A sharpshooter terrified to discharge her weapon.

Something his superiors had conveniently omitted in the briefing when they'd convinced him, against his better judgment, that she was invaluable to this operation.

Goddamn it.

"It's over, rookie," he told her evenly, overriding her control of her own mic. Her breathing was fast and shallow in his ear. He felt a faint pull of sympathy, which he instantly quashed. "Surprise is shot. We're pinned down. Pull back. Now."

Click. "I c-can do it."

If her hands shook as badly as her voice, they'd be lucky if her bullet hit something in the same country. "I gave an order, Cooper. The limo split. Your target's gone. Now get the hell back here."

More muzzle flares lit up the sky, filling the air with the thick smell of ozone and cordite. Twilight, coupled with flying stone and sand, and unpredictable brilliant bursts of light, reduced visibility to near zero. Kane wanted to race across the rubble separating them, grab the woman by the scruff of her neck, and . . . what?

Hell if he knew. Get her out of the line of fire, for one thing.

"Cooper. Pull back!" Radio silence throbbed in his ear once more. "Goddamn it, woman, turn on your mic and talk to me." The sky lit up with another artillery round. Score one for our side. *Good man, Escobar.*

This was a waste of ammunition. Time to bail.

The op had gone tits up soon after the four-man team inserted two hours ago. The sun was mercifully setting, but the temp still hovered in the high nineties. He, of all people, should've known this break had been too easy. Too pat.

Sweat stung his eyes. His shirt clung to his skin like a shroud. And if he didn't get Cooper fully functioning PDQ, a shroud was what they'd all be wearing. Soon.

In the distance, the night skyline of Cairo made for a strange juxtaposition between the crumbling ancient ruins where they were taking cover and the world of modern-day Egypt.

Five hundred yards below them, Raazaq's camp was lit up like Ramadan and Christmas combined. When they'd arrived on this ruined little hilltop citadel, Kane had counted four all-terrain vehicles in the terrorist camp. Also, incongruously, the long, black stretch limo, which was now gone, and approximately thirty turbaned heads. Raazaq's people were armed to the teeth, and well trained.

Time to get the good guys the hell outta Dodge. Kane signaled Escobar and Struben. They signaled back. *Acknowledged.*

AJ's entire body was backlit as a mortar shell exploded just this side of the rise. They'd brought out the big guns.

Close. Too damn close.

What the hell was she *thinking? Move, damn it!* She hadn't budged in three minutes. Even from yards back, and in the iffy light, he saw the whiteness of her knuckles as she clutched the Dragunov. *What you planning to do, Cooper? Club them to death? Shoot, damn it, shoot!*

"Escobar," he muttered, and the other man's head jerked up. "Get her."

"Yo." Escobar, closer to the left and above the rookie, slid down the wall and inched his way toward Cooper's position.

Night slammed down, black and deadly. Dusk didn't last long in the desert. Escobar inched up beside Cooper, but she didn't acknowledge his presence. Probably didn't even hear him with the noise all around them.

Kane's annoyance had evolved into a serious case of pissed. She still wasn't acknowledging his order, or even noticing that her incompetence had forced him to send another team member to grab her ass out of the fire. She was shaking hard enough to make the sand vibrate and clutching the weapon as if she still had something to offer the op. Shit! She was endangering them all. Kane discharged a volley of shots over their heads, laying down cover fire.

Escobar grabbed her shoulder. Startled, Cooper whipped round and slammed her elbow up hard into his jaw at exactly the same moment a bullet slammed into his upper arm. She'd already turned back to the action before

Escobar went down like a rock—from her blow, not the bullet. His weapon bounced off a cracked wall and skittered into the dirt to land three feet away as he slumped against the ruins like a Saturday night drunk.

"Shit." Kane started belly-crawling toward them. Fast. Why the hell had he let them talk him into bringing Cooper in on this mission? Not only was she unseasoned, she was insubordinate and un-fucking-predictable.

He crawled faster, past his injured operative—he'd live—over rocks the size of his fist, over jagged bits of broken brick, cursing under his breath every inch of the way. He grabbed Cooper's waistband in his right fist, put his left arm up to protect his head from her instinctive jab, and hauled her backward just as the crumbling wall beside her exploded in a shower of fragments.

Burying his face against her sweaty back, he covered her head with his arms. She struggled beneath him, all sharp bones and prickly attitude. "*Now* I get your attention? A little goddamn late, Cooper."

"Get off me, I told you I could do it."

Kane pressed her flat with his hands and body until the hail of bullets moved on.

"Off." AJ spat out a mouthful of dirt, and managed to turn her head so her cheek, instead of her nose, pressed into the ground. Her eyes stung, and her heart beat so fast she was terrified she'd hyperventilate and pass out. Nausea rose in everincreasing waves.

She'd missed Raazaq. *Missed!*

It was humiliating enough her team knew she was chicken. Manny Escobar and Richard Struben might understand.... But Kane Wright? No way.

To fail her assignment. To fail at something she was *good* at ... and then to fall apart in front of the great Kane Wright, and on their first assignment together ... She blinked grit from her eyes.

Easy shot, Cooper. Easy. Might've even worked if you'd kept your eyes open! Humiliation didn't begin to cover her sense of self-disgust. She could have done it with a second chance. He should've ... No, damn it. *She* should've ...

She'd always admired and respected his reputation. Kane Wright was a T-FLAC legend. He wouldn't've needed a second chance. He'd been her role model since she'd been recruited from the Police Academy last year. She'd transferred her hero worship from her brother, Gabriel, to Kane Wright without even realizing it at the time. He was everything she wanted to be. Damn it, *could* be—*should* be.

"Let me up. I can still get him." A lovely

sentiment if either of them believed it for a second. They both knew Raazaq's people had spirited him out of their camp at the first missed shot. *Her* shot.

AJ shoved at him, but she might as well have tried to shove a mountain off her back. Frustration gathered in her chest, tight as a fist, while her heart pounded hard enough to choke her.

"He's long gone. You had your shot, Cooper. It's over. Now we get the hell out. Fast."

She'd jeopardized the mission and the team. The ultimate sin. "Damn it. I have to finish what I was sent to do."

"A day late, and a bullet short. Two seconds after you killed that lantern, Raazaq was outta there. You snooze, you lose." He was heavy, his breath hot on her cheek. "Now I see why they offered you that desk job. Accept it when you get back. Tomorrow."

She couldn't be tossed out of T-FLAC. She wouldn't. She had a family tradition to uphold. "Just get off me and let me do my job. I can still get his key people."

"Opportunity lost. No do-overs in the real world. Grab your weapons. Op over."

Yeah, she thought, sick with a churning mix of disappointment, fear, and humiliation, *op over.* The sharp metallic scent of blood lingering in the hot night air impinged on her skittering thoughts.

Had Wright taken a bullet? "Were you hit?" she asked frantically. It came out as a hoarse croak.

"Not me. Escobar."

"Manny?" She tried to scan the area to see where Escobar was. See if he needed help. Her visibility was restricted because her face was being smashed into the ground by Kane Wright's weight, and the darkness.

"He'll live." His warm, moist breath fanned against the side of her face. "Grab your weapons and haul ass. Or do I have to repeat every frigging order ten times before you get it? Did you skip that part of your training?" he growled. "You're supposed to follow orders without hesitation. Take a look at Escobar. Your hesitation is the only reason he's got an arm full of lead."

Thanks. Like I need your help to feel like any more of an inept schmuck.

The weight of Kane's body was oppressive, suffocating. Just like his reputation. Her clothing was drenched in sweat, and sand clung like guilt to any exposed skin. "Kinda hard with you on top of me."

He rolled off her and got to his feet, crouching low to keep from skylining himself for the enemy, then turned and held out his hand, presumably to help her up. AJ busied herself staggering to her feet and picked up the Dragunov where it had fallen when he grabbed her. She kicked the spring-loaded bipod back into position, then snatched up her fallen baseball cap, and crammed it, backward, on her head. Lifted the Dragunov to her shoulder . . .

Kane's hand shot out and clamped the muzzle of the sniper rifle in a hard grip. "Quit while you're ahead, Cooper."

This was ahead?

Shit.

She wanted to vomit.

She wanted to disappear.

Oh, God. *Worse.*

She wanted to *cry.*

He gave her a hard look that was easily translated, and released his hold on the rifle with an eloquent downward shove. "Let's do it," he said flatly, heading toward Manny in a low crouch.

Weapons-fire lit up the sky with a series of loud, reverberating bangs and blinding flashes.

"Grab his weapon." Kane stooped, shouldered Escobar in a fireman's lift, then moved crablike, backward, over rock and sand. "Get

the lead out. Struben can't hold them off forever."

She could at least do *this* right. AJ got off a
few covering shots, snatched up Manny's fallen
weapon, then followed Kane, throat tight,
heart galloping as bullets whizzed by, missing
them by a breath. She flinched with every
round.

Struben covered them until they reached his
position. He gave her a contemptuous glance as
they came level. Blood rushed to her cheeks.
No comment necessary. As one, they scrambled
over half walls and obstacles and careened
down the small hill behind the deserted, ancient
village where they'd hidden their vehicle earlier. Machine-gun fire sounded behind them
like a nightmare chasing to catch up.

"Want me to drive?" Struben reached for
the handle.

"In back with Escobar." Kane pulled open
the back door, tossed Escobar on the floorboard, then vaulted over the door on the driver
side.

"Aw, shit. I'd rather sit in front," Struben
complained, hefting his weapon and scowling.
"People around Cooper end up getting shot,
man." He smirked. "Unless you're a bad guy,
that is."

"Front." Wright jabbed a finger at AJ, and to

the other man, "Can the editorial. Get in or you get left behind."

The vehicle was someone's half-assed attempt at a convertible. The top had been removed as if by a giant can opener. A convertible wasn't going to be a whole hell of a lot of protection. Unless it converted into an armored tank.

"Take care of his arm as best you can," Wright told Struben without turning around. The key cranked in the ignition several times before the engine caught. "Then take position. They'll be on our ass as soon as they notice we've split."

Without comment, the other man climbed in back and got to work.

AJ threw her leg over the door and climbed in on the passenger's side. She set the sniper rifle on the floor, switched to her AK-47, then knelt on the seat. She rested her elbows on the seat back and cradled the weapon in suddenly steady hands.

Sure. *Now* she was calm.

Damn it. Up there on the rise it had been a flat wind. Her rifle should've driven tacks.

Breathing slow, measured breaths, like they'd taught her in sniper school, AJ had felt the adrenaline rush as she'd started a slow belly crawl, following her Dragunov across exposed sand to the outcropping overlooking Raazaq's camp.

Easy shot.

Excitement had risen inside her like a groundswell. Like the crescendo in Beethoven's Fifth. Like the sharp, sweet moment just before a climax.

She'd laid her cheek against the sun-heated rock slab, forcing herself to slow. *Discipline,* she told herself. *No need to hurry.* Down below they were preparing the evening meal, oblivious to the four people above them who held their lives in their hands.

Even without her optics, she'd been able to see the sentries down below, cradling blue-steel Ruger assault rifles as they manned the perimeter of the camp. Raazaq and his lieutenants gathered off to one side, drinking thick coffee and planning God only knew what kind of mayhem.

AJ had felt a swell of patriotic pride. By doing her job tonight, thousands of future lives would be spared.

She'd reached forward and flipped the spring-loaded bipod into position, giving her rifle legs. Shoving a small beanbag under the stock to support the weight of her upper body, she settled into position.

I'm here, she'd thought, jazzed beyond belief,

in the field. For real. For God and country. And she'd felt the power of life and death at the pull of the trigger.

Conditioned not to reach past the safety until just the right moment to kill. Left arm folded up beneath her, elbow forward, fingers pinching the beanbag to adjust the angle, she'd watched the sentries circle the camp. Watched as Raazaq drank coffee.

Through the rifle's scope she'd been able to see her target's face with crystal clarity. Swarthy. Hard features. Cold eyes. Slight. Well dressed. Thousand-dollar suit.

The irony of long-range surveillance was the intimacy.

Raazaq had recently had a manicure. His china cup had little blue flowers painted on it. Small details filtered into her brain, making up the whole.

The Dragunov, a gift from her brother, was like an old friend. Certified to shoot a quarter of a mile of angle at two hundred yards. Which meant under perfect conditions, which these were, her rifle could imprint three consecutive rounds in the same hole. *Say good night, Gracie.*

All she had to do was estimate distance, turn the scope to the appropriate number, hold the crosshairs on the Y-shaped veins standing out on Raazaq's forehead, and pull the trigger. Piece of cake.

Her right hand had caressed the grip. Thumb loosely opposite her index finger, squeezing just enough to feel its pebbled texture. She'd set her cheek weld against the stock, finding the eye relief necessary to center the crosshairs in the scope tube.

"Five," Kane had said in her ear, starting the launch sequence.

She'd aligned her body with the recoil path to minimize muzzle jump when a round kicked out at thirty hundred feet per second.

"Four."

She'd pressed her hips to the ground, spread her knees shoulder-width for stability.

"Three."

She'd slid the first bullet into the battery with her index finger so she could feel the seating. The first shot was called a cold bore. An unpracticed leap of faith imprint on a fresh target. She'd pressed the heels of her boots flat to minimize profile.

All outside influences had faded away. Just her and her weapon. Touching. As in tune as two lovers.

"Two—"

God, she'd been ready. . . .

AJ bit her tongue in the here and now as

their vehicle bounced over a sand dune. She snapped to, and tried to concentrate on the current situation. Time enough later to rehash what had happened back there. Or more accurately, what had *not* happened.

Behind them the dark desert floor stretched to infinity. Sand. Sand. And more sand. It wouldn't be long now. . . .

"Still clear," she told the others through her lip mic.

Struben, crouched awkwardly over the footwell, didn't bother to glance up as his hands moved efficiently to stem the flow of blood on his partner's arm.

Escobar opened his eyes as Struben tied off the makeshift bandage. "Heyya, beautiful."

Struben chuckled, since his partner was looking at him when he said it. "Asshole."

Manny shifted his focus to look up at AJ.

"How're you doing, bud?" AJ's voice sounded scratchy with guilt as she made eye contact with him over the back of her seat. *I'm so sorry, Manny.*

Escobar gave her a goofy smile from his prone position. *We're cool.* "Scratch."

A scratch that hurt like a red-hot poker being thrust into your flesh. Over and over and over again. AJ absently rubbed the healing wound on her left shoulder. "Liar."

"Macho." He grinned before admitting, "Hurts like hell." He glanced from AJ to Struben then back again. "Did we get him?"

"Ask Coop," Struben said flatly.

Manny might not've heard the accusation in Struben's voice, but AJ had. The injured man shifted his focus to look up at her again. His face was ghostly pale, sweaty, and covered with sand.

"No," she told him flatly, envying him his ability to take pain without a flinch.

"Back to plan A, huh?"

If Kane Wright allowed her to stay in country to do what she was sent to do, then yes. She shot Wright a sideways glance. His face was as sweaty and sandy as the rest of theirs, his expression closed. The stubble on his rigid jaw made him look sinister and dangerously appealing. AJ gave herself a mental shake. She was in enough trouble without bringing her attraction to him into the mix.

"Plan A," Kane agreed, but before AJ could relax, he added, "with modifications."

Her cheeks flamed, and her temper rose as anger began to overtake humiliation. She pushed it back and tried for calm and rational. "I can do it."

"Forget it." He spoke into his lip mic, so it

sounded as though he were whispering directly into her ear.

AJ shivered. "You're good. But even the great Kane Wright can't pull this one off. You need me."

"Don't bet on it, Sparky." He downshifted and the car lunged forward like an aging tiger after prey. "Just cover the retreat. Assuming you can do that without shooting one of us."

"Up yours," she muttered, and glanced down to see Escobar's wink. At least Manny wasn't blaming her. But then, he didn't have to. She could do that for herself. No matter what Kane might say to their superiors, it wouldn't be enough to best what she was already telling herself. She'd failed. When it had mattered most, she'd come up short.

She'd be damned if she'd prove her family right. She *was* cut out for this line of work. Not only cut out for it, but capable, and good. Damn it.

She wouldn't fail again. Right now she could do her job by protecting their backs. She'd show Kane she wasn't just ballast. AJ braced herself as best she could as the small car shot down the incline in a cloud of dust. Kane hadn't turned on the headlights, and the sliver of a moon was nothing more than a suggestion of cool, pale light in the ink-black sky. The tires bounced and rattled on the shaley ground. There was no road, just sand for miles around.

No one said a word. What was there to say? The fact that they'd found Raazaq's camp was a miracle in itself. It was surprisingly close to the city, but still a ways off the beaten path. Kane had surmised Raazaq's people were laying in supplies before they took off for Fayoum. If they could eliminate Raazaq before he traveled south it would save them a lot of headaches.

Well, thanks to her, they *hadn't* succeeded. They were back to square one.

AJ wanted to breathe a sigh of relief that they'd made it out of there alive despite her screwup. But she knew damn well they weren't safe yet.

"We've got company," she and Struben said in unison as several pairs of headlights crested a rise behind them, illuminating the cloud of sand in their wake. Shots blasted at them as Raazaq's men roared up in their sand spume. Just show. They were too far away, as yet, to make any impact. But that was about to change.

Like everything else Kane Wright did, he drove incredibly well. The car was a piece of crap, but the best they'd been able to commandeer on short notice. Yet Kane made the vehicle corner like a well-oiled machine. Still, the shocks were nonexistent, and AJ bit her tongue several times, tasting the metallic tang of blood, as they bounced over the dunes.

"Savage wouldn't have missed," she said. Like an abscessed tooth, AJ's guilt throbbed relentlessly.

"Damn straight," Wright said tightly.

There was nothing to say to that. Savage, too, was a T-FLAC legend, but the more experienced T-FLAC agent was in a leg cast and stuck in a hospital in South America. Savage would not have missed that shot. Raazaq had been right there in AJ's crosshairs. *Right there.* And she'd bull's-eyed a nearby lantern instead, setting off a small fire, and alerting them to her presence. It was FUBAR of gigantic proportions.

"Can we save the postmortem for later?" AJ shouted over the gunfire and the rattle and clang coming from what was passing as an engine. She kept her weapon trained on their trail, but Raazaq's people hadn't closed the gap sufficiently to waste serious firepower. Yet.

"Sure," Wright said in her ear. "Right now, it would be nice just to stay alive. Tomorrow—damn it," he whipped the car around a small dune, "you go home with Escobar. Struben and I will finish the mission."

"I'm sure T-FLAC will recall me as soon as

you file your incident report. Until then, I'm still part of this team."

"I don't need someone who's gonna freeze."

His voice was its usual controlled and chilly calm, tinged with just a hint of sarcasm. AJ felt as though he'd whipped her with live electrical wire. If she didn't admire him so much, she'd hate him for being so perfect. But she did admire him. And damn it, he was right. She bit her tongue on a smart-ass comeback, and did a quick swipe of her hand down her damp cotton pants to get rid of the clammy sweat on her palm. She had plenty of experience with forceful men. She'd been around them all her life. Her father and brother were just the first of many. But Kane Wright wasn't a man she could wrap around her little finger. Neither did she want to.

Anyway, this was neither the time nor the place to use the womanly wiles she so despised. She'd joined T-FLAC to put her brain and training to use. It was a refreshing change to have a guy not look at her as a sex object. Even if that guy happened to see her as a particularly inept field operative.

"Aw, man! I'm going back?" Manny complained on the mic. He sounded pissed.

"How bad's the arm?" Kane demanded.

There was a long drawn-out silence. "Bad," Manny admitted reluctantly.

"Your woman can kiss it all better when you get home," Kane told him.

"I'd rather—"

"Get your sorry butt off the floor and help cover our ass," Kane finished for him.

Manny scuffled around, then levered himself up beside Struben to give her a clear shot. AJ winced empathetically when he readied his weapon. His arm must hurt like hell. He'd have cold sweats, be feeling light-headed, sick to his stomach . . . but he'd do what he had to do.

Not like her.

Live with it, Cooper. Live with it.

She saw a flash of light, a quick flare behind them. There. Gone, in the thick darkness. A bullet hit the dash behind her, missing her by inches. She bit her lip to keep from screaming. "Closing in," she shouted, unnecessarily, blinking back fear-induced sweat from her eyes.

"Deal with it." The engine whined in protest as Kane demanded more speed. A rooster tail of sand fanned out on either side of the wheels.

They were close.

Too damn close.

Faster vehicles.

Weapons blazing.

"Go. Go. *GO!* Rocket launcher. Incoming!"
Heart in her throat, AJ identified the blast as
light and heat flew over their heads and disappeared into the night.

Jesus God. A rocket launcher? This close?

They were toast.

CHAPTER TWO

She was able to fire off a volley of shots by hanging over the door, using the window frame for leverage. She wouldn't hit anything important. Not at this distance. Not with the car bouncing and jostling hard enough to loosen her teeth, not to mention all the nuts and bolts in the rusted-out vehicle.

Suddenly Manny obstructed her next shot as he slumped down across the backseat.

Oh, God, oh, God. "Was he hit?" she yelled into the lip mic.

Struben glanced down briefly. "Don't think so. Passed out."

Things were going from bad to worse. And she wasn't handling it any better than she had out on that ridge.

"Get him off me," Struben yelled while he kept up a steady stream of fire. AJ leaned over between the seats and grabbed Manny's collar. God, he was heavy. She pulled and tugged until he slid off Struben's lower legs and flopped onto the floorboard.

AJ straightened, only to be tossed sideways, slamming her boob into the side of Kane's seat as the car tore up a steep incline. She shot out an arm and caught herself on the seat back as the vehicle clung there, half on its side before all four wheels slammed back down to earth. She tumbled back into her own seat, then scrambled to get her act together and re-position herself using her own seat back as a brace for her weapon. With Struben on the opposite side of the car, the field was clear.

Kane drove like a bat out of hell, while she and Struben worked in perfect sync. He reloaded, she fired. She reloaded, he fired. Hot air brushed her throat as a bullet zinged by. Her heart did a hard thud-thump as an extra shot of adrenaline zinged through her.

Missed, you bastards.

Turn the fear into anger, she told herself. *Fear into anger.* But the fear was so vast, so huge, there wasn't room for anything else. "Four hundred meters, and closing."

She spread her knees wider on the cracked vinyl seat, and braced her boots against the shot-up dash behind her. There was no swivel firing point as there'd been in class. This was the real deal. And *un*friendly fire was going to hurt just as bad as, if not worse than, a wild shot in training class.

Fear into anger.

How about fear into sheer, unadulterated terror?

"Three-fifty." She fired repeatedly. The AK-47 range was about three hundred meters, which meant she had a loopy trajectory requiring clumsy adjustment for accuracy at this range and speed. About a hundred rounds per minute with a forty-round magazine wasn't going to last long. They were merely holding them off.

The hot air smelled of sweat, dust, oil, and steel. Her shoulder was numb, sweat ran in stinging rivulets into her eyes, and sand crusted to the patches of sweat like flies on flypaper.

Welcome to Egypt.

Kane kept the gap at three hundred and fifty meters. Man, he was unbelievable. AJ reached back into her kit for another magazine. Kane's hand intercepted hers and he slammed a clip into her hand as efficiently as a surgical nurse making a pass off to a surgeon. He hadn't removed his eyes from the road.

A nasty mix of excitement and fear churned a toxic cocktail in AJ's system.

The psychiatrists and doctors had told her flat out: Odds were it would happen again, and it would hurt like hell. Either live with that reality or take the desk job.

Get over it, or get out.

Fear into anger.

She'd been unstoppable before that fateful training exercise three months ago. She'd been fearless no matter what the instructors threw at her. Top of her class in sniper school. Top of her class in physical conditioning. Top of her class in strategy—*despite* her looks.

Three months and two days ago she'd felt invincible. Confident. Self-assured.

But not anymore. Not anymore.

If she could just get the hell over freezing every time she had a human in her sights she'd be a damn good T-FLAC agent. Unfortunately there hadn't been time to work through her fear before they'd pulled her out of boot camp and shipped her to Egypt.

The middle of her first op was a bad time to be trying bravery on for size.

If only she could be like her hero. She'd come close. So close. And then *BAM!* Her magic cape had been ripped away and reality had reared its ugly head.

Oh, she'd get over this. She *would*. If by nothing more than sheer determination.

But when?

Before Kane sent in a scathing well-deserved report of her failure? Before she was asking, "Do you want fries with that?"

Kane Wright was everything she aspired to be.

Determined. Focused.

She had those down.

It was the fearless aspect of Wright's personality she needed to emulate. Now seemed like a good time to start.

The man never made mistakes. Stupid or otherwise. He'd never zig when he should've zagged. Everything he did was perfect and precise. He was a god at the T-FLAC training academy. AJ wasn't the only rookie who worshiped the ground Kane Wright walked on.

His ability to blend into the scenery like a chameleon was legend. His calm, almost detached calm, had never been ruffled. And he never lost his temper. Ever. AJ knew she should study *that* aspect of her hero's personality a lot harder. She tended to go off half-cocked when pissed off. Or scared. A bad trait, her instructors had warned, for a good T-FLAC agent.

She fired off a volley of shots. The windshield of the front chase vehicle exploded. Of course, half-cocked was better than scared shi—

"Good shot, Cooper. *Now* we're talking!" Wright said in her ear as their vehicle careened onto a blacktop road at close to eighty miles an hour, sand pluming behind them like a rogue wave on a dusty ocean.

AJ sighted the scope of her weapon and discharged a barrage of shots at the headlights behind them. The second chase vehicle swerved, then followed them onto the road in a wide arc, moving in faster.

"They're closing," Struben yelled.

She went into the automatic mode she'd learned during training. Steady. Scope. Target. Fire. Move on. Again and again, she squeezed the trigger with command and precision. But there were so many of them. Every few meters it seemed as if another pseudo-military vehicle full of armed men appeared. Even roaches couldn't reproduce this fast.

With the baddies' barrage of fire right on their tail, they flew across the Giza Plateau and onto Pyramid Road, headed for downtown. Several minutes later they encountered the bright headlights of oncoming vehicles as a procession of cars and tour buses headed toward the light show at the Great Pyramid. Lit up for the tourists, the pyramids appeared eerie and otherworldly as they floated surreally in the darkness.

With the approach of civilians and civilization, shooting came to a halt, but neither Kane nor the chase vehicles slowed down. Traffic on the other side of the road was stop-and-go, but as far as AJ could tell, no one bothered to glance their way as they sped by in the opposite direction.

"Might as well get comfortable," Kane told them. Struben turned around from his ready position in back. His eyes met AJ's, cold and unforgiving.

Apparently his ego didn't appreciate her fine display of marksmanship. *Too bad,* she thought. He could shove his ego up his ass.

AJ twisted in the seat, sliding down to face forward. Silently she reloaded the AK-47, and checked her Sig, keeping both close to hand. She used her sleeve to swipe some of the sand and sweat from her face.

Hopefully, Kane was rethinking his plans. Hadn't she just redeemed herself a bit? Besides, who'd come to Egypt in time to make the hit she'd blown? Savage was out of commission. And the cold hard fact was, only a woman was going to be able to get close enough to Raazaq to kill him now that the sniper thing was history. The reason they'd sent her was because there was no one else.

It didn't matter that she'd blown the first attempt. Or how scared she was.

She was it.

No doubt there'd be time for recriminations

later. In the meantime she might still be able to salvage her reputation—not to mention some of her pride—by not missing her target the next time.

And taking what Wright was sure to dish out like a man.

No do-overs.

Grateful for a few moments' reprieve to let her adrenaline level subside a bit, AJ concentrated on taking slow, even breaths, and regulating her heartbeat.

She didn't know why Raazaq's men had ceased fire. They weren't the type to be bothered by hitting a civilian. She glanced at Kane's face, impassive as he navigated the increasing volume of traffic. Eighteen kilometers from Cairo and closing. Would the teeming city streets deter Raazaq's men from following them?

AJ doubted it.

Buildings whizzed by, Kane took a sharp left, sped up, and zoomed onto the ramp of Sharia Corniche el Nil freeway going north, then crossed the El-Giza Bridge over the Nile, weaving expertly through the traffic heading for Imbaba and their safe house. It was hard to see any difference between one street and the next. Everything was ecru-colored, and decorated in varying degrees of poverty. AJ inhaled what felt like her first real breath in twelve hours.

"We lost them," Struben said into the mic.

"No we didn't," AJ said flatly, pulling her ball cap more firmly over her hair. "They'll take the other freeway and come back at us and try to box us in. Arterials?" she asked Kane.

"Yeah." He paused. "Is that what you were reading on the flight over? Street maps?"

"Among other things, yes." She'd tried to cram as much intel into the twenty-two-hour flight as possible.

"Should have seen Coop in logistics," Escobar said admiringly from the floor of the backseat. "She's amazing. Remembers everything. Right, Coop?"

Having a photographic memory certainly helped in the academic part of her courses. "I remember that you still owe me seventeen bucks and twelve cents, Escobar," AJ teased, her attention never wavering from the vehicles surrounding them.

Kane missed a produce truck by an inch and a prayer as he wove in and out of traffic. He wouldn't lead the tangos home. AJ knew how his mind worked. She'd studied him—and his ops—at length. She probably knew more about Kane Wright than Kane Wright did.

He took an off-ramp, twisted and turned

through back streets and alleys, and shot onto another freeway. AJ twisted to look behind them. They'd lost one vehicle, but the others had done just what she'd said they would. Came in behind them from another direction, and now they remained right on their tail like stink on poop.

So close she could clearly see the large, black mole on the passenger's beak of a nose through the glare of the headlights. He raised a handgun.

AJ took a chance and fired off one quick round, grinning when the driver swerved, sending beak nose's aim off.

"Goddamn it." Kane spread his open palm on top of AJ's head and pushed it down. The shot went wild, hit the fly-speckled rearview mirror and kept on going as she collapsed over onto his lap like a soufflé, her face buried in his crotch.

Jesus, Kane thought, *wouldn't you know she'd find her guts* now? She was damn lucky he'd seen the glint of the weapon in the side mirror and grabbed her at just the right moment.

Her breath felt hot and moist through his thin cotton pants. He realized he was still clasping the back of her head in his palm, and removed his hold. "Clear. You can g—"

She put a hand on his thigh to push herself

upright just as he threw the steering wheel in a quick jitterbug to snag a side street. Her hand slid off his thigh and dove into his groin for purchase. "Christ, woman!"

"Hey!" She yanked her hand from between Kane's legs, retrieved the Sig Sauer off the center console where she'd dropped it, and resumed her backwards position on the seat. "You're the one that grabbed me, remember? I could have shot 'em again if you hadn't."

Her slender back was ramrod straight, the soles of her boots braced against the dash for balance. She readjusted her backwards black baseball cap more securely and hunched over her AK-47.

"Excellent!" Struben's voice came across the mic. "We finally found something she's good at." He made a disgustingly wet sound with his mouth. "After you get him off, babe, climb on back here and make yourself useful."

"Screw yourself, Struben," AJ shot back.

"Why should I when you're around? I hear you can suck the brass off a doorknob, babe— Jesus Christ, Escobar!" Richard Struben suddenly yelped into the mic. "Little prick just bit my ankle like a fucking dog!" he complained to the others.

AJ gave a choked laugh. "Thanks, Manny."

"Yo!" Kane said with deadly calm. "Shut the

hell up, or every single sorry ass one of you will be on that flight back home." He gritted his teeth. Fuck it. He was going to send them all back home and do the job alone, like he'd wanted to in the first place. "Pay attention to your job. You can have your pissing contest after we're clear."

He glanced into what was left of the rearview mirror—Struben didn't look happy. Escobar had crawled up from his biting position on the floor and was exchanging meaningful I want-to-smash-your-face looks with his partner, and Cooper looked ready to spit nails. She opened her mouth to say something.

"Not," Kane cut her off, "another word. From any of you. Unless it's directly related to where we are, and why we're here. Got it?" He gave AJ, who looked ready to speak anyway, a hard personal glare, and added, "Just nod."

The two in back gave reluctant jerks of their heads. A quick glance at Cooper showed her gimlet-eyed and tight-lipped. But she bit her tongue and remained silent. Looking at her, it was hard to remember she was an operative.

She wasn't anything as tame as pretty, or attractive. She was jaw-droppingly beautiful, even with the layer of dirt she was wearing at the moment. Her skin was fine-grained and lightly tanned, her face a perfect oval. Her eyes ice-green. Her hair, a red-gold that even sweat-slicked and tightly bound shone like fire. She had a tall, long-legged, curvy body, and full, firm breasts.

AJ Cooper was a walking centerfold.

A woman that beautiful was used to fending off unwanted attention from men. And if she wasn't, she'd learn soon enough.

"Just a reminder, Cooper," he reminded *himself*, "when you're with me you're not a woman, you're an operative."

Struben snorted, forgetting, or not, that every word was transmitted on his mic. "The cold son of a bitch must be deaf, dumb, and blind."

Kane ignored Struben's comment. For now. The man had just punched the last hole in his ticket home. One more off-color remark and he'd be in the cargo bay on the transport Stateside with Escobar and Cooper.

AJ's mic clicked off. Kane glanced at her out of the corner of his eye. Her mouth was moving.

Smart of her not to let him hear whatever she was saying.

Hell and damn.

In the midst of the pissing contest being played out in the car, he'd been keeping an eye out for the vehicles that had been following

them. The white car wasn't behind them anymore—not anywhere Kane could see it, anyway. But it was there. Somewhere.

Cars, trucks, horse-drawn carts, and livestock vied for position on the roads. It was
early evening, and the streets were crowded.
Fiats and Hondas hemmed in plodding wooden
carts, tinted-windowed BMWs vied for space
with flocks of sheep and boys driving camels.

The sidewalks were Disneyland-packed with
crowds of people from rich to poor. Mingling,
chatting, and drinking coffee in outdoor cof-
feehouses, they were a moving, shifting tapes-
try.

The air was thick with the smell of days-old
produce, smoke, diesel fuel, and the pervasive,
dank odor of the Nile. The river ran through
the concrete jungle as a sewage system as well
as the city's water-supply and laundry.

Kane took familiar, and unfamiliar, side arterials, swooped up onto a busy freeway, shot
over another bridge, the one remaining chase
vehicle tight on his ass.

He took a turn, cornering without slowing
down. Skipped lanes to avoid a flock of sheep,
made another right. The other maniacs on the
road separated the chase car from them. But it
was still there.

Most of the streetlights had been shot or

burned out on these narrow side alleyways. Zebra-striped pockets of light and shadow slashed across his vision. One part of his brain concentrated on losing their tail. The other tossed the problem of AJ Cooper around like worry beads through nervous fingers.

If her reputation was accurate, she could do the job. Given the situation she'd been briefed on, she *could* do it. But was the last hour an indication of how she'd behave under pressure? Kane didn't know the woman well enough to make the call. And there was no room for another mistake.

Could she do her job given the right set of circumstances?

He had to be sure. *Probably* wasn't going to cut it. He had to be 100 percent convinced, without a moment's doubt, sure that when face-to-face with Raazaq, AJ would pull the trigger.

Because no matter what the hell he said, or how strongly he felt about sending her home, AJ Cooper was the only one available who could eliminate Raazaq. If there'd been any other choice, she wouldn't have been here in the first place. Like it or not, Kane was stuck with her. He might be a master of disguises, but even he couldn't duplicate a drop-dead-beautiful, five-foot-eight-inch, well-endowed, green-eyed, redheaded female.

There were many reasons he'd wanted to get Raazaq before the man started his trek into the desert. One of them being keeping AJ Cooper as far the hell away from the sick son of a bitch as was humanly possible. That opportunity was lost.

Now he was about to hand her to the terrorist on a silver platter, with an apple in her mouth.

AJ Cooper was Fazur Raazaq's designated assassin.

AJ felt sweat pool at the base of her throat and between her breasts. She almost wished they *would* shoot her and get it over with. Filled with dread, she was poised to jump out of the car the moment Kane told her to.

Clambering over rooftops was going to be a piece of cake compared to waiting for a bullet to hit her in the back of the head, smashing it like a dropped watermelon on a summer day. Ah, Jesus God . . .

Earlier in the day, they'd left town from the ritzy Hotel Ra, in a completely different direction as they'd circled into position above Raazaq's camp. AJ didn't recognize this area at all. Escobar and Struben had gone directly to the safe house in Imbaba and picked them up at their hotel downtown before they'd headed out.

They traveled a few more blocks before she recognized their location. Thanks to Kane, and his detailed debriefing reports from an assignment a few months ago. Like all his other reports, she'd pored over that one as well, studying his style, his modus operandi. Learning him. Absorbing his techniques.

The Khan al Khalili bazaar should be coming up soon on their left—Yes. There. The smell of roses, cinnamon, and dozens of other sweet and savory fragrances hung in the air. The stalls were crowded with late-night shoppers. If this were a movie, Wright would plow through the vendor stalls, fruit and veggies flying. A: It wasn't a movie. B: Kane Wright had more control than that. He'd circle and twist through the old *suqs* and capillary alleys until he lost the tail. Then he'd abandon the vehicle and make it on foot and take to the rooftops.

"Two seventy-five," AJ told him as the bad guys got close enough for her to count. "Six noses."

Wright spun the little car into a tight one-eighty, and slipped down a narrow side street. She hit her shoulder sharply on the empty window frame, but ignored the pain. There was another sharp jog about . . . now. Moonlight didn't reach into the constricted, dank canyon. The pungent stink of burnt rubber filled the air as the car skidded around the corner.

The chase car was too wide to follow them, but if the bad guys were smart, they'd block both exits.

"Struben, you and Escobar take the fire escape to the left. Cooper, with me. We'll go down a bit farther, then to the right. Cooper and I will take to the rooftops. She's too important to let them see her now."

"They already saw me," she pointed out, her voice flat and raspy with fear. Fear or not, she had a job to do, and damn it, she was going to do it. If she could just swallow this acidic lump in her throat and stop her heart from beating so damn fast.

Damn. Damn. Damn. How could she want to do this so badly and still be scared out of her mind? How did the others do it? None of *them* were sick to their stomachs. At least not so's anyone could tell.

"They saw what they expected to see. Four men in dark clothing. Get ready, you two. Cooper, stick to me like crazy glue. Got it?"

"Yes, sir." She turned and hooked the straps of the Dragunov and AK-47 over her chest, bandolier-style, and tucked the Sig into the front of her belt. "Ready," she repeated more firmly. Her stomach lurched up into her throat to join her erratic pulse.

Fear into anger, my ass. This was so not working.

Fear was fear was fear.

"Now!" Kane told the men in back.

The car jostled as the two men lunged for a fire escape on a brick warehouse. One of them grunted as he hit with the full force of his body. Manny's arm. AJ bit her lip, but didn't turn around.

There was barely enough room for the car as it hurtled down the narrow lane.

"Hand me that water bag behind you," Kane instructed.

AJ flipped her weapons against her back and out of the way, then twisted to reach down onto the floorboard. Her fingers closed around the bag. Getting a better grip, she hauled it up and handed over the heavy water bag they'd brought, but had never used.

"Three." Kane took it, and put the pedal to the metal. "Two . . ." He wedged the canvas sack against the accelerator pedal. Removed his foot, checked to see that it would hold at that speed. "Go!" He stood, crouched on his seat, one foot beside her hip. "Up! Up! Go! Go! Go!"

There wasn't room to open the doors in the alley, good thing there was no top to the car. AJ shot to her feet and lunged for a fire-escape ladder as they shot past it. Her weapon slammed hard against her back as she climbed the wonkie ladder like a monkey.

She felt a large hand on her butt, and appreciated the extra burst of speed with a little help from the man behind her. The ladder abruptly ended. She jumped up and caught the next one in both hands, then swung her body up and over and started climbing again. The two large guns were heavy on her back. The building was Mt. Everest. The ladders were rusted and barely adhered to the crumbling brick. Damn good thing she wasn't afraid of heights.

Climb. Hand over hand. Leg up. Jump, grip, climb. There was nothing else. Heat. Pounding heart. Climb. Climb. Climb. Faster, damn it.

She sensed rather than saw the presence behind her. Kane. Knowing he was with her made her feel better. More confident.

A massive blast from the street below lit the night sky with a demonic glow. Flames and thick black smoke flared high. Their vehicle had made it to the end of the alley.

The noise, and the brilliance of the fire, pulled people from their beds. Raised voices floated up on the still air. A bomb? Who?

Where? Contrary to popular belief, Cairo was a very safe city. People were startled and frightened by the explosion. Hopefully, a panicked, curious crowd would slow down their pursuers.

AJ hung by one hand for a second when her sweaty palm began to slip off the rung. The warm metal creaked under her deathlike grip. She swung her body for momentum and managed a solid two-handed grip before swinging up to the next rung. The muscles in her arms screamed. She ignored their SOS.

Shouts from below. The clatter of booted feet on metal.

AJ climbed faster.

A bullet ricocheted off the building, missing her left hand by inches. Okay. Maybe she could manage it even quicker if she stopped thinking about the feeling of . . . *Never mind, damn it! Climb. Climb!*

This was nothing like training exercises. *Nothing.*

Ten stories. She'd tackled more in boot camp, but she was out of breath, her chest heaving when she finally saw the flat surface of the roof at nose level. Thank you, God.

The sudden sensation of a large hand on her butt propelled her the last few feet. She flew up onto the roof, and staggered to keep her balance. "Tha—"

"Go," Kane ordered, even as he crouched low and raced across the roof, weapon drawn. Panic rose inside her like bubbles in boiling water. She stared at his back for an instant. He didn't look either scared or sweaty. AJ gave a small inward sigh, but didn't waste time wondering how long it would take her to be that good. That in charge. That in control. She started running, emulating his movements, as she pulled her Sig from her belt and hurried to catch up.

No amount of training could've prepared her for this reality. Her heart raced with equal parts exhilaration and sheer, unadulterated terror. The buildings were relatively close together—close if one was a flying squirrel or a bird.

A canyon opened up ahead. She caught up with Kane, and they ran hell-bent for leather across the heat-sticky rooftop. At the exact same time they raised their arms, flung themselves forward doing the splits. Their momentum hurled them across the ten-foot-wide, ten-story-deep cliff separating the buildings. AJ slammed into the wall with enough force to jar her from head to toe. Kane was already standing as she threw a leg over the small lip of the roof.

He reached down and grabbed her wrist, yanking her onto the flat surface. Without missing a beat, he hauled her up, then dived behind a small square structure—probably an air-conditioning unit for the building—and pulled her down beside him.

"Scared?" he asked, still holding on to her hand. His was dry and firm; hers, slick with sweat.

"Shitless," AJ panted. She could barely hear over the sound of her own heartbeat thundering in her ears.

He chuckled low under his breath. "Scared keeps you sharp."

"Then I'm a razor."

The smile didn't quite reach his eyes. Something else flashed there as well. Anger? Pain? Empathy? Masked as quickly as it had floated to the surface. AJ had the irrational urge to reassure him. Silly. He was the man of steel. She resisted the impulse, but left her hand in his. Just for the moment.

"Courage is mastery of fear," Kane told her, smile gone. "Not *absence* of fear. You were sent in because they know you're ready. You have the skills. Trust your training. Focus and breathe. We have a straight shot to the next roof before they get up here. Ready?"

"You bet." She let him haul her to her feet

again. The voices were getting louder. They ran side by side. AJ suspected Kane was dragging her with him, and was grateful when he didn't release her hand. He was the Energizer Bunny pulling her along. She needed all the help she could get. They were flying.

The men behind them shouted to one another in Arabic. AJ didn't speak much Arabic, just a word here and there. But she used their voices to pinpoint where they were. Close. Too close. The minute their heads cleared the roofline they'd start firing, and there was nowhere to hide up here. The roof was flat and endless. Its blackness melted into the dark night.

Her booted feet bit into the slightly sticky surface even as she scanned the area for shelter. Nothing. Just the next roof. And the next. And the next.

The flash of weapons-fire. Not even close. They couldn't see them. Not dressed in black as they were, and not against the unrelieved darkness. They were shooting blind. AJ didn't return fire. The muzzle flare would alert them to their exact location.

"Take a running jump, and spread wide," he ordered, releasing her hand.

"I'm with you. Go. Go. Go." There wasn't time for ladies first. It was every man for him-

self. She knew that. They started running together, but his legs were longer. And stronger.
And, damn it, surer.

Wright took an upright, running jump. She
shot a sideways glance as he almost levitated
across the gap and cleared the fifteen-foot space
between two buildings.

AJ mimicked his every move. Hot air rushed
past her face as she lifted off, her legs in a splits
position, her body forward, arms windmilling
to keep her momentum. She hung, suspended
for a lifetime, above the yawning maw of the
street below before landing in an ungainly
sprawl on the other side. Safe. Not a great landing by any stretch of the imagination, and she
was damn grateful that Wright was yards ahead
and hadn't seen her foot slip. Still, a bad landing was better than no landing at all.

Her heart slammed up into her desert-dry
throat. Crouching, she followed him across another rooftop, her breath sawing in her lungs,
her heart manic. Hot air pushed against her
sweaty skin, wrapping her in a thick cocoon.

Suddenly the sharp pinch of a stitch in her
side almost doubled her over.

Not now, for God's sake. Not *now*. AJ raced
beside him, holding her side as the sharp pain
intensified. Jesus, hadn't she screwed up
enough already? Did she really have to be a

crybaby and yell "cramp"? Of all the ridiculous reasons to get shot in the back. If it weren't so pathetically . . . *girlie,* she'd laugh at herself.

Crap. No wonder Kane wanted to send her home. She might as well go back on the pageant circuit if she couldn't be a better agent than this.

AJ grimaced as she tried to straighten up. If nothing else, she could match him for speed. At six three he was only five inches taller than she was in her boots. Despite the annoying pain of the stitch, her strides almost matched his as they came to the next rooftop jump over an alley.

This would take them down by at least fifteen feet. Down fifteen, across at least ten. Her spit had dried up an hour ago. Nothing to swallow down her dry throat. She dug the heel of her palm into the now screaming pain of the stitch and gritted her teeth.

More shots. Closer now.

"Crazy glue," Kane said grimly into his lip mic.

"Joined at the hip. Got it." A spear of pain radiated from her side directly to her brain, doubling her over.

"Together—" He jumped, and landed on the rooftop below, light as thistledown, then spun around to make sure she was following.

Which she wasn't because the pain was so sharp she was cross-eyed.

He swore under his breath. "What the hell are you waiting for, Cooper?"

She panted through the pain in her side. "Stitch."

"Jesus," he said in her ear. "You'll have more than a fucking stitch if you don't jump. Do it now, Cooper. Now!"

Trying to straighten up as she ran, AJ backtracked to get a running start on the jump. No matter how good an agent she wanted to be, if she didn't shake this paralyzing terror of being shot again, she'd end up dead. Worse, she'd end up responsible for the deaths of other operatives. Perhaps even the mighty Kane Wright.

Forget the stitch. Forget everything. Run like hell. Clear the jump.

That's all I have to do. Run. Clear the jump.

I can do it. I can do it. . . .

Her heart cramped as a bullet tore up the roofing inches from her feet. Raazaq's men closed in. She couldn't control the way she started at the noise and close proximity of the gunfire. Her head went light with fear. Damn. Damn. Damn.

Determined, grim, she rotated to return fire. It was obvious they could see her location. She had nothing to lose. She got off a few shots, then spun back around and started running flat-out for the gap. . . .

Her breath sawed painfully as she ran.

Faster.

Faster.

Twenty yards . . .

Zigging.

Zagging.

Faster.

Faster.

She tried frantically to put the image of a bullet tearing through her flesh out of her mind. God.

Ten yards . . .

She struggled with the image. The memory of the feel of the impact. The sharp, hot pain as the bullet sliced through her soft tissue and muscle. The sensation as it went through the back of her shoulder . . . burning, scorching, agonizingly painful.

"Nonono!" *Concentrate on the now, damn it!* AJ blocked the memory and ran with every ounce of energy in her body. Flat-out.

Three yards and she'd be flying.

One minute she was in full, flat-out motion. The next . . . nothing.

CHAPTER THREE

An agonized scream ripped AJ out of unconsciousness and into heart-pounding awareness.

Not her own scream. Thank God.

What—? Where—?

Preternaturally alert, eyes closed, she remained dead-still where she lay, senses tuned to the sound of violence nearby. Another scream. Male. Cut off mid-shriek. A thump. Something solid connecting with flesh.

Her body jerked in sympathy as another agonized scream ricocheted off the walls and seemed to echo on and on in the blackness surrounding her. Jesus God. A shudder of dread washed through her already sweat-drenched body. Where in God's name was she?

Gingerly, she rolled her head to one side, listening to someone being tortured very close by. She winced as blow after blow rained down on some unlucky bastard. And every groan floating through the darkness reverberated through her body, making her nearly feel each blow. She fought the sensation, aware that at any minute it might be her turn.

Think! Her brain felt slow, annoyingly sluggish. Pain blossomed behind her eyes and stretched out to every corner of her muddled mind. Didn't matter. She had to think around it. Had to marshal her thoughts so she could figure out where she was and what was going on. And most importantly, how to get the hell out of there.

Damn, the floor beneath her body felt hard as a rock. Foul, putrid odors permeated the air and she breathed through her mouth, trying not to think what she was sucking into her lungs. *Come on. Come on,* she mentally chanted, willing her body to get up. To move. To take action.

Another man's screams of agony joined the first. Tag-team torturing. No interpreter was needed to understand that the two men being viciously beaten next door were begging for mercy and shrieking bloody murder to the accompaniment of the blows.

Goose bumps chased each other down her spine, then settled in the pit of her stomach, where they churned into a mass of nerves that had her ready to scream herself. She forced her sticky eyelids open, then blinked a couple of times as the darkness around her wavered and her stomach did queasy flip-flops. The pain in her head was subsiding to a low roar, but she felt new aches and pains popping up all over.

Jesus.

Had she already been tortured?

Where was she, how had she gotten here? More important, how could she escape? Wherever *here* was smelled like old pee and older sweat, and God knew what else. Lucky she couldn't see where she was lying. Or what she was lying on. The stench made her eyes water as she swallowed back nausea.

Something scuttled in the darkness and she drew her knees up, instinctively avoiding what sounded like the Godzilla of rats.

Another scream, blood-chilling and bone-numbing—then abruptly, and terrifyingly, cut off mid-note.

Jesus God.

Silence throbbed like a living presence. Alive with terror. Thick with anticipation of what was to come next.

A sob shattered the unnatural quiet. A plea for mercy. A slap. Quickly followed by a succession of blows.

Muffled Arabic voices bounced and echoed against stone walls. While the men weren't in the same room as she was, their voices were clear enough. AJ tried to decipher the rough dialect through the pain of a king-size headache.

Frowning made the ache in her head worse and didn't improve her hearing. She wasn't able to grasp more than a word here and there, but what she did understand didn't make her any happier. She tried to push herself upright, and instantly regretted it. Quickly, she lowered her head back to the floor as vertigo washed over her, and nausea roiled through her empty stomach.

"Bite the bullet, AJ," she warned herself, pushing the words out through gritted teeth. "What were they always saying at the Academy? Oh, yeah. Make pain your friend." She pressed a hand to her forehead. She didn't care for her new friend.

Next door, the victims were whimpering. Keeping her voice low, she whispered encouragement that they would never hear. "Come on, guys," she said while trying to stop her own world from spinning, "hang on. Don't let 'em win." She hoped to hell they could hang on through the torture, because as soon as the beaters were finished with the beatees, it'd be her turn. And sympathy or no sympathy, better them than her.

She couldn't afford to hurl right now. She willed the dizziness to pass, but because of the darkness, there was nothing to focus her eyes on until the spinning stopped, and she had to wait it out. She concentrated fiercely on the conversation next door, hoping for a clue. Something to tell her where she was and what was going to happen next. Beyond the obvious torture thing.

Someone was going to die come morning. She got that part. The who, where, and why eluded her. However, the fact that they sounded excited about it filled her with dread. Nothing worse than a bad guy who loved his work. She'd hazard a wild guess there weren't that many victims left to choose from.

Carefully touching the back of her head, AJ discovered a huge, tender lump on the left side. Which accounted for the headache, but didn't tell her who'd hit her or how she'd ended up in this pit.

She rolled to her knees, wanting to put at least a body-length distance between her nose and the floor. The air wasn't much better at two feet than it was at ground level, but at least nothing could crawl into her hair. She was either in a bathroom or a cell. She'd vote for the cell. Or perhaps she was two for two.

It took less than a minute to travel around the room and trace the circumference with her hand. Eight feet by eight feet. Stone walls. No furniture. No toilet. There went the bathroom theory. Cement floor. Wooden door. Locked, of course. That was it.

And one female T-FLAC agent who was shit out of luck.

"Don't panic," she told herself firmly as her heartbeat sped up, and sweat popped out on her brow. *Just don't panic.* Yeah, right. Trapped. Beat up. Maybe about to be killed. Why spoil the fun with panic?

AJ braced her arms on the wall, and shifted her feet apart to do press-ups against the rough stone. She needed energy, and a plan. Thinking about what was happening next door or her various aches and pains wasn't going to achieve either. The physical movement helped her concentrate.

"Come on, AJ," she ordered quietly, "think. You're a smart girl. The cream of the Academy. Now's your chance to prove it." Her muscles quivered in protest as she lowered herself slowly. First she had to figure out where she was. Somewhere hot . . . it was stifling in here . . . she raised her body away from the wall, slowly.

Arabic . . . She got a mental flash of the pyramids. Egypt . . . Yes! She was here to eliminate Raazaq!

That was it. AJ gusted out a relieved breath. Okay. The blow to the head hadn't scrambled her brains totally. She was here with a team to take out Raazaq.

And the team consisted of—?

And the plan was to—?

She let her forehead rest for a moment on the rough stone wall. Totally or not, her brains were scrambled. "Oh, shit."

Kane slumped against the wall facing the small rural jail on the outskirts of Cairo and took another clumsy swig from the bottle cradled in his gnarled hand. Damn fool woman had got herself locked up. And not by the Cairo police, either. Raazaq had damn long arms.

They'd kill her in the morning. They'd sure as hell worked over the two guys locked up inside with her. Their screams of pain could be heard quite clearly in the hot, still night. Damn it to hell.

Oh, yeah, they'd kill AJ Cooper without a blink. *After* they tortured every scrap of intel she had out of her. In the most painful and brutal ways possible. He suspected the only reason they hadn't interrogated her yet was they were saving the woman for last. To prolong their entertainment.

If they knew how scared she was already, it would probably take all the fun out of it.

She'd spill her guts in two seconds flat at the first *hint* of torture.

He shuddered at how cleverly cruel they could be. How they'd withheld food and water in exchange for intel. And when he hadn't given it up, how they'd brutalized his team. One at a time. Until he'd thought he'd go mad with their screams of agony. It went on for days, and days. . . .

In a cold sweat, he shoved his personal nightmare aside. Wasn't going to happen. Not on his watch. But Jesus, he fucking *hated* being put in this position again. Responsible for somebody else's very existence . . .

He was good at a number of things. But keeping his teammates alive wasn't one of them.

Which is why he'd worked alone for the past two years.

He swore viciously under his breath. Angry at himself for giving in to the order to bring her. Angry at Cooper for being the rookie that she was . . . Hell, angry at God for putting up another roadblock to his sanity.

Never again. Never a-fucking-gain.

And never with a rookie in this lifetime. No matter how good they said she was. No matter how many sniping and sharpshooting medals she'd won. No matter how hard up he was for a sniper.

Damn it. He *needed* her.

Which just went to prove how fucked up this operation had become.

He glanced down to see a scorpion, tail curved to strike, walking across the hand he had braced in the dirt beside him. He flicked it off before it struck, and again lifted the sealed bottle to his mouth, watching the jail through narrowed eyes.

Jesus, it was hot. His scalp itched under the wig. The skin on his face, neck, and chest pulled under the heavy makeup. He ignored the discomfort and concentrated on the task at hand. The same task he'd managed a few hours ago. Getting AJ Cooper out of trouble.

The two guards across the way came out for a smoke. They ignored the old drunk slumped across the alley as they hunkered down on their haunches and lit up. The smoke curled lazily in the still air as they relived the torture they'd just perpetrated on two of their prisoners. Hell, they were practically whistling.

The two prisoners were low on the food chain of Raazaq's army. They hadn't seen the earlier attack out at the ruins, hadn't been prepared for it, and had generally screwed up. They were being used as an example to everyone else in the terrorist's organization of what would happen when an order was not obeyed. Raazaq's first-in-command would be there in the morning to take the bodies back to camp as an example. These two yahoos had a free reign of terror until then.

Was this smoke break just a brief respite before they went back in and started in on Cooper? His insides bunched. He'd been tortured himself. Knew just what they'd be planning for Cooper. And when the beatings were over, he figured the raping would begin. He knew how fond these dirtbags were of beating and raping, but he was not about to let them destroy his best shot at getting Raazaq.

Kane relaxed against the wall. Patient. Waiting. Watching for just the right moment as he listened to the men. He wondered if Cooper was listening, and understanding just what was in store for her.

She had a photographic memory, but how much Arabic did she understand? She'd claimed at least a cursory knowledge of the language. Kane suspected that was an exaggeration. She'd been too eager to please, too damn bright-eyed and bushy-tailed about the prospect of her first field op. Her need to prove she was ready meant she'd probably said anything to get this assignment. But her linguistic skills, or lack thereof, weren't why T-FLAC had sent her—ready or not—in with them.

They'd needed a beautiful woman who was a crack shot. Savage hadn't been available. Plain and simple, Cooper was second choice, and here because she had a great body, a beautiful face, and could put a bullet through a keyhole at three hundred feet.

He'd worked with Savage before. She was good. She was reliable. She was seasoned. But Savage was banged up and not due out of the hospital for months. And they'd needed someone now.

Cooper was it. Lucky him.

Kane hoped to hell the rookie *couldn't* hear or understand the conversation going on right now. These guys were practically salivating at the prospect of interrogating their witness at daybreak. What they had planned for her was enough to chill the sweat on his skin and raise the hair on the back of his neck under the scraggly wig.

"Hey!" he shouted in slurred Arabic. "Gimme a smoke."

The men laughed as they got to their feet. All that alcohol would cause an old man like him to explode with a bang if he lit up, they taunted. Not to mention Allah would see him in hell for his vices.

Kane grumbled, but toasted them with his bottle before wrapping his galabayya around himself and pretending to settle down for the night. Through slitted lids he watched them reenter the small jail. It was too hot to close the door behind them, and they didn't bother. A narrow stream of light speared out into the stinking alley.

With any luck, AJ was in a cell alone. He wasn't in the mood to jailbreak anyone else. No doubt she'd be a gibbering wreck when he sprung her. Enough of a handful without extra baggage. And he couldn't afford to wait any longer. He wasn't risking the guards moving on her before morning.

Kane staggered to his feet and shuffled across the alley, making no effort at stealth. All they'd see was an old beggar, coming to pick up their still-glowing cigarette butts.

He took his time crossing the narrow alley, then stooped to pinch a smoldering smoke between gnarled fingers, straightening slowly, and with apparent difficulty. The guards noticed his motion near the door, and cursed him half-heartedly. Apathetic in the sultry heat, bored now, they were ready to be diverted. Morning, and the entertainment of interrogating the female prisoner, seemed a long way off.

Kane took a drag off the foul Kévork Ipekian

and expelled a cloud of camel-dung-scented smoke into the still night air as he shambled inside.

Fortunately, boredom and heat had the two men too lazy to give him much thought. He didn't waste his time. It took less than a minute to dispose of them with a knife to the kidney. Kane left them slumped over the desk and went in search of his errant agent.

All was quiet. The stone building retained the heat of the day, and the smell in the narrow confines of the corridor leading to the cells was rank. Didn't matter where in the world the jail was, they all smelled the same. Terror, blood, pain, helplessness.

He palmed the keys he'd snagged off a convenient hook, to prevent a jangling of warning, and chose a door at random. Flashed the mini Mag light into the small cell as soon as the door swung open. The stench of bodily fluids hit him like a punch. Two bodies, crumpled on the dirt floor. He took precious seconds to check for pulses. Dead. The guards were sloppy but enthusiastic.

He unlocked the next door, and shoved it open. "Cooper? You in h—"

She jumped him from behind the door, and Kane fell for the ruse like a veritable rookie as she knocked him to his knees on the hard floor.

"Jesus, woman! I'm here to save your ass." He broke her hold, shot to his feet, and had her in a headlock before she could knee him in the nuts.

Her nails dug into his forearms. "You son of a bitch, I'm not telling you anything. I'll make you sorry you ever opened that goddamn door."

"I *am* sorry," he muttered, and winced as she clawed and moved around trying to dislodge his hold on her.

She slammed her heel down on his instep and he grit his teeth, but didn't let go. Her neck was slender and fragile. One pop and she'd be gone. The thought chilled him.

"Settle down before you hurt yourself," he instructed the ungrateful agent. "Or before I hurt you."

She stopped waltzing around him and froze, slender body bowed at the waist as she finally recognized that he was speaking English. He could almost hear her thinking.

"Kane?"

"No. The Godfather. Who do you *think* would waltz in here to save your ass in the middle of the night? We seem to have fallen into a me-rescuing-you loop, Cooper," he said, pissed off. "We'll figure out how to break the pattern later. Let's get the hell out of here be-fore someone else shows up."

She froze. "Crap!" she muttered under her breath, and then more loudly, "All the blood's rushing to my head. Want to let go now?"

He let her go abruptly and she staggered back into the wall. Wasting no time, he reached out, snagged a fistful of her shirt, and yanked her forward again. He ran the small beam of light from the mini Mag across her face. Other than filthy, she looked in reasonably decent shape. All things considered. "You injured?"

"Thanks for the sympathy, but no," AJ said tartly. She straightened, then pushed past him and strode down the corridor toward the light glowing from the office. Her black cotton pants and a loose, long-sleeved T-shirt were covered with pale dust. She was a mess. A ripped-off strip of fabric fluttered on her left sleeve, ex-posing a bloody scratch high on her arm. A bullet graze.

She'd lost her baseball cap, but not even cap-tivity was going to dislodge so much as a hair from the tight braid on the back of her head. Following close behind her, Kane could see where a dark bloodstain smeared her hair, indi-cating the point of impact. She didn't smell any better than she looked. But then, neither did he. They were a fine pair, he thought sourly.

Her movements were solid as she walked, instinctively looking for an ambush. He felt a flicker of admiration, and, frankly, relief, that she wasn't a gibbering idiot. Thank God she wasn't clinging to him in terror like a motherless monkey. He'd already decided if she freaked out, he'd knock her unconscious and carry her out. Too damn hard to pull off a rescue when the rescuee was hysterical with fear.

She continued down the corridor ahead of him with a loose-hipped sway that was sexy as hell. Kane shook his head. Every other man in T-FLAC might think Cooper was the hottest thing to hit the agency since sliced bread, but he wasn't one of them. He never mixed business with pleasure. And he had a feeling Cooper would be too high maintenance for him, even if she wasn't his subordinate and on an op.

Fortunately, so far, so good. She seemed to have it together. Unfortunately, more of Raazaq's men would be here at first light. Which gave them a half hour, tops, before the bloodhounds were out trying to run them to ground.

He and the rookie would be at the apartment across town in fifteen minutes. He'd lay low, then radio the extraction team to remove her later today. He'd spent several hours debating the wisdom of trusting Cooper to finish the assignment. It was too important to leave anything to chance. She might very well be the best sharpshooter T-FLAC had ever had. But even as much as he needed her, she'd proven herself unreliable.

It was a chance they couldn't afford to take twice.

Time was running out, ticking like a metronome in his head. In his gut. He was wasting precious minutes of it saving Cooper's tattered ass. Again.

He'd already lost one member of his team—Escobar was on his way home—and he pretty much wasn't happy with either of the other two members left.

Cooper slipped down the hall on the balls of her feet. Silent, efficient, alert. She held up a hand to keep him back while she glanced at the two men slumped over the desk in the front office. "Nice job."

"I thought so," he said dryly, handing her a Sig Sauer as she nodded her thanks. They emerged into the thick darkness of the alley and shut the door behind them.

"Transportation?"

He pointed. "Block over."

"Let's go." She took off at full speed. Kane caught up with her and a few minutes later they arrived at the spot where he'd left their commandeered vehicle.

They both reached for the handle on the driver-side door. Kane quirked a brow. "What?"

"I'll drive." AJ held out her hand for the keys. "Let me at least do *something.*"

Kane blocked her with his arm across her soft breasts and she stopped in her tracks, frowning up at him. "Right now you can't even see straight," he told her flatly. "Get in and buckle up."

"But I—"

"Get in. Buckle up," Kane repeated. He didn't mind being driven by a woman. Made no difference to him. But a woman with a head injury? No, thank you.

AJ hustled around the front of the vehicle, opened the door, and slid into the passenger seat. "I appreciate you coming for me," she told him as soon as he got in and put the car in gear.

Kane pulled into the street, shooting her a glance. "Since when has T-FLAC ever left a man behind?" They were more obsessed with retrieving their operatives than the Navy SEALs were.

"Never." She rubbed at her forehead with a grubby hand.

"Headache?"

"No. Yes. Of course I have a headache. Some goon hit me with what felt like a frigging two-by-four." She shot him a glance and he noticed she had blood smudged on her eyelids—possibly from the blow to the head. Didn't seem to faze her any, but it sure as hell bothered Kane.

The air-conditioning was on high, and he noticed her nipples poking at the front of her T-shirt. Heat shot to his groin and he got a semi-hard-on just looking at her. Christ. This was all he needed. He was shocked, and pissed, at his reaction to her. He pulled his attention back to the road, and gripped the wheel more tightly.

"Did the others make it to the safe house?"

"Escobar caught transpo home a couple of hours ago. Struben's waiting for us at the apartment."

"How long was I in there?" AJ stroked the barrel of the Sig absently, her attention on the buildings they passed. Kane turned down a main street and kept to the speed limit. Even at this hour of the night there was traffic. He stayed in a middle lane, hidden in plain sight. He wished to hell she'd put her hands in her lap and stop stroking the gun. Her slender fingers on that barrel were not only erotic as hell, the movement was distracting.

"Four hours."

She looked at him. "The two men in the other cell?"

"Raazaq's people. Dead."

"Shit." She closed her eyes. "I'm sorry. I'm so damn sorry."

"For what? You're not responsible for the death of those men."

"I'm responsible for Raazaq getting away. Jesus God, Kane. I'm humiliated. . . . Worse, I'm disgusted with myself for screwing up that badly."

"You're a professional. Use what you learned here and you won't let it happen again," Kane advised unsympathetically. God only knew he had his own suitcase of rocks to haul around. But he'd be damned if he'd listen to her feel sorry for herself. He wasn't going to give her any slack for being female, and he sure as hell wasn't giving her any slack for the screwup.

"You'll be back at the Academy tomorrow," Kane told her. "Have yourself a little chat with the shrinks. Deal with it."

AJ twisted in her seat to look at him, her face gray in the light from the street lamps. "You're really sending me back?"

Kane canted his head to glance at her. Her face might be filthy, but her skin still looked smooth. He knew it was flawless. Soft. He realized his attention had dropped to her mouth and jerked his eyes back to the traffic milling in front of them. God*damn* it. "Yeah. Really," he said harshly.

"Let me stay. Prove myself."

"You had your chance."

"And I only get one?"

"This go around, yeah."

"The best man for this job is a woman, and you know it," AJ said, talking fast now in an attempt to convince him. "You might be a master of disguise, but even you can't pull that one off. Admit it. You need me here."

"Having a female operative smoke out Raazaq was one choice. You were there for the briefing. The other choice was me going in alone."

"Not alone. With Struben and Escobar," she reminded him. "And you won't get within five hundred feet of Raazaq. He's even more paranoid than you are, Wright. Raazaq trusts *nobody*. You know that. This op is far too important to let egos get in the way." She shot him a glance, her pale, cat eyes gleaming in the lights from the dash. "Don't be pissy because I made a mistake—Okay, a frigging *huge* mistake. But a mistake, nonetheless. The next time I have the son of a bitch in my sights he'll be dead as a doornail. I promise."

"I have no fucking idea what that means but I told you last night. No do-overs. You're on your way home, Cooper. Buy yourself a souvenir at the airport." Kane picked up the pace, crossed an intersection, and slipped into the dark cavern of the next alleyway for a shortcut to the freeway.

She fumed silently beside him, but he could almost hear her mind clicking away, looking for an argument to beat his. Too bad for her, he already knew there wasn't one. This was his op, damn it. He'd do it his way.

"Is there anything I can say to change your mind?"

"No."

"Then drop me off at the Ra," she told him far too mildly. "Why spend my last night in Cairo in a dump when I can sleep in a bed without fleas?"

"Nice try. But forget it. You won't find him on your own," Kane informed her coldly. Not surprised that she wanted to do what he would have done in the same position. "And if you were stupid enough to try, you'd be looking for new employment within the hour."

She turned to him. "But I—"

"Quit while you're ahead, Cooper. Nothing you say or do is going to change my mind."

She blew out a frustrated breath. "Know one

of my favorite games I played with my brother when we were kids?" AJ asked, apropos of nothing, and far too sweetly.

Kane didn't give a damn, but he snapped out, "What?" anyway. When he shot her an annoyed glance she smiled that annoying Julia Roberts smile that drove him nuts and raised an eyebrow.

"Chicken."

Chapter Four

Kane Wright was intractable.

Stubborn.

Pigheaded.

And in charge, AJ reminded herself, let's not forget *in charge*.

Great White Shark. Minnow.

Got it. Didn't like it. But got it.

She would have given a lot to be able to read his mind right now. Then again, she wasn't wearing asbestos. She was probably better off not knowing. What he'd said already was just the tip of his iceberg, but the gist stung quite enough. And the knowledge would probably give her more performance anxiety than she already had.

She mulled over how she could go about convincing him she was invaluable after she'd proved herself just the opposite mere hours ago.

It was before dawn, but the Cairo streets were already teeming. Life went on. Kane's disguise was so effective that between the iffy streetlights and the pancake makeup he wore, she couldn't read his expression. Displeasure, however, radiated off of him in waves. She felt like a kid who'd disappointed her favorite teacher.

And to be absolutely fair, she'd have felt the same way in his position if an unseasoned rookie had been foisted on *her* in such an all-fired rush.

On the other hand, she thought grimly as Kane took a corner and narrowly missed three kids riding a single bicycle, which wobbled all over the road, if the rookie was exactly what the mission required, if the rookie was top in her sniping class, if that rookie could be used as bait to set the trap, if that rookie was 100 percent right for the job . . .

AJ sighed. She'd send the rookie home for screwing up!

Crap. She hated being logical about this.

God only knew Kane Wright was a brilliant field operative. But T-FLAC sure as hell hadn't hired him for his people skills. Besides, he had plenty of reason to be cranky with her.

People skills or not—in his case, a big *not*—the hero worship she'd been feeling for months had slipped a cog into something a little more personal when she'd met him for the first time three days ago at the briefing for this op.

While she had devoured his reports and his analytical papers on terrorism at the Academy, AJ hadn't thought of him as a man so much as an icon she'd set on a pedestal. Someone she would try to emulate. Someone whose career was everything she wanted her own to be. When they'd called her in from a training exercise to inform her she'd be going on assignment with Kane Wright, her heart had pounded so hard, she'd figured she might pass out with excitement at the great man's feet.

She'd wanted nothing more than to get out of that meeting and prove herself.

Then Kane strode into the briefing room. Dressed from head to toe in unrelieved black, he was a striking man, and her heart had done a different kind of hop, skip, and jump just looking at him. Heat speared into her from head to toe. The kind of hot awareness she'd never experienced before. AJ had never reacted to a man on such a purely physical level in the past. But then, her reaction hadn't been solely physical then, either.

Meeting him in the flesh had put another dimension to the man on the page.

He'd just returned from Istanbul, and long days under a blazing sun had turned his skin a deep tan, and shot golden highlights in his dark shaggy hair. His lean strength and six-foot-three height had added an elegant cache to the black chinos and dark T-shirt he wore. A girl would have to be dumb and blind not to sit up and take notice seeing the snug fit of cotton stretched across those broad shoulders, displaying his flat stomach and impressive abs. His long legs made short work of circling the conference table to find the only vacant seat—the one opposite her.

He'd flicked a dismissive glance her way, his eyes a dark, dark blue, holding no warmth whatsoever, and then without expression returned his attention to the head of the table, where their superior immediately started outlining the mission.

She'd found out Kane Wright's displeasure was as ruthlessly clipped as his dark chocolate voice. It had taken her several minutes to grasp the fact that while *she'd* been sitting there trying not to drool into her coffee cup, *he* was informing the table at large that he didn't want to use such an important mission as a training vehicle for a rookie.

He'd wanted to go to Cairo alone, and made no bones in saying so. His dark eyes told her, in no uncertain terms, he considered her unsuitable. Worse than useless. AJ wasn't used to a man looking at her that way. There was a first time for everything.

Disinterest. Dismissal. Disdain. All emanating from Kane Wright was bad enough. The fact that everyone sat there discussing her unsuitability for the job and their doubts she would be able to pull it off made her want to scream.

She'd almost died after she'd been shot. And while AJ didn't expect their sympathy, she did expect them to give her the benefit of the doubt. She'd bitten her tongue on her anger, and rationally explained why she should accompany Kane Wright and his team to Cairo.

In the end they'd relented—only because she was, by default, the only one suitable for the job.

Kane had been harder to convince. But he'd finally agreed under duress. Severe duress.

Now, she thought, he'd believe, they'd all believe, he'd been right. Not only had AJ messed up her own chance to prove herself, she'd no doubt put a crimp in every other rookie's chances. From here on out, they'd be more careful about taking an unproven agent out on an op of this magnitude. And it was all her fault.

She sighed again.

"Don't sulk," Kane said, mistaking her sigh for petulance.

AJ shook herself out of her reverie to look at

him. It was impossible to see the good-looking guy under that eighty-year-old face. Gray hair, crepey skin, rheumy eyes. She tried to see where the makeup ended and he began. But the application was flawless. She wasn't three feet from him and she would swear that papery, wrinkled skin was the real deal.

"I never sulk," she told him, to set the record straight. She had a few other skills in her female arsenal, but sulking wasn't one of them. "I was just thinking—"

"Save it."

"Oh, yes, sir! Didn't know thinking wasn't allowed."

"If you'd done less thinking and more shooting, we wouldn't be in this mess."

"Nice of you not to beat me over the head with my failures, though. I *really* appreciate it, *sir.*" What'd she have to lose by telling him what she was thinking? He was already sending her home in disgrace. What was left? A spanking? Another tongue-lashing? A curl of something dark and hot and yearning opened up inside her at *that* imagery, and she figured she must have hit her head harder than she'd thought.

He shook his head and firmed those old papery lips into a grim line that told her he was done talking. She shut up, too. Streetlights blinked past as they drove through the predawn city, and AJ kept her face forward while she weighed her options.

Not only was she determined to kill Raazaq, a man in the top ten of the U.S.'s Most Wanted Terrorists list, she had to prove she had what it took to be one of T-FLAC's best operatives.

She had to prove it to herself.

To Kane Wright.

To Mac MacKenzie, her psych instructor, who had warned her that her aggressive need to succeed would get her killed if she didn't learn to control it. Fine. She was controlling it. *Look at me, Mac. See? AJ Cooper biting her tongue.*

All she needed was one more chance.

It didn't help that her hero worship for the man stoically driving the car was mixed in with a healthy and very unwelcome case of lust, which she hadn't been able to shake on the twenty-two-hour plane ride over here. In the last three days her emotions had gone to hell in a handbasket, and the last man, the absolutely last frigging man she should have any romantic interest in was Kane Wright.

The man was a loner. Did not play well with others. Was a perfectionist. Brooked no mistakes from himself or anyone else. And was intractable, unfriendly, and cranky.

Hells bells, AJ thought, scrunching down in

her seat, closing gritty eyes, now that she thought about it, she didn't even like him!

The car slowed and she opened her eyes to look around.

The safe house was on the West Bank of the Nile on the edge of the newly reclaimed Imbaba district. It was a high-rise hovel. Peeling paint, graffiti, and broken lower windows proved it wasn't one of the newer buildings in the recently spruced-up neighborhood. In fact, it was just a taller version of the crumbling tenements surrounding it. Kane pulled their vehicle into the building's basement parking garage just as dawn broke over the city through a smoggy golden haze.

Things were looking up. He'd brought her here before hauling her off to the airport.

AJ huffed out a grunt of relief as he pulled into an empty parking slot and shut the car off. She was flat-out exhausted, and figured he must be, too. Flea-bitten or not, the safe-house apartment must have a shower and a toilet in working order. And a bed. She needed a shower, food, and a horizontal surface to crash on for a few hours. Then she'd sit down and figure out how to salvage her reputation and do the job she'd been sent to Egypt to do.

"Do I get to shower and nap before you haul my ass off to the airport?" she asked, unsnapping the frayed seat belt as soon as they stopped. The fact that she hadn't had a full or decent night's sleep in over three months was immaterial.

"You'll have plenty of time for a nap on the plane," he said shortly, reaching for the door handle without even glancing her way. "Just stay downwind of the civilians."

AJ got out of the car and slammed the door behind her a little harder than necessary. *Dickhead.* He didn't smell any better than she did.

If he were her brother, Gabriel, she'd give him a good solid punch to the solar plexus. But her quick temper had landed her in trouble and written up more than once, and she was already one of Kane's least favorite people. AJ bit her lip even harder. She didn't have to be one of his favorite people.

Don't kill him, she thought determinedly, *and don't kiss him, either. Just do your job. Do it well and go home. Mission accomplished.*

Kane's dusty black galabayya swept about him like the wings of a raven as he walked around the back of the car to join her. Still in character, although they were the only two people in the parking garage. AJ noticed his shoes. Battered and old, they looked insubstantial and as fragile and worn as he did. He

looked Arab, talked apple pie, and was as emo-
tionless as a robot.

In short, a perfect T-FLAC operative.

"Move it," he said, indicating the elevator on
the far side of the cavernous, and almost full,
parking garage.

AJ gave him the finger behind his back, but
she bit back a smart-ass retort and caught up
with him. She pushed the elevator button and
blinked moisture into her dry, tired eyes as she
leaned against the wall to wait for the car.
Damn, she could fall asleep standing up. She
pushed herself away from the wall. "When do
you leave for Fayoum?"

"You're not coming."

The doors jerked open, and she stepped in,
leaving him to follow. "I didn't say 'we,' did I?
I heard you the first dozen times. Give it a rest,
okay? I got the message."

He hit the floor button. Eleven, she noted
absently as the car started ascending in rum-
bling fits and starts that didn't fill her with confidence. Great. Blow her big chance, then die
in a plunging elevator in a rat-infested hotel.
Just perfect. She'd go down in T-FLAC history
as the biggest loser to ever walk through their
doors.

Gabriel would have to change his name in
self-defense.

"Some people need to be told more than once."

AJ heard her back teeth grind together as she said tightly, "Well, I'm not one of them." He could talk until he turned as old as he looked. Whoever got to Fayoum first could take out Raazaq. She'd be there first. She'd make sure of it. When he dropped her off at the airport she'd split. He wouldn't have to know she'd disobeyed orders until after the hit was done.

It was a risk, disobeying a direct order. But on the other hand, when she'd taken out Raazaq and done her job, the powers that be at T-FLAC would see she'd used her own initiative and be pleased.

The elevator was slower than molasses in winter and jerked and hesitated every few feet as if it were too tired to make the trip. Standing side by side, they faced the doors. AJ shot him a surreptitious glance under her lashes. His normal closed look was made even more obscure by the makeup.

What was he thinking? Nothing good, judging by the set of his jaw.

A couple of years ago Kane had been imprisoned for two months on an op. His report had, frustratingly, been sealed. Just the bare facts were on record. Six men had gone into

Libya. Five men killed in action. Kane imprisoned for two months. Kane returned home.

End of story.

Maybe bringing that back to him, getting him to relate to what had just happened to her, would soften him up a bit. Remind him that once upon a time, he'd been vulnerable, too.

"I guess I was lucky." AJ shuffled back to lean against the wall as they rose in fits and starts. "Thank God they didn't get around to torturing me. You showed up in the nick of time."

"It wouldn't've been pleasant," Kane said laconically, not bothering to look at her.

Right. "Not pleasant" was one way to put it. She shivered just thinking about the shrieks and screams of agony she'd listened to in there. Of course, she wasn't being tortured now, either, but it was damn unpleasant, just the same. "You were held captive in Libya, right?"

"Yeah."

Okay. That didn't open up a dialogue, either. The man was as uncommunicative as a clam. He'd been tortured for months in that hellhole in Al Jawf. During her second month at the Academy, she'd pored over what there was in the report. Reading between the lines, and empathizing, sick to her stomach at man's inhumanity to man. How had he withstood what they'd done to him? How had he survived?

How had he ended up in that prison? Had it been his mistake or a mistake by one of the others on his team?

"I'm sorry, it must've been hell," she said softly to his back. A massive understatement, she knew. Damn it. She was a fairly intelligent woman. Knew how to conduct a lively conversation most of the time. But with Kane Wright she felt ridiculously inept and tongue-tied. It didn't help that he was pissed. Or that he was being stubbornly unresponsive to her olive branch.

AJ curled her fingers into her palms. She desperately wanted to reach him on some level. Wanted him to be pleased with her, with her performance as an operative. She wanted, *needed*, his validation. Frustrated, she dug her short nails into her soft palms until she concentrated on that pain instead of the pain of disappointment crushing her chest.

She shouldn't need his validation. Damn it. She really shouldn't. He was nothing to her. Nothing more than her boss on this op. Nothing more than her hero. Nothing more than a man she'd looked up to, sight unseen, for the last eighteen months of her life.

He looked at her over his shoulder. "I was

outside the whole time you were in there, Cooper," he said quietly, as if he'd read her mind. "I wouldn't have let it get that far."

AJ felt a huge wash of gratitude. "I wasn't worried."

He faced front again. "Right."

Feel the warmth, AJ thought, glaring at his back. Talk about unbending. He must've been raised by wolves.

"Okay, maybe a little worried," she admitted. "But you must have been worried when you were in prison, too, right?"

"Can't remember."

"Would you mind me asking how you landed there?" *A mistake you made, right?*

"Yes."

AJ waited a beat. Honest to God, the man took the word "uncommunicative" to a whole new level. "Don't hold back, Kane. Feel free to tell me how you really feel, in as many words as you need."

"Fine. You want to know? Trust was misplaced. Someone didn't obey orders," he said after a few minutes of heavy silence. "The result was that five good men were tortured to death right outside my window. After a while I started praying that my turn would come soon. Is that enough info for you, Cooper? Or would you like the gory details?"

AJ pressed her fist to her stomach. She'd read the bare bones of the report. Over and over and over again. She didn't need the details. The images of what she *thought* might have happened were etched in her brain. It had probably been considerably worse than anything she could've come up with.

Kane Wright had never, as far as she knew, made any mistakes or missteps in his eight-year career, so whoever had screwed up had died. Did he feel responsible somehow?

"Sorry for dredging that up. That was a shitty thing to do. Just because I'm feeling sorry for myself doesn't mean I have the right to stir up your old memories."

"Doesn't matter anymore."

Yes it did, she wanted to argue, but talking to the back of his head was getting her nowhere fast. "I'm sorry I asked."

"So am I, Cooper. So am I."

They rode the rest of the way up to the eleventh floor in silence, and when the door opened he was the first one out. AJ caught up with him, and walked beside him when he turned left down the hall. With her Sig Sauer in her hand, her gaze shifted constantly as she kept a sharp eye on their surroundings. Raazaq's men could be anywhere.

If she went to Fayoum alone and then

screwed up this opportunity again, she could wave her T-FLAC career good-bye. Of that she was a dead certain. Of course, if she screwed up while she was on her own, it was pretty much a certainty she'd be dead. So worries about her career were pretty much moot.

If she got on the plane and went home with her tail between her legs, they might send her out on another op again sometime. In fifty years or so. Maybe. Or, more likely, they'd insist she take the damn desk job they'd offered her in the first place. Even more likely, they'd boot her ass out of the organization so fast, she'd get whiplash.

She'd go to Fayoum.

And this time she wouldn't miss Raazaq.

It wasn't an option.

Decision made. Debate over.

Strangely enough, now that she'd made up her mind, fatigue dropped from her shoulders like an old jacket she'd shrugged out of. There was bounce in her step, and a tiny burst of energy dazzling through her bloodstream. This wasn't over. She wouldn't be going home in disgrace. She'd show Kane. She'd show them all!

The endless corridors smelled of urine, cumin, and poverty. Babies cried behind closed doors, and large, black cockroaches crawled the walls and crunched underfoot on the filthy, cracked linoleum. Nothing like the posh Hotel Ra.

One more turn in the labyrinth of filth and they came to a blue-painted door. E1101. It looked like the Hounds of the Baskervilles had clawed at the chipped and faded paintwork to get in. "Got the k—" Her mouth snapped shut.

The door was closed, but not latched. AJ tightened her grip on the Sig. She wouldn't be caught flat-footed again. Weapon held in both hands, she motioned she was going in.

He nodded.

They burst through the door, Kane high, AJ low.

She did a quick visual scan of the large, shabby room. Her nose wrinkled at the rank smell in the place, and she quickly started breathing through her mouth.

Nothing was out of place that she could see, but there was definitely something wrong. Something . . .

Weapon at the ready, she rounded the dirty beige sofa, making certain her eyes followed the same line as the barrel of the Sig. Constantly in motion, she scanned her surroundings.

Shabby. Cheap. Transient. A typical safe house. Nothing unexpected.

Living room. Open-plan kitchen. Two bed-rooms.

Quiet as a tomb.

Smelled like one, too.

Narrow-eyed, she turned in a slow circle, the Sig leading the way, keeping Kane in her peripheral vision. He moved soundlessly about the room and into the kitchen. For a large man he walked as silently, and as gracefully, as a dancer. AJ completed her circle.

Something on the sofa snagged her attention. She stared for several moments at the obscene splash of dark brownish-red on the oily cush-ions.

Droplets of blood sprayed out in a high-ve-locity pattern from a central point on the mid-dle seat. Resting smack dab in the center lay a small object. A small *bloody* object.

Clearly something severed right where it lay . . .

"Jesus God!" she whispered. The blood drained from her head.

Kane came back around the bar separating the kitchen from the living room. "Nothing. I'll check the be—"

AJ pointed. "Is that what I think it is?"

"Yeah," he said grimly, coming up beside her. "If what you think it is is someone's tongue."

"Oh, crap . . ." She breathed a little heavier through her mouth, and looked a bit paler under the dirt, but she took it well. Thank God she didn't freak out. He had enough to deal with.

AJ's head turned toward him, but her eyes were still glued on the gory calling card, as if she couldn't quite believe what she was seeing. She blinked, then switched her focus and looked at him steadily—in control again. He'd never noticed just how green her eyes were before. Must be her pallor and the dirt. He'd never seen anyone with eyes quite that clear, pale, summer grass color.

Christ. He *really* didn't want AJ Cooper here. A woman—hell, nobody—should have to see shit like this. Looking at her standing there in her filthy black clothing, her face pale and streaked with dirt, her sleeve torn from a gunshot, Kane felt every protective instinct inside him rear up and shout. She was made for silk sheets and candlelight, not cordite and blood.

She shouldn't—Christ. What the hell was he thinking? She wasn't his to protect. Cooper was an operative. It was her job to deal with things like this. She'd made the choice to enter the game. Now it was time to learn the rules.

She cleared her throat. "Whose?"

"Only two choices. Struben or the house-boy."

"God, what's that smell?" She frowned, absently rubbing her forehead. "Never mind. Let's get the search over with. I doubt they left any other evidence, but we can check, anyway. I'll take this one. You take that one."

"Yes, ma'am," he said tongue in cheek. He'd gotten the closest bedroom and, he suspected, the source of most of the stench.

Weapon up and ready, he moved through the doorway. His glance was swift and all-encompassing.

The bed had been slept in. Struben. He'd been napping, had been hauled up and out of it, taken by surprise. A Glock was exposed by the strewn bed pillows, but there'd been no time to fire it.

The prints of several pairs of feet on the carpet indicated at least four men besides his operative. Struben had had the shit beaten out of him against the far wall—blood splatter indicated blunt force, probably many well-placed fists, then he'd been dragged across the carpet—here, more indications of a scuffle, more blood. A *lot* more blood. Fresh. A body's worth of blood and fluid puddled on the matted carpet.

Kane's gut twisted. They'd hauled the man,

battered and bleeding, into the living room to interrogate him. When he'd refused to talk they'd cut out his tongue to show they meant business, and then dragged him back into the bedroom. Kane could see how it all had played out. It ran like a video in his brain.

Struben had still been alive. His nails had left striped furrows in the matted carpet on either side of his body as he lay bleeding. He'd tried to crawl. Fallen over. Here. And here.

They'd offed him. Right *here*. Three feet from his fully loaded weapon.

The foul smell wafted from the small adjoining bathroom. The door was ajar. Kane kicked at it. Hard.

Stuck.

Bingo.

Wedging his shoulder into the eight-inch gap, he used his full weight to force the door, and whatever was behind it, to move enough for him to see inside.

Struben. Or what was left of him.

"Jesus. You didn't go quietly into that good night, did you, you poor, sorry bastard?"

He'd bled out, but defensive wounds on his hands indicated he'd got in a few good hits. Too few, too late.

"Anything?" AJ called, coming into the bedroom soundlessly.

"Don't come in here." Kane's voice was grim. She'd been cool so far, but this was sure to set her off.

"Why no—" She narrowed her eyes, then the penny dropped. "Oh, hell. Who?"

"Struben."

"Let me in there." She came up behind him and lay her hand on his arm. "Call for cleanup."

Kane glanced down at her fingers on the black fabric covering his forearm. Her slender hand was filthy, the short nails broken and chipped. He didn't know why he noticed her hand, or how fragile it looked. All he knew was, he didn't want her to see what the tangos had done to Richard Struben.

"He's beyond help," he told her flatly, braced for her tears, and probably hysteria.

"Yeah, I know," she said gently, but he saw the shudder that coursed through her body. "Dead operatives are an unpleasant reality in our business, aren't they?" The rim of her full lips was white, and a rapid pulse skittered at the base of her slender throat as she stood, straight as a soldier, looking at the carnage. "It doesn't get easier to deal with, either, does it?"

"Wait in the other room."

"It's okay—I'm okay. Let me do my job." She looked at him through cool green eyes that looked a hell of a lot steadier than he'd expected.

She'd seen death close up and personal a few months before. Was her therapist right? Had she worked through it? Kane would have said no yesterday. But now? Maybe. Curious, he stepped aside. AJ slid between his body and the doorjamb, then crouched down beside Struben's body. Teeth biting her lower lip, she felt, unnecessarily, for a pulse at his throat, then gently closed the man's staring eyes.

She stepped over the body, and turned on the water in the sink to wash her hands. She caught Kane's eye in the mirror.

"I'll call it in," he told her. "Go ahead and collect what we'll need. I want us gone before the garbage detail arrives."

Calmly she finished washing her hands, her booted heels inches away from a dead man, who looked like a raw side of beef, and smelled like a latrine.

Her throat worked as she dried her hands then stepped over the body a second time. "I wasn't finished in the other room. Be right back."

A few seconds later he heard her puking her fear out in the kitchen. He was tempted to go in there and help her, but he knew damn well she wouldn't appreciate it right now.

While water ran in the other room, he made the call. Arranged cleanup of the body and told Control they were on the way to the Ra.

Christ. The hits just kept on coming. "Clear," AJ said, coming back into the room. Her face had been scrubbed clean. Her eyes were shadowed, but she met his gaze with a steel he hadn't noticed in her before. She'd puked, yeah, but so would most people when faced with what had been left of Struben. And damned if Kane wasn't a little impressed that she was holding it together.

"How well did you know him?" she asked.

Kane stuck the phone back in his pocket as AJ picked up the unused Glock, checked it, then inserted the gun into her belt in back. She went to the closet and pulled open the door. Finding a black canvas duffel bag, she tossed it on the bed and started filling it with the few items she found in the closet. Clearly she needed something to do with her hands. They wouldn't have any need of Struben's clothing.

"Well enough to be pissed off seeing him like that," Kane said, going to the nearest bed-side table and removing a flat black bag. He tucked it inside his galabayya and waited while she finished packing the duffel. She opened her mouth, then snapped it closed again without saying anything. "What?" he asked.

"They tortured him." AJ didn't bother to hide a shudder as she zipped the duffel closed. Her face was dead white but she was maintaining. A man had to admire her for that.

"Would he have talked?" Kane wondered aloud. He'd never met Struben before the briefing. He hadn't liked him on that occasion, but that didn't mean he didn't feel pity for the poor bastard being turned into hamburger meat. And for having the bad luck to have Kane Wright on his team.

Damn it to hell. Yet another man to add to his list.

The sooner he got rid of Cooper, the better he'd like it.

"He—he's been with T-FLAC for about four years. He was a sexist jerk, and an a-hole, but he was an exceptional operative, and well trained. So, no. He didn't talk." She straightened, holding the duffel.

"Are you prepared to risk our lives on the belief that Raazaq didn't discover our next move from Struben?"

He'd said "risk *our* lives." Did that mean he'd changed his mind? AJ kept her gun in her hand as she walked beside him, and felt ancient spirits and centuries-old traditions brush her skin. Imagination, of course. Something to do with the big black cockroaches skittering underfoot, and the towering walls surrounding them. It was hard not to be affected by a structure that had been built more than two thousand years ago. Despite the rising temperature outside, down here in the bowels of the earth, the air was cool and a little musty.

"What is this place?" Her quiet voice echoed off the high, vaulted ceiling of the underground cavern.

"Necropolis," Kane answered. "City of the Dead."

"Lovely." AJ had no trouble imagining the square alcoves off to each side of them as receptacles for sarcophagi—a *lot* of coffins. The little burial rooms soared several "stories" above their heads. Condos for the dead. Hundreds upon hundreds, row upon row, as far as the eye could see. People long forgotten, their bones turned to dust, the artifacts, buried with them to take across the River Styx, long since looted and defiled by grave robbers. Faded and worn traces of ancient inscriptions above each crypt were etched and timeworn against the sand-colored walls. Memories of loved ones, the name of the mortician, even spells to ward off evil, spelled out in hieroglyphs.

The colors must once have been brilliantly

vibrant, some still were. Terra-cotta and gold, black and peacock blue. At any other time, AJ would've enjoyed lingering, learning, knowing about the people who had been interred here. Now all she could think about was the possibility of being back in the game.

Kane walked beside her, galabayya swirling about his feet. The Hotel Ra was, as the mole crawled, six miles across town.

When they'd emerged down the stairwell thirty minutes earlier and approached the parking garage, they'd found their car being watched, as well as the entrance and exit from the building.

T-FLAC operatives learned early and well there must *always* be a way out. Which, in this case, there was. AJ rather wished she'd been the one to know about the maze of catacombs beneath the city. She needed to rack up some Brownie points pretty damn quick.

If they didn't get lost in the labyrinth of the catacombs, they'd arrive beneath their hotel in about an hour. AJ looked at him. "How'd you know about this place? I thought the Necropolis was in Alexandria."

"There's one there, too. They discovered that one first, then this one a couple of years later. They're still excavating both. Alexandria is taking precedence because they think

Alexander the Great may be buried there. But there is some incredible history here, too. You interested in Egyptology?"

"Right now I'm more interested in the here and now than in a bunch of very old dead people."

"Seven centuries of dead people, in this case."

"I'll be sure to come back on my next vacation."

He didn't stop walking, nor did he slow down. The man *was* the Energizer Bunny. They passed broken shards of pottery stacked by the archeologists in higgledy-piggledy piles on the sandy floor. They passed rows of what looked like Roman lamps, they rounded a corner and saw hundreds of terra-cotta figurines lined up ready for inspection.

Maybe if she could figure out what made him tick. "Don't talk much, do you?"

"No. This isn't a cocktail party."

All righty, then. "Are you chatty at cocktail parties?"

Kane slanted her a glance. "What do you think?"

I think you don't get a lot of invitations. "Not."

"Right."

"Just as well." AJ heard something behind her and glanced back over her shoulder. A rat.

The rodent variety. She tried to relax but the back of her neck felt as though it were being gripped in a vise. Every small noise was spooking her. Odd that she was more freaked out by a noise than she had been seeing Struben lying in a pool of his own blood.

The known and the unknown? Probably.

"If you weren't on this op," AJ asked Kane, to break the thick silence, "would you enjoy being here?" Her hand encompassed the immense chamber they were crossing, the frescoes and friezes, the trompe l'oeil.

The old-man disguise Kane was wearing right now was an illusion to fool the eye just as the ancient paintings on the walls were.

"Very much. I was invited here by the Egyptian government when it was first discovered several years ago. Did a photo essay for *National Geographic.*"

He speaks! AJ looked at him. "You did?" She knew his work as a photographer was another part of who Kane Wright was, but of course there were no reports to study on that aspect of him. Although she'd accidentally come across some of his work in magazines when she'd been in the hospital, and had been fascinated. His photographic work seemed to cover the spectrum of subjects. From high fashion to famine. People always featured prominently in his work. In the *National Geographic* piece she'd seen, his pictures of a tiny South American village had brought tears to her eyes. Somehow, he'd managed to capture the quiet dignity of an old chieftain and the simple joy of the children. In a few beautiful photos, he'd made time stand still—and had drawn her into a world she'd never known.

"Yeah," he said, fishing a length of cream-colored fabric out of the bag he carried. "Really. Had to use ultraviolet light. It was incredible to see all the glyphs for the first time in centuries. Here." He handed her a *niqab*. "Put this on. Cover your hair and face. We'll cut through the subway station and cross the street to the back of the hotel."

She was almost stunned into silence. Kane Wright had been *talking* to her. Like she was a person. Like a person he didn't hate.

"Right." Not all Arab women covered their heads these days, and many wore pants. Still, if she wanted to hide in plain sight, the long dress and veil of the *niqab*, worn by conservative Muslim women, would do the trick. AJ took a moment to brush off her black pants and shirt. Dust rose from the fabric in little clouds. "I hope nobody looks at us too hard. I'm filthy enough to raise questions."

"You'll be up to your neck in hot water in

ten minutes," Kane said, probably thinking about a shower himself.

Too late, AJ thought ironically as she pulled the fabric over her head and settled it into place. Way, way too late.

She'd been in very deep, very hot water for hours already.

CHAPTER FIVE

An uneventful ninety-two minutes passed as they swam the tide of early-morning commuters, traversed the crowded Rameses train station, then strolled across the street to the back entrance of the Hotel Ra.

AJ kept her eyes modestly lowered as they went through the service entrance of the hotel. Not only was it the custom, she didn't want anyone getting a good look at her. Green eyes would stand out like a bikini in the marketplace around there. She'd be made, and remembered, in an instant.

She and Kane had arrived, with attitude and a mountain of Louis Vuitton luggage, through the front door yesterday morning. The world-renowned photographer Kane Wright and his model du jour. For their entrance this morning they chose the service elevator and low-key.

The elevator smelled of spicy food, B.O., and some kind of pungent furniture polish. Quilted brown fabric covered all four walls, absorbing sound.

"There's a commercial flight out at two. That'll give you a couple of hours to clean up and rest," Kane told her as the doors closed. "I'll be taking you to the airport myself."

So much for that second chance. AJ slanted him a look. "Don't trust me to catch a cab by myself?"

"No," he told her shortly. "And that's wasted on me, Cooper."

"What's wasted on you?"

"That flirty under the lashes look. I'm not your boyfriend. Nor am I charmed."

AJ hadn't realized she'd done whatever it was he was accusing her of. But his crappy attitude was really starting to piss her off. Irritation rose like a wave. "Where the hell do you come o—" AJ snapped her mouth shut.

Jesus God. What was she *doing*? Pissing him off even more?

On the other hand, she thought, what did she have to lose? Who knew? Maybe he'd even respect her standing up for herself. Arguing for the right to prove she was more than one bad mistake.

"You were saying?"

Maybe not. The words backed up to sit like a rock in the pit of her stomach. "Not a damn thing." Her jaw ached from clamping her teeth together, but she didn't say a word for the rest of the trip upstairs.

The elevator stopped. AJ glanced around as they emerged into a wide corridor on the eighteenth floor. Plush red and gold carpeting cushioned their feet. Not a bug in sight.

"Yippee," she said drolly. "No creepy crawlies." Just then they passed an ornate mirror over a gilded table and she got a good look at herself in decent lighting. "Oh, man!" She choked back a laugh at her filthy, disheveled appearance.

"Wait here," he said, flashing a quick look at her as the door quietly snicked open under his hand.

AJ followed him into the suite. She wasn't about to put herself in the position of the little woman, told to stand in a corner and quietly wring her hands while the big strong man took care of everything. She was a trained operative. Okay, maybe not as experienced as Kane. But she knew what she was doing.

Hand on her weapon she scanned the large cream and gold living room of the suite, listening, hoping like hell there were no intruders. If she stumbled over a tongue-slasher right now, she'd probably just shoot him, and then cranky Kane would be even crankier. No thanks.

By the look of things, the room hadn't been disturbed since they'd left yesterday afternoon.

Unlike the low-rent safe house across town, these accommodations were top of the line. The Queen's Suite consisted of elegantly monochromatic tones in cream and gold, cool and soothing to the eye. Pale, silk-lined walls were bathed in the soft, warm glow of recessed lighting as morning sunlight filtered in through the sheers at the bank of tall windows.

Antiques mingled with tasteful modern pieces. Everything had a subtle Egyptian flavor, from the curved lotus shape of the gilded legs on the tables to the understated hieroglyphs on the wallpaper and fabrics. The elegant room was filled with the fragrance of fresh flowers reflected in the gold, embossed mirror on a half-round table across the room.

"Grab that shower," Kane told her. "I want to check your head. You might need stitches."

"I don't."

He raised a fuzzy white brow. "You a doctor?"

"Nope. Not a patient, either." She didn't want him to touch her, and that was the honest truth. There was too much emotion swirling around inside her, and AJ wasn't sure just how she'd react if he did. She'd either pummel him, or grab him and . . . kiss his bad tem-

per away. Which would either start a war, or
the opposite. Until she could manage to get her
all-over-the-place emotions in check, she'd lay
off having him touch her, just to be on the safe
side.

Her stomach growled.

Kane reached for the phone. "I'll call room
service," he said briskly. "Any preferences?"

She shook her head. "Food, and lots of it. As
long as it's not green."

"Meet me back here in fifteen minutes for
debriefing."

"I'll be back in ten."

In the end it took AJ half an hour to shower
and wash her hair thoroughly. It was lovely having French milled soap and delicately scented
floral shampoo, but given the way she smelled,
she needed industrial-strength cleaners and a
good hard wire brush. A flea dip might not
have been out of line, either.

Finally clean, she spent a few extra minutes
applying antiseptic cream to various small cuts
and scrapes. She could feel the knot on the
back of her head with tentative fingertips, but
couldn't see how badly she'd been hit.
Considering where Kane had found her, she
was damn lucky this was the worst she had to
show for her overnight experience.

Female T-FLAC agents always knew in the

back of their minds that they could, and possibly would, be sexually assaulted if an op went wrong. It was a frightening, and very real, hazard of the job. An implant protected against pregnancy. But there were far worse things a woman had to be concerned with. Her psychological training had included a hundred different scenarios. Thank God she hadn't needed to utilize any of that information. Yet.

Knowing what she did of Raazaq and his followers, AJ knew just how damn fortunate she'd been to escape his methods of interrogation. Once. But she was pretty sure her ration of luck was used up. She couldn't count on getting that lucky again. If Raazaq managed to snatch her a second time . . .

"But you won't have to worry about that, will you?" she asked the disheveled woman in the mirror. "Pretty hard for Raazaq to snatch you out from behind a desk at T-FLAC headquarters."

She scowled at her own reflection, trying to figure out just how she was going to lose Kane. The man was being as pissy as a maiden aunt and she didn't doubt for a minute that in his current mood he'd walk her right onto the plane and buckle her seat belt for her.

The thought of Kane's hands on her caused another shiver to skitter through her. AJ shook

her head. Even though he was mad at her, even
though he was rude, insensitive, and bossy—
God help her, she was attracted to the jerk.

"You need help," she told the idiot still staring back at her from the foggy glass. "And step
one is to get over it. For God's sake, the man
can't stand the sight of you. Do you really need
more punishment?" A good argument—unfortunately, neither she nor her reflection seemed
to be paying attention.

The psychiatrists would have a field day with
this one.

"Cooper! Move your ass."

"Yes, sir, O captain, my captain," she muttered, thinking briefly about how tempting it
was to slam something heavy into his hard
head. She could make her escape while he was
out. Of course, when he came to, there
wouldn't be a country big enough to hide in.
The satisfaction, however, just might be worth
it. Grumbling to herself, she yelled, "I'm coming, already!"

A couple more hours in his company and
they'd go their separate ways. She could bite
her tongue—instead of his, AJ thought with a
sudden grin—for just a few more hours. A few
hours of keeping her thoughts to herself were
do-able.

Drying off quickly, she wrapped a towel

around her wet hair, rubbed most of the moisture out of it, then tossed the towel over the rack and padded naked into the luxuriously appointed bedroom.

She pulled on clean underwear and jeans, then tried to find a top that didn't expose her boobs. She hadn't chosen any of the clothes hanging in the closet herself. T-FLAC wardrobe department had selected and packed for her while she'd been in briefing. She'd stepped aboard the plane bound for Cairo a few hours later carrying just her backpack. Everything had been waiting for her in baggage claim on arrival yesterday.

Normally, she wouldn't be caught dead in any of this stuff. Everything was a little too tight, and a little too low cut. But it wasn't her tastes being catered to. It was Fazur Raazaq's.

AJ finally settled on a white tank top, turning it around so the low, scooped neckline exposed her back instead of her breasts. She started finger-combing the heavy mass of her damp hair. Hanging halfway down her back, it was long enough to be a nuisance, and she rarely wore it loose. She absently started plaiting it into a tight French braid as she walked into the living room.

Kane stood by the window across the room, talking on the Sat Comm link.

The real Kane.

Tall, loose-limbed, and broad-shouldered, dressed in black pants and charcoal shirt. AJ sighed inwardly. If her attraction to the man hadn't been dimmed when he'd been in full makeup and looked like her grandfather, why had she thought it would go away when he was back to his normal gorgeous self?

Her knee-jerk reaction to him was the same now as it had been the first time she'd laid eyes on him. Damn. She'd hoped everything that had happened recently would've put paid to the lust problem. It hadn't.

Maybe it would fade when he started snarling at her again. A girl could hope.

He glanced up, impatiently waved her into the room, then seemed to physically withdraw as he turned his attention back to the conversation on the phone.

His shaggy hair, wet from his shower and finger-combed back, exposed the contours of his face in bold, unrelieved strokes. He'd needed a shave several days ago. He looked damn good. Too damn good. He also looked sinister, rakish, and dangerously appealing. Fortunately for her good sense and libido, his features shouted "Do not disturb" in no uncertain terms.

He looked his normal unapproachable and

taciturn self. This was a man used to giving orders and having them obeyed without question.

Well, wasn't he going to be in for a surprise.

A small table, elaborately set for two, drew her attention. Her stomach growled. Loudly. She sat down, not waiting for him to complete his conversation, though she did try to hear what she could.

"I'd appreciate anything you can get me by noon our time today." Kane paused, and AJ felt his gaze on her, but didn't look up from spreading apricot jam on a slice of warm bread. Rivulets of melted butter ran down the backs of her fingers.

"No. I am *not* happy, but you're giving me no choice," he said into the phone, then paused to listen, impatience tightly reined.

Hmmm, AJ thought, hiding a smile behind her bread. *Apparently I'm not the only one who can drive the man to the absolute end of his rope.*

"Yes. I agree. Give me what you—" He paused, and AJ glanced up to see him watching her lick the butter off her fingers. "—can," he finished tightly.

"Problems?" She absently sucked at her pinky finger. What concerned Kane affected her, and vice versa. Besides, if someone was making him mad, she wanted *that* guy on her side. "What's going on?"

"You're back in the game, Cooper." His voice was grim, his eyes an opaque dark blue as he snapped the phone closed and stuffed it into his back pocket. "God help us both."

"I am?" AJ cleared the frog out of her throat. "I am?"

"Against my better judgment, yes."

She turned her attention back to her breakfast to hide her elation. He could be as crabby as he wanted to be. The point was, she'd won. She wasn't going home. She was going with him. Largely under his duress, but that didn't matter. All that mattered was, she had the chance to salvage what she hoped would be a long and proud career. Inside she was turning cartwheels and doing the Snoopy dance. She kept her expression sober. "You won't be sorry."

He faced her, all steely eyes and grim determination. His expression telegraphed he was already sorry. "Tell me the truth, Cooper. Are you capable of killing Raazaq?"

She met that gaze with a cold, hard look. "Yes."

"Unequivocally?"

"Unequivocally."

"You do realize we won't have another

chance, right? Once he leaves Fayoum, we won't know where the hell he is. And if when we get there he puts together the fiasco the other day with who we'll be when he meets us, we'll wish we were dead. Got it?"

"Jesus, I'm not an idiot." She stiffened and told herself the hell with it. If she was going to be burned, she might as well be burned for being cocky instead of being unsure of herself. "I know what this means. I know we wouldn't be in this mess if I hadn't screwed the pooch. But I did. I can't change it but I can assure you it won't happen again."

"Why should I believe you?"

"Because you have my word. I'll get close enough, and Raazaq will die."

He looked at her for a long minute that seemed to tick by in eternity-filled seconds. AJ didn't look away. She stared right back at him. *Don't let him see your fear. Don't look away first. Be the Alpha dog.*

Right.

After staring at her hard enough to do a mind-meld, he nodded. "All right. Tell me what you know about your target."

He had a made-for-radio voice. Deep, dangerous, mysterious. Very sexy. *Oh, for God's sake,* she thought irritably, *forget Kane. Concentrate on getting what you wanted. Another opportunity.*

She took a bite of warm bread, chewed, and swallowed. "We were at the same briefing. I know what you know."

"I doubt that. But what I'm telling you to do is to distill what you know and regurgitate it for me."

She could play the game as well as he could, AJ thought. He wouldn't catch her flat-footed again. This time, she'd be prepared. This time, she'd knock his socks off. "Fazur Hessan Ali Raazaq. Forty-three. On the FBI's Most Wanted list for the bombings of United States embassies in Dar es Salaam, Tanzania, Nairobi, and Johannesburg."

AJ rattled off the list as if she were reading it. "Attacks on Federal facilities resulting in death. Aircraft piracy, hostage-taking. The use of destructive devices. Attacks on U.S. citizens abroad. Aiding and abetting. Murder. Kidnapping. Torture." She paused. "Latest atrocity—the bombing of a private, and very exclusive, girl's boarding school in Switzerland. Five hundred and eighteen girls, average age twelve, killed. That was two weeks ago. Public outcry for his ass has been heard from every country large and small. I think that about covers him."

Kane lifted the silver dome and set it aside. "You forgot sexual deviant. He's big into S and M."

"Don't ruin my appetite with minor details. Let's eat first." She closed her eyes, breathing deeply. "God, this smells incredible." She unwrapped her silverware and settled the napkin on her lap. "Coffee? It's American."

He glanced up. AJ held the heavy silver pot poised. She was strong. The container didn't waver. Her hand was slender, her nails short and clean. There was still a faint gleam of butter on her tanned skin. Kane felt an untoward spark of sexual attraction and immediately squashed it. "Sure. Thanks."

He'd read the reports and had been concerned about her temper. As well as her looks, her inexperience, and the fact that she was under his protection.

And damn it, this was the wrong business to feel any emotion. Temper. Joy. Disappointment. Fear. The enemy was everywhere. The slightest hint of any kind of feeling, and it would be used against you. Kane hardened himself against her satisfaction at being back in the game.

This op was going to require all of his skills just to keep them both alive. He had to be sharp, in control, and focused. Normally none of those would present a problem, but he'd known the first time he'd set eyes on Cooper she wasn't going to be the norm. Just the thought of once again being responsible for her safety knotted his stomach. Goddamn it.

Too hungry to communicate, they ate in silence.

He was silent, anyway. She couldn't seem to stop talking, even to chew. He blocked out the sound, but had a harder time with the visual. Barefoot, she wore blue jeans and a white tank top, which left her tanned shoulders and lightly muscled arms bare. Pale, ginger-gold hair was unceremoniously slicked off her face and twisted into a braid that hung almost to her waist. She absently tossed the long rope over her shoulder, leaving the front of the thin white cotton shirt damp. She was tall, toned, and drop-dead beautiful.

And way too much trouble.

"What?" she asked, looking up to catch him staring at her.

"You clean up well." Her moods were fascinatingly mercurial. She'd been furious in the elevator—why, he wasn't sure. Because he'd called her on her flirting? Possibly. He'd been well aware of her control. Yet the mood had passed almost before they reached their suite.

She smiled a smile potent enough to shoot straight to his groin. "Thanks. So do you." She gave him a thorough once-over in return. Kane sat still for her perusal. She inspected him with the careful attention he'd just given her. "You're really a master of disguise, aren't you? Just looking at you an hour ago, I would've sworn you were a hundred."

"That was the idea." He wasn't used to being scrutinized with such intensity. Although he was damn sure Cooper was. He knew there'd been disciplinary action taken with several male students in her class. Now that he'd seen her up close and personal, he pitied the poor bastards who'd given in to their hormones and fucked up promising careers.

"Eat before it gets cold." His tone was slightly annoyed. Which irritated the hell out of him. For years he'd gone for the Mr. Spock school of emotion. None at all served him well, and he had no intention of changing that now.

His cover as an internationally renowned photographer was more than a job. Photography was his passion. His artistic and creative outlet. He'd photographed many beautiful women over the years, they were a dime a dozen, but none of them had what Cooper had. She'd been chosen for this op specifically because she was a crack sharpshooter, but God only knew, it was her physical appearance that had proven to be her biggest selling point.

She smelled of roses.

Damn it.

"Have we had an update on Raazaq's location in the past six hours?"

"We know where he's going and when he'll be there." Good. Mind on business. Safest that way. Kane cut into his steak. Nice and bloody. Just the way he liked it.

"Are we still going to intercept?"

"Plans have changed." He motioned to her plate. "Eat. I'll fill you in."

She picked up her fork and resumed eating. "Go."

He told her the new plan, changed because of what had happened the day before. When he was done, and it had taken him all of four minutes, he rose from the table and crossed the room to retrieve a small bag.

"I bet if you read *War and Peace* you'd summarize it in a minute thirty," AJ said waspishly. "You could give Cliffs Notes a run for their money."

He returned to stand behind her. "I gave you the salient points."

She twisted around to see what he was doing. Kane made a motion with his hand for her to show him the back of her head. She sighed and obediently lowered her head. He began unplaiting her hair. "There's more to life than salient points, you know. Color, drama—"

"This is a mission," he informed her coldly.

"You don't require either color or drama to do your job. In fact, the least amount of color and the absence of drama are preferable. Every legal avenue has already been attempted," he told her, annoyed because if he were on his own, *like he wanted to be,* he wouldn't be standing here smelling her hair and explaining himself. He sifted through the warm, wet, rose-scented strands to find the wound.

"Raazaq is slippery as hell and has, thus far, managed to elude every effort to capture him. This needs antiseptic."

"Done."

Strands of her long hair clung to his hands and wrists like licks of a flame as he inspected the lump on the back of her head. The jagged cut was already healing but he'd keep an eye on it. His fingers sifted through the fiery strands for a brief moment. He was almost surprised to find her hair cool to the touch, not blazing hot.

Kane removed his fingers from her hair with a silent curse. "You'll live."

"Good to know," AJ said wryly. She pushed her empty plate out of the way and reached for her coffee cup as he resumed his seat opposite her. She didn't do what any other woman would've done: mess with her hair. "Why did he target the school?"

"The daughters of high-profile heads of state

from all over the world attended San Souci. He demanded the U.S. free the hundred members of the Freedom Fighter cell we're holding. The U.S. refused. Three of the girls were daughters of members of the British Parliament, another a minor princess. Thirty-two of the kids were from the States. Everyone wants swift retaliation. The United Nations just passed a resolution—get him, but keep it by the books."

She gave him a short smile and a nod of admiration. "You said on the flight over that's what they'd say."

Kane nodded. "They're predictable, I'll give them that." Security forces all over the world were aware Kane was heading up a team to go in after Raazaq. While the world champed at the bit for news reports of official inquiries, T-FLAC was doing its job. Covertly.

"Sure. Easy for them to say. Chaos reigns and we all get wet," AJ said, helping herself to another cup of fragrant coffee. "Do we know where he is now?"

"Just received confirmation. Moving south. Slowly."

"Looking over his left shoulder for us?"

"Enough clues were left that he'll think we were just one of a multitude of enemies. He'll be watching his back, but not for us. Luckily for the good guys, everybody wants a piece of Raazaq's ass and he knows it. The son of a bitch has more enemies than Satan."

"I hate to point this out, now that I'm back in the game, but his people will certainly recognize me when we come face-to-face. How will I pull that off?"

"I seriously doubt you'll be made. There was too much action, too far away. Your most recognizable features are your eyes and your hair. Your head was covered, your face and hair were masked by the sand and dust. The guys chasing us were low on the food chain, not hired for their observation skills."

She relaxed. Good. This could still be salvaged. "Did intel fill you in on why he's going to Fayoum in the first place? It's just a small oasis, a green smudge in the desert, isn't it?"

"He has a sister he raised himself when their parents were killed in a bus accident. Apparently they're very close, yet this is the first time anyone knew he had family. For obvious reasons he wouldn't want anyone to know of her existence. She's about to have her first baby and he's planned to visit her in the next couple of days."

"Unless we get to him first."

"Unless we get to him first," he agreed.

"We're registered at the Auberge du Lac Hotel in Fayoum, where we'll arrive early this evening. I've arranged for a local to scout out scenic backdrops for our fashion-photo shoot for the next couple of days. The man's known as a talker. By the time we get there, everyone will be aware that a beautiful redheaded American model is in town."

"You're still not telling me what the—"

He cut her off and reached for the coffee. "Raazaq's sister lives in a village not far from there. He'll be one of the first people to find out about you. The temptation to meet you will draw him to one of our outdoor shoots. Or he might show up at the hotel. Either way, he'll ask you out. You'll go. Pick your opportunity carefully. You'll have only one shot at this. Once he's tipped to your real reason for being there, he'll be trying to take *you* out."

"I'm expected to walk up to him in front of witnesses and shoot him?"

"You're expected to do what you were sent here to do. Assassinate one of the world's most vicious terrorists. Shoot him. Poison him. Fuck him to death. Whatever it takes to do your job."

"Will I have poison?" AJ asked flatly.

"You will."

"Then two out of three can be considered options." She stood up and looked down at him. "Relax, superspy. I'm going to kill the little bastard, just like I said. Now, I'm off to take a nap. How long do I have?"

CHAPTER SIX

AJ sat on a silk-covered stool at the marble dressing table in the large, well-lit, and luxurious bathroom off her bedroom. Kane leaned against the sink counter, arms folded over his broad chest. Having a man—and such a large man, at that—in such an intimate space made it feel overcrowded and confining.

And damn it, she could *smell* him. It was a unique smell. Not soap, not cologne. Agents didn't use fragrance when they were on an op. It was the scent of his skin. How weird was that? She'd never been aware of a man's smell before. Pheromones. Being aware of what it was didn't make it less annoying. Distracting. Arousing.

"Smudge on a little more brown," Kane instructed. "Yeah. Like that. A little more underneath—no, more . . . Here, just give me that thing."

"Excuse me?"

"Lemme do it. You're not blending it right."

"Who're you, Max Factor?"

"Hand it over."

"I can do my own makeup."

He looked at her.

AJ sighed. "Here." She handed him the small eye shadow brush. "I've no doubt you can apply makeup better than I can. You certainly tend to wear more of it than I do."

She turned on the seat so he could apply the color himself. Kane stepped in front of her, his jean-clad groin at eye level, and about six inches away. A rush of sexual awareness washed over her. Jesus God. Her eyes shot to his face. It was impassive. Was it possible that he didn't feel anything? How could this attraction be so one-sided?

And what an effective way to keep her in her place, AJ thought with a small, self-deprecating smile.

One-sided or not, she had a mental flash of him on top of her. Bare sweaty skin to bare sweaty skin. She felt his weight, the slide of his hair-roughened leg along her smooth calf. . . .

"Yo, Cooper. You paying attention?" he demanded, bending down to peer at her face.

She swallowed hard, then glared up at him, suddenly feeling antsy and cranky herself. Her insides felt like they were on speed. Damn it. It just didn't matter how hot he made her. She was not about to screw up her second chance at building a career by doing anything stupid. He already thought little enough of her as it was. She wasn't about to compound the feeling. "Yes. You're fascinating. But it's hot in here."

He'd been nit-picking her makeup application for the last fifteen minutes. Man, give a guy a little authority and it went straight to his head. She wanted to *go*. She'd slept for three hours, and awakened alert and ready for just about anything. They were already getting a late start—it was past two—so they'd be traveling in the worst heat of the day. "If you'd just let me do it myself, we could be out of here in a few minutes." She cocked her head and gave him a one-eyed glare. "Do I tell you how to shave?"

"A: If you could do it yourself, I wouldn't have to. And B: The day I need your help is the day—" He broke off.

"Can't finish that one, can you?" she challenged. It wasn't easy to maintain a one-eyed glare, but she gave it her best shot, as he had her other one closed. "Because you *do* need me. Even Command thinks so."

"Command doesn't know jack."

"That's loyal."

"That's honest." He took her chin and tilted up her face. "Open your eyes. Hold the pot and look up. And while you're at it, shut up." He stroked the tip of a brush through the shadow and layered it beneath her left eye in small, sure strokes. Dabbed and stroked again. Leaned back, checked out his handiwork, then started on her other eye.

"You can let go of my face. I can hold my own head still," AJ pointed out. His hand felt cool on her hot skin. He was looking at her hard enough to notice every pore. She hoped to hell he didn't count mind reading as one of his many talents. He dropped his hand and scrabbled around in the cosmetic bag beside him.

Her erect nipples rasped against the inside of her bra. She glanced down. Oh, this wasn't good. She was hot, bothered, and blatant. Thank God Kane was oblivious. Or he would be if he didn't glance down and see her body's response to his.

His warm, coffee-scented breath fanned her face. He was close enough for her to see the dark blue rings around his irises. *Talk,* she told herself. *Keep him too busy to notice that you're panting like an idiot.* "How do you know so much about applying a woman's makeup, anyway?"

His eyes narrowed as he inspected his handiwork. Apparently not satisfied, he reapplied the small brush to her lid. "It's all part of the art of disguise."

"So you *don't* moonlight on Broadway as a chorus girl."

"You're a laugh a minute, Cooper."

"Well, you do have great legs."

"You're still talking."

"Right." She almost nodded, then figured he'd put her eye out. "So, you studied and perfected it." His hundred-year-old man had been amazing. "I wish you'd teach me how you did the old guy look. It would be fascinating to live in that skin for a while."

"Wrong op. You look just like we need you to look for this one."

"I wanted to work for T-FLAC so I didn't have to use my appearance for my job."

"Then you're a fool," he told her. "Your appearance is not only an asset, it can be a weapon. Have you had any classes with Savage?"

"Not yet."

"Well, hold on to your hat," he told her, and AJ wondered if there was something going on between Kane and Savage. As soon as the thought wandered into her brain, her blood began to simmer. Kane kept talking, oblivious. "That woman'll show you moves you've never even considered. She uses every God-given attribute to her advantage. Most men think with their little heads. Keep them off balance enough and you can use it to drag them where you want like a pull toy."

"I figured that out already. I've been a girl a lot longer than you have."

"Trust me, I noticed. Here." He handed her a tube of mascara, keeping eye contact. "I imagine you can do this part unsupervised?"

"I don't know, *Mom*. Maybe you shouldn't leave me alone with this. I might poke my eye out." When he just frowned at her, she blew out a frustrated breath. "Thanks for the tips."

He went back to his perch, half sitting, half leaning on the marble counter beside her. At least she wasn't eye to eye with the *Little General* anymore.

Her breasts ached for the touch of his hands. . . .

The image of their entwined naked bodies was starting to make her sweat.

It was so vivid. So sharp. So damn real that she was revved up and wanting more, just thinking about it.

She jerked the mascara wand from the container and applied goop to her lashes in short, annoyed strokes.

Why did she always want to sneeze the second she'd applied mascara? "You know, all this crap is going to melt off the second I step out into that heat."

"I want you in character when we leave the hotel. And I want you to stay in character until your job is done. Sultry, and seductive. Bimbo with a brain. Not girl next door."

"Fine. Is this sultry enough for you?" She turned her face to glare at him and worked her lips into a guppy kiss, while batting her now completely gooped eyelashes. Did his lips just twitch? Nah.

He gave her a mild look. "You'll do." He leaned his butt against the sink and inspected her face as if it were the Holy Grail. "Yeah, you'll do just fine. We'll have air-conditioning in the car for a few hours at least. By the time we get to Fayoum it'll have cooled off a bit. Is your hair naturally curly?"

"Unfortunately, yes." She frowned. "Which is why I keep it long and braided. Otherwise I look like Orphan Annie. What about supplies?"

"Taken care of. Leave the hair loose when we leave. It'll be like a flashing neon sign telling Raazaq and his minions where you are." He stopped, cocked his head. "Is that what the 'A' stands for? Annie?"

"No. My hair will get full of sand and make my scalp itch." She met his stony face and caved. "Oh, okay. Fine. Loose it will be." She glanced at him for a moment. "Do we have a staff of elves or something?" She shot him an exasperated glance. "Who took care of obtaining our supplies?" *Can we please get the hell out of this bathroom now?*

"Our Cairo-based people. I checked everything while you slept. We're good to go. What *does* it stand for?"

He was like a dog with a bone. And a small one, at that. "AJ."

He raised a brow. "Your parents christened you AJ?"

"Unfortunately, no. But that's what it is now."

"You had it legally changed?"

"Yep." At thirteen, she had stood firm. Name change and she'd go back on the pageant circuit. No name change and she'd refuse to budge. She hadn't answered to any other name since. "You ready to go?"

Kane levered himself off the counter. "Here," he said, sounding cranky again. "Put them on." Temper flashed in his eyes as he handed her a pair of small gold hoop earrings. It was gone so quickly AJ thought she might've imagined it. Wow. Anyone who could control emotion like that was someone to tread lightly around.

"Each holds one dose of poison. One's for Raazaq. One's for you. Just in case."

Just in case Raazaq and his gang decided to do unspeakably painful things to her body. AJ shuddered and took the earrings from his outstretched hand. A zing of electricity charged up her arm when their skin brushed. Their eyes met. He frowned. Annoyed again.

"Will your face actually break if you smile?" she asked, muttering the question more out of frustration than in the hope of an answer. "What's wrong with you, anyway?" AJ demanded, getting crankier herself by the minute. Unfortunately, she wasn't able to control her moods as efficiently as he seemed to. It was like watching a blind come down over a window.

"Me?" He sounded surprised. "Not a damn thing."

She stopped him with her hand on his arm. "Right. Look, if you're cranky because I'm on the op, that's not my fault. Your superiors made the call. And if you're being a pain because I won't tell you my former name . . . then get over it."

His eyes narrowed with irritation. "Your name should be Angina."

"And yours should be Pain in the Ass." She huffed out a breath and leaned in to make her glare more impressive. "You don't know jack about when not to push a lady, do you?"

"You're too damn beautiful," he finished as if she hadn't spoken.

Okay, a few minutes ago, she'd been doing a lot of daydreaming about rolling in the sheets with this guy. But for some reason, hearing him call her beautiful didn't hit the right buttons. It went in the opposite direction. She'd been judged on her looks all her life, and damn it, she was sick and tired of it.

AJ's teeth ground together, "Well, excuse me all to hell," she shot back hotly. "It's a gene thing. It's not like I had anything to do with it! If I had, I'd have arranged to look like a mud fence so guys like you wouldn't think I didn't have two working brain cells to rub together. So if looking at me bothers you . . . Look at something else, for God's sake. The reason I'm here is to kill Raazaq."

"It'll work."

"Huh?"

"You. The beautiful thing. It'll work on Raazaq, and that's all that matters."

"Fine."

"Fine."

"Look," she said, "if it'll help, pretend I'm a ninety-seven-year-old man under the makeup."

"Cooper, nobody's imagination is that good."

"Well, you're the great Kane Wright," she said, shoving past him to stomp out of the damn bathroom. "Find a way to make it work."

Kane hadn't said more than a dozen words in the hour since they'd left Cairo, and with another hour to go before they reached Fayoum, she'd be climbing the walls before then. The Hummer had excellent air-conditioning, but it was visibly hotter than hell outside the confines of their vehicle, and the sun was completely on her side of the car. Heat shimmered like water on the blacktop ahead of them. She wanted to strip off her too tight clothes, and jump into the mirage to cool off.

They were traveling south, parallel to the Nile. A wide swath of verdant green farmland stretched out on either side of the slow-moving river. Beyond its reach the dry barrenness of the desert appeared like a soft golden-brown blanket covering the world as far as the eye could see.

"Is it just me, or do you not communicate with humans?" AJ demanded, breaking the silence only because she could hear herself thinking.

"I'm not uncommunicative," Kane said mildly. "I'm meditative."

"Great. I'm teamed up with Ghandi."

He snorted a laugh and she cheered up a little. "Wow. Was that an actual reaction?"

"Don't press your luck."

"Quit meditating and talk to me, or I'll talk to you and you already know how good I am at that," she warned, and even while his gaze narrowed, she went on another rant—the kind that used to drive her brother, Gabriel, nuts. "So if you think about it, all of these planted fields probably look the same as they did three thousand years ago. Do you think the pharaohs used irrigation systems, or did they just beat small children until they cried enough to water the plants?" No response. Fine, she could keep this up all day. "Did you know that some people believe the pyramids were built by space aliens? It would explain a lot, but what do you think? Was it ancient astronauts, or were the Egyptians just really good architects, or—"

"Okay!" he snapped. "I surrender."

"There. That wasn't so hard, was it?"

They passed a small collection of mud-brick houses. Children waved as they drove by.

"What're you feeling so chatty about?"

They were in the middle of nowhere. Straggly vegetation, date palms, and sand as far as the eye could see. "Have something else you'd like me to do while you drive?" AJ had several lascivious thoughts. She folded her arms across her chest and tried to imagine being immersed in ice cold water.

"It's not my job to keep you amused. Take a nap."

T-FLAC operatives were trained to sleep for as little as a couple of hours at a stretch and wake refreshed. This cycle allowed them to function on smaller amounts of sleep, allowing them to handle stress and pressure if they had to go thirty-six hours straight without sleep on an op.

Navy SEALs had nothing on T-FLAC's Hell Week. Which was fondly called Beyond Hell *month*. Of the recruits who made it through basic training, another 90 percent rang the bell after BHM.

AJ hadn't, though. She'd thrived on it. She'd made it through her class—despite the "incident." And she wouldn't lose her momentum now.

"I slept three hours. That's enough."

"You're a restless sleeper."

"Wha—" She swung her head to look at him. "How do you know that?"

"Came in to ask you something. You were waging war on your pillow."

AJ felt her cheeks grow warm at the thought of Kane seeing her at her most vulnerable. "I have nightmares sometimes." *Most of the time.* Asleep and awake, she had nightmares. These days she had to be pretty damn exhausted to get any rest at all.

"Because of what happened?"

This was her fault. She'd wanted him to talk to her. Now that he had, of course, she wanted him to shut up. She didn't want to talk about what had happened. About the night sweats and the cold, shrieking terror that locked her muscles. She didn't want his sympathy. She didn't want him even knowing what had happened to her. But, of course, he did. Even if he hadn't heard of it, he would have looked up her service record before she'd come on the op.

The knowledge that he'd read her report made her cheeks burn hot. "I'm working through it. And I'll do my job. If you don't mind, I'd rather not talk about it." And before he took satisfaction finding something that effectively shut her up, she changed the subject as fast as she could. "If I'm going to off Raazaq, what's your job now, since Escobar and Struben are out of the picture?" She bent to pick up the water bottle at her feet, uncapped it, and took a swig.

"I'm your spotter." He paused. "And your bodyguard for the duration."

"Snipers have spotters. They *don't* have bodyguards."

"Lucky you."

AJ bit her tongue. Yeah. Lucky her.

She turned in her seat to look at him. If the situation were different, she might consider making a play for him. Of course, she'd have to be crazy, but damn, he looked good. *Really* good. Still, the situation wasn't different—he was her boss and she was the lowly rookie. She'd do well trying to keep her brain wrapped around the job at hand.

His shaggy dark hair looked silky to the touch. He was tanned, fit, and smelled so damn yummy, AJ was salivating. Just looking at his long-fingered hands made all her juices flow and her breasts tighten. His hands were relaxed on the steering wheel, large and limber, and his fingers cupped the hard plastic like a lover's . . .

She took another deep swig of cool water just as the car went over a bump in the road. Water trickled down her chin and wet the neckline of her T-shirt. Nice and cool. It put an abrupt halt to her fantasy. She was tempted to douse herself, just for the hell of it. Instead, she swiped her chin with the back of her hand and glared at him. "Really?"

"Really. Raazaq has a preference for beautiful, redheaded American women. He's also a sadistic son of a bitch, and given half a chance will rip your wings off because it amuses him."

"I don't have wings."

He shot her an annoyed glance. "Would you prefer I said he'd perform weird, perverted sex acts on you and then rip your throat out with his bare hands, or watch while his people cut out your tongue . . . or worse?"

"Wings are good."

"Get him alone," Kane said grimly. "Do the world a service. Kill him. We'll be Stateside by the weekend, with no one the wiser."

The Hummer hit a rut in the road and she bounced high enough to slam the top of her head into the ceiling. When she landed again, she asked, "Now, why does this sound just too simple?"

"The best plans usually are."

The Fayoum Oasis was one of Cairo's weekend getaway destinations. Only a couple of hours outside the busy metropolis, the waters of the Nile had been diverted here centuries ago, creating a rich agricultural area. Considered the "garden of Egypt," El-Fayoum had lush fields of vegetables, sugarcane, groves of citrus fruits, and nuts and olives. It also had one of Egypt's largest saltwater lakes, which was used for recreation.

"Did you know the Auberge du Lac was originally built as a hunting lodge by King Farouk?" AJ asked as they pulled under the portico of the hotel.

"No," he muttered, "but I bet you're about to tell me how many bathrooms there are."

She did.

As with all her comments and observations for the past couple of hours, Kane just tried to ignore her, throwing a grunt in when nothing else would do. The woman *talked*. Incessantly.

She'd given him a blow-by-blow history lesson as they'd traveled the desert roads. Past children working in the cotton fields with cows and camels, past mud huts and date palms, past sand and vegetation. Past inquisitive women turning to stare at their vehicle through a narrow slit in their veils. AJ Cooper had chattered on. Non. Frigging. Stop.

He'd always considered himself something of a student of Egypt. Well, if he was a student, he'd just met the professor.

"Winston Churchill stayed here in 1945," Cooper informed him as they were swamped by bellhops and children the second they opened the car doors.

Every one of their all-male audience dropped back a step, eyes wide, mouths falling open when Cooper unfurled her long bare legs from her seat and straightened as she glanced around, apparently oblivious to the commotion she was causing.

She wore a sleek, fuchsia-colored silk tank top tucked into a multihued pink floral skirt, which dropped in soft folds to swirl around her shapely calves. Her loose red hair caught the sun, and shone a brilliant, blatant, *hot* orange. Against her creamy, lightly tanned skin the long skeins were enough to have every man in a hundred-mile radius panting to run his fingers through the fiery strands. She screamed female sexuality. An Egyptian goddess sent to earth to torment mere men into doing rash and foolish deeds for just one smile.

"Winston loved the place," she told him, whipping that amazing hair back from her face. "Said he felt like King Tut—which was pretty funny, considering poor Tut died at thirteen and . . ."

Kane strode toward the front door, leaving the staff to remove their luggage from the vehicle, and Cooper, still talking, to follow. He caught a glimpse of the shimmering blue waters of Lake Karoun. According to his loquacious travel guide, the oldest man-made lake in the world.

He wanted a cold shower and an hour of peace and quiet.

The woman talked as much as his sister, Marnie, did, all while tap dancing on his last nerve. The two women would get along great. And if they were ever in the same room together, Kane would have to kill himself.

AJ Cooper rattled his cage and set every sense on red alert. There was no doubt that the second Raazaq saw her, he'd be a goner. In more ways than one.

If Cooper didn't inadvertently screw this one up again.

On the phone, he'd discussed her situation with the T-FLAC shrinks. They believed she could do the job.

He was here to see that she did.

All in all, Kane thought, as they followed a fleet of moon-eyed hotel personnel to their rooms, things were going according to plan.

All they needed now was for their prey to see the bait.

The small plastic-surgery scars, one on the inner curve of her shoulder, the other on her back, had barely healed. The marks were still pink and shiny, and an obscenity on her clear, smooth skin, despite the skills of T-FLAC's best team of doctors. Kane had an old scar on his left shoulder in exactly the same position. But it was a knife that had dug into his flesh, not a bullet.

The bullet that had shaken AJ's confidence had taken her right up to death's door and helped her knock. It was a lot harder to go into a battle situation when you knew what the impact of a bullet felt like. Kane knew. He'd had several.

She was swimming laps in one of the hotel pools. She was a strong swimmer. Good form. He bit back a smile. Terrific form. Jesus. Even the women poolside were watching her. Poetry in motion in a white bikini.

AJ's slender arms sliced through the water, she jackknifed into an underwater dive, showing a nicely curved ass, then surfaced on the pool's edge beside his lounger, arms folded on the lip of the pool. She blinked diamond droplets of water off spiky lashes. "I'm starving. Let's eat."

"Out here, or one of the restaurants?" The air was hot and still. The setting sun glowed red and magenta over nearby Lake Karoun, and the pigeons were returning to their tall domed pigeon house nearby. Hungry for their dinner, not knowing they'd be someone else's dinner the next day. It was a dog-eat-dog world.

"Here's fine." She hauled herself out of the pool, dripping wet. Kane almost swallowed his tongue.

That damn white suit was transparent, and

blast if his gaze didn't lock right onto the dark circles of her nipples, standing taut against the wet fabric. He needed to send a memo to wardrobe. There was attractive and there was blatant. Cooper didn't seem to be aware of the view she was affording the other swimmers.

The thought annoyed the hell out of him. He, and every other male who laid eyes on her, apparently, wanted to jump her bones. He gave a "back off, asshole" look to a young stud who appeared stupid enough to come over. The guy tried to hold eye contact, then wisely subsided into his lounger. He wasn't as dumb as he looked.

There were a dozen excellent reasons not to have sex with Cooper. Not the least of which was they had a mission that couldn't be screwed up a second time.

They both had to keep their minds on business. But if she was going to walk around three-quarters naked for the next couple of days, he was sure to be a basket case.

Being around her made him irritable. He couldn't have her. Shouldn't want her. Didn't want to want her. And just looking at her slender, voluptuous body spiked his blood pressure and made him hornier than he could remember being. Ever.

It was a damn nuisance. Not an insurmount-
able problem, but a nuisance, nevertheless.

He tossed her a towel, and she absently blot-
ted her face, leaving her long hair glued to her
wet skin like seaweed to a mermaid. She
shrugged into the toweling robe she'd thrown
over her lounge earlier, and reached for the
menu on the small table holding their drinks.
"What's your pleasure?"

He wondered what her reaction would be if
he told her.

Twenty-four hours, and still no sign of
Raazaq.

If he was anywhere within a hundred miles
he knew about the American redhead staying
at the best hotel in town. Everybody was talking about her. From their auspicious arrival
yesterday, to the shoot this morning, Kane and
AJ had been blatant and out there.

If their mark didn't contact them by early
this evening, they'd have to go and seek him
out.

They were in the car again, this time traveling a few miles to the Pyramid of Hawara. This
morning Kane had taken shots of her near the
lake. AJ might be oblivious to her looks, but
the camera loved her.

She was a natural, and a photographer's

dream. Not self-conscious in any way, AJ was more concerned with their need to draw a crowd to attract Raazaq than she was with his recording her every move.

And damn, she did a good job of attracting a crowd. Little kids loved her and she gave it right back, laughing and playing with them whenever she had a break. She ignored the young men with their hot eyes and teased the old men who looked at her in fond memory of what they would have liked to have done with her if they were thirty years younger.

She was more than he'd thought she'd be. More than just a great face and an incredible body. More than a halfway decent agent and a good shot. She was the whole damn package. Through the viewfinder he found her face even more compelling. Other than her obvious physical beauty and the symmetry of her features, there was a strength of character, and a complete lack of guile one didn't expect to find in a woman who could turn intelligent men into puddles of testosterone.

By the time they'd been at the morning location for half an hour, upwards of a hundred people had joined them. Standing respectfully in a semicircle around them, AJ's admirers had offered to assist, fetch, carry, and generally make themselves useful in the hope of getting closer to the woman or getting a *baksheesh*, a tip, for running errands, or carrying water.

Now, back in their car, on the way to the Pyramid of Hawara, nine vehicles, three horses, and two camels followed in their wake. It was a damn parade, and if Raazaq didn't know about her, then he clearly wasn't around.

"Did you know that seventy-eight percent of all women, if given the chance, would rather drive than be driven?"

"Is that so?"

She blinked her eyes at him. "You don't believe me?"

"Nope." Kane brought his attention back to the desert road ahead. If the fools wanted to eat his dust, more power to them. "You're a natural at this. Why didn't you pursue modeling? It's a hell of a lot more lucrative than working for T-FLAC."

A nerve flexed in her jaw. "There's more to me than a face. And money isn't everything."

She'd got a bit of sun this morning and her nose and cheeks were pink and glowing. It made her look younger and, damn it, even more appealing.

"Tell me about being Miss Illinois."

She rolled her eyes and chuckled. "Oh, please. That is *so* yesterday."

He did his best not to react to that laugh.

Her low, throaty laugh was a man's fantasy come to life.

"Don't like tiaras?" he asked.

AJ snorted. "Trust me, I still have night-mares about my pageant years." She mulled it over. "Of course, being forced to wear high heels and be slathered in makeup *is* my idea of a nightmare. Wanna hear about the Pyramid of Hawara?"

"Do I have a choice?" He glanced in the rearview mirror. The convoy was still behind them, kicking up a mile-long cloud of dust.

"Sure. You can hum under your breath while I talk. Built by Amenemhet the Third, the pyramid was the most visited site of the an-cient world." She turned in her seat, held her hair back from her face, and grinned at him. "It was also called the Labyrinth because it's so enormous inside. It's been estimated to have over three thousand rooms in the two stories. Twelve covered courts—"

"Cooper?"

"What?"

"I don't give a damn."

"I thought you found Egyptology fascinat-ing."

"I do. But right now the only Egyptian I'm interested in is Raazaq. I want him to show so we can do our job and go home. If you still have this newfound fascination with frigging pyramids, come back some other time, and spout to your heart's content."

"Fine." She uncurled her legs and faced forward. "You know, we have to be together. I thought I'd be friendly. But apparently you don't know jack about friendly. I just thought it might be nice if we got to know each other a little. But, hey, don't mind me, I'll just—"

"You said you were gonna shut up."

"I am."

"When?"

"You have something against conversation?"

"I like quiet."

"Quiet is too noisy for me."

They lapsed into silence.

Kane discovered quiet *could* be noisy.

AJ leaned against the sun-warmed brick and smiled nicely for the camera—and about a hundred men, women, children, and livestock who'd followed them out to the pyramid. Raazaq better show up pretty damn soon. She wasn't cut out to be a model. It wasn't that she couldn't do it. She was just bored out of her mind.

"Curve your left arm over your head."

She obeyed and went back to thinking about

the nightmare of walking in high heels and a tiara.

"Why the hell are you scowling? Turn into your arm and smile. Could you try to make that a little more sincere? Yes, like that. Tilt your chin down a little. Too much. Yes. Hold it."

"I thought digital cameras don't have moving parts."

"They don't."

"For a guy who likes quiet, you've sure got a noisy camera. How come yours clicks, whirrs, and beeps?"

"So I know when I've taken the shot. Go put on the yellow dress," Kane instructed, switching cameras as he spoke.

She left the shade of the makeshift canopy Kane had erected and walked across the scraggy grassed parking lot to the tent to change out of a blue shorts outfit.

The tent was hot despite the battery-operated fan sitting on the small table. AJ let the flap drop closed behind her and unbuttoned the short, sleeveless blouse, standing in front of the fan as she finished undressing.

Kane had to be as bored as she was, she thought, as she checked her makeup—looked fine to her—and her hair—annoyingly curly.

The yellow evening dress—Badgley Mischka, Kane had told her, as though she should know . . . or care—was filmy lemon chiffon. The skirt was made up of miles of flounces, and the top consisted of a couple of Band-Aid-size scraps of practically see-through silk crossed over her breasts, leaving her entire back and tummy bare.

AJ would've given her next five paychecks to be wearing her favorite jeans and a T-shirt, and packing her weapon. She sighed and went back outside, holding the hem of the fragile dress up as she strode across the sandy lot, still wearing her boots.

Kids scrambled to get a place beside her as she walked. They jabbered as they ran to catch up. AJ just smiled, and indicated she didn't understand what they were saying. It was easier to pick up bits and pieces of intel when people thought you didn't understand what they said.

The decision suited AJ just fine. She *did* understand a word here and there. Arabic, and all its dialects, was a good language to know. Unfortunately she had no ear for languages and was second from the bottom of her class. She'd work harder at that when she returned. Kane's linguistic skills were phenomenal.

A few hundred yards ahead, she watched him fiddle with his camera and adjust a white umbrella for better reflected light. He wore a long-sleeved, collarless, green cotton shirt. The snug fit of the shirt accented his broad shoulders and flat belly. Tan pants tucked into heavy boots emphasized his long legs and tight butt. His shaggy hair looked lighter in the sun as he bent over to retrieve a straw cowboy hat to shade him from the unrelenting rays of the sun. He moved with an easy, fluid grace that was at once relaxed and purposeful.

The hat shaded the top half of his face, and highlighted the stubborn curve of his jaw and the sensual curve of his mouth.

AJ forcibly dragged her attention from Kane Wright's lips to the pyramid behind him.

Didn't look much like a pyramid now. More like a large mottled green hill in the middle of scrub brush. Just the mud-brick core remained, the external limestone had long since disappeared, but Kane liked the primitiveness of the broken stone as a backdrop to the expensive clothing she was to wear for the shoot.

AJ made a mental note to ask him if he'd actually do anything with all the pictures he was taking. He certainly knew his way around a camera.

The hot sun felt good on her bare shoulders, but staying out here unprotected for long was dangerous. Heatstroke was always a possibility in the desert. They'd set up a large awning against the side of the pyramid for the shoot, and she picked up the pace to get into the shade.

She watched Kane as she approached and almost did a double-take. Right before her eyes he changed from a tall, virile, take-charge kind of a guy into a bony, bad-postured camera geek. He looked like a paler, less interesting version of himself. Different, and yet the same.

He squinted at her absently as she approached. "More lip gloss," he instructed, holding out the tube as she passed him. "Take your time. I believe the party's about to get interesting."

AJ paused. My God, even his voice was different. Lighter. Slightly hesitant. Less substantial. How did he transform himself so subtly with no makeup or costume change? Nothing but his own body and demeanor. It was remarkable.

Slowly, she applied the sticky gloss to her mouth as she glanced back to the crowd of observers. From the corner of her eye, she saw the long, black stretch set apart from the other spectators.

Her heart did a little hop, skip, and jump of anticipation.

Raazaq had sought her out.

The game was afoot.

CHAPTER SEVEN

Kane glanced at the large man who'd lumbered out of the front seat of the limo and now stood, *loomed,* out of camera range, clearly waiting for AJ.

"Tourist?" he asked the guy facetiously.

The goon, in a dark, shiny suit, folded his arms across his massive chest. He was the bad guy straight out of Central Casting. No neck, shaved head, small reptilian eyes, and lipless as a trout.

"Waiting for ze girl." The accent was French. His weapon, tucked in plain sight in a front holster, Russian, and his dental work, American.

The small, gold cartouche earring in his cauliflower ear was a nice touch.

Kane raised a brow. "The lady'll be a while."

"I will wait."

Kane bent to look through the viewfinder. "Suit yourself." His heartbeat kicked up a notch or two. Damn. What could be better than this? Combining his two loves. Photography and an-

nihilating tangos. Life was great when everything came together.

He'd had his doubts, still wasn't 100 percent
sure that when push came to shove AJ could do
her job. But he was with her. Between them,
the job would be done. And done right.

Raazaq would be wary after the attempted
hit the other day. But there was nothing that
would make him suspect a beautiful model.
The net was in place.

Kane adjusted the focus and pulled back for a
full-length shot of her. His lips twitched. Peeking
from beneath the hem of the delicate concoction
she wore were heavy, lace-up boots. The look
was sexy, in your face, and provocative.

"Cross your right arm over your chest." He
raised his voice so she could hear him. "Cup
your left shoulder, and tilt your head back a little. Little more." Her breasts moved beneath
the thin fabric of the dress as she shifted.

Kane was surprised Raazaq—and he didn't
doubt for a minute that Raazaq was inside the
air-conditioned vehicle—hadn't fallen out of
the limo by now. "Good. Good. Hold it."

She gave no indication that she was aware of
the man beside him. Her gaze didn't so much
as flicker to the dark windows of the limo.

"Okay, now toss your head. Give me some
movement—something with your hair."

AJ scooped up the long slippery strands and gathered the copper mass on top of her head. Arms raised, head back, she made every nerve and cell in Kane's body jump to attention as he imagined that cool flame blanketing his body. His hands itched to touch her soft, smooth skin.

He lost his own focus and had to readjust and realign to bring her back into the camera's focus. Enough of this crap.

He fired off a quick succession of shots. *Women's Wear Daily* was eager for anything he sent them. He'd kill two birds with one stone. And Kane suspected that these shots of AJ Cooper wearing some of the top designers were going to be his best work to date. The camera loved her.

And God help him, he wanted her. In print the photographs of her would be combustible.

She was the center of attention but wasn't the least bit self-conscious. He suspected she'd prefer being dressed in jeans and a T-shirt, and wearing her ass-kicking boots while she tromped through the woods. The Messrs. Badgley and Mischka would be rolling their eyes if they could see AJ in their creation. The hem of the dress was liberally coated with taupe-colored sand, the flounces slightly wilted in the heat. Kane was pretty sure they hadn't imagined an impatient tomboy wearing such a feminine gown. Seeing AJ Cooper in the frou-frou creation was actually quite captivating.

"Tilt your head to the left—Stay."

She froze in place, but her pale eyes sparked irritation and heat at the command. "How much longer?"

"Till I say we're done."

He set the camera on the tripod and strode across the scrub grass to the large shaded awning where she stood.

"Now what? Don't mess with my makeup anymore," she warned, taking a step back and crossing two index fingers as if to ward off a vampire. Her hair tumbled down her back and slithered over her shoulders. "If it's melted, we're done."

"Don't look so hopeful," he chided. "It's waterproof, and we're almost done." He resisted moving a curled strand of hair off the gentle swell of her breast. "Raazaq is sitting in that limo salivating. No. Don't stiffen up. Relax." Kane tunneled his fingers through the roots of her hair at her temples and spread the warm, fragrant mass over her shoulders like he'd been itching to do for the last hour. She'd been doing fine on her own, but damn it, he wanted to touch her. *Had* to touch her. Her hair felt as fine as warm silk as it brushed his hands and wrists.

"Pretend that's your lover watching you." He draped the strands artistically over her left shoulder to curve against her breast. And cover the scar. The back of his fingers brushed against the sharp point of her nipple. They both drew in a breath.

"Kane—"

"I want him to want you more than his next breath," he told her roughly. "I want him to think sex when he sees you. Hot. Wild. Steamy sex." *Just words,* he reminded himself. *Just words. No physical reaction necessary here, Wright! A pheromone thing.* His body tightened, just the same.

"Why can't he think dinner?" AJ inquired a little breathlessly as he walked behind her. She tilted her head to watch him warily. "What are you doing?"

"You're playing a role, Cooper. Sexy siren. Immerse yourself in the part. Become it. Be it. Think sultry. Think hot. Think bare naked skin to bare naked skin." If she got any hotter, Kane thought, they'd both burn to a crisp.

"I'd rather think about a dip in the hotel pool followed by room service," she said with amusement.

"You can't look sexy if you don't think sexy." He ran his hand around her waist from the back. His fingers splayed across the warm, smooth skin of her stomach. He knew a sudden, overpowering urge to brush her hair aside and press his mouth against the vulnerable skin of her nape.

She shivered at the intimate touch of his hand. "Of course I can," she said firmly. "Don't tell me every underwear model is thinking sexy thoughts when she's posing in nothing but skimpy underoos and a pair of wings! She's thinking of a Big Mac, and supersized fries."

Kane stood directly behind her. "Forget about food for a few minutes," he told her dryly. He ran the flat of his palm up, over her diaphragm. The sheer fabric bisected her plump breasts in a cross–her–heart X, leaving tantalizing triangles of flesh bare. "Close your eyes and take a deep breath."

He felt her drag in a shuddering, deep breath, and presumed her eyes were closed. Her skin felt unbelievably soft, and as smooth and warm as slightly damp satin as his hand skimmed the flat plane of her stomach and glided up her midriff, then moved smoothly between the plump mounds of her breasts.

"You're beautiful. Feel it," he said against her temple. "Sexy. Confident in your own sensuality. You love sex. Want sex. *Crave* sex—"

"Sex as a disguise?" she asked, her voice low and husky. "I bet *those* classes are packed with female operatives."

"No classes. But don't underestimate the power of sexual attraction, Cooper. Armies have been conquered and countries lost for it."

Kane forced himself to remember that he was doing this for the op. A disguise was only as good as the person believing in it. He'd given dozens of lessons to rookies on the art of camouflage, disguise, and sleight of hand, ways to blend with their surroundings. This was just another training exercise.

Except that he'd never been quite so aware of the fragrance of a rookie's skin, or become so in tune with her every breath. "You have to project sensuality, Cooper. Feel it from here." He pressed his flattened hand against the erratic beat of her heart. "And especially here." He touched his chin to the crown of her head. "Disguise is 50 percent mind games."

"Are you doing this to make your pictures turn out better?" she asked thickly. "Or for Raazaq?"

"Yeah."

"Yeah wh—" The back of her head thumped onto his chest as he slid his left hand around her waist, and spread the fingers of his right hand between the soft mounds of her breasts. "Jesus God, Kane. Do you know what you're doing?"

He was swimming in shark-infested waters. "I'm trying to make you feel sexy."

"And—" She cleared her throat. Her rose-scented hair tickled his chin. "And do I?"

"Oh, yeah."

"From in here, too. You'd better stop that pretty soon." She lifted her head from his chest and he felt the loss. "Don't look now," she sounded out of breath and a little vague, "but we have a fascinated audience."

"Hold that look," he told her, then strode back to his equipment and the loomer.

"Still here?" Kane asked the trout companionably.

"Mr. Raazaq gets impatient."

Good, he thought. Impatient meant careless. And careless for Raazaq meant dead. "Who's Raazaq?" Kane asked carelessly. "Your driver?"

"Mr. Raazaq is my boss. He is . . ."

Kane waited a beat, still peering through the camera at AJ. Jesus. She had "look sexy" down pat. "He is . . . ?" *A Terrorist? Evil personified? The anti-Christ?* He clicked off a quick succession of shots, before AJ forgot what she was about, and *he* forgot to breathe.

"He is Mr. Raazaq," Trout Face repeated.

"Yeah?" Kane said absently.

"It has been an hour."

"Maybe your boss needs to come talk to the

lady himself," Kane told him, still clicking shots as fast as he could. Damn. The light on her face was perfect. Diffused by the awning, it accented the honeyed tone of her skin and turned her hair to fire.

The camera loved her. He zoomed in. Just her mouth. Soft. Plump. Damp.

After several long seconds, he remembered he was supposed to be taking pictures. He clicked a succession of shots of her mouth . . . and struggled to get his brain back where it belonged.

"Don't think she'll be that impressed your boss sent you," Kane told Raazaq's man. "No offense. But look at her." *And I'd better not.* "Think she's used to waiting for a guy?"

He was talking to air. Kane shot a glance over to the right. Fish-faced goon-boy was lumbering back to the shiny black limo. Kane returned his attention to the camera and gave her curt instructions for another fifteen minutes before calling, "Okay. That's it. Change, and we're outta here." Kane raised his voice slightly.

AJ heard him just fine. His voice was deep and rich and perfectly pitched to carry.

The bodyguard type had returned to stand watching her. A long-stemmed rose in his hand.

AJ ignored the guy in the suit, only too

happy to get back into comfortable clothes. Kane had hired several young men who, at his signal, started removing the shade canopy, and were helping him load the car.

Feeling a little like a mother hen followed by her chicks, she moved quickly across the parking lot to the small tent to change, followed by a gaggle of pushing, shoving, giggling kids.

She paused as the limo driver stepped in front of her, brandishing the long-stemmed flower like a sword. He shoved it at her chest. "Mr. Raazaq would like you to join him for dinner this evening."

AJ took the stem of the wilted flower. In this heat she knew just how it felt. "I have no idea who Mr. Raddeek is. But thank him for me, sugar, and tell him I'm busy tonight. Maybe another time." She turned and waved at the man concealed behind the blackout windows in the car. "We're at the Auberge du Lac. Have him call." She didn't wait for a response but sped up, a flock of kids, two dogs, and a braying donkey in tow.

It was customary to refuse a first invitation in Egypt. Raazaq would have been more suspicious if she'd immediately agreed to dinner. He'd call. She'd go.

She understood that she'd been sent to do this job because of her sharpshooting skills. But if she could manage to eliminate Raazaq in the most expedient way possible and divert suspicion to someone who worked for him, all the better.

Poison or a bullet. Either way, the job would be done.

Dead was dead.

There was no wiggle room. No room for failure.

The poison inside her gold earring was slow-acting. Depending on the man's body weight, anywhere from five to nine hours. AJ and Kane would be back in Cairo while Raazaq breathed his last.

They would wait for intel of his death and then leave on the next flight out.

Quick, and relatively easy if everything went according to plan. If not, there was always the Dragunov and a fast bullet.

She wouldn't miss.

Not again.

"What are you doing in there?" Kane called from outside. "Digging a tunnel to China?"

"Changing. You might as well go ahead and load the car. And turn on the air conditioner, would you, please?"

"Yes, ma'am."

She was more than happy to strip off the chiffon dress and change into a cool floral skirt and T-shirt, though they didn't look any better with her boots. Feeling a bit more like herself, she packed up her makeup and emerged from the tent into the heat of the late afternoon.

"Thank you." She indicated to the two men hovering outside that they could take down the canvas tent, then went over to the car where Kane waited for her.

The limo was gone, but the rest of the on-lookers were still milling about in a wide semi-circle. Reluctant to leave and miss anything interesting, but now hot and bored, they wandered about, chatting, eating, and staring at her.

AJ opened the door and slid into the cool interior. "He took the bait." She twisted the hot weight of her loose hair up, pinning it on top of her head with a pen she found on the console.

"Without a doubt." Kane started the car. "We'll keep a low profile until he surfaces again. Let him cool his jets until then. Make him more eager. Less observant."

She leaned her head back on the seat and turned to look at him. "God, I can't wait to get started."

The cool breeze from the air-conditioning ruffled Kane's hair about his strong face. He turned to glance at her. "You're looking forward to it?" The words were simple enough, it was the subtext that made the blood rush to AJ's brain.

It made sense that he'd continue to need reassurance, but knowing it was his right to ask didn't diminish AJ's surge of righteous anger. "Yes," she said shortly. "I'm looking forward to it. I want to do my job."

The op depended on her reasoning ability and quick reflexes. He was her partner. Their lives depended on her. He had to be able to predict her behavior in a crisis situation. Hell, they both did. But she wasn't asking him every second of every day if he could do *his* job.

"I understand that the great Kane Wright is infallible, invincible, and damn well perfect. But the rest of us lowly humans make mistakes. *I* made mistakes. I won't make any more. Let's move on."

"You won't be killing this man through a rifle scope, Cooper. It'll be up close and personal. If you don't get him first, he'll sure as shit get you."

"Have I given you the impression," AJ demanded through clenched teeth, "that I'm half-witted? I was shot in the chest, not through my brain."

"You were pronounced dead."

"Yeah, but I didn't stay dead, did I? See? Even almighty God-like beings like doctors screw up. Because here I am, hale, hearty, and rarin' to go. You bet your sweet ass I can't wait to kill the sick son of a bitch. He needs to die, and I have to prove myself to every gun-toting good guy in the free world that I'm just as good as they are. Not perfect. Just good at what I do. I've waited my whole life to prove I'm more than two boobs and a pair of long legs. I'm not going to blow this. Is that enough damn confidence for you, Mr. Always Right?"

Heat shimmered ahead of them on the dirt road. Behind them was a dust cloud containing their enormous band of followers. Somewhere out there, their prey was unaware of just where his dinner invitation would lead.

"You'll have your chance," he said calmly. "And believe me, Cooper, I'm not anywhere close to being perfect." He steered the car down the middle of the road to avoid the line of people on either side, waving as if they were a parade. "Tell me what happened that day."

"What day?" AJ said offhandedly.

"The day you died."

Crap. She'd known he would dig away. "It was hotter than the hobs of hell that morning." AJ leaned forward, damp palms clamped between her knees. Her heart raced. She stared with scratchy dry eyes at the sandy road ahead, seeing instead sagebrush and scrub. Different sand. "A hundred and eight. No shade. Five-day field trip where we had to find food. Water. Survive on our wits." She snorted a laugh. "We'd gone up there unarmed."

The sun had beat down on them fiercely. "It was day four. None of us knew what a five-day field trip with Curtner could possibly be like. He was a sadistic son of a bitch, and proud of it. We'd had target practice the day before, six hundred yards. Not all the rookies had a good eye. Some of us didn't get 100 percent of our targets. Curtner was going to make us stay up all night until all eight of us got it picture perfect—100 percent bull's-eyes, 100 percent of the time.

"I'd never been that tired in my life. The heat. The flies. The ass yelling and screaming at us nonstop—We were all hungry and dying of thirst. He wouldn't let us sleep, eat, or drink until we did it as a team. We were up on that ridge for fourteen hours."

"No water for fourteen hours?"

"Not a drop. Forrest eventually passed out from heatstroke. Curtner went ballistic. Went for him with those big, bad-ass boots of his. The kid didn't stand a chance. The screaming and yelling were bad enough. But Forrest was down and out. He couldn't defend himself—I saw red, and went for Curtner. Took him down." AJ squeezed her eyes shut.

"It happened so fast. The others were still blindly trying to hit those targets. I had Curtner in a headlock and was so angry I couldn't see straight—"

"You were in the line of fire."

She shuddered. "Oh, yeah. Worse, Stillwell and Evans charged in to the rescue—"

"Whose?" Kane asked dryly.

"Mine," AJ told him tightly. "Mine." Curtner was disciplining her in the only way he knew how. With his fists and feet. But at least he'd left Forrest alone while he concentrated on her. "They were both killed by friendly fire. Both of them. Jesus God."

Kane frowned. "I read the report. That wasn't it."

"I know." Curtner, with nothing more than a bloody nose, had claimed she hadn't liked being out of her comfort zone. Then told everyone she'd gone apeshit, tried to beat the crap out of him, and pulled him into the line of fire so he would be shot. The other two men had come in to pull her off, and gotten shot for their pains.

"It was a little difficult putting a stop to the rumor while I was unconscious in the hospital. By the time I was released, the story had morphed into something else entirely."

She glanced at Kane to see how he was taking this. Probably thinking the same thing many other T-FLAC operatives had thought. Hotheaded, temperamental, *female* operative.

Even though the incident had happened over three months ago, she was still fighting to maintain her place and dignity with the others. Still trying to overcome flinching every time she heard a gun discharge, for God's sake.

"Why didn't the men report what'd really happened?"

Her eyebrows rose. Man, he didn't get it. She'd tried to set the record straight. Rookie. Twenty-two-year veteran. Yeah, right. "Against Curtner? The trainer who held their future in his hands? Surely you jest."

"Shit happens, Cooper. The deaths of those young men was a tragedy waiting to happen. But not your fault. And as for you being shot— hazard of the job. Brace yourself. Everybody knows Curtner's an asshole. They might have believed you if you'd stood up as a team. But it'll happen again. And again. And a-fucking-gain. Until you move faster, and think more clearly."

Two men were dead because of her. Dead. Never going home to their young wives. Never completing basic training and going out in the field to eliminate terrorists. Never coming home to a pot roast dinner on a Sunday night with their moms . . . Never doing *any-thing*. Because they were stone-cold dead.

So it didn't matter what the hell anyone said. She knew it was her fault.

And as for getting shot . . . she'd never experienced all-consuming pain like that. Never been hurt, or beat up, or attacked in her life. She'd pranced across runways and looked pretty. She'd bitched to her mother for years about how much she hated the beauty-pageant circuit. She'd hated it. But she'd never been physically hurt wearing a swimsuit and a smile.

When she'd come out of the coma her entire body and mind had gone into shock from the experience.

"You're right," she bit out. "Absolutely right. I'm working on it." AJ wanted to hit him. While her temper bubbled and boiled like the contents of a witch's cauldron, Kane sat there calm and collected and matter-of-fact. The man drove her absolutely nuts, he was so controlled. "Have you ever been shot?"

"Of course."

"Of course," she mimicked. "I presume you got over it fast? What'd you do? Chew the bullet out of your own shoulder with your teeth, then stitch it up yourself, with your own little emergency sewing kit?"

He quirked an eyebrow. "Sorry. If you feel

that strongly about it, you can do the honors after you off Raazaq, and I promise, I won't gnaw it out of my body for days."

Oh, do not tempt me, Wright!

The car was small and confining. She needed room to move about. Room to release the churning activity squiggling around inside her. Beating him up because he was convenient was vastly appealing.

"Do you kickbox?" she asked with relish, imagining beating the crap out of him and getting rid of some of this energy.

"Yeah, I do. But I'm not taking you on in that mood."

"Mood?" AJ asked dangerously through clenched teeth. "What mood?"

"The I'm-lookin'-to-kick-some-ass mood."

"Scared?"

"Please." Kane narrowly missed two kids on a camel. "There's a tennis court back at the hotel," he told her casually.

"Is there?" She smiled, and her eyes sparkled with challenge. She'd never played, but she suddenly had all sorts of ideas of what to do with a racket and a couple of nice hard balls. "You're on, partner."

CHAPTER EIGHT

Wearing baggy shorts and one of Kane's black T-shirts, AJ's tanned skin gleamed with perspiration. Her gaze blazed with determination as she shifted from foot to foot, dancing in anticipation of the next serve. This was a lady who thrived on competition, and who aimed to win.

She had an amazing eye. Kane had never seen anything like it. It was almost as though she saw the ball coming, read its trajectory, seconds before he even hit it to her.

One of his personal heroes, football great Joe Montana, had a similar spatial instinct. Capable of seeing the ball's direction before anyone else could do so.

He knew it was something Cooper's trainers couldn't fully understand, but certainly appreciated. And it was one of the main reasons she'd been admitted into sniper school months ahead of schedule. They'd never seen anyone like her. She had the uncanny capability of seeing farther, better, and more accurately than

anyone else on the T-FLAC teams. Given a bit
of seasoning, AJ Cooper's sniping skills would
be in high demand.

Kane whacked another ball over the net, enjoying watching her long legs as she raced
across the clay court. Those legs of hers had
probably won her a lot of the beauty pageants
she refused to talk about. Her beauty queen status wasn't a secret—he'd heard about the rifle-
toting beauty queen long before he'd met her.
And while most men were well aware of what
she'd done before coming to T-FLAC, it was
also common knowledge that she didn't talk
about it much. Preferably not at all. She was
uniquely refreshing in that regard. In his experience, women usually managed to work bits of
flattering information like that into a conversation.

Right now, as he kept his eye on the tennis
ball, he was more interested in the colorful reports of Cooper's temper. He'd been curious in
the car to see just how explosive it was. He'd
felt the heat, but she'd pulled it back to a simmer. And that was good. It hadn't always been
the case. He'd heard her temper was loud, vo-
cal, and she had the habit of leaving broken
china in her wake.

"Fire in the hole. Tiiiimberrr!" AJ yelled a
second after her ball hit him, *smack,* between

the eyes. "Concentration," she said wryly, "is the secret to any form of combat."

The fuzzy ball smarted like hell, but God only knew his eye *hadn't* been on the ball, in any sense of the word.

Kane stopped the roll of the ball with his foot, then bent to scoop it up. He straightened, tossing the tennis ball in one hand. "Competitive" was his middle name. "Another set?"

"Pass, thanks," AJ said cheerfully, swiping her face with a small towel as she left the court. "You've whipped my butt. This time. Now I want a shower and food."

Kane dropped his racket to his side. Thank God. He'd thought she'd keep playing forever. "You're on."

The phone started ringing the moment they opened the door to the suite. Their eyes met.

Kane nodded, and AJ walked over and picked up the old-fashioned black receiver, saying a cool, "Hello?"

"Ah, Miss Cooper. I am Fazur Raazaq. I noticed you at the pyramid this afternoon, and your beauty compelled me to seek you out. I apologize for sending an emissary earlier."

"You're the guy behind the tinted windows?" she asked, hoping she sounded charming, interested, and sexy. The latter made easier by the fact that Kane was next to her, sharing the receiver. Heat sizzled from his large frame.

"If you would permit, I offer you dinner this evening, here at the hotel we share. The food at La Brasserie is excellent."

"Tonight?" she echoed.

AJ ignored Kane's hand signals telling her to accept Raazaq's invitation. Like she was going to turn him down.

She turned her back with a scowl, so she wouldn't have to watch Kane miming and gesturing to her while she tried to think. "Thank you, Mr. Rabbit—Oh, Raazaq? Excuse me." She glared at Kane as he stalked a circle around her, trying to get her to pay attention to him.

"Please, call me Fazur," her caller said in unaccented but slightly . . . off English. "It would please me."

"Fazur, then. I'm really sorry, but I'm busy tonight. Perhaps another time?" Still ignoring Kane, she tossed the rented racket on one chair and flopped down on another, then bent to untie the laces of her tennis shoes, the phone tucked against her shoulder.

Kane crossed the room, mumbling to himself. His hair clung damply to his neck and throat, and he wore khaki shorts and a red ribbed tank, and looked ready to pop. But he'd just have to trust her.

He opened the minibar and held up a bottle of water. AJ nodded.

"Tomorrow evening, then," Raazaq said in her ear, the faintest tinge of displeasure in his voice. "You must not disappoint me again, my dear. I will think I have done something to offend you."

"Oh, Fazur, honey, how could that be? We haven't even met yet."

Kane rolled his eyes and glugged the cold water.

"I feel as if I know you already, just from watching you this afternoon," Raazaq said.

Oh, please. God, the man was so oily, he practically oozed through the line. "That's so sweet of you to say, Fazur."

"Tomorrow night, then, Miss Cooper? Nine o'clock?"

AJ paused, drawing out the silence as she toed off her shoes, and accepted an icy bottle from Kane. She listened with satisfaction as Raazaq's impatience hummed clearly across the telephone lines.

"Hmmm, I don't usually like eating that late." She took a swig of water. "How about eight tomorrow evening instead? Down in the lobby? Lovely. See you then." She put down the phone and smiled. "Tomorrow."

"I heard." Kane rubbed his cold bottle across his chest and dragged his attention away from the rapid pulse throbbing at the base of her throat. The suite wasn't large enough to pace and get rid of the pent-up energy he hadn't used up playing tennis for a couple of hours. "I'm going out."

"Got a little stress to walk off?" She spread her arms across the back of the chair and smiled at him sweetly. "The kickboxing offer is still open."

"I already whipped your butt once today, Cooper, I'm trying to leave you with a little ego intact."

She pushed out of the chair with a laugh. "Oh, you dreamer you. I didn't want you to overtax your heart. You are, after all, an older man, so I gave you a break, Mr. Perfect." Still smiling, she wandered toward her room. "I'm off to shower. Hungry?"

Hell, yeah. But not for food. The thought of Cooper standing naked under running water was enough to make him able to jump buildings in a single bound. "Order me something from room service. I'll be back."

"See you, Andre," she said with a laugh.

"Enjoy your walk, don't take candy from strangers."

Kane shook his head as she closed her bedroom door.

As much as she smiled and seemed at ease, he could see that the closer she came to endgame, the tenser AJ became. There were some highly efficient ways he could use to get her to relax. Sex being only one of them.

Honesty was another.

She wasn't as adept as he was at hiding what she was thinking. And she thought everything he did was right? Jesus. He let out a short bark of laughter. Was she way off. *Perfect, my ass.* He was no fucking hero. He'd spent the last two years diligently and tirelessly working his nuts off to make up for the stupid mistake that had changed the lives of too many people.

He'd had ample opportunity to tell her how similar their experiences were. He *should* tell her, and ease a little of her guilt and fear. But instead he'd let each of those moments pass.

God only knew, he'd talked about it to the shrinks enough. Just words. But the heat of guilt, the fire of his shame, sorrow, and anguish were kept tightly inside himself to deal with. He was coming to terms with what he had done. Hell, he was doing fine. Just fine.

Other than the inability to sleep. The es-

trangement of everyone he'd ever cared for,
and a feeling of watching the world go by
through a thick piece of plate glass. Yeah, he
was doing great now.

And asshole that he was, he hadn't wanted to
see the light of hero worship dim from her
beautiful eyes.

And while he kept telling himself the night-
mares would eventually stop, that the guilt
would eventually fade, he knew he was lying.
His life had changed irrevocably two years ago.
And nothing had ever been the same again.

Kane returned to the room an hour later,
meeting up with the room-service waiter
wheeling a covered cart. AJ was dependable as
far as food was concerned. Whatever it was
smelled damned good, and made his stomach
grumble in appreciation. He preceded the man
into the room, told him he'd take care of the
setup, tipped him, and saw him out.

AJ was nowhere in sight and he didn't hear
the sound of water running, so she wasn't still
in the shower.

He suddenly had a vision of a sleepy AJ
spread, naked and still wet from her shower,
across the wide bed, fast asleep.

A twist of something hot and needy speared
through him, but he put it away. Like his

brothers, and men in general, Kane had always enjoyed sex. Recreational, and, on a couple of occasions, something fairly long-term. But it had been a while—two years? Jesus. *Two years?*—since he'd wanted sex. No wonder Cooper had him hot and bothered! Christ Almighty, *two years* since he'd been laid! Where the hell had the time gone?

He stopped to listen to the silence in the suite. There might not be any sound coming from his partner's room, but there was a faint, furtive noise coming from his own. What the hell?

All right! He was in just the mood to beat the crap out of somebody. Maybe Raazaq had sent one of his trained apes on a scouting mission. Christ, he hoped so. He pulled his Sig from the shoulder holster under his loose cotton jacket. Weapon raised, Kane nudged his bedroom door open with his foot.

The door moved soundlessly on its hinges.

He tapped it again with the toe of his shoe until it opened wide. Ran a glance across the queen-size bed; a crease in the faux satin cover where he'd sat putting on his shoes earlier. The local paper, unread, on the bedside table. He scanned the rest of the room. Didn't take long. Wasn't that big.

Empty.

The noise came from the bathroom. A scrape. Kane frowned, trying to decipher the noise. Hell, he was wasting time.

He kicked open the bathroom door, weapon raised.

The door slammed against the wall. In the ready position, Kane aimed the Sig into the small, steamy room.

And found himself eye to eye with a fully loaded Walther PPK. And a very naked AJ Cooper sitting in his tub.

For a long moment the two of them just stared at each other. Kane's blood pressure throbbed behind his eyeballs. He reholstered his weapon, and glared at her. "What the hell are you doing in here?"

She slid the gun onto the small table she'd set up beside the tub. The table held a flickering candle, a bottle of water, and now a fully loaded weapon.

"What does it look like I'm doing?" She sounded just as irritated as Kane felt. "Changing the oil in a car? I'm taking a bath."

"Take a bath in your own bathroom. Jesus, Angina, I almost shot you." And almost gave himself a coronary in the process. It was a testament to his self-control that he didn't storm over there, yank her, dripping naked, out of the tub, and take her right there on the bath mat. A shudder of want ripped through him.

"Excuse me?" AJ stiffened indignantly. "The stupid handle broke off the faucet in my tub. They can't come and fix it until tomorrow. Maybe." She waved a bubble-covered hand. "I left you a note out there."

A pulse throbbed at the base of her throat. He wanted to put his mouth there. Among other places. She was playing with fire. Tossing a live grenade from hand to hand, waiting to see just how many tosses it would take for the damn thing to explode. If she had a clue just how damn short his fuse was, she'd've stayed the hell out of his way. "Where?" he demanded about the note.

"On the table by the doo— Are you going to just stand there staring?"

He leaned against the doorjamb and gave her an appraising look. Hell, he owed her one for scaring ten years off his life. "It's a hell of a view."

She crossed dripping arms on the rim of the tub. The tub wasn't that big, and the bubbles were obligingly disappearing as if by magic. He could now see the shiny wet curve of her hip, and the gentle slope of a truly spectacular ass accented by the faint, creamy paleness of the outline of a bikini bottom. Kane wanted to put his mouth on that pale swath of skin, too.

"It's not the damn pyramids, Kane. No tourists."

"Too bad. You could make a fortune charging a fee."

"I'll keep it in mind." Her eyes narrowed, pale-green slits surrounded by spiky dark lashes. "Now, if you don't mind, I'd like to finish my bath."

"I don't mind a bit."

"Go . . . do something."

"I am doing something," Kane said, his voice silky as he made himself comfortable against the door frame, arms folded across his chest, at ease, relaxed. Steam curled her red hair into corkscrew ringlets around her clean-scrubbed face. She'd stuck that glorious mane up on top of her head and tied it with—what the hell was that? A sock?

He was lusting after a woman who wore a sock in her hair? Christ.

The sensible thing, the *professional* thing to do was turn around, close the door gently behind him, and remember that they were here to do a job.

Which would be a hell of a lot easier to do if AJ was nothing more than her looks. Unfortunately, she had levels and depths that intrigued Kane on a far more dangerous plane. Pretty women were a dime a dozen. Even women as stunning as AJ Cooper were relatively easy to find.

Kane had never been that interested in attractive outer trappings. The inside ticking fascinated him. The whirl and twist of a woman's mind intrigued him, and he'd found over the years that a beautiful woman counted on no one digging any deeper than skin deep.

But AJ Cooper presented a challenge. A puzzle. A package with layers and layers of interesting, convoluted depths that he was dangerously tempted to unveil.

She was the most arousing, the most tantalizing sight he'd seen in years.

Still . . .

I can do this. He would show *both* of them control. Prove to both of them that he was seduction-proof.

Easier said than done.

Like the moon to his tide, she was hard to resist.

Tension stretched between them. A single, gossamer thread, as fine and insubstantial as a spiderweb, and just as strong.

She was a houri, Venus on the half shell, a siren . . . her very annoyance at his presence a powerful lure. The flickering candlelight danced in her pale-green eyes as she glared at him.

She wasn't embarrassed, or coy, that he was seeing her naked. She'd turned into the rim of the tub, facing him, covering up all the interesting parts, and only her naked shoulders and bare arms, slick with moisture, showed. He could almost hear the rapid throb of her heart from where he stood.

Kane wanted to sip the dew from her skin. He wanted to undo that ridiculous sock out of her hair, and drown in the glory of her body. He craved filling his hands with her flesh, sinking into the firm, lightly muscled body that had been driving him insane for days.

Him. Kane Wright. The man who considered self-discipline and control a religious calling. He scoffed at his carefully constructed containment as it slowly, untidily unraveled while he watched her.

"So am I going to need my gun to get you out of here?"

Dangerous. Seductive.

"I'm getting cold," she snapped. "Hit the road already."

He unfolded his arms and shoved his hands into his pockets for safety. "I'm an artist, remember?"

"And how does that impact what we have

going on here?" She raised a ginger brow, her eyes very green. *Hot* green.

"I have this fascination with form and color. Your form, to be precise." He took his hands from his pockets and squared a frame around her face with his fingers. "Pretend I'm framing a shot." *Look. Don't touch.*

"You took enough shots of me today. So get over it. Go photograph a bowl of fruit or something."

He bit back a grin. "We have a serious problem here."

"We do?" Pale eyes, narrowed suspiciously, and bright with something unreadable, met his. "And what's that?"

"I want you."

She shook her head slightly. Her eyelashes, long and thick, were dark and spiky wet. "Sounds more like *your* problem."

"You want me, too."

"No ego problems here." Her mouth twisted and she huffed out a breath. "Is this your idea of foreplay?"

"I do believe, Angina, that I'm just going to have to show you."

He didn't move.

Neither did she.

"You're not going to show me anything."

She tipped her head and scowled at him. "And don't call me that ridiculous name."

"What *is* your name, then? I'd be happy to call you whatever you like."

"Cooper will do just fine, thanks. Now back off." She narrowed her eyes and gave him a steely look that he was sure would have most men obeying. On their knees. He wasn't most men. "You don't even like me," she reminded him. "And right now, I'm not real fond of you, either."

"Didn't say I liked you. Said I wanted you."

"Yeah, well, it's good to want things. Builds character."

"Sometimes, want is the only thing that counts."

"This is not a discussion I want to have with you. Not here, and particularly not now."

"The fact that we don't talk about it won't make it go away."

"Knock it off, Wright. We're both adults. It doesn't mean squat if we find each other attractive or not. As adults, we don't have to act on our urges."

"Speak for yourself," he taunted.

"Let me rephrase that so we both understand. I choose my lovers. And I haven't chosen *you*. I have too much at stake to risk screwing everything up by . . . by . . . by screwing you."

She was right, damn it. He didn't even know what the hell he was doing here. He'd never acted so damn unprofessionally in his life. There was just something about AJ Cooper that got to him. And because of that, he'd have to work harder at ignoring her. Shouldn't take more than a coma.

Whether she worked for him or he worked for her—even if they were equal partners—this was way out of line. They both knew it. Fraternizing between operatives, *especially* on a mission, wasn't just frowned on, it was verboten. There were a few married couples with the organization. But they were few and far between, and special cases. This wasn't a special case. Just a horny one.

"Yeah. Understood." Frustrated, annoyed with himself for showing an unacceptable emotion, and pissed that she, damn her sultry smile, was in enough control to draw the line in the sand while he stood there with a yen and a hard-on.

He took the three strides necessary to reach the tub—

"What do you think you're—"

—leaned down, and hauled her up out of the water, against his body. Water sheeted onto the floor unnoticed. She gave a small scream of surprise as he wrapped her wet, slippery body in his arms and crushed his mouth down on hers.

Not enough. Not nearly enough.

He slid his tongue against hers, feeling her heat, tasting her reciprocating desire. A tremor swept over her body, and she opened her mouth, slanted it against his, her tongue dueling, challenging. Making the kiss deeper, wetter.

Alarm bells started clanging in his brain. *God.* He had the sense of being drawn into something bigger and more immense than he'd imagined. Like wading into a kiddie pool, only to unexpectedly find dark, shark-filled waters, sweeping over his head.

Kane slid his palms down her arms, captured her wrists, and pulled them around his neck. She rested her full weight against him, her body slick and hot. Rose-scented steam enveloped them. Her feet were still in the tub, her body braced by his.

He felt the sharp points of her nipples through his now wet T-shirt. The sensation set up a humming throb through his entire body. He wanted to groan with the pleasure of it. With the relief of having her here, under his hands, against his hardened body. But his control was too good. Too complete to give up that last small store of restraint. He ravished her mouth soundlessly, his control shattered but not completely broken.

He was intensely aware of her scent. Not the scent of roses, but the spicy fragrance of her skin, which made him dizzy with need and fogged his brain with desire. He wasn't ready to let her go.

Her lips were firm and warm, her tongue bold. Over the initial surprise of the assault, she was giving back as good as she got. Her fingers tightened in the hair at his nape and she nipped his lower lip, before slanting her mouth under his once more, her tongue wily and aggressive.

The woman knew how to kiss.

Eventually he pulled away. Their lips clung like a promise.

"Had to get that out of the way."

She nodded, breathless. "Feel better?"

"No."

"Me neither," she admitted.

"Dinner's been delivered," Kane told her, steadying her as she slipped out of his arms and back into the now cool water of her bath like a mermaid off a rock. "It's getting cold."

Their eyes met. "I'll be right there," she said quietly. He turned to go. "Kane?"

He glanced over his shoulder. Her gaze

slammed into his and he felt the solid punch of it from across the room. "Just so you know," she told him quietly. "Next time, P.C. or not, we'll finish what we start."

CHAPTER NINE

AJ chugged half a bottle of cold water from the mini-fridge. She glanced at Kane. "What?"

She was sprawled sideways across an easy chair, ankles crossed and swinging over the padded arm.

"You only have an hour to get ready."

She raised her left eyebrow. He'd purposely kept her out all day, taking hundreds more shots of her, then claiming he had to get that last sunset before they headed back to the hotel. "And you're blaming me for this? Who was the one who was attached to his camera all day?"

"That's my cover. And yours," he snapped. "Don't you have to get ready now?"

"Going to do my makeup again?"

"If I need to."

"I'll pass." She smiled that lethal smile that made his heart skip a beat or two. "Think I didn't know what you were doing, keeping me busy all day, Wright?" She paused. "Thanks. It helped."

Yeah. It had. The look of strain in her pale eyes had diminished as the day had worn on. It was coming back now, however.

"There's nothing wrong with being a little nervous before a hit, Cooper. Keeps you focused."

"I'm okay with this. I really am." She held out her hand, palm down. "Lookit. Dead steady."

"Excellent. Forty-six minutes."

"Slave driver. It'll take me all of ten minutes to shower and dry my hair."

"Take a little longer than three minutes with your hair, would you please? I want you to wear it loose." It rattled him how badly, how *strongly*, he didn't want her to do this. Kane shook it off. It was her job. But, Jesus, he would've preferred she do it from three hundred feet away. This was too close. Too dangerous. Too fucking . . . personal.

"What are you?" AJ laughed. "My new best girlfriend?"

"Believe me, Cooper," Kane said soberly, watching her slender ankles swing back and forth. His gaze rose to her face. "I'm neither a girl, nor your friend."

The smile slipped. Christ. Her face was so expressive. He saw her mental retreat a second before he realized how that must've sounded to her. Tempted as he was, he wasn't going to clarify the statement. She could think whatever the hell she wanted to think.

"Of course you're not. Sorry." She swung her legs off the chair and rose. "I was only kidding. Guess this is a full-service op. You don't want me as a partner, don't want to be friends. Don't even want to be my lo—" She shook her head. "Never mind. I get it, okay?"

"AJ—"

She put up a slender hand to forestall whatever he'd been about to say. "Can it. Just can it, okay? You don't have to keep beating me over the head with a two-by-four. I totally, 100 percent get the message."

"I don't . . . fraternize with coworkers. Especially right in the middle of an op," he told her harshly. In truth, he didn't fraternize with *anyone* anymore. Hadn't for a long time now. Which probably went a ways to explain why his dick was in a knot. He didn't spend time with anyone. Not his coworkers, not even his family. He'd been emotionally drifting away from everyone he loved for years. Why hadn't he seen that before? He was an island in the middle of a becalmed sea. Nothing around him. Nothing on the horizon. Alone. All frigging alone.

No highs. No lows.

He liked the view just fine from where he was.

Just fucking fine.

This time tomorrow they would be heading home. He'd request they not work together again. Angina Cooper was just too damn hot to handle. Despite that kiss, nothing had changed between them. Nothing.

And everything. At least for him. He was questioning himself in areas he had deemed off-limits years ago. "Wear the short black silk," he told her, suddenly not wanting to think further than tonight.

Without a word she gave him a mocking salute and went into her room. The door didn't slam behind her. But it felt as though it had.

She showered and dressed, then came back into the living room, to find Kane waiting for her. Without a word he looked her over, *inspected* her, from head to toe. AJ felt exposed and raw. Although there was no reason to feel that way.

"Will I do?" she asked, then damned herself for being vulnerable enough to ask, or care, what he thought.

"Do you need to ask?" He cocked his head. "Didn't you look in the mirror? Every man in the restaurant is going to need CPR when they swallow their tongues the second you walk in."

His dark eyes told her that he didn't think that a good thing.

"Yeah, well, tonight there's only one man I want looking at me. And he's going to be in a whole lot more trouble than swallowing his tongue." Her temper, fueled by something she refused to put a name to, flared. "If you're finished with the inspection, I'm off." She paused when he didn't say anything. "Unless you want to check my teeth before I go?"

He didn't want to inspect her teeth. Which was a damn good thing. AJ thought if Kane came close enough to do that, she would've bitten him. If he read that in her eyes, he seemed sublimely unconcerned as he looked her up and down.

The short black silk was made to seduce. The dress, what there was of it, was skintight, low-necked, and short. *Very* short. Just about a breath south of public decency. AJ pushed a hank of hair off her shoulder—damn nuisance, and hotter than hell—and tried not to tug the neckline up and the hem down while she stood still under his scrutiny.

What shook the man? Anything? Nothing? He was so one note, one almost had to check his vital signs to see if he was alive. Except for that flash of heat last night.

Her pulse skittered annoyingly when he walked across the room. He stopped right in front of her and ran the fingers of one hand up the side of her throat. "What—" She licked her lips. "What are you doing?" Her bones melted just at the thought of his mouth plundering hers again.

"I can see the earpiece."

The earpiece? He could see it from across the room? AJ slapped a hand over his where he seemed to be fondling her ear. Of course, the android wasn't doing any such thing, but the way her nerves were stretched tonight she should be forgiven for a leap of imagination. "I'll fix it." She took a step back.

Kane's hand fell to his side, then he stuffed both of his hands into his pockets. "You'll do."

Gee, thank you very much, Excellency. "See you in a while," AJ told him, opening the door.

"AJ?" She turned back to look at him, eyebrows raised. The slight concern she imagined she saw in his dark eyes made his usually aloof expression seem more human. Even if the worry was a figment of her imagination. "Be careful," he said softly. "Watch your back, and keep your wits about you."

"Don't worry," she told him flatly. "I'll do whatever it takes to get the job done."

Kane grabbed a bottle of juice from the fridge and twisted off the cap. There was a reason operatives didn't get involved with other team members, he thought as he paced the room. He'd never felt a fist to the gut worrying about any *guy* he'd worked with. Not that he was worried about Cooper. She'd do what she was sent in to do. He knew that. Damn it, she was willing to do anything to make up for screwing up the first opportunity. And maybe that's what worried him, he told himself. The *anything*. Did that mean she'd take unnecessary chances? Risks?

He clearly heard the rhythmic sounds of breathing over the small speaker on the coffee table. Slight echo. She was in the elevator already. Must've speed walked down the hallway to get there that fast. He didn't answer her. But he listened to her slightly elevated respiration and found himself breathing with her.

She'd be standing in the middle of the elevator—Yes. In. Out. In. Out. Nice, calming breaths. *That's my girl.*

She was going to do fine, he thought, as he paced from one end of the room to the other and back again and resumed his normal breathing before he passed out. In an hour or so, she'd be back up here driving him nuts.

Then why the hell did he have a hole the size of the Grand Canyon in his belly? And why was he the one having arrhythmia?

★ ★ ★

Raazaq, flanked by Trout Lips and two other equally unattractive bodyguards, was waiting for her in the lobby when AJ arrived at seven minutes past eight.

Fazur Hessan Ali Raazaq was not an Adonis by any stretch of the imagination. If he weren't rich and powerful, he'd be one lonely guy. Shorter than AJ by a few inches, he was thin and almost effeminate, with small hands and dark, soulful, heavy-lidded eyes. For some reason AJ didn't trust a guy with small hands. Now, *Kane's* hands were huge. . . .

". . . suite, where a dinner has been prepared by my personal chef."

Dinner in Raazaq's suite instead of the very public restaurant. Hell.

I hope you're paying attention, Kane.

AJ smiled and accompanied the four men back to the elevator. Raazaq put his hand on the small of her back. She resisted shrugging it off as she would've a big black hairy poisonous spider. It felt exactly the same, and gave her exactly the same visceral sensation.

A chill ran up her spine.

The elevator rose smoothly to the top floor.

AJ preceded Raazaq into the opulent red and gold living room of one of the penthouse suites.

"A cocktail before dinner, my dear?"

"No, thank you." Instead of seating herself on the red brocade sofa, AJ wandered about the room, ostensibly looking at the objets d'art, while she was really counting noses and getting the layout of the room. Six bodyguards in all stood arms akimbo, evenly spaced about the suite. If she had to make a run for it, it would be like trying to run through the Chicago Bears' offensive line.

"Come, my dear." He patted the plump cushions of the sofa beside him. "Sit here beside me. I want to know everything there is to know about you. Why is it that I have never seen your exquisite face gracing any international magazine covers?"

AJ moved across the room, all eyes following her every action. Had the lights just dimmed? Slightly, she supposed. Too many A/C units going tonight. "Oh, goodness, honey, don't tell me you read those silly things?" She smiled as she sat down on the sofa. Not too close.

The lighting dimmed another notch, and the sweet strains of an Italian aria came up as the lights went down.

Raazaq smiled. Unfortunately, his smile didn't reach his eyes. Something a great deal more disturbing glittered in those opaque black depths as he watched her. "Fazur, please. And I have some interest in the fashion industry, yes. Where is it you come from, Miss Cooper?"

AJ crossed her bare legs. She should've accepted that drink. At least it would've given her something to hold. "Illinois, originally. Now I live out of a suitcase most of the time. I travel a great deal for work. Not terribly exciting, I'm afraid."

The lights dimmed another notch.

Definitely deliberate.

"Fazur, honey, am I going blind?" She blinked up at the ceiling. "It's getting awfully dark in here." *Translation: Kane, pay attention!*

"I'm afraid my eyes are . . . sensitive. I prefer the lights to be lower."

"Dinner is served, monsieur."

Raazaq glanced up, then turned to AJ, hand outstretched as he rose. "Shall we, my dear?"

Still holding her hand, they went into the dining room, where two white-jacketed waiters flanked the mahogany table. One pulled out AJ's chair with a flourish, and settled her napkin on her lap with a dramatic flick of his wrist. He looked at Raazaq. "The wine, monsieur?"

Raazaq glanced at her. "Would you like wine, my dear?"

"No, thanks. Water's fine."

"Please. Do not feel obliged to drink water

on my account. I do not object, should you wish to drink wine."

"Water's great. After spending all day out in that heat, I find it more refreshing than alcohol."

Raazaq waved the man away. Another waiter served their meal. Lamb and rice. It smelled delicious.

"Thank you for joining me on such short notice, Miss Cooper." His smile was too white, too practiced, and too perfect. "I imagine that you and Mr. Wright will be finished with this project and moving on within a short time?"

"A few more days. I hate to leave, though. I've posed in front of many interesting places, but I really haven't gotten to see anything." She smiled even though when he'd adjusted his chair he'd moved it closer to her. Too close. He was invading her personal space and she wanted to shoo him—or shove him—back. She couldn't do either. While she knew exactly just how dangerous Raazaq was, and what he was capable of doing, she realized she was pretty safe. If he wanted to sleep with her, and by the strokes and touches and lecherous looks, he did, then he wasn't likely to do anything to scare her off on the first date. She hoped.

"I'm fascinated by Egypt, and would love a

chance to explore once Kane has finished with the fashion shoo—"

She glanced up at a hovering waiter, then feigned surprise when he handed her her earring. She touched her bare lobe as if expecting it to still be there. "Oh. Thanks. I hadn't realized." She had, of course, dropped it on purpose. She inserted the post, finding the small gold backing on the table, where she'd "dropped" it then left it to lie next to her plate.

"I would be delighted to show you the region," Fazur murmured. "I am quite familiar with out-of-the-way places of interest that few tourists ever see."

Oh, she was willing to believe that. He probably knew every back alley that made a good dumping ground for bodies.

"Do you live in the area? Or are you visiting?"

"I have family living locally. However, like you, I am but a visitor, and will be here just a few short days myself. Having the diversion of your company would surely make my stay more pleasurable."

"I'd enjoy that," she said lightly, forcing another smile. "Thank you."

He leaned over and brushed a finger across her cheek. It took everything in AJ not to flinch. "Your lovely skin is burnt. The sun is

strong here. Yesterday Mr. Wright had you under a canopy. Why not today?"

AJ looked up. He'd been observing them as
carefully as Kane predicted. "You were there?
Why didn't you come and say hello?"

"I was not there. I sent my man to make sure
you weren't bothered by the peasants."

"Oh," she waved a hand at him, "I enjoy
meeting the locals. *Everyone* here has been just
charming, Faz," AJ told him pointedly as she
absently picked up her earring from the table
and loosely reinserted it into her lobe.

"When is your return flight to . . . ?" he
asked, so close AJ's eyes watered from his
overly sweet aftershave and she noticed he'd
nicked his chin shaving. Her natural reflex was
to lean away from him, but she forced herself
to stay where she was. She wondered if she
would feel such a strong and violent dislike for
this man if she didn't know who and what he
was. The answer was yes. She would. Evil em-
anated from him like stink on shit. You didn't
have to see it to know it was there.

"Boston," she told him smoothly.

"Wonderful. Then I insist you be my guest
when your photographer returns to Cairo the
day after tomorrow."

AJ gave him a cool look and sat back in her
seat. She ignored the earring falling to the table,

and let it lie between her bread plate and Raazaq's hand on the white tablecloth between them. "You seem to know an awful lot about our business."

"I beg your pardon, mademoiselle." He smiled, but the expression went nowhere near the black void of his eyes. "It is just that I had many hours to spend as I waited to meet you tonight."

"And you chose to use them by inquiring about a pair of strangers' travel plans?"

He gave her another smile. It sent a chill down her spine. Fazur Raazaq might think he was suave and irresistible. He wasn't. "Forgive me. Please?" He touched her hand briefly and her skin felt as if an ice cube had brushed against her.

AJ smiled at him. She, too, was a professional. Her stomach was jumping with anticipation of the sleight of hand she was going to have to perform in the next few minutes.

"Since our time here in Fayoum is so short, I would like to invite you to travel with me for a few days, a few weeks? So that we can get to know each other." He picked up her hand and damply kissed her palm. AJ forced herself not to shudder or yank her hand out of his grasp. *Ew!*

"I will be traveling on a business trip," he told

her smoothly, still holding her hand. "I believe the destination might interest you. I would deem it an honor if you would join me."

"I'd love to hear about it," AJ told him with utmost sincerity. While he was doing his best to charm her, she was contemplating his death.

Judging by his slight size, the poison would take about six hours before it started to work. The trick was getting it from her earring into his food without Raazaq or his bodyguards seeing her.

This time the earring slipped from her ear and fell, with amazing precision, onto the rim of Raazaq's water glass.

"Sorry." AJ shot him a half-embarrassed smile, but took a few extra seconds before she plucked the gold curve off the rim of the goblet. Picking her small clutch purse off the table beside her, she tossed the earring, now empty of poison, since it had just done its job, into her purse. Then detached the other one from her ear and pitched that into her bag as well.

"You were telling me about our trip?"

"Let's discuss the details after dinner, shall we?"

"Why not now? I'm fascinated."

"I will give you everything you want, my dear. After we have dined."

That's what she was afraid of. "You say you

have family living in Fayoum?" She let her attention slip for a nanosecond to his glass. The clear liquid of the poison, slightly thicker than the water, slid slowly down the side of the clear glass, then dissolved invisibly into the liquid.

"A sister. Aziza is seven years younger than I." He played with the braided stem of his glass. "A beautiful girl, and the apple of my eye. She made a good marriage, and is about to have her first child. That is why I have delayed my business interests to be at her side at this happy time."

"Exciting." AJ picked up her water glass and drank. *Cheers, Fazur Raazaq.* "So you will be a proud uncle." *Drink up, you bastard.*

"Indeed. Aziza was wise not to tell her brother the sex of her child. I didn't know whether dolls or guns were more appropriate." He stroked the stem of his glass then lifted it to his mouth.

Gun. *One size fits all, no matter the sex,* AJ thought, tempted to pick up his glass and shove it against his smiling mouth. Hard.

"Would you care to travel with me to meet her tomorrow? It's only half an hour away. She lives in a small village not far from here. Quite picturesque and charming, though the people there are poor and uneducated. My brother-in-law is a sugarcane farmer. The wealthiest man in the village."

"Thank you," AJ said casually, wishing he'd drink up so she could relax. He needed to consume at least half the glass to do the job. "We only have a day before Kane leaves. He's got some insane schedule planned for tomorrow. And I'm sure if your sister's baby is about to be born, the last thing she'd want is a stranger showing up."

Raazaq placed his untasted water back on the table as the waitstaff swept one course of their meal away to deliver the next. AJ wanted to scream.

Raazaq finally spoke to them in a spate of French. The area cleared as if by magic. "There. Now, you were saying?"

"Kane and I will be busy all day tomorrow, and then he wants to do a night shoot on his own—you know, pyramids and stuff—before he leaves. Perhaps we can do a little sightseeing then."

"We will discuss this further after dinner," he said, still using his charm. But it was clear he didn't like being thwarted. *Aw. Too bad,* she thought unsympathetically. *Things are going to get a lot worse, pal.*

AJ, who prided herself on her ability to consume anything closely resembling food, smelled her dinner and found her stomach flipping and flopping uncomfortably. Tension. If the son of a bitch would just drink his water, she could settle back and enjoy her meal.

She ended up consuming the entire bottle of water on the table, while Raazaq flirted, ate his meal . . . and didn't pick up his glass.

Until their plates were cleared an interminable hour and a half later.

He picked up the goblet.

Oh, thank God. About frigging time. Her nerves were stretched as tightly as rubber bands.

Clear water made a wedge in the glass as he brought it up to his mouth. It all happened in slo-mo to AJ. Candlelight glinted off the rim of the crystal goblet as he tilted back his head. Rested his mouth on the rim—

"Mission aborted," Kane said urgently in her ear. "Do you copy? Mission aborted."

Chapter Ten

"Op terminated," Kane yelled urgently. He listened intently, waiting for some indication from AJ that she'd heard the order. He didn't realize he'd moved until he was out the door and slamming his fist on the elevator call button, way the hell and gone down the hall.

Screw the elevators. He raced farther down the corridor, slapped open the door to the stairwell, taking the stairs three at a time. "Do you cop—"

Shit. He'd blasted out of the suite so fast, the receiver and headset were still on the table in the living room. Damn it! He hesitated a nanosecond. Either she'd heard him and had things well in hand, or she hadn't heard him for whatever reason, so trying again was pointless. Except that he couldn't hear *her.*

This was why he worked alone now. God damn it! This was why.

She can handle this, she's okay, Kane told himself over and over again as he burst through the door on the top floor minutes later. Two armed guards stood halfway down the corridor. He started walking. As he passed the elevator bank, he hit the call button, then continued on. The guards turned to watch his progress, but made no overt motion to stop him.

The doors to Raazaq's suite opened behind them—the elevator pinged its arrival at exactly the same moment AJ emerged from Raazaq's rooms. Kane backtracked, stepped inside the car, and held the door open with his foot, weapon raised.

Come on. Come on. Come on. Move it, Angina. Move it.

The second AJ was in his line of sight he grabbed her arm, pulled her inside, and hit the CLOSE button all in one smooth motion.

Her eyes widened. "Wh—"

"Did he drink?"

"No. I sp—"

"Talk later."

The doors slid closed. The car started down. Kane swung her against his body until the angle he held her had her up on her toes and flush against him. Her wide, startled eyes were the last thing Kane saw as he closed his own eyes and crushed his mouth down on hers.

AJ's body stiffened for a second, then her lips softened as he plunged his tongue inside the warm cavern of her mouth. Her hands came up and fisted in the back of his T-shirt as she returned that kiss with enthusiasm.

He slid his hands up her bare thighs, bunching the stretchy silk in his finger and taking the short dress with them. Her breasts flattened against his chest and he could feel the hard points of her nipples, which incited him even more.

He hooked his thumbs into the thin elastic of the thong she wore and yanked it down.

"Jesus God, K—" He bit her protests away, drugged by her response as she kissed him back. Her tongue mating with his, her breathing erratic. Her arms wound around his neck as he slid the thin bits of lace down her legs.

Their bodies fell against the side wall, and she blindly reached out to hit the STOP button on the panel. The elevator jarred. An alarm sounded. Neither of them noticed.

He reached down between them and unzipped his jeans over the hardness of his erection, freeing himself. She sucked in a harsh breath when he touched her intimately. Slid two fingers down the swollen furrow.

She was wet, ready for him.

He pushed her into the corner, slid his hand down the back of her right thigh and pulled her leg up, positioning her. She tipped her head back, baring her throat. He kissed the smooth skin there, filling his senses with the fragrance of her skin. She made a soft sound in the back of her throat as he thrust inside her. AJ wrapped her raised leg around his hip, using her strong calf muscles to draw him harder against her.

The feel of her surrounding him was close to pain. So exquisite, so sharp, he wanted to race to the finish. Yet he wanted to prolong it, savor the sensation, make it last.

But he dared not prolong it, no matter how much he wanted to. If nothing else, people would soon be clamoring for the elevator. Raazaq was waiting for his comeuppance, and HQ was expected to call back in less than seven minutes. He couldn't think. Couldn't stop. Hell, couldn't breathe.

He plunged into her, hard and fast, his breath ragged, his heart manic with the power racing toward him.

The hot velvet fist of her climax triggered his own, and his body shuddered with the force of it.

AJ's head dropped to his chest as she dragged great gulps of air into her starved lungs. Kane had her squished hard into the corner. Their bodies were intimately joined and her right leg was still firmly around his waist. The ripples of her climax were spreading concentrically deep inside her as she lifted her face.

He bent his head and kissed her again, his mouth hot and hungry. He lowered her down his body, slipping out of her as she found her footing. AJ felt heat flush her cheeks. Jesus. What had she been thinking?

Nothing.

The second, the instant, he touched her, her brain had shut down. She'd never experienced such intense, immediate arousal in her life. Everything they'd said and done to each other until this point had been foreplay. When he'd entered her, her body had welcomed his. She'd been ready, willing, and raring to go. She still was.

"Pull yourself together." He rearranged himself, tucking all the interesting parts out of sight, and zipped his jeans. With some difficulty, AJ noticed with a little satisfaction.

"I'm flattered that you just couldn't wait to do that," AJ said dryly, her voice slightly breathless as she adjusted the dress to cover what she could. "But please don't tell me you terminated the mission just to have sex in an elevator. What happened? Why did we abort?"

"Status has changed," Kane told her shortly as the elevator began its decent.

Well, no shit, she thought. *Their* status had certainly changed. But what could possibly have happened to have HQ cancel her hit? And how could she think about business when her body was still humming?

How long could that possibly have lasted? A minute? Less? Jesus God. AJ leaned against the wall, shaken. She'd never had sex like that in her life. It was as though he'd sucked every ounce of sense out of her and replaced it with live, crackling electricity and primal satisfaction.

What do you get when you put together two Type A personalities? AJ asked herself. *Nitro and glycerin.*

He gave her a lazy look. "You're wet."

AJ blinked. *Duh!* Of course she wa—Oh. She brushed at the front of her dress. "I spilled the water." The car stopped at their floor. "What on earth were you doing up on Raazaq's floor, anyway?" *And why did you just screw my brains out without comment?* Not that she was in any way complaining. Speed sex with Kane Wright beat any kind of sex with anyone else hands down.

The doors opened and Kane took off. AJ bent to scoop her underwear off the floor then raced after him.

Sex was great, AJ. The best I've ever had. Thank you, Kane. It was incredible for me, too. Can we do it again when you can stay longer? Sure, AJ, can't wait. She caught up with him, almost grabbed his arm, decided against touching him just yet, and dropped her hand. "What—"

He glanced at her sideways. No one would have been able to tell by the look on the man's face that he'd just had sex faster than you could cook a soft-boiled egg. How flattering was *that*? "Wait till we're inside," he said shortly.

Once inside, with the door locked, Kane stalked to the window, flipped the curtains back, and stared, as if looking for a sniper. AJ felt her temper start to sizzle. "So?"

"Intel confirmed Raazaq intercepted a shipment of chemicals between Russia and Iraq this morning."

A chill of foreboding shimmied up AJ's spine. "What kind of chemicals?"

"Right now we're not sure what was in the shipment, nor how much of it Raazaq's people managed to get hold of. All we know is, it was stolen and he has it."

AJ started pacing. "If it's Russian, it could be either DZ-9 or Ricin." Kane walked to the brocade sofa and sat down. He lifted his legs to the coffee table in front of him, crossed his feet at the ankles, and folded his hands across his middle. He looked calm. Cool. Collected. "Or worse."

"Yeah. Or worse. Doesn't matter what it is," she said, talking more to herself than to Kane. "If that son of a bitch wants it, then we have to retrieve it before he uses it. God knows, it's not a shipment of Girl Scout cookies." She leaned down and snagged a pen off the coffee table near Kane's booted feet, twisted her hair up on top of her head, and stabbed it into the untidy mass, using the pen as an anchor. "What do we know?"

"We know the approximate size and weight of the container. Small, easily transported, and deadly."

She stopped pacing, her mouth suddenly dry. "How deadly?"

"Category four."

"Oh, shit." She rubbed the sudden chill from her upper arms. "This is bad. Really, really bad. Chemical warfare? Viral agents? Splinter governments have got excess amounts of both since the fall of the Soviet structure. The Federation government still hasn't been able to round up all the chemical agents, especially not with so many dissident offshoot factions playing finders-keepers."

"Everyone is on it. We'll know soon," Kane told her grimly.

She glared at him. "He would've been dead by morning if you'd let me finish the job."

"Couldn't risk it. He's the only person who knows where the container is, and what its final purpose is." His eyes were hard, his jaw tight. Sex hadn't relaxed him any. And AJ fleetingly wondered why he'd bothered. She'd save the question for later. If there was a later. "For all we know," Kane went on, "one of his people has already passed it off. We have to confirm what he's set in motion before we eliminate him."

Made sense. Damn it. She'd have felt a lot better if that little weasel was already halfway into dying. But if he'd already arranged for distribution of whatever the hell it was he'd taken possession of, then his miserable death wouldn't help them stop what might be coming.

AJ blew out a frustrated breath. "How fast can intel get back to us on content and possible targets?"

"Twelve hours. Maybe less."

"It better be less. If it's DZ-9 or Ricin, there is no anti-dote," AJ said grimly, reaching behind her back for the zipper. She needed to change into more-appropriate clothing, and then start putting things in order just in case they had to bug out fast.

But she couldn't reach the damn zipper. She had to try twice, three times, before she gave up. Disgusted, she marched to the sofa and turned her back. "Get this, will you?" she asked, pointing to the hard-to-reach zipper and bracing herself for his touch.

While she waited, her brain churned. Jesus God. *Chemical warfare.* In the hands of a sociopath like Fazur Raazaq it could spell mass destruction on an unimaginable level. He had to be stopped.

Now.

Kane was right. If Raazaq had died, they'd have no idea where the hell the chemicals were, or who had them. And she'd been so close to taking the rat out, too.

"Bend down."

"Hmmm?" She glanced at him. "Oh. Right."

She crouched beside him, back turned, bracing on the arm of the couch as her mind raced. T-FLAC personnel had already placed tracking devices into each of Raazaq's vehicles. Their own vehicle was ready to go. All they needed was fresh water, and they could split within seconds. . . .

Shit. She had no experience with chemical warfare. And while Kane had been around for a long time, this was not his field of expertise, either. They were here on a wing and a prayer.

Kane's hand felt cool against her bare skin as

he lowered the zipper—far too slowly. She squirmed a little as her skin heated up. She shifted on her bare feet, feeling the nubby texture of the carpet under her bare toes, and Kane's warm breath on her nape.

He was mighty damn close for zipper duty. And her body was still humming and ready for more. She craned to look over her shoulder and came nose to nose with him. She met his gaze and decided not to notice the flash of something dangerous she saw there. "Is it stuck?"

He shook his head. "I got it."

Cool air fanned her back, and thankfully helped put out the first flickers of heat he'd generated. Zipper undone, she rose to her feet. "You don't have any experience with chemical agents, either, do you?" she demanded, holding the top of the dress up.

His jaw clenched. "No. Not many do."

AJ felt a sizzle of adrenaline mixed with a healthy dose of fear of the unknown. This is what she'd joined T-FLAC for. To be a part of something so big it could affect millions of lives. To be one of the few people in the world who stood between normalcy and insanity. She'd joined up because just by doing their jobs, she and Kane would make a difference. Lives could be saved, and threats averted.

Now she was finally going to get the chance to make that difference.

"We can track Raazaq, we can get the intel of his proposed target—or targets—but neither of us knows a damn thing about containment and disposal of a dangerous chemical. We have to call for backup," AJ told him grimly. "This isn't a two-person op anymore. We need Hazmat, and we need them now."

"I figured that out on my own," he said dryly. "Backup is on their way as we speak. The minute HQ knew the situation, they dispatched an experienced Hazmat team."

He gave her a measured look she couldn't hope to interpret.

"So we wait?"

"We wait."

"Waiting sucks. The Hazmat team is coming, but soon enough?" She started pacing the room again, paying no attention at all to the fact that her barely there dress was wide open at the back. Hell, there were way too many important things to think about. *Keep calm. Focus.* Mentally, she ran down the supplies in their vehicle. Weapons, ammunition . . . Damn it, the flight here from the U.S. would take twenty-plus hours.

The terrorists could be anywhere and have

done *anything* by the time the T-FLAC team landed in Cairo.

"We can't wait almost twenty-four hours for the team to get here. We have to have them right this second."

Kane nodded his agreement. "We will. Cairo dispatched a six-man team. They'll be here within the hour. The Hazmat team is en route from Europe. Be here by morning."

"Better," she said, thinking out loud, pleased to have Kane to bounce her thoughts off of. "But not near good enough. Raazaq said he'd only be here for a couple of days in the middle of a business trip."

"We'll be right behind him." Kane said it shortly, firmly, and she turned to look at him as he continued. "Everyone can play catch-up. We're keeping tabs on the GPS."

"Let's call in again and get an update—" She grabbed the bodice of the dress tight as it slipped off her shoulders. She ignored the hardness of her nipples and the still-pumping heat of her blood as she turned to look at him, only to find he'd risen silently from his relaxed position, and now stood inches away. They were almost nose to nose. Again.

AJ stood her ground.

His eyes glittered. Challenging her? Daring her? Playing chicken?

Or something even more dangerous?

Their eyes met.

His gaze burned even as his pupils dilated. He didn't move so much as an eyelash. His control annoyed the hell out of her.

"If you're trying to scare me off, it's not working."

"Angina, if I wanted to scare you off, I wouldn't have had you in the elevator."

"Or now?" she asked.

"Or now."

To hell with it. AJ reached out and grabbed him by the front of his black T-shirt and stepped into him. As she pulled him closer, she rose on her toes and slanted her mouth over his. Two could play this game.

His arms came around her like a steel vise. The hot cavern of his mouth welcomed her. There was no tentative tasting. The kiss was full-blown and carnal. Tongues mated, bodies rubbed together, radiating heat. His hand slid inside the open back of her dress, skimming down her spine to cup her behind and warming her from the outside in. His other hand had somehow become buried in her hair, cradling her head in his broad palm as he shifted her face to his satisfaction.

AJ grabbed his hair in her fist, and held him where she wanted him. Dizzy with longing, she fought for balance and knew she wouldn't find it. She slid her hand, still fisted on his shirt, out from between them, and brought it up to cup the back of his neck, drawing him down to her mouth as she rose impossibly higher on her tiptoes. *More. More. More.*

Her head spun.

She was intensely aware of his scent. Rich. Enigmatic. Erotic. She'd recognize him from his smell alone. In a dark room. With twenty other guys in there. Blindfolded.

Shivers rippled beneath her skin as his lightly calloused palms skimmed down to her bottom. Warm hands, strong and sure, learned the curve of hip and waist as he pulled her into the cradle of his thighs. One hand cupped her bare behind. The other drifted to her front and thumbed an already sensitive nipple. His erection nudged her mound through his jeans. She felt the internal melting of her body as she deepened the kiss, trying to regain the control she'd lost with the element of surprise.

She shivered lavishly as his tongue drew her deeper, tempting her. *Come to the dark side, Luke.*

The dark side had never looked more tempting.

CHAPTER ELEVEN

After twenty minutes of sweaty, mind-blowing sex on the floor, they separated to go to their rooms to shower. Kane had rug burns on his ass to prove what a gentleman he'd been by letting AJ stay on top.

For the first time in years, he actually felt alive.

Stupid, but alive. Making love to a fellow operative was going to cause nothing but trouble. It'd never happened before now and he knew damn well that if the woman assigned to this op had been anyone but AJ Cooper, it wouldn't have happened this time, either. But AJ was . . . different. She reached him even when he didn't want her to. She infuriated him, aggravated him, and in general annoyed him. She also made him laugh. She made him think and, damn it, she made him want her every time she walked into a room. Jesus Christ. He rubbed a hand over his face. What the hell was he thinking, making love to Cooper?

The woman had a massive chip on her shoulder, and something to prove. She was as focused and determined as he was. Didn't matter that the attraction was mutual. And powerful.

Why now, Lord? Why the hell now?

His brothers would laugh their collective asses off. . . . If he ever told them. Which he most certainly would not.

But damn it, the woman used weapons on him that he had no defenses against. Humor. Guts. Integrity. Honesty. Hell. Kane buried his face in his hands with a groan.

He was in trouble here. Deep fucking trouble.

A feeling thumped in his chest. It took him a moment to realize it was a chuckle.

Oh, damn.

Just as AJ strolled back into the room there was a hard *thump-thump-thump* on the door. The Cairo team.

AJ checked the Judas hole, then flung open the door, and practically hauled them into the room bodily. Sex had revved her engines. She was up and raring to go. Wired for sound. Eager, on edge, and climbing the walls, desperate for activity.

"Anything?" Apollo Hawkins demanded, briefly nodding acknowledgment to AJ and striding across the room to shake Kane's hand. They'd worked together several times and Kane had requested him on the team. Kane's estimation of the man went up several notches when Hawk didn't give AJ more than a cursory glance after they'd been introduced. And if AJ noticed that the guy was tall, dark, and fairly decent to look at, she didn't seem to give a rip, either.

She introduced herself, unnecessarily, to the others. Killian, McBride, Tariq, Christof, and Wondwesen.

"You guys eaten, or do you want to order something before we get started?" AJ asked as the men arranged themselves in the suddenly incredibly small room.

Kane bit back a satisfied smile. A regular United Nations of operatives, the six T-FLAC operatives were draped about the gold and white suite like a roomful of hungry black panthers, champing at the bit to get into the action just as much as he and AJ were. They were all experienced, seasoned operatives.

The men settled down to outline options and share what they knew. AJ efficiently called in a room-service order, then seated herself cross-legged on the floor beside the huge, square coffee table. She waited her turn, then started out-lining a plan. Kane realized with

not a little surprise that AJ Cooper knew her
stuff. She might be a kitten as yet, but she was
a tiger kitten.

He leaned back in his corner of the couch
and watched and listened as AJ laid out the pos-
sibilities of Raazaq's route. She knew Egypt as
well as, if not better than, he did. And he'd
been here several times in the last few years.
Her study of the maps on the flight over was
standing her in good stead. She knew back
roads, unpaved roads, and variables for thousands of miles. All in her head. Amazing.

"I'm damn impressed," Roman Killian said
quietly as AJ went to her room to find a map
that included the Sudan. Just in case they had
to head that way. "How's she doing?"

"Good," Kane told him honestly, picking up
his soda and drinking. "I've been pleasantly impressed, too." She was good except for that minor glitch. "She takes this dead seriously.
Doesn't whine, thank God. Yeah, I'm pleased
with her so far."

"Her recall and grasp of detail are sure as hell
assets, rookie or not. That can't be taught in
any Academy classroom," Killian added.

"And unlike yourself, Wright, Coop seems
to be a real people person," Hawk inserted
with an evil smile. "She almost makes you look
friendly."

"Bugger you," Kane told him mildly.

The other men hooted with amusement.

Watching her interactions with the other team members had solidified Hawk's point. AJ's beauty was attractive, but not as important a tool as her ability to put strangers at ease. The woman knew how to read and react to people. Effortlessly, she responded to comments and questions, earning respect without demanding it.

There was a hell of a lot of testosterone in the room right now. And he wasn't sure he liked the way Ari Tariq watched AJ's butt as she left the room. The guy's sleepy, hooded eyes were deceptive. The Turk had a mind like a steel trap, and reflexes like a cobra. Kane scowled as he turned toward Killian.

"I've never worked with a female operative before," Tes Wondwesen said morosely. His large bald head glinted in the light as he watched the bedroom door. The enormous Ethiopian had the look of a basset hound. Droopy eyes and his lack of eyebrows made him appear deceptively lazy. French roast coffee-colored skin made it hard to read his features. His strength was his tactical ability. But he was also known as quite the ladies' man. And even a sleepy guy could have the hunger of a predator in his gaze.

"No different than working with a male operative," McBride said tongue in cheek, light eyes
laughing. There weren't that many female T-
FLAC operatives, and most of the field agents
didn't look anything like Cooper. Savage came
close. But tangling with Savage would be like
tangling with a black widow spider.

"I enjoy working with the female of the
species," Tariq said lazily, crossing one booted
foot over his knee and leaning back against the
silk pillows like a pasha. "They bring a different perspective to an op."

"Keep your mind on the mission statement,"
Kane told him flatly. "Cooper's the most important part of this op. Don't any of you even
consider muddying the waters."

"Here it is," AJ said, returning to the table
and unfolding the map. She glanced around.
"What'd I miss?"

"Nothing," Kane told her shortly. He looked
at Conrad Christof. "Sit, for God's sake."

Christof towered over the rest of them. He'd
jumped to his feet when AJ stood, now he
waited to sit down until she did. Pretty damn
good manners for a blond giant with no neck
and too many, too white teeth. Kane decided to
keep a weather eye on the Austrian as well.

AJ seemed oblivious—which made Kane feel
better. Until he glanced over to see Hawk grin-

ning at him. Kane flipped him off. Hawk chuckled.

AJ was one of the guys. One of the guys with breasts, a shapely butt, and sparkling green eyes. There was not one scrap of artifice in her. She was animated, serious, knowledgeable, and in charge. While they chowed down on a mountain of sandwiches and drank several gallons of thick, sweetened coffee, *six* pairs of male eyes tracked her every move as she paced, gestured, made notes on a pad she carried, and talked with authority and conviction.

She was doing a damn fine job. And Kane respected the other guys for listening and treating her opinions with respect.

Of course, Kane was forced to admit, it helped that her ideas were damn good ones.

They were all aware that this was to be a team effort. Getting Raazaq now was imperative. AJ had a map of the Western Desert imprinted on her photographic brain. That and her sniper ability, coupled with Raazaq's attraction to her, made her indispensable.

And every man in the room knew it. They would all protect her, and get her to her objective, at the cost of their own lives if necessary.

". . . split up into four teams," AJ said, coming back to the table and dropping down into a cross-legged position that got Kane's attention in a hurry. He mentally ratcheted back. Instead of grabbing her, tossing her over his shoulder, and making a forty-yard dash to the bedroom, he drank deeply of his Coke and slitted his eyes until she was no more than an animated blur.

Better.

Not great.

Just better.

The satellite communicator rang. She was up and had the receiver in her hand seconds ahead of the others. "Yes?"

Her eyes narrowed. "When? How many vehicles? Got it." She tossed the clunky black receiver back on its cradle. Her pale eyes shone like stars, her cheeks pinked with excitement.

"Sorry, guys, no rest for the wicked. Raazaq just moved out. Headed south and booking. Let's get the lead out. We've got to get this sucker before he cuts loose."

AJ drove, while Kane kept in communication with the two vehicles behind them, the Sat Comm, NOAA, and the blip on the screen of his handheld GPA indicating Raazaq's southerly direction. They were far away from the lights of any towns or villages, and scudding clouds obscured the moon. It was eerily dark.

Wind buffeted the Humvee, and sand from the dunes on either side of the paved road, illuminated by the twin beams of the headlights, blew in increasingly thick clouds across their path. No matter how bright the lights, though, they barely penetrated the billows of yellow sand whipping in a mad frenzy across the empty road.

AJ kept a map of the area in her head as she drove. The signposts were few and far between. Fortunately they were in English as well as Arabic, but it looked as though the terrorist was heading into uncharted territory. The farther south he led them, the worse visibility got. The north-south route had been a trail of agony for tens of thousands of slaves who'd moved along its route thousands of years before. It had been called the last, and worst, portion of the *Darb-al-Abrain*, or the forty-day road. The farther they went, the farther behind they left civilization.

They'd speculated where Raazaq might be heading, and what the shipment could contain. But since they didn't know the answer to either question, speculation was, at this point, moot. All they knew was, whatever it was, in Raazaq's hands it would be bad. Very bad.

Dirty bomb? Nerve agents? Smallpox? A nuclear bomb?

Jesus God, it could be anything.

Behind them, five miles apart, two more

Humvees rolled through the darkness, head-lights glinting on and off as they hid behind dunes and turns in the road or were obscured by wind-driven sand. In one vehicle, Christof and Wondwesen; in the other, Hawk and Tariq. The other two men had remained at the hotel to await the arrival of the specialists from Europe, whose plane had been delayed by NOAA's warnings of the approach of Khamsin. Sandstorm season.

"Khamsin" meant "fifty" in Arabic, the number of days the season lasted. Timewise, they were right in the middle of it. And Raazaq was heading directly toward the heart of the storm. AJ was sure that had been a deliberate move. Where the hell was the man going? And why?

The farther south he went, the less popu-lated the area. It didn't make sense. Raazaq al-ways went for the big bang. The most people terrorized. If it was some sort of bomb, he was heading in the wrong direction. If it was some sort of viral agent, ditto.

"Maybe he's going to blow up a dam? Poison the water supply?" Her fingers tightened on the steering wheel. The vehicle shook and shuddered, and her muscles ached with the ef-fort of maintaining control as the car weaved and swayed in the high winds.

"We'll get to him before he does whatever he plans to do."

"From your lips." Eyes dry with the strain of trying to pierce the swirling sand, AJ stayed in the middle of the narrow paved road, and gripped the steering wheel in white-knuckled fists, feeling the jar and pull all the way up to her shoulders. "This is getting worse. I'm going to p—"

"Pull over," Kane ordered at the same time.

"Damn. I wanted to make an oasis about a hundred miles down the road before stopping. But you're right. This is suicide waiting to happen. Alert the others." She pulled off the road, battling the seventy-mile-an-hour winds with all her strength to steer the vehicle to higher ground. The wind tended to blow hardest at ground zero. The tires bit into the soft sand, sliding and slipping before digging in as they climbed.

"Good to know Raazaq is probably doing the same thing. No one is going to be traveling for a while." Kane's calm manner was starting to piss her off more and more. Nothing seemed to ruffle the man's feathers.

Not spectacular sex. Not Raazaq transporting an unknown chemical. Not a sandstorm.

What the hell rattled the man's cage?

Kane's hand shot out and he grabbed the

wheel as it spun out of her hands. "Give it more juice. That's it." His hand, between both of hers, held the wheel relatively steady as the heavy Humvee bounced and swayed. Thank God the vehicle was wide, and low to the ground. Built for just this sort of terrain.

They crested a small dune. AJ doused the lights and turned off the ignition. Kane's arm brushed hers as he withdrew his steadying hand from the wheel.

The darkness was loud, almost alive, as sand and wind buffeted the vehicle in ever-increasing gusts. Grains of sand pelted the windshield, and AJ knew that come morning, they'd be lucky to be able to see through the damn thing. The Humvee shuddered as the growling beast of a storm battered it. Sand sifted through the vents and sighed as it dropped to the floorboards. A few hours of this and they might be buried under a dune of their own. But there was nothing to be done about it.

"Now we wait," she said, more to herself than Kane. The man had an amazing capacity for stillness. Inactivity drove her nuts. She adjusted her seat to give herself more room in the cockpit and leaned her head back against the seat rest.

She couldn't see him—hell, she couldn't even hear him breathing. But damn it, she *felt* him. "This could go on for up to eight hours, you know."

"Uh-huh."

"You hungry?" AJ asked, voice raised over the wind.

"We just ate a truckload of sandwiches, and you had dinner before that." His voice, low and deep, coming out of the pitch-darkness, was curiously intimate.

"That was hours ago," she said, absently rubbing the aching muscles in her upper arms. "Besides," she told him, talking to avoid thinking, as she fumbled around for the small roll of mints in her pants pockets, "sitting around doing nothing makes me hungry." Antsy. Impatient. Reckless.

There were several beats of silence while she silently admitted that there were different kinds of hunger. And sitting here beside Kane Wright in the windswept darkness was awakening way too many of them. She thought about all the things they could be doing while they waited for the storm to blow over.

"What's wrong with your arm?"

AJ stared in the direction of his voice. She couldn't see him—he was just a deep voice in the dark. But she felt him looking at her. "Nothing." She shifted in her seat. "Jeez. You must have eyes like a cat."

"All the better to see you with, Annabelle. Arm?"

"My arm's fine. Just strained a bit from fighting the wind." AJ smiled into the darkness. "Annabelle?"

"Why not? AJ's gotta stand for something."

She turned in his general direction. "Want a mint?"

"Nuh-uh."

She dug a couple out of the tube, popped them into her mouth, and crunched down. "Do I look like an Annabelle to you?"

"No. You look like Angina to me, but you don't like that one, either. Give me the real deal, and I'll call you whatever you like."

"I like AJ." She yawned.

"Fine. Why don't you climb in back and get some rest? We're here for the duration, might as well make the best of it."

"What about you? There's room back there for both of us." The idea of stretching out, full-length and horizontal, in a small confined space with Kane Wright was probably not a good one. Not thinking about having sex with Kane was like trying to put a summoned genie back in his bottle.

Sex or no sex, it would be nice to have the human contact. The night outside sounded wild and untamed, and despite the heat, AJ shivered. "That's not an invitation for hanky-panky or anything," she pointed out into the yawning silence.

"No hanky-panky?"

"Not an invitation." Which were two completely different statements. AJ grabbed the flashlight from the console between them, then without turning the flash on climbed between the seats to get to the back cargo area. Wind and sand struck the vehicle, making it rock and shimmy. "Hell on the paint job." She intentionally switched the subject.

AJ moved Kane's camera equipment and various other boxes out of the way by feel, then stretched out on the carpeted floor with her head on her bent arm and closed her eyes.

It had been a long day. The adrenaline rush had come and dissipated, come again, then not been necessary once more, leaving her feeling agitated and cranky. She was tired, but too restless to sleep.

"You don't have claustrophobia, do you?" she asked Kane. It was close back here. Close, and hot and dark. She kinda liked it. Would like it more so if he were back here with her.

"No," he told her unequivocally. "We have plenty of water and enough food to last days. We'll be fine."

Days?

It was possible. Not likely, but certainly possible.

Days alone with Kane on a horizontal surface. With no interruptions . . . It boggled the mind. "Of course we'll be fine," AJ said cheerfully. "How much trouble can we get into with the wind blowing like there's no tomorrow?" She paused, and then said with a smile, "Unless it blows us way the hell and gone to Oz. Damn, where did I pack my ruby slippers?"

She wondered if he'd come back here and want to make love to her again. Slowly. Because this time they could take it slowly. Her breasts ached for his touch. "Anyone ever sweated to death?" she asked rather desperately. Lord, she'd had more sex in the past twenty-four hours than she'd had in the last year. How could she already want him again?

"Not that I'm aware of. Drink plenty of water."

She still had on a perfectly decent tank top, and under that an unadorned, unromantic, unsexy sports bra. Not that Kane Wright was going to see the bra—AJ bit off a smothered laugh and added a mental, *Not in the dark, anyway.*

He'd seen all there was to see already, anyway, and apparently was unimpressed.

"Sure." She pulled her T-shirt over her head.

"I don't know about you, but I'm stripping down." *Oh, Ka-aaaane.*

"Go for it. It's going to be a long night."

A long, *slow* night, AJ hoped.

It wouldn't be because they were stopping their pursuit of Raazaq to indulge. So if they were here, anyway, why waste time? She grinned into the darkness and removed her bra.

The vehicle was large and spacious—still, it was close confines for two people who were already hot.

She stripped off her heavy boots and socks so she could be comfortable. "Do you know my brother?" She wiggled her toes. Thought about taking off her pants and undies for half a second—then removed those, too.

The carpet was scratchy against her bare skin, but just being naked, when Kane wasn't yet aware of it, turned her on even more.

"Only by reputation," he answered out of the darkness. "He's been undercover for three, four years, right? Are you guys close?"

AJ rolled onto her stomach and cupped her chin in her hands. The darkness alone made this conversation much more intimate than if they'd been having it in a well-lit room. Chances were, Kane wouldn't have a conversation like this with her in a well-lit room. Naked or not.

"Not as close as I'd like to have been." AJ raised her calves and crossed her ankles. "He's eight years older than I am, first of all. And our folks separated when I was barely five. I'd see him when I went to my father for weekends. The age difference and sporadic visits prevented us from getting too close. How about you? Are you close to your brothers? You have three or four, right? I've heard their names bandied about at HQ."

"Three brothers, one older, one younger, and a sister, Marnie."

"That's two brothers."

"And my twin, Derek."

"A twin, huh? Are you identical or fraternal?"

"He's prettier."

"Is he, now. Are you all close?"

"Yeah. We are. Don't see each other as much as we'd like. Everyone is pretty much spread out. Marnie and Jake live up in Northern California. They have a couple of great kids, and a pretty cool dog that rules the roost."

"Are all your brothers married, too?"

"Kyle and Michael are, Derek and I are the last holdouts."

"Five kids? Your mother must be a saint."

"She died when we were pretty small."

"That must have been tough."

"Yeah, it was. But our grandmother moved in with us, and we didn't lack for a female influence."

"And I had a little too much female influence," AJ said, shifting around to get more comfortable. "My mom was obsessed with me getting every title she could lay her hands on. She loved everything about the pageant business, just as passionately as I hated it."

"You won about every title there was, didn't you?"

"I won a few," AJ told him self-deprecatingly. She'd won more than a few. Every win was a feather in her mother's cap, and further humiliation for her. She'd hated parading around winning *anything* on her looks alone. It was as though she didn't exist. Just a face and a body.

"My mother loved, worshiped, pampered, and paid attention, to that ... shell. Her daughter, the beauty queen. It got old after a while." The inner AJ, the soft, tender, hungry core of her, had gone neglected and unnourished while her mother fed her own ego with her daughter's trophies. Until AJ had put her foot down and realized she hated what she was doing more than she loved her mother.

"You stopped short of your eighteenth birthday, right?" Kane asked.

Why don't you come back here and talk to me? "I dropped out just before the Miss America." The memory of *that* confrontation still gave AJ hives. "I went straight into college so I could eventually join the P.D. Once I'd ruined my mother's life I moved out and into a dorm."

"Quite a switch."

"Culture shock to the max." AJ smiled. "God, I loved it. Not college particularly, but oh, man, the second I stepped onto the shooting range at the Academy I felt at home.

"I didn't tell my family what I was doing until I passed the final exam at the Academy, and had finished my first week in the P.D."

"How'd your family take it?" Kane asked, his voice carrying clearly over the noise outside. Perfect pitch. Of course.

"My mother was predictably furious. Our relationship's been strained ever since. We try, but it was never about being mother and daughter, anyway. Our bond was the pageant crap. Once that was gone . . ." AJ shrugged in the darkness. "Gabriel and my father, on the other hand—Now, *their* reaction came as a shock. I thought they'd both be proud of me. Since Darrel was a retired Navy SEAL and Gabriel had just started with T-FLAC about the same time, I truly believed that if anyone would understand, they would. But instead they were both livid, and both of them tried to get me to quit."

"But you didn't."

"Nope." She'd been hurt that neither man in her life had bothered to look beneath the surface. "I guess people see what they want to see, huh?"

"Sometimes it's safer that way," Kane said flatly.

Wind sandpapered the Humvee, grains of sand stinging the steel body like thousands of tiny bullets, shaking the vehicle and its contents.

The intense darkness, like a thick, black, extremely noisy cocoon, sealed them off from the world. They were literally inside the island in the storm.

"Move over, I'm coming back there."

About time. AJ's heartbeat sped up as Kane moved into the back. When he settled with his back against the forward-facing seat, his knee brushed her arm. Kane stretched out his legs parallel to her prone body. The back area wasn't *that* big. She felt the heat of him all the way down her right side as he lowered himself to the floor beside her.

She braced her chin on her hand. The smell

of him so close—sweat and Kane Wright—made her salivate. Clearly the man was catnip to her cat. How long before Mr. Perfect realized he was sitting next to a naked, available woman?

After several moments of silence, when Kane didn't fall on her ravenously, AJ sat up, reached out, and touched his face. "What's going on in that head of yours, Kane Wright, sir?" she asked softly.

He took her hand and kissed her palm. "I'm thinking, Anaglypta Joy, Why are we sitting here in the dark *talking*, when we have better ways to occupy our time?"

"And what was your answer?"

"This." He tugged her down until they were both sprawled flat on the floor. "Hey," he whispered against her mouth. "You lost your clothes. I'm shocked."

CHAPTER TWELVE

Ah, damn. He smelled so good. His body radiated heat, which seared her skin despite the layer of his clothing separating them. Sprawled half over him, AJ pressed closer, loving the sensation of the hard plane of his chest against her sensitized breasts. She rubbed against him like a cat, and lowered her head, already so aroused she could barely think. Openmouthed, she brushed his lips with hers. Fire erupted in her stomach and she tangled her fingers in the cool silk of his hair, holding him, even though he hadn't moved. She licked the Fort Knox of his lips. Hungry. Eager. Hot.

Unresponsive?

The man beneath her lay still, unmoving. She couldn't say *totally* unresponsive, since his erection was rock hard and ready, nudging her thigh, and she felt the thick, heavy throb of his heart beneath her right breast.

She kissed him again, and when he still didn't respond, lifted her head. The dark pressed down unrelentingly, and the wind howled a deep, mournful bass. "Kiss me back, damn it," she demanded.

"I don't play at this, AJ."

"Who's playing?" She grabbed fistfuls of his hair and kissed him again, sliding her tongue between his lips to sweep into the warm, wet cavern of his mouth. He opened for her. But that was it.

Every one of AJ's previous lovers—all three of them—had wanted it fast and often. While they'd been around. Kane was no different—as he'd proven already today. Five times in twenty minutes at the hotel.

Fine. She'd take it any way he wanted to give it to her. AJ tried to clear the sultry fog from her brain to figure out why this wasn't working. She didn't believe for a moment that these sensations were one-sided. She felt the tension in his body the entire length of her own—he practically emitted a crackly electrical current. Hell, no, this wasn't one-sided.

Was he changing the rules on her?

Perverse bastard.

His hard grip on her upper arms belied his calm tone and lack of . . . vigor. Other than his enormous erection, which moved and pulsed against her thigh, he was unnaturally still.

She huffed out a frustrated breath. "Damn it, Kane. I'm not asking you to take vows,

here. I'm just asking for a little body heat. A
little . . ."

"Distraction?" he suggested coolly.

"As I recall, you didn't mind being distracted
in the elevator."

"That was different."

"Why, because *you* started it?"

His silence rang out loud and clear.

"What's wrong with this if we're both willing participants?" *And my heart won't be in tatters
when I'm no longer the right trophy for you. It won't
hurt as badly when you walk away.* She felt an annoying prick of tears. Why was she never
enough?

"Not only is this ridiculously unprofessional
while we're in the middle of an op," he told
her, his voice gratifyingly ragged, "your
brother would castrate me if he ever found
out."

*I'm sorry your heart's cracked, short stack. Not
every guy out there is as superficial as that asshole.
Trust me. There'll be a man one day who'll see beyond the packaging and know how beautiful you are
on the inside, too.*

When? she'd cried. *When will a man look beyond this damn face and see that I'm a real woman,
and not his play-boy fantasy come to life? Love
sucks! I'm not falling in love ever, ever, ever again. I
don't need or want a man to validate who I am.*

Memories. Crowding in, tugging at the raveled edges of her mind, and damn it, making her doubt herself. *Not now,* she cried. *Not now when my body is humming, and the man driving me to distraction is just an erection away.*

Nothing wrong with two consenting adults having sex, was there? A biological urge that had nothing to do with emotion. Good old-fashioned lust. There was a lot to be said for simplicity, damn it. If Kane would just let himself go. For heaven's sake, the first time ever *she* made the pass, and the guy had to go all noble on her.

Fortunately it was dark enough so that she didn't have to see his mocking gaze as he rebuffed her. "Believe it or not, Boy Scout, my brother doesn't run my sex life." She paused to press her fist to her chest, where a familiar ache was spreading. Damn it. Damn it. "Why the sudden change of heart, Wright?" she asked thickly. "Did you just want to see if I'd let you do me? Was I just a couple of notches on your belt?"

"That's no—"

"No? Then please explain your reticence to me. What's going on? First you can't get enough of me. Now you don't want me anywhere near you. Which is it?"

"I made a fucking mistake," he said through gritted teeth.

A bitter laugh welled up in her throat. "Oh, yeah. You made that *fucking* mistake more than once. You're going to hell anyway, why not go for one more?"

"We don't have to compound the mistake."

"God," AJ said, not bothering to keep the anger out of her voice. "That just makes a girl feel warm all over, knowing she's a mistake."

"I don't want the responsibilit—"

"Good!" AJ swung around to stare in his general direction. "Because I don't want to *be* anybody's responsibility. So we're even."

"No, damn it. That's not what I—God damn it, woman!"

"Do you find me attractive?"

"Christ, Cooper—"

"Do you?"

"Yes," he shouted. "God *damn* you, yes!"

She reached between their bodies and stroked the hard, rigid length of him. He hissed in a breath.

"Let's go for it. And I won't tell if you won't." She nipped at his chin, scraping the edges of her teeth across his skin. When Kane still didn't respond, didn't move in any way, AJ felt a chill course through her body.

What did she need? A two-by-four across

the back of the head? He didn't want her. He had a male's reaction to a warm female body, but he didn't want *her*. This had never happened to her. Not that she'd ever made this blatant an invitation before in her life.

And no way in hell was she getting out of this with her pride intact. What could she say? *Let me just slide off your body, you poor little sexually harassed thing, you.* Her pride was hurt. Her ego was dented. And her body was burning, with no sign of a fireman rushing to the rescue.

"Hey, I can take a hint." Face hot, she jerked her hand away, and tried to roll off him. "No need to get pious on me," she added sarcastically. Tears of sexual frustration and embarrassment pricked her eyes. Damn it. "The quickies were enough for you. Cool. I'll live with the disappointment."

His fingers bit into her upper arm, holding her in place. "Cold feet, Antarctica Joy?"

"Cold feet? You're the one in the fridge, bubba." She stopped trying to pull away. He'd release her when he was good and ready. But now she was damned if she'd respond, even if he wanted her. "You know," she said coldly, keeping her voice level with effort, "you keep guessing like that, and you'll hit on my real name."

"And?"

"And a gypsy once told me the first guy to figure out my real name would be my future husband."

"That so?"

"Don't panic." This time she spoke through gritted teeth. "The invitations aren't ordered. The chances of anyone tr—getting it are a million to one."

"No one's even tried?"

She struggled in earnest. Trust him to always pick up on the one damn thing she didn't want him to. "A," AJ gritted, "That's so none of your business. B: I want you to let the hell go of me, *pronto.* I apologize for starting something you didn't want to finish, but right now you're holding me against my will. C: One wrong move now and my knee will make you perfect for the doorman at the local harem." When he still didn't let go, she said tightly, "Damn it, Kane." Her breath caught on a sob that shocked the hell out of her. "Please." Chest tight with fury, she tried to wrench her arm free of his hold.

"I didn't say I didn't want to make love to you again. You jumped the gun. As usual."

"Excuse me?" He was still as hard as a rock against her, damn him. "Pretty much felt to me like I was getting through, but you still said no." She was absolutely furious. "Now I'm over it. Let go. I need to get some sleep."

Without her realizing it, his hands had stopped gripping her upper arms, to slide up her shoulders, glide up her neck until his fingers combed through the hair at her temples. He wasn't holding her, but she couldn't seem to move away from him. Which really pissed her off.

He wasn't hurting her, but his hold on her head was implacable. She'd roll off him in a minute, turn her back, and go to sleep. In a minute. "What do you want from me, you son of a bitch?"

His penis jumped to attention between them.

Her insides contracted in reaction, and her nipples ached. "Stop that!"

His thumbs stroked maddeningly gentle at her temples, across her cheekbones, inside the shell of her ears. "What are you willing to give me?" His voice was thick and husky.

"A black eye?"

"Tough talk."

"Let me go and we'll see."

"Now, why would I want to do that?"

"Make up your mind, here, Wright. Nah. Let me do it for both of us." She tried to knee him. In a lightning-quick move, he blocked her leg with his own and locked her in place with his calves, sandwiching her legs.

"You're not going anywhere."

She blew her hair out of her eyes. Trying for calm when her temper was jumping like an Olympian. "Look," she said, embarrassment turned to irritation just this side of red-hot, "I offered, you declined. End of story." She lay still, panting slightly from sheer unadulterated temper. "Hell. By the time you finish giving me this lecture or warning or whatever the hell it's supposed to be, we could've had sex five times and been fast asleep! I'm not going to flog a dead horse." She managed to twist her body sideways, off the heat of his.

"The horse is far from dead." He tightened his legs and jerked her back where he wanted her. Back into the cradle of his thighs. "And we've had it hard, fast, and five times already. Superlative, by the way. But not enough."

It was damn hard to maintain her temper when she wanted to melt into him and say, "Forget whatever you're trying not to say, and just *do* me." Problem was, she had adrenaline, anger, embarrassment, and sexual frustration all blended together, with nowhere to go. And the man was giving off such complicated mixed signals, she had no idea what the hell was going on.

She punched his shoulder. Hard.

She wanted sex—*now*—or she wanted a good fight.

At this point, either would do. "You're giving off mixed messages here, Wright. Tell me straight out what the hell you want."

His hands slid from her hair, down her back, and gripped her bottom tightly. He held her still against him. "This is what I want from you. But no involvement. No obligation."

"Perfect," she snapped, frustration getting the better of her temper. "Put it right there on the table where we can both see it. No involvement. No obligation. No messy emotions involved. Excellent. That's just what *I* want. I—"

He silenced her with a kiss that rocked her to the marrow of her bones and sent her temperature spiking. She opened her mouth to taste him. Hot. Intoxicating. Addictive. The kiss was lascivious, juicy, and hot enough to melt all her girl parts. Jesus God. She'd never been kissed with this much diligence in her life. Not even by him.

The noisy blackness around them took on a whole new dimension as he continued kissing her. He devoured her mouth in hungry, deep kisses that took her breath and made her lose all reason.

Desperate need fueled them. It arced between them, bright and hot, pulsing off their bodies, filling the close confines of the vehicle with heat that was nearly unbearable.

AJ clung to him, her fingers twining through his hair, anchoring her. Her body dissolved into his. Her heart raced in time with his. Her hips rocked against his, pounding his erection closer, harder to the aching center of her.

She lifted her head enough to growl against his mouth, "I want you inside me. *Now.*"

The sound of the raging storm outside was drowned out by the cacophony of her blood racing in her ears. In the darkness, AJ was blind, and acutely aware of Kane's touch. His smell. The sound of his ragged breathing. The taste of his mouth.

"Soon." His voice was thick, sexy, and hot. "Soon." And he brought his mouth back to hers like a homing pigeon.

The son of a bitch turned her on as easily as a light switch.

The wind howled long and low outside, and the thrumming of the sand on the Humvee became AJ's heartbeat, a part of her. Nature's fury raged inside the car as well as out.

"Hurry." She sank her teeth into his chest as need raged through her, found his nipple, sucked on it the way she wanted him to do to her. He gasped and moaned, grabbing her head, both of them breathless now as they rolled about in the back of the Humvee, boxes falling about them unnoticed. His hands were rough on her, and her skin came alive, burning hot, feverish.

She ripped at his shirt with one hand, wanting, *needing* the feel of bare skin. Buttons flew. The sound of rending fabric was so satisfying, she grabbed the front of his shirt in both hands and used all her strength to shred it again.

Good.

And again.

Better.

"God. Hurry." Her hands slid feverishly over his warm, hair-roughened chest, up and over the smooth skin of his broad shoulders. Back down, over his shirt-covered biceps, thick with muscle, down his sinewy forearms, and back across his chest to tangle her fingers in the wedge of chest hair she found there.

"No, Cooper, no. We will *not* do this fast. Not again. We have time. Let's use it." He brushed her mouth. Once. Twice. "Let's use it, and take it slow this time."

She didn't want it slow anymore. She wanted it hot and fast. They had time to do it slowly . . . later! Something raw and primitive spiraled through her, and she shuddered with want. Oh, Lord, he felt so damn good under her hands, hot, smooth, hairy. She almost melted. While her own heart was going ballistic, his beat hard and heavy. And steady.

The car rocked violently in the wind as she ripped and yanked at the rest of his shirt, trying to get it off completely. Since his arms were locked around her, the shirt wasn't going anywhere. Mouths fused, breath mingling, she pushed his shirt off as far as possible, then skated her hands down his sides and yanked at the waistband of his pants.

"Why won't you hurry?" she demanded, almost sobbing as she tried to squeeze her hand between their hipbones to get to his fly. Although his body parts and her body parts desperately wanted to party, it wasn't happening.

"Slow down." His hands swept to her behind and he stroked and kneaded her flesh until she whimpered. "Ka-aaane!" She wanted him. Now. This instant. More than she'd ever wanted anything or anyone in her life. They were practically glued together. And she wanted that. Desperately. But first she had to get this man out of his pants, and into her.

"Off. Off. Off!" she muttered thickly, frantically. "That's an order."

"Yes, ma'am."

She laughed, the sound bubbling up from deep inside her. "Nice salute." Her laughter mixed with the yearning need to have this man inside her. It was different, incredible, this mix of joy and red-hot desire. "Let's not waste it."

Her fingers encountered his roller-coaster-shaped zipper. His body immediately reacted to her touch as she sought the zipper tab by touch. "Hells bells, Wright." She tugged, then tugged again. "Is there a padlock on this thing that I don't know about?"

He laughed shortly. "Protecting the family jewels."

"Oh," she said dryly, "you are a funny, funny man." She yanked at the stupid zipper again, with no success. "These pants didn't look this tight when I saw you earlier. What'd you do, shrink-wrap them when I wasn't looking?"

"Think of it as unwrapping a Christmas present."

"Yeah?" she warned, leaning in close to his mouth and taking a little punishing nip from his bottom lip. "Well, when I really want my present, I rip it open. Sometimes small working parts of my toy might get damaged. Sure you want to see that happen here?"

"On second thought," he said with a hoarse laugh, "why don't you let me unwrap it for you." He shifted, and she heard the happy rasp of the zipper teeth opening.

She couldn't get his clothes off fast enough, and trying to finish unzipping his pants while she was lying on top of him, with his erection pushed against the zipper, suddenly seemed farcical and made her laugh. Breathless, and semi-hysterical, but laughter nevertheless.

"You find this amusing, do you?" Kane asked. Easy for him to say. She was naked, while he was still fully, and annoyingly, clothed.

"Hell, yes," she said, still laughing under her breath. "Not exactly a graceful moment." She fumbled with his damn zipper again, eventually succeeding in getting it tugged all the way down, then slipped her hand inside. Kane groaned as her fingers closed over him. His thick penis, smooth as satin, jerked in the warm glove of her fingers. "Gimme."

"Good things come to those who wait, Angelica Japonica." He rolled her over onto her back, his body welcome and heavy against hers. Camera bags and boxes toppled and scraped together as they shifted in the small cargo area. She heard him shove things out of their way. AJ raised her knees to cradle his body, and he rocked against her heat while his mouth devoured hers. She felt fire crackle in her veins, saw fireworks behind her closed eyelids.

She groaned, and arched her back as one large, calloused hand slid up her side and closed over her breast. The sensation was piercingly sweet. "Ahhh . . ."

His strong, beautiful hands slid up the inside of her arms, sending goose bumps skittering across the surface of her skin. He wound his fingers between hers, pressing her hands up above her head and flat against the carpet.

And he kissed her. Her mouth. Her neck. His lips lingered for several minutes on each breast as he laved her nipples with his hot, wet tongue. His chin brushed her midriff, her belly . . . and lower.

He spread her knees with his broad shoulders, then buried his face against the damp curls.

AJ tried to free her hands to grab his head. "Kane! Wait—Stop—You can't—"

He could. He did. His avid mouth pressed against her, making her hips rise from the floor as his hot, competent tongue laved her.

He released the shackles of his hands to scoop up her hips and draw her more firmly against his mouth. Holding her against the heat and insanity-causing action of his very clever tongue.

AJ couldn't think, she could only feel. And God, what a feeling. She brought her hands down and grabbed hold of Kane's hair, helpless to stop herself from arching her back and making little whimpering sounds from deep in her throat.

The corded muscles in his arms bunched under her thighs as they flexed and shifted, moving her hips, holding her as her body bucked and rolled through the tempest of sensations.

This was more than sex, AJ realized as her body shuddered and shook with the onslaught. Oh, God. This was *way* more than uncomplicated sex. She tried to shift her hips away from his mouth. Too much. More than too much. "Kane. I—I—"

She came in a tidal wave of sensation, her body shuddering and quaking. Her mind completely, utterly blank.

She came back to earth as lightly as a feather. Limp as a piece of overcooked spaghetti. Kane still between her legs.

"Ah . . ."

He raised his head, then trailed a burning, damp path up her stomach, up her rib cage. With strategic stops at her breasts and nipples along the way.

Then he took her mouth, and as he did, his

body slid into hers so swiftly, so completely, she gasped with the overwhelming sensation of fullness. Before AJ could catch her breath, he moved inside her, pushing her, stretching her body wide to accommodate him. Her nails dug into his back as she shuddered at the intoxicating sensation of him filling her. Pleasure drenched her as she rocked against him, until he drew in a ragged breath.

Her climax came hard and fast. Her body clenched around him. She dug her nails into his shoulders and clung to him with a vicious grip as she sobbed with the sheer perfection of it.

"Sometimes hard and fast is good," he said softly against her ear. "And sometimes— Are you asleep?"

Her head was heavy on his shoulder, her long hair clinging like hot silk filaments to his damp skin. Her leg thrown across his body. Kane ran his hand lightly down her arm and slid his fingers to the curve of her hip. Her skin was unbelievably smooth and soft, damp with their exertions.

The next time they made love, he wanted to see her. Wanted to look into her face and watch her eyes darken and go hazy with desire. He wanted to feel her nipples peak as he sucked on them. He wanted to see her blush when he buried his head between her legs.

Her reactions to his lovemaking made Kane suspect her past lovers had been a selfish lot of asses. There was a lot to be said, he thought smugly, feeling the weight of her head on his chest, for savoring the moment.

CHAPTER THIRTEEN

The ringing of the Sat Comm link woke them. They'd managed to grab four hours of sleep. Better than nothing. Naked, Kane climbed over the seats to grab the link.

AJ searched around in the thick darkness for her clothes, pulling them on as she listened to his terse questions, and surmised the answers. Jesus God. Her heartbeat thudded in her ears. Things moved in slow-mo while she raced to dress.

She listened intently to Kane's tone as she grabbed a handful of his clothing, and slipped between the seats and into the passenger seat of the cockpit, then turned on the overhead light.

Kane's face was frighteningly grim as he disconnected from the call. "It's a viral agent," he said flatly, taking his clothes from her and starting to dress. "Raazaq's got enough to annihilate a small town and infect countless others. Apparently it kills as many as it infects. Some die within days, others are fine, except they're carriers. It's highly contagious."

"Holy shit."

Kane finished dressing and cranked the engine. It was still dangerous to drive. Sand replaced air, and visibility was zero. It was pitch-dark, and winds whipped past them at upwards of eighty miles per hour. But they had no choice.

She buckled her seat belt, then reached across Kane as he drove, grabbed his belt, and clicked it into place.

The sharp, metallic tang of fear filled her mouth, and her heart beat irregularly. Something this toxic in the hands of a sociopath terrorist like Raazaq was enough to give Mother Teresa, as dead as she was already, a heart attack.

AJ squeezed her eyes shut for a moment. She wanted backup, goddamn it, and she wanted it now. But they'd just have to do what they could.

"Two degrees south." AJ checked the GPS on the dash, absently correcting Kane's heading. "There's not a damn thing this far south," she mused, gripping the dash in both hands as the wind threatened to turn the vehicle over like a turtle.

Mentally, she flipped through maps of the area, trying to figure out where Raazaq could possibly be headed. "He could be going to

Bawiti," she mused, thinking out loud. "But I doubt it. Not populated enough. Why waste something that could kill thousands on a few hundred 'peasants,' as he calls them? Maybe farther south? The Sudan?" She shook her head, discounting that notion. "Then why not fly? Hell, why not take the river?"

They skidded and skated down the incline as the heavy winds tried to force them back. Even nature was working against them. Kane's jaw clenched and his eyes narrowed. In the dim dash light, AJ studied his expression and gave thanks that she wasn't the focus of his anger.

It was going to be slow, agonizingly slow, progress, made worse by the sense of urgency nipping at their heels. It was like being in a dream and trying to run while your legs wouldn't move. *Keep busy,* she told herself. *Keep talking. Stop thinking so damn much.* "There are a few settlements. A couple of decent-size oases out here. Not much more." She braced herself as the Humvee bounced convulsively, broadsided by the gale. Her gaze shifted from the wash of sand beyond the windshield to the man behind the wheel. "We need that team. Here. With us, to contain this when we catch up to the bastard."

"Don't panic yet. Believe me, I'll let you know when it's time to panic." Kane spared her a quick glance, then looked back at the outside world as it tried to claw its way in. "The team'll be there when we need them. There's only so much anyone can do in this weather. Even Raazaq can't beat the storms. Right now we're the closest to him.

"The second this storm backs off," he said, each word bitten off, "the skies will be filled with aircraft and more backup than anyone will know what to do with. In the meantime, we go as fast and as far as we can and ride his ass."

"I'll alert the others." She grabbed the comm link and connected with Hawk, instructing the men to catch up and stay close if they could. AJ used a simple series of T-FLAC code words to briefly fill in the others about the danger and the ramifications of Raazaq, and within seconds the convoy was once again in motion. She couldn't see them, but she knew the team was back there, covering their ass, moving up to join them in T-FLAC solidarity. She and Kane weren't alone, despite the isolation of driving in this storm.

Hell, just driving was a potentially lethal business as the winds gusted and the sand whirled in a blinding, beige wall. The road, not that great to begin with, was obscured by moving sand. They could have been about to drive over an oasis full of happy villagers and they wouldn't know it until the wheels made a thumping sound over their bodies. Jesus.

AJ glanced at Kane in the lights from the dash. The muscles in his arms bulged as he fought for control of the wheel, and strain bracketed his mouth as he took the Humvee to dangerous speeds. They didn't speak as he concentrated on keeping the heavy vehicle on the road.

At times they almost seemed to levitate in the raging wind. AJ bit her tongue, swore, and pressed a hand to her somersaulting stomach. The wind was actually trying to push them backwards. Was Fate trying to tell them something?

No.

The only fate was the one you made, AJ thought. And she'd be damned if she'd let that madman Raazaq continue holding the world hostage.

She grabbed the Sat Comm when it rang— grateful for the interruption. "It's Hawk," she shouted over the raging storm. "He wants to talk to you."

"Put him on speaker."

AJ flicked the switch and adjusted the buttons to bring in the other operative more clearly. She turned up the volume as high as it would go so Hawk's voice would carry over the thundering roar surrounding them. The satellite communicator crackled like an old-fashioned radio. "Shit!" she shouted as some sort of flying vegetation—Was that a palm tree?—came right for the car. "Watch out!"

The vehicle slewed across the nonexistent road, bounced convulsively as Kane wrestled the wheel to get the car back in the right direction.

"The—broken dow—" Hawk's voice broke up.

"Say again," Kane demanded.

"—two—sand—engine—" The other vehicle's engine had seized in the sandstorm. Hell. There was a pause as they all contemplated this news. "Have—back—them."

"No," Kane said flatly. "Raazaq is already in the wind. They'll have to wait. Radio in and have the others pick them up when they come through."

There was a long pause. "Cou—three da— or more."

"Could be," Kane told him flatly. "I need you more than they do. Get your ass in ge—" He swore. "The line went dead."

"I'll try again." AJ used the satellite communicator, she tried the land line, she tried both cell phones.

Nothing worked.

All communications, satellite and otherwise, were suddenly, inexplicably, dead.

They were on their own.

"Raazaq is approximately eighteen miles ahead of us." Kane flicked a grim glance at the blip on the screen. "Which places him . . . where?"

"The oasis," AJ said triumphantly. "If we gun it, we can be there in twenty minutes. Tops."

"You sure?"

"Yes."

"Have a heading?"

"We're on it. Just keep going. We can do this."

Forty-five minutes later, Kane knew they'd arrived. The front bumper of their vehicle and a very large palm tree suddenly came eye to eye. He slammed on the brakes. The Humvee vibrated, its back end swinging wide in the sand, but it stopped dead just inches away from the trunk.

"Well done, bubba." AJ let out the breath she appeared to have been holding for miles, and started braiding her long hair. Hair as soft as the finest silk and smelling of roses and cinnamon.

"Raazaq better be here." AJ dropped her hands. "If not, where?"

"Wish to hell I knew." Kane squinted through a veil of swirling sand and observed the black tents and staked animals of the nomadic Bedouins.

She searched the bag at her feet. "What do we want to take in?"

"I'll take the Sig, thanks, and my knife." AJ handed him the weapons. Not much if things turned to shit. But they couldn't go in armed to the teeth and look friendly, either. He strapped the knife to his calf, then tugged his pant leg down over it. He leaned forward to secret the gun in the small of his back under his T-shirt. Wouldn't bear close scrutiny, but in the dark nobody would notice. "Take something small and discreet. Ready?"

"I'm weaponed up, if that's what you mean. Are we getting out, or do we sit here until the wind blows us to Oz?"

"Out, wiseass. Grab the canteen first."

They both wet large bandannas, squeezed out the excess water, and tied the damp cloths around their noses and mouths to keep out the sand. They looked like outlaws.

He held out his hand. "Grab that bag of supplies behind your seat. Give it to me. Here, I'll take it." He tucked the small leather sack inside his shirt.

AJ grabbed his hand and slid across the console, exiting beside him on the driver side. Instantly, she was battered by the never-ceasing wind. Kane put himself between her and the blast, but it was like trying to hold off a tornado with a screen door. The sand was everywhere. Living, breathing, an entity all to itself. It surrounded them, pelting against her skin like thousands of needles at once. Digging, stinging, slapping.

The wind wrenched the door handle out of Kane's hand and slammed the car door hard enough to shake the vehicle, missing her by a breath. Kane grabbed her hand and steadied her, pulling her toward the largest tent, in the center of the small encampment. A faint glow of a lamp within shone like a beacon, guiding them in out of the storm. The rest of the world was darkness and gale-force-driven sand.

Despite the wet cloth covering their faces, both choked and coughed on powder-fine dust particles as they leaned into the wind, weaving on unsteady feet like Saturday night drunks. Sand gritted between her teeth and coated her nose, despite the bandanna.

The narrow squint of their eyes made walking hazardous, and the damp cloths over their faces quickly clogged with sand, making breathing damn near impossible. He held on to AJ's hand tightly enough to crack her slender bones. And she was glad of it. He was the one stable point in this night filled with sound and fury and little else. Every step was torture. Every breath painful. She clung to Kane, a part of her terrified that she'd be plucked from his grasp and carried away on a wall of sand.

Christ. Kane'd never experienced anything like this. Particles stung his skin like microscopic shards of glass. He felt as if he were being sliced to pieces by an enemy too small and too numerous to fight. So much for this storm passing in eight hours. It'd been seven, and it didn't look as though it would let up anytime soon.

There was no sign of Raazaq's entourage. He had four vehicles, at least. But the fact that Kane couldn't see them didn't necessarily mean anything. The cars could be hidden behind the tents, or between some of the small mud huts scattered about the oasis. Hell. They could be sitting right in front of him and he wouldn't be able to see them. Impossible to tell in the dark with the sand blowing up a screen that covered everything unless they tripped over it.

There was a strong possibility that Raazaq wasn't here. That he'd somehow managed to ditch the tracking device. If that was the case, finding him now would be like finding a needle in a haystack. Or, in this case, one particular grain of sand in the middle of a khamsin.

The hot wind buffeted AJ smack into him. Hard. They staggered before Kane caught her and wrapped a strong arm about her waist, supporting her weight against him. Their booted feet sank into ankle-deep sand, which moved and shifted beneath them like quicksand.

The cluster of tents, which had seemed so close when they left the Humvee, appeared much farther away now. Almost as if the camp were slipping away from them. Hell, they wouldn't be the first people to get lost and die when safety lay a few feet away. The desert was alive and malicious. A killer with no compassion. Very much like the monster they were tracking. The only way they'd stay alive would be to remember that.

Kane called out a greeting in Arabic as they came within feet of the tent—fortunately they'd managed to arrive at the front door. More by accident than design. He pushed into the tent, dragging AJ in with him.

A man, reclining on the ground in a nest of blankets, looked up, startled, from the book he was reading. *"Salaam Aleikum."*

"Aleikum es Salaam," Kane replied, drawing AJ inside. Still supporting her with one strong arm, he reached up and pulled his bandanna

down to lay around the base of his neck. God, it felt good to draw a breath that wasn't filled with sand grinding its way down his throat.

"Assef. Ma-batkallamsh àrabi." It would be expected that he didn't speak Arabic, but a wise man didn't plead too ignorant. A tourist would pick up a smattering of the language in his travels.

"I speak your American," the man said in deep, if halting accents. He waved them forward. *"Marhaba,* welcome, travelers."

After much *salaam*ing, greetings, and offers of food and lodging, Kane and AJ found themselves seated on a pillow-strewn rug as the man woke his servants and ordered food prepared.

AJ slumped against Kane, yanking her bandanna down and scraping one hand across her dirty face to push her sand-encrusted hair back and out of her way. She looked gorgeous.

Kane was so damn glad to be out of the wind and sand that he grinned at her before turning his gaze to their new surroundings.

The goat- and camel-hair-paneled tent was large, and well insulated against the storm. Seven feet high, and held up by nine poles, the large space was divided into a women's side and a men's side, with rugs on the ground, and facing away from the worst of the winds. The raging sand screamed outside, and they had to raise their voices to be heard, but they were sufficiently protected from the worst of it.

Kane introduced himself and AJ, found out their host's name was Jafar Shaaeawi, and politely refused the first offer of food, as was custom. Their host politely insisted, which was also custom. Kane explained he was a photographer, AJ his model, and they were on their way to the Siwa Oasis. Of course, they were going nowhere near the oasis, but it was in a somewhat southerly direction and could explain why they were heading this way.

Jafar, a small, middle-aged man with a grizzly gray beard and large, meaty hands, informed Kane, in excruciatingly polite tones, that they were way off course. He offered to have one of his many strong sons go with them in the morning and get them back on the correct road for their destination.

A woman rose from a pile of blankets in the corner and moved to light a fire. AJ straightened up and smiled at her. Kane presented her with the small pouch he'd brought in with him. It contained a brick of sugar and a pouch of tobacco as gifts to their host, who would prize both, as they were so hard to come by. Both the men and women of the nomad tribes chewed tobacco, and the woman accepted the gifts with obvious delight.

Then she turned with a swirl of her black robes to squat and stir the fire. The flames danced, flickering golden on the roof of the tent. Jafar's wife then served them curdled milk in small, filthy mugs. Saharan nomads used precious water only to drink, not to wash their utensils, and a filter of sand covered the curds. Even in the dim lighting Kane could see the dirt and small insects swimming in the gray mess.

Their host slurped his down, and Kane and AJ drank, too. Kane hoped AJ attempted to do what he was doing, filter the liquid through clenched teeth. Since there was no way to politely spit out what he'd filtered, he swallowed, anyway. He bit back a grin when he heard AJ noisily swallow beside him. This was foul stuff. Good girl, she'd managed to do so without gagging. His estimation of her went up several more notches.

The woman, never introduced, and covered from toes to eyes in her black garb and veil, filled a miniature enameled teapot with green tea leaves. She broke a large lump off the rock-hard loaf of sugar Kane had given her, with a precise knock of a small tea-glass bottom. She then lined three glasses up on the rug in front of her. Silence hung in the tent while the woman went through the hospitable ceremony.

Outside, the wind and sand continued to batter at the walls of the tent, but inside, it was still, and warm.

After the tea was brewed, she poured it into a glass from a height that made it foam, then back into the teapot. She poured the tea back and forth three or four times, let it come to a boil again, then served them each a glass with a flourish.

Kane knew that the sugary green tea was one of the few sweets the nomads indulged in. He let the silence deepen as they sipped their drinks, letting their host savor the taste with loud, slurping noises. As was the custom, the tea was served three times.

"The first glass tastes bitter, the second one just right, the third one a little weak," their host told them with a smile.

Kane declined food. It was late, they'd disturbed their host more than enough for the night. But the man insisted. Kane felt AJ droop beside him as she leaned heavily against his side. He glanced at her once. She was fighting sleep, but game, and he knew should the need arise she'd be wide awake and raring to go.

Admiration pooled inside him and he gave her full marks. No matter how this op had started, she'd more than pulled her weight since.

Ful beans had been boiled—at some point—with vegetables, mashed onions, and tomatoes, and then heavily spiced. The woman reheated the mixture, and brought it to them in a communal serving dish with rounds of bread. They tore the round loaf into finger-size portions and dipped the bread in the bowl, eating with their fingers. The bean dish was delicious, lack of refrigeration notwithstanding, and AJ and Kane both ate their fill. He'd been hungrier than he'd realized, and he noticed AJ must've been, too; she ate everything except the finish on the bowl. And she was looking a little more perky.

All to the good.

Fatigue dragged at Kane's gritty eyes, but he fought to stay alert. Their host was friendly and courteous, but for all Kane knew, Jafar had offered Raazaq the same hospitality. He couldn't afford to relax too far.

A *nargileh*, or water pipe, was brought out, but this time Kane declined with utmost sincerity. He and his twin, Derek, had smoked half a pack of Lucky's behind the garage one momentous afternoon when they'd been fourteen. Between the two of them, they'd been sick enough for ten people. It wasn't something Kane wanted to repeat. Since then, just the smell of tobacco was enough to remind him of the indignity of heaving into his mother's petunia bed. Not to mention the lecture he and Derek had gotten from their father, when the old man had hauled them inside the house stinking of smoke and puke.

Jafar's *ma'assul* tobacco was burned over live coals, then filtered through the water and drawn up a three-foot-long snakelike tube. The gurgling sound of the water bubbling blended with the howling of the wind in a strange and unfamiliar tune that was almost hypnotic.

Kane glanced down at AJ, then gently removed the glass she held tilted on her lap from her lax fingers. Head slumped on his shoulder, she'd fallen asleep while he and Jafar talked.

"She is very beautiful, your woman."

"She has a beautiful soul," Kane said easily. He relaxed against the pillows, tucking AJ more comfortably into the curve of his shoulder. She was dead weight. Exhausted beyond her limit, she was out like a light. Kane sipped his tea. "It is a good thing you were here, Jafar. We couldn't have traveled any farther this day."

"Allah be praised." Jafar touched his lips and forehead and gave a half bow. "We are always happy to welcome weary travelers."

"Have there been many in this storm?"

"We have given a few travelers sanctuary.

You will meet the rest of our guests come morning."

Kane glanced around casually. They sat in a small pool of flickering, amber firelight. The rest of the tent, and its occupants, were shadowed in darkness. The hairs at the back of his neck prickled as he studied the various blanketed lumps huddled around the edges of the tent. Raazaq? Was the bastard hunkered down, listening? Planning?

"While I'm enjoying your company, I would ask that we be shown where we may sleep. It's been a long day."

Their host clapped his hands. A servant, a boy of about ten or eleven, materialized out of the shadows. "Show our guests to their beds." He turned to Kane and bowed. "I will look forward to talking with you more in the morning."

"Thank you for your hospitality." Kane supported AJ as he rose, then dipped down and lifted her into his arms. He followed the child, who carried a small lantern, across the carpeted floor and into another tent, and then another. They were all linked together by canvas passageways. It was a fabric catacomb, leading him . . . Hell, it could have been leading him anywhere.

The boy finally ushered Kane into what

looked like a supply tent, which had been hastily rearranged to accommodate a sleeping pallet.

Kane lay AJ down on the blankets, then reached into his pocket and handed the boy a few coins, *baksheesh*. The child left the lantern on a stack of baskets piled haphazardly in the corner, and closed the tent flap behind him.

Kane knew he needed to sleep. And sleep hard. He'd had precious little in the last seventy-two hours, and while his mind could compensate and allow for the lack, his body was protesting. Even a couple of hours now would stand him in good stead. He was a light sleeper, their accommodations were at the end of the row of sleeping tents. If anyone entered he'd hear them.

He removed the Sig from his belt and lay down beside AJ, keeping the weapon close at hand. She sighed in her sleep and turned into him, flinging one arm over his midriff and snuggling her head in the curve of his neck. Kane wrapped one arm around her and pulled her snugly against his side, where she fit perfectly. He nuzzled the tender skin at her temple and whispered, "What is it you're really so afraid of, Aphrodite Jacintha?"

Chapter Fourteen

Early morning

There was no horizon. Just a mustard-colored haze, a murky blend of sand and sky as far as the eye could see. The wind had died down to a playful breeze. Kane drank from his canteen and surveyed the sand dune that had once been the Humvee. Half a dozen laughing, shrieking children were having the time of their lives digging out the vehicle. Dust flew as they slid down the sides and tossed handfuls of sand at one another. Reminded him of winter weekends spent with his sister and brothers at his grandmother's cabin up in the Sierras. Snowball fights and hot apple cider, laughter, love, warmth. He smiled.

It had been a lifetime since he'd felt that kind of simple joy.

The air was pleasantly cool. But then, it was still early. It would heat up soon enough. He glanced at the fancy do-everything watch on his wrist. Tapped it. Damn thing must've quit last night. He figured it was before seven, though.

"That looks like fun." AJ came up beside him. She'd managed to persuade their hosts to give her water to wash with, and her skin looked fresh and dewy, and extremely touchable. She'd scraped her hair back into a long braid—the woman never seemed to use a comb—tied at the bottom with a bit of rawhide. She still wore khaki pants, but she'd dusted off her cotton shirt and knotted it loosely at the waist, exposing a smile of tanned tummy. Somehow she managed to look chic instead of sloppy, and eminently kissable. He should be worn to a nub. Instead, just looking at her revitalized him better than any vitamin.

To hell with Viagra.

Bottle AJ and the world would have a hard-on.

"Time?" he asked, smiling at the antics of the kids, very much aware of the closeness of AJ's body, and the brush of her sleeve as she stood beside him.

AJ glanced at the utilitarian watch on her wrist, then frowned. "Damn. Must've got sand in it."

A chill crept up the back of his neck. "What time did it stop?"

"Oh-two-eighteen. Why?"

He tilted his wrist so she could read the face of his. Oh-two-eighteen.

"That's weird."

"Isn't it."

Several women came out of the tent behind them, chattering like kids escaping from school for the summer, and gesturing to the children as they walked down to the water hole several hundred yards away. Kane observed them for several seconds. The other occupants of the tent were still inside. And while many of them probably didn't speak English, he wasn't going to risk it. "I hate to spoil their fun, but let's help the kids. I'd like to make up time, and get to Siwa as soon as we can."

It was unlikely Siwa was Raazaq's destination. But if anyone was listening they had to be on their way *somewhere*. No one came out into the Western Desert aimlessly. No one. Their eyes met. "Slave driver," AJ teased.

"Too bad the cameras are buried," Kane said easily. "I'd like some shots against this sky."

"Yeah." AJ glanced at the weirdly yellow sky and scrunched her nose. "Too bad. You and Andy Warhol."

He brushed an imaginary bit of dirt off her cheek with his thumb, just because he had to touch her. "Walk with me before we start excavating."

"Where?"

"To those trees over there."

She put on the sunglasses she'd been holding, covering her pretty, pale eyes. "Sure." Kane saw his reflection in her lenses. Despite keeping it light, he looked as grim as he felt, and clearly AJ felt the heightened urgency, too.

They walked side by side, not touching. He had the sudden urge to hold hands with a woman. This woman in particular. He pushed the urge aside, tucking his fists into the front pockets of his Dockers as he walked.

"Raazaq's vehicles are behind those huts over there." He nodded to the cluster of mud huts to the right as soon as they were out of earshot of the tents. "He's long gone."

"Damn it!" AJ's long legs matched his stride. He could almost feel the vibration of her energy as she walked, *strode,* along beside him. Like a sleek jungle animal, she always seemed poised to take off running. "The slimy turd was here when we arrived?"

"No. Jafar says he showed about an hour before we did, switched the vehicles for camels, and split."

"My God. In that wind? I suppose it's too much to hope he was smothered by the khamsin and then blown down to hell."

Their hats were in the buried car, and the

morning sun turned her pale amber hair to pol-
ished copper. "They say only the good die
young."

"I'm going to prove that a lie," AJ said
grimly as she shoved her sunglasses up her nose.
"In his case—What is he? Thirty-eight?—
thirty-eight is far too *old* to die."

"Have to find him first."

"And we will." They stepped into the shade
of several tall date palms on the edge of a
muddy water hole. The women had gathered
in the shade on the other side to chat and wash
clothes. Several others, with a handful of children, herded goats to a patch of long grass and
weeds nearby. The air smelled of campfires, wet
wool, and the musty, brackish odor of the water. And under it all, the faint, barely percepti-
ble fragrance of tuber rose.

"He lit out of here directly into one of the
worst sandstorms of the year," Kane reminded
her. "He's in a hurry. My gut tells me he knows
we're after him." His gut feeling had saved his
ass many a time, so he wasn't going to ignore
the knotted warning this time. Raazaq was in
possession of a deadly poison. And they were
playing cat and mouse with a man who held no
value for human life.

Kane had a bad feeling. A feeling of impending doom. Which wasn't like him. He

prided himself on his pragmatism. Their directive had been simple. But there was nothing simple about this anymore.

"Maybe not us, specifically. But he probably suspects *someone* is. A man in Raazaq's line of work spends his life looking over his shoulder." AJ removed her sunglasses and hooked them to the front of her shirt.

Jesus. The world was dangling from a thread in the hands of a psycho and Kane Wright could only think about how AJ Cooper had slipped seamlessly into his life.

"Of course," AJ said, scowling, "that would be giving the bastard a character trait like a regular human being. Maybe megalomaniac psychopaths don't get paranoid. What do you think?"

"Hell if I know. I'd like to think so. Although from his dossier I'd say paranoia wasn't one of his traits. Megalomaniacal and psychopathic are two that do apply, though.

"There're precious few choices south of here as far as his destination goes." Kane dragged his gaze away from her and stared out at the desert around them, trying to get into the tango's mind. "And absolutely none that make any sense," he finished irritably.

"Could be headed to Bawiti," AJ suggested.

"Or the Sudan, for that matter."

AJ glanced up at him. "But you don't think so."

"Hell, no. I don't. If it were anyone else, I'd think he was going walkabout as the aborigines do in Australia. But knowing Raazaq, he's not going out into the barren Western Desert to find himself, or commune with nature."

"Then he's heading *toward* something. All we have to do is figure out what or where, and we'll have him."

Above them, fronds of the palms clicked slightly in the hot breeze. The voices of the women melded with the giggles of the kids, the bleat of the goats, and the soft *shuush-shuush* of the sand as it drifted and swirled across the surface of the desert in an endless pattern. Little eddies, made up of lighter grains, danced across the surface of the desert in a wavy pattern reminiscent of a choppy sea.

"There's something going down, something we're missing," Kane told her grimly. "What could possibly attract a man like Raazaq? There aren't any big, heavily populated cities this way. No rivers or lakes to pollute. He has twelve men with him. A baker's dozen of trouble on the hoof. What in God's name is their target?"

"A person?" AJ mused, her brow wrinkled with concentration. "A place? Hell, I don't know. The only thing I can think of, and it's not realistically a place he'd be interested in, is that new dig south of here."

"What dig?" Kane's instincts perked up.

"Kane." She blew out an exasperated breath. "Raazaq wouldn't give a damn that one more ancient king's tomb has been discover—"

"Tell me anyway."

"Fine. One of the nomadic tribes literally fell over a small pyramid last year. It'd been completely covered by sand and vegetation, and the oasis it sits in is so far off the beaten track— Never mind all that." She started pacing like a caged lioness.

"Finding it wasn't that big a deal. They discover new tombs all the time. But this one was completely intact. Inside and out. *That* was unique. They had a long article about it in the *New York Times*. For a month or so, everyone made a fuss about the discovery. No grave robbers or vandals. Then all of a sudden, nothing. Everyone stopped reporting on it."

She frowned, squinting against the bright sky. "At the time it seemed odd, then I forgot all about it. That was right after I was recruited from the LPD to join T-FLAC. I kept up with the articles and then forgot about it."

"Do you know where it is?" Kane asked.

"Southwest of here. About three hundred miles."

"Remember more?"

AJ smiled. "You mean like the coordinates? Yeah, actually I do. Only because I looked it up on a map when I was reading about—You don't really think that's where he's headed, do you? What would be the payoff?"

Kane shrugged. "He has a six-hour lead. Let's head in that direction—since we don't have anything else—and call in on the road. Our people will have updated intel by now, and will possibly have pinpointed his target area. At least we'll be going in his general direction. In the meantime, let's help the kids unearth the Humvee and make tracks."

They strode back to the half-revealed mound that was their transportation and started digging. It didn't take long to ex-cavate the vehicle once the kids understood it was no longer a game.

As soon as the door was clear, Kane got in and tried to start the car. The engine didn't turn over. He got out and popped the hood. The engine was sealed, and there wasn't much sand inside it. Certainly not enough to clog the components. He dusted everything off as best he could and got back into the Humvee. "Contact the others and see what their ETA is."

AJ reached in and grabbed the Sat Comm.

Kane glanced at her as he tried to start the engine again. "Shaking it isn't going to make it work," he told her dryly.

With a frown, she gave it another jiggle for good measure. "How about if I kick it?"

"Nope. Not that, either. Car won't start." He removed the key.

"Sand in the engine?"

"No."

She slipped into the passenger seat, and hand-signed, *Our host? Sabotaged?*

"No way," he said in his normal, calm tone. "Think about it. There's just too much that's gone wrong. Watches, car, communications. All out."

"The khamsin knocked something out somewhere."

"Seems like," Kane said with a frown. "I'd understand communications. But watches? Car batteries?"

"Maybe the signals from the satellite were knocked out by the storm?"

He raised a brow.

"Sorry. Electronics weren't my thing."

"Frankly, doesn't matter what or who caused it. Or how it was caused. It just is. Now we deal with it. Identify the problem then find a way around, over, under, or through it. See what you can put together for supplies."

Better prepared for the khamsin, Jafar's people would offer them food, and if necessary sell them—

"Transportation," AJ exclaimed at the same time he said, "Let's see if they'd sell us a couple of fast camels."

"Frankly," AJ rubbed the back of her neck, "I don't relish the thought of being exposed to the elements on the back of something that breathes."

She twisted in her seat to look at him. "Maybe this blackout thing will pass in an hour or so. It'll be suicide to set out across the Western Desert on camelback." It was a statement, not a protest.

"People who live here do it all the time. Got a better idea?" He paused. "Can you ride?"

"I did some riding as a kid. Horses, not camels. I'm not great, but I can stay on. I'm game. How about you? You ride?"

"Yeah. My twin has a ranch."

"Bet he doesn't have camels." She pushed her hair back from her face.

Kane gave her a half smile. "Bet you're right. I'll talk to Jafar about transportation, and hiring a guide."

She glanced out the window. The desert stretched out forever. Miles in any direction, there was nothing but sand, and the already rising sun glancing off it like light off a mirror. Other than the oasis a few hundred feet away, there wasn't a damn thing out there. It was like being on the moon. "Let's hope he can lend us something with wheels instead of feet."

"It's not going to be much fun, either way. How close will your memory get us to that pyramid you were talking about?"

"Visual contact."

"Good enough." One corner of his mouth tipped into a smile. "Get the supplies together, then check and double-check our maps. You have ten minutes. Double what you think we need for water rations."

"Aye, aye, captain."

He smiled slightly. "Make it so."

The Bedouin had a dozen four-wheel-drive vehicles. But when anyone attempted to start them, they were met with the same results Kane and AJ had with their Humvee. Nothing moved. Their host offered them the use of the camels he used for plowing as well as for transportation. Not prepared to look a gift camel in the mouth, they accepted his offer. Kane assured the man the animals would be returned soon.

Jafar supplied them with six camels, and

three of his middle sons—Anum, Yusuf, and Ziyad—as guides.

Surrounded by the women and children on one side, and the men of the tribe on the other, they prepared to mount. Everyone had come to see them off, cheerfully issuing instructions in rapid Arabic.

The camels, stubborn animals that they were, knelt under duress, then were efficiently loaded with supplies. Kane, followed by the three young men, clambered aboard their camels while AJ watched their every move so she could mimic their actions. From the ground, she looked at her kneeling camel.

They were eye to eye. Kika had ridiculously long black eyelashes and sleepy black eyes. "Hello, pretty girl," AJ crooned. The camel greeted her with a severe lack of interest and a refined air of sophistication and superiority as she looked down her long nose at this new human.

"Give her a pat on the nose. She'll like that," Kane said as he settled himself into the blanket-covered leather saddle on his camel, named Roopsi, and gave it instructions to rise. The maneuver looked dangerous. Not to mention uncomfortable as the big animal stood, rocking Kane in the saddle like a loose bag of grain.

AJ figured she'd wait to see if he fell off before she attempted to get on Kika. Kika silently stared at her. AJ patted the camel on her nose. It felt like hairy leather. Kika huffed. She had god-awful breath. "We'll discuss the merits of mouthwash when we're on the road," AJ told the beast firmly. "Okay, girl. Here we go."

Climbing on a camel wasn't that tough since it was fairly low to the ground, crouched as it was. AJ accepted assistance from another of Jafar's "many, large, healthy sons." They all looked like carbon copies of their father. Sharp-featured, a little ferrety, and running to fat.

AJ managed a coordinated jump and swing, and was on her camel. Funny, but in all the old movies she'd seen, camel riding had looked pretty . . . romantic. Nothing romantic about it this close up, though. She wiggled her butt on the saddle—felt pretty comfortable—and slipped her feet into the stirrups, which the young man had to lengthen to accommodate her long legs.

He commanded the camel to rise. Kika turned her head slightly and lifted her lip at him, exposing large, yellow teeth. The young man gave the beast a sharp kick. AJ braced herself. He kicked the camel again and waved his hands.

"Hold tight," Kane warned, laughter in his voice.

Good advice. AJ grabbed the saddle horn in front of her. The animal straightened her knobby hind legs first, thrusting AJ forward with a teeth-jarring jolt that almost pitched her headfirst into the dirt.

She held on for dear life as Kika unfolded her front legs and rose majestically to all four feet, tossing AJ back in the saddle with a whoosh. The quick backward swoop made her stomach leap into her throat. The feeling was comparable to a roller coaster. AJ laughed at the sensation.

She felt a swell of excitement as Anum took the lead rope and prodded the camels into motion. He clicked his tongue. *"Har-EEB, Har-EEB, Har-EEB."* Go! Go! Go!

He went first, followed by AJ, then Kane, followed by the other two brothers and the pack camel.

Kika moved in a casual saunter that triggered a comfortable swaying motion that was quite pleasant, and AJ settled in to enjoy the novelty of the ride. Jafar's wife had suggested she'd be more comfortable, and certainly cooler, in a loose caftanlike garment. Dubious, but unwilling to hurt the woman's feelings, AJ had swiftly changed into the borrowed all-encompassing cotton garment. Slathered with sunblock, coupled with a straw cowboy hat Kane had provided out of his endless bag of tricks, she must look somewhat ridiculous. But she didn't care.

AJ was on a serious and crucial op. She'd been given the opportunity to redeem her miserable inaction on that first night. She felt Kane's eyes on her back. Somewhere between hero worship and brain damage, she'd managed to slide ridiculously close to an emotional precipice she hadn't even considered when she'd made T-FLAC her life.

Kane enjoyed sex with her. Great. He didn't want responsibility? Even better. She had absolutely no intention of depending on anyone for her happiness.

Never again would she mistake being a man's trophy girlfriend for real emotion. She was worth more than that. She had worth and value with T-FLAC. She liked knowing that she was defined by her ability, not her build.

"Check that out," Kane said, coming up beside her. He pointed with a jerk of his chin. They observed the churned-up sand indicating several camels had come this way then veered off and headed southwest.

AJ frowned. Annoyed with herself for not seeing something that now it had been pointed out to her was obvious. *That's it,* she thought. *Stop thinking about Kane and start thinking about the op.* She had to prove herself—not only to

Kane, but to herself. She would have noticed had she not been lost in thoughts that had nothing to do with a diabolical madman. Instead she was trying to make some sense out of her—what, relationship with Kane? It wasn't a relationship. But it didn't feel like casual sex, either. AJ knew she no longer worshiped the hero image she had brought from the Academy. Nope, this felt like a whole lot more. Maybe she was falling in love? That was almost as frightening as anything they currently faced.

"Follow the tracks," Kane shouted ahead to Anum in Arabic.

"How did you see that?" she demanded, trying to cover the embarrassment of her inattentiveness.

"Put your sunglasses back on. See now?"

The U.V. filtered out the sharp light, leaving a deeper shadow on the surface, making the agitated sand stand out clearly. Yes, she saw, and stored. She wouldn't miss it again. "Must be Raazaq and his cronies."

"Yeah."

The sand had a mica sheen, tiny diamonds exposed. The sun was high, and beat down on her covered shoulders. A light, playful breeze made the heat bearable.

Fascinated by the lurch and sway of the camel in front of her, AJ admired the engineering of its spindly legs, which gave it such perfect balance in the shifting sands of its world. "Did you see the soft white pads under their hooves?" she called to Kane, who rode beside her. "Look how they spread with each step, just like dough. Cool, huh? Prevents them sinking into the sand, and provides traction."

"Do you remember everything you read?" Kane asked curiously. He looked like some kind of exotic cowboy in his straw hat, black galabayya, and several days' growth of beard darkening his jaw. He'd stroked her body with his face last night, and just remembering the tickle and scrape of that beard on her sensitized skin was enough to make her go weak at the knees. Good thing she was already sitting down.

She gulped a breath and focused on camels. "Pretty much. For example, did you know that from head to hump, *Camelus dromedarius* is perfectly adapted to this harsh desert life? Their long eyelashes and nostrils can close to deflect dust. They collect moisture from the air with each expelled breath and then inhale that moisture and take it into their lungs. Oh, and their single, fat-storing hump helps regulate their body temperature and can keep them hydrated for weeks. Which," AJ assured him, "I would prefer not to observe firsthand." She shifted in the saddle.

"Butt hurt? Try crooking your leg over the seat."

"In a while. I'm fine. It's spectacular, isn't it?" She indicated the vast, never-ending expanse of caramel-colored sand. The silence made her want to whisper as one did in church.

"Yeah," he said, not glancing away. "It is."

They didn't stop for lunch. There wasn't a scrap of shade anywhere. Just flat, camel-colored sand. A few outcroppings of rock once in a while broke the monotony. They ended up lapsing into long periods of silence.

"I'm not sure I'll ever be able to walk again," AJ confessed when they finally stopped to eat in the late afternoon. Raazaq's track went directly through a wadi. "Oh, look. Shade," she exclaimed happily.

Kane smiled. "Only an optimist would call that pathetic two inches shade."

A cluster of five pretty sad-looking palms stood sentinel over a small grassy area, where a muddy puddle indicated a water source. The shade, like the fronds on the date palms, was meager.

"Shade is shade."

"They had a cooking fire." Kane kicked at the coals with his toe. Cold.

Yusuf got the camels to kneel. An interesting rocking motion AJ quite enjoyed, despite her sore butt.

In his twenties, the young man had bad skin, the sharp features of a small rodent, and the family's slumberous black eyes. He did not look happy. "I am not the servant. Ziyad will prepare tea and food," he told them dismissively in pretty decent English. He went off to sit beside Anum.

AJ glanced at Kane. "What was that about?"

He held out his hand to help her down. "Wrong side of the blanket brother, apparently."

AJ swung her leg over Kika's back. "Ow."

"Saddle sore?"

"You have to ask? If you tell me your legs and butt don't hurt, I'll shoot you." AJ's skin felt stretched tight, and she would sell her soul for a gallon of Coke clinking merrily with ice.

Kane helped her down. Her legs buckled. "Want me to carry you?"

She was grateful for his help, and her legs wobbled as she stood upright, holding on to Kane to gain her sand legs. "Yes," she told him primly. "But it has nothing to do with my atrophied legs."

"What does it have to do with?"

"You holding me. Think they'll mind?" She nodded to the brothers.

Kane ran his hands up her arms. "Want me to ask them?"

"Nah. Let's fool around without permission."

"Let's," he whispered roughly, capturing her mouth.

She opened her mouth to welcome him.

Kane groaned. God, she tasted good.

She wrapped her arms around his neck and slumped against him, her hands gripping the back of his galabayya in both hands as she really got into the kiss. Up on her tiptoes, she pressed her body against his and responded to him as if she were dying of thirst and he were the well. He curved his hands over the firm mounds of her butt, drawing her against his body. She moaned low and thick against his mouth.

Heat and desire rose in him until he was dizzy with it.

Except this was neither the time nor the place. Damn it.

He eased her away from him with regret. "Rain check?"

Her pale-green eyes were hazy with desire,

large with want, but she stepped away and nodded, her gaze holding his. "Let it pour."

He brushed her cheek with his finger. It was warm, and slightly damp. Damn. He understood desire. Hell, he was no monk. He'd had a few long-term relationships, and more than a few short-term ones as well, but this felt . . . different. His need went beyond the mere physical. Which astounded him, since his physical desires for AJ were like nothing he'd ever known. His entire body seemed to think it couldn't function without her taste in his mouth and the feel of her skin. This wasn't only about giving and receiving carnal pleasure.

Damn it to hell. He didn't want to go there. Getting emotional about Cooper was the last thing he wanted or needed.

There be dragons there.

Unaware, or unconcerned, with where his thoughts had taken him, AJ rubbed her bottom with both hands. Her ass must hurt as badly as his did, but she hadn't complained. Yards of fabric covered her from neck to toe, but when she put her hands back like that the soft material pulled across her flat belly and flowed over her spectacular breasts. Seeing how the kiss had affected her nipples made him hotter than ever.

"I'm hoping for a monsoon," he murmured,

briefly touching her damp lower lip with his thumb.

Her tongue snaked out and darted a quick temptation before she stepped out of reach. "Torrential rains," she agreed, her eyes sparkling.

CHAPTER FIFTEEN

The camels were already at the water hole. They leaned down, legs comically splayed, to drink. Yusuf and Anum sat on the other side of the green patch, watching Ziyad prepare tea.

"I'm thirsty enough to lick that mud hole," AJ said as they walked into the shade.

"May I make another suggestion?"

"No, you may not." Mouth damp from his kiss, she smiled that infernal smile that drove him to distraction. "How long a break can we afford?"

"As long as the camels want to drink, we wait."

"Thank God they filled up before we left. Otherwise we'd be here for hours." She walked stiff-legged over to the scrubby grass, tossed her hat to the ground, then flopped down, some-how managing to do so without bending her knees. Spread-eagled on her back, she closed her eyes. "Hold that piña colada until I wake up from my nap, Raul."

Kane dropped down beside her. "Would that be before or after madam's massage?"

She opened one eye. "Oh, my God! A massage?" She quickly rolled over onto her stomach, pillowing her head on her arm. "I think I love you."

Kane eyed her speculatively. What an interesting thought. "Spread your legs."

"I do believe that's the first time a masseuse has said that to me." She opened one eye again. "The spirit might be willing, but the flesh is weak." She gave him a half smile, eyes dancing. "Not to mention Curly, Moe, and Ralph are right over there getting an eyeful."

"They can't see anything from where they are. And I'm talking massage, not wild monkey sex."

"Darn."

"Yeah," he said laconically, kneeling between her spread legs. "Darn."

He lifted the hem of the all-enveloping cotton garment she wore, running his hands up her smooth calves. Her skin felt warm, silky, resilient under his palms. He rested his hands lightly on the sweet curve behind her knees, and felt the unsteady beat of her pulse there as it picked up speed from the contact. He enjoyed touching her as much as she enjoyed being touched. He ran his hands up the back of her thighs, massaging the tight muscles in her legs in sure, easy strokes. She groaned softly. The sound was sexy as hell, and he came to life in a hurry. *Down, boy.*

She made an erotic picture with her body bared to the shoulders and exposed to his hungry gaze. He even found the fact that her slender feet were encased in heavy combat boots sexy. A narrow black thong bared her ass cheeks, which flexed at his touch. So responsive. *So not going to happen right now,* he reminded himself. He glanced over his shoulder. The brothers were lying down, taking a nap. Good.

He turned back and concentrated on giving her a proper massage. Her muscles were sore and tight and he kneaded and manipulated her glutes until she practically purred.

He spanned her narrow waist with his palms, digging his thumbs into the muscles on either side of her spine. Found a knot and worked on it until she softened, almost melting into the grass. "Hmmm-hmmm, good."

Sunlight filtered through the palm fronds high above, painting tiger stripes on her tanned back. Kane stroked instead of kneaded, just because he loved the sensation of her skin under his hands. It felt alive and responded instantly to his touch. He smiled. "Were you a cat in another life?"

"King Tut's." Her voice was thick. "Worshiped and revered. And I warn you, I became accustomed to it in a hurry."

"You mean you weren't Cleopatra?"

She snorted. "Maybe Caesar."

"Ah. You prefer ruling with an iron fist." This time he smiled fully. How like AJ. She wanted none of the girl trappings. She wasn't a woman who enjoyed games or prevarication. She was direct and straight to the point, with no stops along the way for political correctness. "As Queen of Egypt, Cleo had power," he pointed out.

"Oh, please. She was too busy drinking pearls, and playing at politics. She should've gone out with her troops and kicked some butt instead of waiting for her guys to save the day."

Kane laughed. "You're one in a million, Agatha Jethro."

"Ah–huh. One in a million reincarnated cats. A little to the left . . . Yeah. Oh, God. That feels sooooo good."

Kane leaned over and brushed her hair aside to kiss the back of her neck. He brushed his lips over her soft skin, drinking in the fragrances of roses and AJ that was becoming more and more addictive. He laved the spot with his tongue, then blew cool air against the damp spot, making her shiver. He glided his mouth up the side of her throat, and dropped a kiss on her parted lips.

"Yum. More," she demanded without opening her eyes.

"Later, little cat." Kane reluctantly lifted his body away from hers. "Camels are ready to rock." He pulled the caftan down over the tantalizing mounds of her spectacular butt and gave it a little pat. "Let's do it, Amy Jean."

She opened her eyes, rolled over, and stretched. "I owe you one."

"And I'll collect, too. I suggest we both tap a kidney before we split."

"Give me a minute." She held out her hand, and he pulled her to her feet. Christ. He was tempted to grab her and take her back down to the ground, rip her clothes off, and sink into the hot, wet heaven of her body. To keep from doing just that, he took a step back, and called to the Brothers Grim.

AJ walked to the other side of the small wadi, not exactly as private as closing a door, but as private as it was going to get.

When she returned the camels were ready, Kane on Roopsi, and Yusuf waiting to help her board Kika.

"Onward and upward." AJ grinned. The

massage, and that ten-minute break had done
her a world of good. She was refreshed and
rarin' to go.

They followed Raazaq's churned-up tracks
out of the wadi. He was still heading south. His
trail couldn't have been clearer if he'd stuck a
neon signpost saying, *I've Gone This Way.*
Either he was arrogant enough to believe no
one would follow him, or he was stupid
enough to think jamming their vehicle and
communications would stop them.

"Think our guys are following us?" AJ asked
as Kane came up beside her. She was getting
used to the camel's gait, a back-and-forth swaying movement that was almost hypnotic. She
hooked her knee over the front of the saddle
for a little relief on her aching butt. The foot
would fall asleep soon, and she'd have to switch
legs, but it helped a little if she moved around.

The hot afternoon sun baked down, a dry
heat that burned her nostrils and dried out the
moisture in her eyes. She was grateful for the
shade of the straw cowboy hat Kane had provided. It could be scrunched up to fit in her
back pocket, if she'd had a back pocket, and
was much better all-around protection than her
baseball cap.

"I'm hoping they were out of range of whatever shut us down. They'll put two and two to-

gether when they can't locate us, and go back to Cairo and get a plane to search."

"Talking about planes—I haven't noticed any fly over, have you?"

"Probably not a commercial route."

"Probably not." AJ drank greedily from her canteen. In this climate one didn't wait to become thirsty, which indicated dehydration. She stuck the container back into the pack in front of her. She frowned. "Unless whatever it is that's stopped everything on the ground also stopped things from flying. Is that possible?"

Kane shrugged, his face hard. "Sure, you can block instruments, but our pilots can fly blind—if the engines aren't in some way jammed. I know they'll figure out a way to find Raazaq. The problem might be in relaying the info to us."

The desert stretched out for miles around them, barren and majestic in its vast, unspoiled beauty. Golden ripples of wind-driven sand curved and spiraled up dunes and across flat surfaces in a monochromatic canvas. The only thing spoiling the pristine landscape was the darker, frothed-up tracks of the men they followed. And the threat Raazaq carried across the desert.

The brothers stopped for prayers at dusk, and Kane and AJ got off the camels and stretched their legs. The setting sun made the air cooler, but heat waves captured by the desert glistened in the distance. A mirage materialized way off, replete with mountains and shimmering water. She wondered how many people had died while trying to reach the mirage that would constantly slip farther out of reach.

"You're really enjoying this, aren't you?" Kane murmured as they walked.

"The desert? Yeah. I like it." She kicked sand with the tip of one sturdy boot and watched the setting sun filter through the drifting grains. "Hate to live here, though—too quiet for me—but it's fascinating to visit."

"That, too. But I meant, really love working for T-FLAC."

"Ah, the love of my life."

He glanced at her. "Is it?"

"You know my father was a SEAL? My brother bucked him, and joined T-FLAC straight out of the Marines. Of course, I had no idea what Gideon did until years later." She yanked off the cowboy hat and shook her head, letting the soft wind caress the sweat-dampened curls at her forehead. "The eight years between us made us practically strangers, and of course it didn't help that we each lived with a different parent. But I loved listening to Darrel talk about his years in the service. I craved that kind of commitment. Wanted to do something that made a difference."

She glanced up, to find his gaze locked on her. Heat skittered along her spine like an electrical current. "From when I was really small, I wanted to be a cop. It took me a while to chuck off the other crap in my life. But I did it. Then I was recruited by T-FLAC, and *bam*, my life changed."

"T-FLAC is a hell of a long way from being a beauty queen."

"Hooray for that." AJ shuddered dramatically. Not needing them, she took off her sunglasses and hooked them on her neckline.

His lips twitched. "Didn't like it much, huh?"

"Even getting shot in that training exercise, which was god-awful and scared the crap out of me, was better than parading around half-naked showing my assets." She huffed out a breath. "Maybe it wouldn't've been so bad if any of us had had anything to do with the way we looked—but it was a toss of nature's coin. Genetics."

"Genetics that must have helped you in life."

"Well, I suppose it helps not to be butt ugly," she said honestly. "But if anything, what I look like has held me back. A sort of reverse discrimination, you know? I never had a date for any of my proms. Guys just presumed someone else had asked me. And doing what I was doing—all that beauty-pageant crap—people made assumptions about my I.Q. And why wouldn't they? People tend not to look any farther than skin deep. They didn't even care if I had a brain or not. Until I joined T-FLAC."

"And then?"

"And then," she grinned ruefully, "I'm not sure if *they* cared there, either. But I have two things they do covet. My photographic memory, and my sniping abilities. I had nothing to do with the former, but I worked my ass off in sniper school and it's paid off. I plan on being T-FLAC's best sniper. I'm going to build my reputation on it."

She paused, face pink. They both remembered with crystal clarity what'd happened on that first day.

"AJ—"

"I screwed up. I know that. But I won't screw up again. *That* I can promise you."

"I believe you."

She slowed to look at him. "You do?"

"Implicitly."

She stopped walking, closed her eyes. "Jesus God, Kane. You have no idea what those three words mean to me." She turned and flung herself into his arms and gave him a smacking kiss on the lips. "Thank you."

The Shaaeawi brothers were closing the gap, and the sun was a brilliant tangerine streak across the horizon. Raazaq's tracks pointed south across the windswept desert floor. Kane wrapped his arms around AJ's slender waist and took her mouth greedily.

His kiss was slow and voluptuous. As if they had all the time in the world. As if they'd shared a lifetime of kisses. He knew her body so well already, and a little part of AJ rebelled that he knew that sucking her lower lip would make her shiver, and licking a slow, silky trail across her open mouth would make all her girl parts contract and throb. He didn't have to touch her breasts to make them ache. He didn't have to be inside her to have her on the brink of coming.

Her body hummed with pleasure as his tongue slid between her teeth. She met him boldly with her own tongue, gliding and caressing, imitating sex until she shuddered with longing. She clutched the back of his shirt with fisted hands as he drew her hard against his body, moving her hips against him in an erotic slide, like a virtuoso stroked a violin.

Lips. Tongue. Teeth.

AJ ached, and her heart pounded hard

enough to hear it in her ears. They broke apart. Both panting slightly. AJ blinked several times, like a sleepwalker, to clear her vision.

"I wasn't bullshitting you," Kane told her softly, holding her body against him without moving. She could feel each individual pulse point in her body throb in frustration.

"I know you'll do whatever it takes to kill Raazaq. What happened the other day was stage fright. First-time nerves." He brushed a long strand of hair off her cheek then let his finger linger on her skin.

"The first time someone is shot is a traumatic experience. It's the first time we realize just how vulnerable we are." His lips tilted in a smile. "Getting shot hurts like hell. Our brain shies away from letting it happen again."

"Some things in life are just begging to be experienced, right?"

He smiled. "Right." Then, as if he couldn't *not* touch her, Kane ran the edge of his thumb across her lower lip. He glanced over her shoulder. "Our ride's here."

"My butt protests, but let's do it."

"We need to get some rest," Kane said, following her to Kika. "Spell me while I grab a couple of hours, then I'll spell you."

"No problem." AJ climbed onto Kika with a

smile. "I'll call ahead and make a reservation at Motel 6."

He swung his leg over behind her and slid against her behind rather nicely. "We'll take a camel nap."

"Camel nap, huh?"

Riding double with Kane on a slow-moving camel was quite an experience. As the sun set and the black sky became a star-studded canopy, she appreciated the warmth of his hard chest at her back. He'd wrapped his arms loosely about her waist, not for balance—the saddle was as wide as a chair—but maybe, she thought, to keep them connected, as if he, too, didn't want to be separated from her. It was a nice thought, but knowing Kane, not terribly likely.

They'd removed their hats and stuffed them in her backpack. Kane rested his chin on top of her head. "What got you from beauty queen to queen of snipers?"

"I told you. I honestly wanted to make a difference." She smiled, resting her head back onto the curve of his shoulder. "It's all very well standing up on the stage *saying* I want world peace while I twirled a baton—"

"Baton twirling was your talent?"

"Hell, no." AJ gurgled a laugh. "At the time my talent was shooting marbles. But the judges didn't seem to want to watch me flick goonies for ten minutes at a stretch. I suppose there was something unappealing about having a young woman in a swimsuit onstage with her butt in the air, one eye closed."

Kane chuckled. "I don't know. Sounds pretty damn appealing to me."

"That's because you have a very sexy, very one-track mind."

"Apparently so. Okay, not marbles. What, then?"

"I did some fancy footwork gymnastics—"

"Can you do the splits? I once saw a girl in a circus who—"

AJ smacked a muscular thigh bracketing hers. "Can I finish this boring story?"

"I'm not bored."

"We are riding together so we can get a few hours' sleep, remember?"

"You take first watch. Finish your autobiography. It'll be my bedtime story. World peace," he prompted.

AJ snuggled her bottom into the V of his thighs and rubbed the top of her head against his chin like a contented cat. "Don't laugh. I did, *do,* want world peace, but I didn't want to *chat* about it. I wanted to be part of the people who can make it happen."

"Of course you did," Kane said dryly.

"Why'd you do the whole beauty-circuit thing if you hated it so much?"

"My mom's gorgeous. She wanted to be Miss America more than anything. She was obsessed with it. Not mildly obsessed, but rabidly, one-track-minded obsessed. It broke up her marriage, lost her friends—hell, gave her enemies, for that matter. But as much as she so desperately wanted the crown, she never made it past Miss Junior Illinois. So then I was her shot at it. At first I was just happy to have her attention. Then I realized she wasn't seeing me. Her daughter. She was seeing her entrée into the world she wanted to belong in." AJ paused when he didn't say anything. "Bored you into a coma, did I?"

"Keep going."

"Okay. But if you find yourself slipping into a stupor, don't say you weren't warned. Where was I?"

"Stage mother," he prompted.

"Did I say that?"

"Not in so many words."

"She was my handler in more ways than one. My life was micromanaged. What I ate, when I slept, when I exercised—"

"Sounds like boot camp."

"A hundred times worse. I was froofed, fluffed, and frillied ad nauseum, and dressed in scratchy, girlie crap from morning to night. My hair had to be straightened—too curly. That was one of the few perks. It took me a while to hate that life enough to hurt her by saying, 'no more.' Man, that was a different lifestyle. As far back as I can remember I was a tomboy. Don't get me wrong, I didn't want to be male, particularly."

He snorted, which actually made her feel good.

"Unfortunately," she continued, "being a tomboy wasn't something I could hide from my mother. I was always coming home with a skinned elbow or knee, or a colorful bruise. It drove her nuts. I was the only kid in the pageants who wore makeup on her knees." She laughed.

"I woulda kissed them better."

"Aw, how sweet is that," AJ said with a bit of bite that made him chuckle. "I just knew I could do everything the boys at the playground did. My mother, though, would put any stage mother to shame. She had a goal, and nothing, not even me, was going to stand in her way of achieving it. She put everything she had into my career, micromanaging my every waking moment. And every sleeping moment, with motivational tapes."

"Christ."

AJ shrugged. "She didn't handle the separation very well. She's the type of woman who needs a man to tell her what to do, and when to do it. She and my dad never divorced. But they separated when I was about five. Darrel still pays her bills and balances her checkbook. Our house was all frills and flowers. My father and brother's house was tweed sofas and paper plates. I preferred the paper plates. Gave my mom fits when I went there, because I'd come home more rebellious than ever."

"Good for you."

"Between them, Gabriel and Darrel treated me like a china doll when I visited, but I saw how they 'played,' and more than anything I wanted to be like them. Darrel wanted my brother to be a SEAL, too. But Gab was approached by T-FLAC when he was in college, and he joined up and loved it. I'd go over there for my one weekend a month, and he'd give me little glimpses of what he did. Not the classified stuff, but enough to whet my appetite. The more I heard, and the more stories my father told me, the more frivolous my life became, and the more frustrated and smothered I felt."

"Not surprising."

"I wanted to be a SEAL like Darrel. He and my brother said, over their dead bodies. 'Said' being a mild word for two extremely volatile Alpha males. I said, fine. Because I couldn't be a SEAL, I signed up for the Police Academy. I was three for three. My mother was pissed, the two men I admired most were terrified I'd be gunned down in the streets before I got out of training."

"Then you were recruited by T-FLAC."

"Best day of my life." She grinned.

"I'm sure your dad and brother are proud of you now."

"I don't think Gabriel knows, and my father says war's no place for a girl. My mother hasn't talked to me since I entered the Academy last year. I stole her dream of the crown and she'll never forgive me."

He'd fished a blanket out of the saddlebag behind him, and draped it around both of them, enveloping them in the warmth of wool. The back of his fingers brushed her breasts as he gathered it in front of her. "She loves you," he told her. "She'll get over it."

AJ gave a half laugh. "You don't know my mother."

"Bad, huh?"

"Think the evil queen in *Snow White*," AJ said dryly. "Mirror and all."

"Will she get over it?"

AJ shrugged. "I hope so." There was a world

of hurt in her voice. "She's pretty unforgiving. It's tough when someone wants something that badly and it's stolen from them."

"You didn't steal anything." Kane brushed aside her hair and dropped a kiss on her nape. "That was her dream, not yours."

"Doesn't matter. As far as she's concerned, I could've given her the crown, and I didn't."

"No matter what you say, your father must be proud as hell of you. An A-1 Sharpshooter? Top of your class at the Academy? Recruited by one of the most respected elite private antiterrorist organizations in the world."

AJ's smile was sad. "Ironically, he wanted that crown, too. For such a macho guy, he's got a lot of very old-fashioned ideas. He still thinks a woman's place is in the kitchen. Preferably while wearing high heels, pearls, and a chiffon apron."

"And nothing else? I'm enjoying the image myself."

AJ turned to stick her tongue out at him.

He laughed. "That, too."

"Take your nap," AJ told him tartly, drawing her Dragunov across her lap and relaxing into her spine.

"Two hours," Kane instructed.

Other than the soft thud of camels' feet on the sand, the quiet was absolute. AJ had never seen so many stars. The sky seemed infinite and unbelievably vast. If one wanted to commune with God, this seemed the place to do it.

But somehow it didn't seem appropriate to ask God to help her kill Raazaq.

She had no idea how this was going to play out. A spurt of adrenaline shot through her system and tasted right. That was one of the things she enjoyed most about her job. The unexpected. The fact that an operative had to be on their toes and ready for anything.

And she was convinced she *was* ready.

But nothing could have prepared her for the reality of the man who slept behind her. She'd known all his ops inside and out, having studied them at length. But she hadn't known the man. She didn't know he loved children—that had been evident from the way he'd enticed the kids to help free the Humvee. Didn't know that he had a sense of humor that went beyond sarcasm. She had come into this thinking of him as a robot. Now that image was dissipating. There was a great deal to Kane Wright, including some secret she had not yet uncovered.

AJ figured that she was slowly eking her way through the chinks in his shell. He was a hard nut to crack.

And now that she was, nothing would ever be the same for her. AJ didn't have a clue what the future might hold. Didn't even figure she should be thinking about a future, since they still had to face and survive Raazaq.

Kane Wright was a lot more complex than the men she'd dated in the past. He was like the iceberg, nine-tenths submerged. She was a pretty good diver, but she wasn't sure she was equipped to handle what she might find at those depths. And really, she reminded herself, why try? He'd walk away eventually.

They always walked away.

They'd get sick of other men staring at her, trying to hit on her, for one thing. For another, there was always someone prettier, more well known, or with better contacts.

She'd gotten used to how men looked at her. How they perceived her before getting to know her. Sometimes it was useful, like getting this op. Other times it was annoying on a sliding scale.

Oh, yeah. They always walked away. Unless she walked faster.

Her brother tried to tell her she'd never given a man a chance. Cutting them loose first. But that was a guy thing. AJ called it self-preservation.

It had never bothered her before, she tended to measure their worth by their staying power. But she had a sinking feeling she wouldn't be quite as blasé this time when it was *Kane* disappearing into the sunset. And while she'd spilled her guts about practically everything, despite what they'd shared she knew little more about him now than she had before. Clever Kane.

Being a T-FLAC operative was something she'd wanted more than anything else. It had become an obtainable dream. She was a T-FLAC agent, and with Raazaq's death, her reputation would be assured.

One day rookies would read *her* reports, hear stories about *her* ops, and want to be just like her. She'd be a great role model for the new female students.

What a woman looked like had nothing to do with how she did her job. It didn't give her any more or less value as an operative. Being an excellent operative did that.

She was doing a job she loved, and doing it with her hero. And, for now, her hero was her lover. What could be better than that?

AJ knew exactly two hours had passed when Kane kissed the side of her neck. His internal clock was incredible.

"Good morning, Sleeping Beauty." She kept her voice low.

His chuckle was warm against her neck. "Your turn. I'll wake you." He reached around her and took the sniper rifle out of her loose grip.

AJ immediately closed her eyes and rested more of her weight against him. "No bedtime story for me?" For some stupid, stupid reason, she felt like crying.

"Sure." His voice held a smile. "Once upon a time . . ."

She fell asleep and dreamed she was looking at Kane's back as he strolled into a sand-colored sky. Rain fell on her face.

Chapter Sixteen

AJ climaxed before she was fully awake. Her body clenched around Kane's fingers as tremors shook through her, shattering in tiny explosions as she surfaced to complete awareness from a dead sleep. The camel's rolling gait only emphasized the rocking motion shaking her body. She blinked open bleary eyes to a star-studded sky and a barren desert lunarscape washed by moonlight, her body singing.

"Wow," she turned her head to languidly kiss the bristly underside of his jaw, "that beat the hell out of an alarm clock."

"Wait'll you see what touching the snooze button'll get you."

She shivered a little and hugged the arm he had draped like a bandoleer across her midriff. While she'd slept, Kane had drawn up the all-enveloping caftan, baring her legs to the cool night air. But her skin was steaming—it wasn't the chill in the air that had her shivering, it was the look in his heated gaze that sent ripples of sensation along her spine.

A mile ahead, the Brothers Grim cast three elongated shadows against the moon-bleached sand. But here, it was just the two of them. And the night.

"You sleep soundly, I'll give you that," Kane muttered.

"If I knew my wake-up call would be this interesting, I wouldn't have slept so long." She glanced at the sky again. "You didn't wake me after two hours, did you?"

He shook his head. "No need. I'm good."

"Oh," she said softly, "you're better than good."

Hungry, eager to taste him while her body still shuddered and burned, she turned her face up to his.

He captured her mouth in one of his succulent, deliciously carnal kisses. His fingers delved into her slick wetness until her body did that quick trip down Electric Avenue again.

AJ's spine arched and her hips lifted for better access as Kane pressed his palm to her mound. His other hand cupped her left breast, manipulating the nipple into a hard, aching peak through her sports bra and the thin fabric of the caftan. She wiggled against the hard length of his penis, rubbing her bottom against him. He groaned, low and deep in his throat.

AJ reached back between their bodies and

worked determinedly at his zipper. Eager to touch him, she cupped him and stroked his length through the fabric of his pants, and still it wasn't enough.

"As hard as I am, you'll never get that zipper down, Agile Jamboree," Kane said on a strangled chuckle. "If wishes were horses . . ."

His zipper opened with a satisfactory *zip*.

"I so love a challenge," she said on a soft burst of laughter as Kane groaned tightly behind her.

AJ laughed again as she snuggled her butt closer. "Isn't this fun?"

Kane choked out a short laugh. "You're out of your mind, woman."

"Hey. You started this, remember?"

He chuckled, a wicked gleam lighting his eyes. "You know this is impossible, don't you?"

She gave him a saucy glance over her shoulder. "Nothing's impossible if you want it badly enough."

"Oh, I do," Kane assured her. "But this is nuts."

"Move this leg." She patted his right knee.

"To where?" Kane demanded. "There aren't a hell of a lot of options on a camel."

"Okay. Watch this." AJ shifted her bottom, and stood in the stirrups.

Kane grabbed her waist as her body swayed,

then shot a look at the distant trio. "Don't fall off. Jesus. Can't we wait until we stop?"

"Have you ever done it on a camel?"

"*Nobody's* done it on a camel."

"Camels probably have."

"No *people.*"

Responding to the humorous glint in his eyes, AJ laughed. "Cool. We'll be the first."

"They'll find our dead bodies come Christmas, naked and dried up like prunes."

"Your penis will show them we died happy," she said with a wicked smile and a gurgle of laughter. "A little pink staff saluting in the breeze."

"Hey, what *little?*"

"Move your leg."

"It's moved as far as it can possibly move. A contortionist, I'm not."

AJ got the giggles as she tried to hoist the caftan clear of her bottom. Then she stood in the stirrups again. "Help me lift my—"

He gripped her waist and lifted her as easily as he would a bag of potatoes. "See?" she crowed, yanking the bulk of the fabric of the caftan free. The blanket between her thighs felt smooth and warm on her bare skin. A shiver of excitement coursed through her.

"I see a lovely ass," Kane assured her, running both hands lightly from her midriff down to the curved indentation of her waist, then cupping the aforementioned ass. "World-class," he said dryly. "Now cover up before we fall off this thing."

AJ crossed her arms, and swiftly drew the caftan up and over her head. Chill air raced over her skin, causing a delicious rash of goose bumps. Her nipples peaked from the cold as she unfastened her bra. She stuffed both garments into the bag in front of her, then reached back to loosen her hair. Long strands untwisted from the braid and tumbled down her bare back in a warm, ticklish fall.

"Christ. Lady Godiva," Kane said reverently, sliding his palms around her narrow rib cage and slowly up her midriff until he cupped a breast in each hand. She sucked in a breath as he lightly brushed each taut nipple with a calloused thumb. The sensation shot straight to her core in a sharp, sweet wave.

The feel of him, so close behind her, their torsos not quite touching, sent a shimmer of need racing from her head to her toes. With his palms warm on her breasts, he nuzzled her neck, his breath warm and moist. His penis moved restlessly against her bottom. "Have I mentioned lately that you have a spectacular ass?"

"Not . . . lately . . . no." She wiggled back-wards.

Damned if he could ignore an invitation as tempting as that one. He paused for a long mo-ment, loving the heavy weight of her plump breasts in his hands, loving the responsive way her nipples peaked, the hard, tight buds nuz-zling his palms before he released his hold there to slide his hands down her slender rib cage, taking satisfaction in her sigh of pleasure as his hands moved to cup her hips.

He cradled her behind in both hands, caress-ing her silky smooth skin and stroking the cool mounds until she trembled in his grasp, rocking her hips.

She leaned back against him, her head rest-less on his shoulder. "Kane . . ."

"Right . . . here." He feathered one hand over the gentle curve of her hip, and traced the warm damp crease at the top of her legs. She made a soft sound of need as his fingers slid un-der the thin black ribbon to find the slick heat of her desire.

He touched her, and she moved her legs far-ther apart to give him greater access, as he glided two fingers deep inside her. He pushed his fingers deeper, pressing his palm hard against her, pressing his straining erection hard against her bottom. She moaned low in her throat.

She trembled and strained against his hand. A primitive satisfaction took hold of him as she moaned and quaked as she climaxed, her body clenching around his fingers.

Kane almost came just listening to her pleasure. With his other hand he freed himself as his mind emptied and his body took charge. Hard and aching, he needed her damp heat as much as his lungs needed air. He wanted to feel the sweet cradle of her wet flesh surround and clench him. He wanted to empty himself into her depths and hear the soft, sweet moans drift from her throat as she came.

And he wanted it—needed it—*now*.

The sensation of him that close but separated by a millimeter of cotton ratcheted her need up another tight notch. She twisted around to look down between them. "Can you get it out?"

"Oh, it's come out to play, honey. But that's not the problem," Kane said, laughing at the ridiculousness of what they were attempting. Only AJ . . . "It's the getting it *in*."

AJ leaned her body forward, laying across the neck of the camel, its harsh, coarse hair abrading her skin as she bared her bottom to Kane. "Now?"

He positioned her with both hands on her hips, and she leaned forward, stretched out over Kika's broad back.

He withdrew his hand, trailing his damp fingers across her hip, and used them to guide himself into her. She gasped as he filled her, and the sensation was like nothing he'd ever known before. Beneath them, the stoic camel walked on, its rocking motion driving Kane as he moved within AJ's depths.

AJ shifted, slowly lifting her hips and then lowering them on him again. Then, in inches, she sat up, pushing herself upright until she was pinned to his body like a butterfly on display.

"Kika's watching us," AJ said suddenly.

"Kika," Kane said sternly, "face forward. Watch where we're going." The curious camel lifted her lip, exposing large yellow teeth. She and Kane made eye contact. Kika blinked her ridiculously long lashes and faced forward, without missing a step.

"Thank you," AJ said. "Now, where were we?"

"One of us is naked, the other is inside the naked one," he said, his tone Sahara dry as he pulled her hard against him.

"Yum. Indeed you are." AJ flapped a hand at the camel's face. Kika lifted her lip and rolled her eyes. Disgruntled, AJ twisted to look back at Kane. "I don't think I can have wild camel sex with Kika watching."

"Are you nuts?" Kane demanded. "After all this contorting, you're telling me *no*?"

"I'm not telling you no . . . exactly. I'm telling you I can't have sex while a camel is watching me come."

"Kika," Kane said firmly. "Go. Go. Go."

AJ grabbed Kane's hands, which just happened to be cupping her breasts right then, as the camel picked up speed and started trotting. The fastest she'd gone since they'd started the journey.

"U-uncle," AJ cried as Kane's penis was jammed high inside her with each jarring thud of Kika's splayed feet in the sand. It felt incredible. Wonderful. Full.

Too much . . . Ahhhh. *Perfect.*

"Oh, Lord. This is amazing. Isn't it amazing?" Stars overhead winked slowly out of existence as light shimmered at the edge of the horizon. But all AJ saw were the sparklers splintering behind her eyelids. Kane's body pushed at hers, rubbing, thrusting. Cool air on her skin, warm hands on her breasts, and the rocking of the camel all combined to send AJ's body into overdrive.

"Amazing," Kane agreed, chuckling as he buried his face against the back of her neck and bit gently on the soft skin behind her ear. He dropped one hand to her center and thumbed the tiny nub at the heart of her heat. She trembled in his grasp.

"Okay?" Kane asked tightly.

"Better than," AJ gasped as she arched her back, taking him deeper, her fingers gripping the camel's muscular neck.

"Run, Kika," he said, and the camel quickened her steps even further, doing all the work for Kane, until all he had to do was hold on and ride out the storm as AJ's body tightened over his and they came together like liquid lightning.

Their bodies trembled from the force of their pleasure, and it was several long minutes before AJ could manage to speak coherently. "Takes the word 'humping' to a whole new level, doesn't it?" She laughed as she sank back against him, their bodies still joined.

Overhead, the sky looked like faded black denim studded with rhinestones, while in the distance, dawn crept like a thief up over the horizon in a gaudy display of shocking pinks and brilliant pumpkin orange. AJ rested comfortably against Kane's warm chest, the blanket wrapped around both of them. His body radiated a comfortable heat, but the desert air felt chill and fresh on her cheeks.

She'd pulled her clothes on hours before. It was one thing to give Kane a view of her, butt-naked on a camel, but a whole other ball game to have the Brothers Grim see her that way.

Suddenly, Kane stiffened behind her. He'd been hyperalert for an hour or more. AJ trusted his instincts, but she hadn't seen or heard anything other than sand and the soft, hypnotizing *plod-plop-plop-plod* of Kika's footsteps all night.

"What is it?" she asked, immediately alert.

He flung off the enveloping blanket. "We've got company." He drew his weapon. The sound of the clip slamming home sounded loud in the predawn quiet. Locked and loaded.

Cool air washed over AJ as the blanket fell away—she barely noticed as she grabbed up the Dragunov from across her lap and followed his narrow-eyed gaze.

"There." She saw them. About a mile to the east, and backlit by the spectacular dawn, a group of men on camels headed straight for them. A thick plume of dust followed in their wake. They were moving fast and with purpose.

"I'd hazard a guess they aren't the Welcome Wagon," AJ said dryly. Her heart pounded with excitement as the men approached, galabayyas catching the wind around them. From this distance, they were nothing more than large, billowing, black blotches with long, spindly legs following their shadows.

Kane leaned away from her to give himself some elbow room. "Hold your fire until we know what they wa—"

Their intent was pretty damn clear as a bullet whizzed over AJ's head. Then another and another. Top-of-the-line weapons, by the sound of them. Russian. New. High-powered. Even in the most inept hands, lethal.

Adrenaline kicked in, and AJ felt a surge of heart-throbbing, Jesus-God-this-is-it kind of excitement. She waited, bracing herself for that lick of paralyzing fear to kick in. . . .

Her heart raced, her brain was clear and sharp, her hands, rock steady. . . .

No fear.

No fear?

She felt a wash of relief. No fear.

She was a real T-FLAC operative after all.

No time for elation.

She raised the Dragunov, tucked the stock into her shoulder, and felt the intensity of the moment as all her concentration ran down the length of the barrel. Index finger resting lightly on the trigger guard, she observed the bad guys through her scope. Kika's rocking motion made

it hard, but AJ worked it into a rhythm. The
man in the lead rose and fell in her target zone.
He had a familiar mole right beside his beak of
a nose. She could see him that clearly, despite
the muted light.

"They're Raazaq's," she told Kane, recogniz-
ing the guy from the car chase the other day.
Definitely Raazaq's. "A little closer . . ." she
said softly under her breath.

Seven hundred yards.

Six-fifty.

Six . . .

"Thank you." She fired, hitting Mr. Mole
bull's-eye. A good, clean shot was messy. A der-
matologist would've done a better job, and the
man's life expectancy would've been guaran-
teed. Unfortunately for him she wasn't a der-
matologist. When she removed a malignancy, it
was fatal.

She fired again, a deterring pattern, and the
man's camel veered off from the others and
went plodding off, back the way they'd come.
Mr. Mole's companions split up, their camels
drifting apart until ten yards or so separated
them. As if making them harder to hit than
when in a group. Instead, they'd just made it
easier for AJ.

Behind her, Kane continued firing the AK-
47. Awkward without room to maneuver. But

they managed to eliminate several of the bad guys in a one-two burst of fire that seemed perfectly synchronized and well choreographed.

Five hundred feet.

As their attackers closed the gap, AJ counted fifteen-plus men. . . . Shit, no—*eighteen*. She and Kane were pitifully outnumbered and needed an advantage. She glanced around. Cover. They needed cover. And fast.

Four hundred feet . . . "Holy dromedary, Batman. Their camels must be on speed! Kika's never moved *that* fast."

" 'Specially carrying two." Kane didn't sound particularly perturbed. "There's a rocky outcrop about half a click ahead," he shouted, still firing.

A hole appeared in AJ's sleeve as if by magic, missing her arm by a cotton thread. She felt the cold heat of the bullet passing over her skin. Her heart leaped into her throat, and sweat broke out on her brow, but she ignored it. She fired again. And again.

"The brothers have headed over there to high ground," Kane shouted. "Kika, get the lead out. *Har-eeb! Har-eeb! Har-eeb!*"

Apparently, Kika, bless her little camel heart, didn't like the noise of bullets whizzing by, and picked up the pace, breaking into a clumsy, swaying gallop, which made their aim even iffier. Still, AJ got another three bad guys in quick succession. Kane, two.

"Damn, we're good," she shouted, feeling the rush of doing her job and doing it well.

"Don't count your tangos before they fall," Kane shouted back, firing an impressive round and still managing to support AJ with his thighs so she didn't fall off the careening camel.

The men were a lot closer.

Four hundred yards and closing.

She aimed for the lead camel, a bigger target, and hoped it would be a clean kill. She loved animals, so it was a tough, but necessary, shot. The shot was true. The camel and rider went down in a heap and were promptly trampled by the camel and rider behind them. AJ winced as she got off another series of shots. One more down. This time she aimed at the human vermin.

The air smelled of cordite, gun oil, and hot metal. *Better than Chanel,* AJ thought with satisfaction, as another bad guy dropped off his camel like a fly. The camel continued running.

Kika let out a god-awful loud, braying cry as a bullet winged her right flank. The poor beast, burdened by two riders, picked up even more speed. This time in sheer terror.

Plod-plop-plop-plod-plodploplopplod, faster and faster.

AJ was flung against Kane as Kika started to climb. He pushed her back with the butt of the AK-47 and held her there until she centered herself on the saddle.

"I'm good," she told him as soon as she felt balanced. She resumed firing. She felt the hardness of the stock on her shoulder as Kane paused, making sure she wasn't about to tumble to the rocky ground. "I'm good," she repeated, and Kane grunted before twisting around to get off a few shots himself.

The small hill was an island in the middle of a sand sea. The rocks dry and crumbling beneath Kika's feet as she did a mad scramble to safety, scattering bits of rock and showering the desert behind them with sprays of sand and gravel.

Several hundred yards away, in a small depression of rock, the brothers hunkered down out of range. Kane could just see the tops of their camels' heads.

They came to a small, flat area. "Down, girl," Kane instructed Kika, nudging the camel hard with his foot. She immediately rocked forward and then back, folding her legs beneath her.

AJ and Kane swung their legs over the animal's back before flattening themselves on the ground on top of the rocks and pebbles. In his peripheral vision, Kane saw a head pop up.

"Keep your heads down," he shouted in Arabic. The brothers didn't need to be told twice—they ducked, and stayed out of sight. "Call Kika," he added.

One of the boys whistled long and sharp, and Kika lumbered to her feet and sauntered up and over the rocks to safety.

Kane reloaded, glanced at AJ, then continued to get off several rounds as she did the same. While her appearance wasn't exactly by the book by any stretch of the imagination, Kane was hard-pressed to imagine anything sexier than AJ with her red hair wild and tangled around her shoulders, and her eyes glittering with excitement as she lay flat on her stomach, caftan hiked about her thighs, bare legs spread for balance.

He grinned. Jesus, she was great. And he had it bad. "Left. Three o'clock," he told her. And she immediately swiveled the Dragunov and dropped the guy. There was no sign now that she'd ever been afraid. It was as if the woman who'd landed in Cairo days ago and the woman before him now were two different people.

Her aim was incredible.

He'd never seen anything like it.

She didn't miss.

There was nowhere for the tangos to hide. He suspected they'd planned to be at this outcrop of rocks before their prey and had miscalculated. The morning sun rose higher in the sky as the remaining men got off a few more shots. They were wasting bullets. They couldn't breach the place where Kane and AJ lay. And unless they planned to outwait them, they were screwed.

"Pick them off," Kane instructed, wiping sweat from his eyes and feeling the unrelenting beat of the sun on top of his unprotected head. Their hats were in Kika's saddlebag with their sunglasses and sunscreen. He wanted this over.

"Leave the big one on the right. Maybe we can get some answers."

AJ nodded. Sweat gleamed on her skin, strands of honey-red hair clung to the dampness on her cheek and neck, and lay in a gleaming pool on the dirt beside her head as she rested her cheek on her weapon like a mother with her child.

"The fat ugly one, or the tall ugly one?"

"Which looks the most intelligent?" Kane asked facetiously. The men were covered from nose to toes in black.

"Fat and ugly." AJ picked off the other three as easily as shooting at tin cans, although they were three hundred yards away and the sun was in her eyes.

"Nice work," he told her easily.

She turned and gave him a brilliant smile that shot straight to his heart, before turning back to keep the Dragunov trained on the last man, a hundred and fifty feet away.

"Off the camel," Kane shouted in Arabic. "Hands up."

He and AJ rose to their feet, weapons still pointed at the last man. The bad guy's camel danced in place as he manipulated the reins.

"Son of a bitch is going to bolt." She squeezed off a warning shot. But it was no use. The man wheeled his animal and took off across the desert in a cloud of dust. She hesitated.

"Drop him," Kane told her grimly.

"We need him," AJ shouted, aiming for the camel's hindquarters. She squeezed off the shot. The camel's legs buckled. Damn it. Damn it. She hated, hated, *hated* hurting animals. The man jumped free, his legs tangling in the enveloping galabayya as he fell to the ground, and rolled over and over. His camel bolted.

AJ trained her weapon on the man, keeping his face in her sight. Fifties. Small, close together black eyes. "Tell us what Raazaq's up to, you bastard," she yelled, not even aware he probably didn't understand a word she said. The weapon didn't so much as waver in her hands.

"Put your hands up, and walk toward us," Kane shouted in Arabic.

Ignoring the order, the man remained where he was.

One moment he was standing still, his hands at his sides, the next he had a pistol in his right hand.

"No. No. No!" AJ yelled as the guy blew out his own brains in a spectacularly messy display. "Damn it to hell. Why'd you *do* that?"

"Apparently," Kane said flatly, "failing Raazaq was a worse alternative than anything we might subject him to."

"Hell."

Now they had no more information than they'd had an hour ago. "Yeah," Kane said laconically, dropping the AK-47 to his side as AJ did the same with the Dragunov. "Sure they were Raazaq's?"

"Hundred percent. I recognized several of them."

He believed her. Her eyesight was remarkable. "Then we're close enough to make the bastard antsy. Come on, let's hit the road and ruin Raazaq's day."

It couldn't be any later than seven A.M., but the day was already hot as the sun rose into a

cloudless blue sky. They needed hats, sunscreen, and water. Now.

Kane called to the brothers. No show. "Poor
bastards must be scared out of their wits."

"I hope they weren't hit." AJ walked faster
up the small rise. Kane grabbed her arm as her
booted foot slipped on the rocks.

"I doubt they raised their heads the whole
time," he told her dryly, releasing her. "They're
fine."

They crested the rocks and stared down into
the small depression where their guides and the
camels had been.

"Had been" being the operative phrase.

Kane swore. The Shaaeawi brothers were
gone.

No great loss.

They'd taken all the camels with them.

Oh, shit. Now, *that* was a *huge* loss.

Chapter Seventeen

A couple of saddlebags hurriedly tossed aside—and a cooling pile of camel dung—were the only things the brothers had left behind. By the look of overturned rocks, and the tracks in the sand, they'd taken off in an all-fired rush, headed back the way they'd come.

Kane glanced up to gauge their distance. While he and AJ had been fending off the attack, the brothers had barely waited for the bullets to fly before they'd made tracks. They were already mere dots on the far horizon.

And in way better shape at the moment than he and AJ.

Jesus. Two people, alone in the middle of the Western Desert's Great Sand Sea. No transportation. No navigational equipment. No form of communication.

No one knew where the hell they were. No one was looking for them. Worst of all, no one was on Raazaq.

They were screwed.

Talk about your Bad Day at Black Rock.

"Alone at last," AJ said wryly, apparently unperturbed by their dire situation. Except that Kane could see the rapid beat of her pulse in her sweat-dampened throat, and recognized the underlying note of tension in her cheerful voice.

Good for you, Kane thought with some relief. She wasn't about to panic at the daunting prospect of crossing the inhospitable desert in the heat of the day. There weren't many *men* who could look at this situation with a cool eye and no panic. But she was doing it. And damned if he didn't experience a rush of admiration for her. AJ Cooper was way more than he'd ever expected. And sometime soon, he hoped he'd get the chance to tell her so.

Right now, though—training or no—the situation certainly scared the bejesus out of *him.*

She crouched down and started rummaging through her saddlebag. "At least they left some of our stuff. We'll need our hats. It's going to be a hell of a long walk."

"Take necessities," he told her evenly. "Nothing else."

They couldn't stay where they were, and the walk was going to be long, hot, and dangerous. They couldn't be more exposed, more unprotected than they would be during the duration of that walk across the almost flat, barren land-scape. Hell.

They'd be sitting ducks for miles.

Head bent, AJ saluted without looking up. Kane went over to his own bag and extracted his hat first thing. After settling it on his head, he grabbed sunblock, extra clips for the Sig and AK-47, and all the water containers they'd brought with them. Chugging down a couple of swallows of the warm water, he stuffed all the protein bars they'd tossed into the saddle-bags into his pack. The less they ate, the less water they'd need to drink. And they'd have to make their water last. Yet their bodies would need fuel for the grueling trek.

One did not conserve drinking water in the desert. One drank it. And prayed there'd be enough to last the trip.

"Ready?" he called, glancing at his wrist-watch. Still inoperable. He hadn't expected dif-ferently. How far did the block extend? And to what extent? And, fuck it, for how long?

Under normal circumstances there would be planes overhead, vehicles in pursuit, the snap, crackle, and pop of verbal communications from the Sat Comm link. Action. Movement. Noise.

Instead, there was this unearthly, surreal si-lence.

AJ blew out a breath as she stood up. "Ready as I'll ever be."

Kane ran a quick look over her. She'd braided her hair, then tucked it beneath her hat. Her skin glistened with a coat of sunblock, and she was standing hip-shot, slugging back water. She was also carrying a small lightweight backpack. In fact, the same make, color, and size as his own.

He hid a smile. "Let's move out."

"Know any jokes?" AJ asked, trudging along beside him, her long legs matching his strides in a comfortable rhythm. Neither fast nor slow, as they paced themselves.

The sun was high overhead in the brilliant blue, cloudless canopy. The temps had reached the high nineties. Thank God the brothers had left their supplies—if not, they'd be doubly screwed, without protection from the unrelenting sun and a respectable supply of water.

Which was the only reason Kane wouldn't kill the little bastards if he ever caught up to them again. A good thrashing would be enough.

Kane kept an eagle eye on AJ, even though he pretended not to. She was holding up well. Her initial panic had evened out to a healthy apprehension. She'd done well today. Damn well. It would keep her sharp. However, the heat and the monotony of walking were soporific and might well slow their reflexes. They should've stopped and made shelter an hour ago. But his gut told him speed was necessary.

The intense and oftentimes seemingly cruel and inhumane training T-FLAC gave their operatives in desert survival gave them a better shot of making it now.

If the next oasis wasn't too much farther.

If their water lasted that long.

If they didn't get heatstroke.

"No," Kane told her, drinking from his canteen. He sloshed the water in the container—half-full—and clipped it back on his belt.

"Come on," she cajoled. "Everyone knows a joke or two."

"I don't. Stop wasting your breath. It's not going to get any cooler, and so far we haven't come across anything resembling a Hilton."

"See?" she prodded. "That was mildly amusing."

"It's too hot to be amusing. Tell me more about the beauty-pageant business."

"I was trying for light and friendly." AJ sounded mildly irritated now.

Kane laughed.

"Now, *that* wasn't supposed to be funny." AJ glared at him through the shaded brim of her straw cowboy hat. "Talk to me. Tell me something interesting about you. Since you didn't emerge from the womb as a T-FLAC agent. How about an episode of Kane Wright—The Early Years."

His lips twitched. Damn it, she was fun. "Like what?"

"*Anything,*" AJ said heatedly. "Geez, Louise. We're out here in the freaking middle of nowhere, under a broiling noonday sun, gasping our last parched breath. Can't you think of *something* interesting to break the monotony? And in case you haven't noticed, you never answer any of my questions. Why is that, I wonder."

"Tell me this," he asked, not answering the question. Again. "Are we headed in a *facsimile* of the right direction? Or are we going around in circles?"

"We're going around in circles," she told him tartly. "I wanted to torture both of us and see how long it would take you to notice that our tongues were turning black and our skin was peeling off our bodies in sheets."

"Great visual. Thanks," he muttered.

She huffed out a breath. "Oh, ye of little faith." She punched his arm, and he imagined behind her dark glasses she was rolling her eyes.

"Of *course* we're heading in the right direction. Look at the sun."

He had. They were headed southwest. He'd merely asked to distract her. The monotony of putting one booted foot in front of the other, for mile after mile, was tedious. And if he hadn't been sure of their direction, all they'd had to do was follow Raazaq's tracks in the sand. Although it would've made their stroll through hell a bit more bearable, thank God there hadn't been even a slight breeze in twenty-four hours to blow away the impressions Raazaq had left in his wake. Arrogant bastard.

He hoped to God the pyramid AJ had mentioned was where she thought it was. Otherwise they were walking into the Valley of Death, he thought with real trepidation. Even if the damn pyramid was there, though, they wouldn't reach it for at least another six to eight hours, walking at this pace. They had hardly any food, but fortunately, they had just enough water to last that long.

Particles of sand refracted the sun like tiny diamonds in a light so brilliant, so fierce, it hurt the eyes, even with the specially fabricated lenses of their glasses. The heat rose off the umber-colored sand in glassy waves. It beat down unrelentingly from above, and radiated brutally from below. Inside his boots, Kane's feet burned fiercely. So must AJ's, but she hadn't said a word.

"It's too hot to go on," he said, practically. "We'll stop, make a shelter, and rest until dusk."

"We've got a rhythm going here." AJ wiped her face with her sleeve. "Let's walk another hour before we stop."

Kane shook his head. If he'd been alone, he may very well have continued another hour or two. And it would've been suicide. It was just past noon, and the sun was straight up and lethal.

"We're probably losing two pints of water an hour in sweat equity. We'll need to drink more water if we expend this much energy in this heat. We can't afford to waste a drop. Come on. That dune looks like a good spot."

The dune was already casting a small, very small, shadow, and they erected an open-sided canopy, utilizing the dune's protection. Within minutes they crawled inside, out of the sun. It wasn't noticeably cooler by any stretch of the imagination, but at least they were out of the direct rays.

AJ removed her hat and scratched her scalp with short nails. "My kingdom for a shower." She flopped down flat on her back and hiked up the hem of her caftan to expose her legs to the thigh. She wiggled her feet in the heavy boots. "How long do we have to wait?"

No time at all, he wanted to say. The knot in his stomach, the one that warned of danger, was coiling tighter and tighter by the hour. He lay his backpack next to hers, then started undoing the laces of his boots.

"At least four hours." He drew off the heavy boots and ditched his damp socks to dry in the sun. As much as his body needed the rest, needed to cool down as much as hers did, Kane's instincts urged him to keep moving. To speed up. To get there—*Where,* for Christ sake?—*now.* Not four hours later than now.

He leaned over and started unlacing AJ's boots. The hightops were military issue, specially made for desert terrains. Impervious to sand, they were lightweight, but bulky-looking, and made her slender ankles look insubstantial and sexy as hell. He drew off her left boot and set it beside his own, then reached for the right.

"Oh, you prince. You're going to massage my poor aching feet for me?"

"You really *were* a cat in a previous life, weren't you?"

"Let me put it this way." AJ stretched. "If someone offered to give me a full-body massage right now, and we were in the middle of Grand Central Station, I'd strip down butt-naked right there and then lay on the cool, marble floor."

Kane drew off her damp socks and tossed them up onto the canopy overhead with his own. Her feet were a little pink. He inspected her soles for cuts and abrasions, and she sighed as his thumbs made a slow circuit of the balls of her feet. She was a tactile woman, and he found he enjoyed touching her as much as she enjoyed being touched.

"Did your trainers know about this little quirk?" he asked, manipulating her toes between fingers and thumbs. "Because," he continued while she sighed blissfully, "this could be a problem. We get intense training and psychological counseling in the event we're captured. Torture prep, et cetera. All the bad shit. But hell, if someone found out about your massage fetish, think how simple it would be to get anything out of you. You'd spill your guts for a foot massage."

"No I wouldn't—*Yes.* Riiiigh-t there. Not a mere foot massage. Now, a full-body? Hell, yeah. I'd tell them anything."

He dug his thumbs into her instep. "What's your real name?"

"A—" She opened her eyes, her lips twitched, and she wiggled her toes in his palms. "Nice try, camel boy."

He patted her feet and scooched back. Before lying down, he dug a clean pair of socks out of his pack, and lay the AK-47 and a clip beside him on the tarp.

After watching him, AJ imitated his actions, then lay beside him on her back, not touching but close enough for him to smell the heat of her body.

"Do you know that bushmen in the Kalahari find the deepest part of an old water course and dig a hole in the sand about an arm's-length deep to find water? Then they take a reed tube as tall as they are—which isn't very tall, now that I come to think about it—and insert it into the hole and pack the sand around it. Then they suck on the tube for two minutes until water comes into their mouth."

Kane rolled onto his side, his head supported on his arm. "There aren't any rivers—dry or otherwise—around."

"I wasn't suggesting that *we* tr—"

"Close your eyes, Abbreviate Jabberer."

She wriggled her brows. "Wanna fool around?"

"Sleep," he ordered.

She obediently closed her eyes, but she was smiling. "Can we, after?"

"If you can work up the energy," Kane said

dryly, brushing a sweat-dampened curl off her forehead.

"Maybe you should just give me a little smooch to see me through." She opened her eyes to peer at him through her lashes.

He ran his thumb over her full lower lip, and she drew it into the damp cavern of her mouth and sucked on it. The sensation shot directly to Kane's groin. He groaned.

"Is that a ye—" AJ's jaw cracked with the huge yawn.

He extracted his damp thumb, and smiled. "Go to sleep. It'll be cooler for all sorts of interesting things when you wake up."

" 'Kay. You take first watch." Her voice slurred as she closed her eyes. She was fast asleep in seconds.

Hours later, with nothing to do but walk and think, AJ realized that as far as Kane Wright was concerned, she was insatiable. This couldn't be a good thing. She was a career agent. She didn't want anything more. Which, when she thought about it, was probably fine and dandy, since she doubted Kane wanted anything more than a roll in the hay—sand— himself.

She scowled. What was he hiding. Something interesting, she bet.

Raazaq's tracks marked their path. An easy, no-brainer route, which gave her far too much time to think, damn it.

And with this much thinking time, her brain naturally turned to Kane.

After knowing each other such a short time it wasn't as though she expected a declaration or anything. They were both getting exactly what they wanted. Spectacular sex. *She* was perfectly satisfied. She frowned, trudging along beside Kane in the moonlight. God only knew, they both wanted the same unemotional . . . encounter, so what the hell was her problem? Why wasn't that now enough?

Wake up and smell the coffee, Cooper. This man is going to offer you nothing more than the here and now. He'd said so in no uncertain terms. Like it or lump it, that's the way it was.

She liked it just fine, she told herself firmly, *just frigging fine.* They were both getting exactly what they wanted.

Oh, crap, here I am, tromping through a desert looking for a psycho, and I'm worried about my love life? Get your mind back on business, Cooper.

But walking was soporific, and no matter how much she tried to push thoughts of the silent man next to her aside, it was impossible.

Kane talked about his family with affection. Something she envied. Her father and brother had been only a peripheral part of her life, and her mother's obsession with beauty and all that entailed had made their relationship strained, to say the least. When AJ thought about her mother, "affection" wasn't a word she'd use. "Pushy." "Obsessive." "Driven." All worked.

Interestingly enough, having spent twenty-seven years ignoring compliments about her physical appearance, she found it refreshing that Kane didn't seem to care one way or another how she looked. Hell, just *that* was enough to make a girl fall in love.

She stumbled at the thought.

Not that she was in love. Hell, no.

"How're you holding up, Alison Jumpup?"

I don't know anything about him, AJ thought wildly. *Nothing. This is insane. . . .* "How can you still talk?"

"Stamina, babe, stamina. Check that out." He pointed to the churned-up sand veering off their path. "Looks like that's where Raazaq's men broke off to circle back for us."

AJ nodded, not wasting breath talking.

"Want to stop for a few?"

"No way. Let's keep going. Straight ahead until dawn."

"Tell me when you're ready for a break."

"Absolutely."

Kane chuckled. "Liar."

"I'll stop when you stop."

"How 'bout I want to stop now?"

"I'd call you a sissy-pants and keep walking."

"A sissy-pants?"

She turned to grin up at him. While that smile was strained and exhausted, it still had the power to hit Kane in the solar plexus. "Yeah."

"By all means, let's keep walking, then." He returned her brave grin. "I've got a rep to protect. How about we get to the third dune ahead, then stop for ten?"

"Okay." There was a long, pregnant pause. "Would you tell me about Libya?"

Apropos of what? "Jesus, why?"

"Because we're out here in the middle of nowhere, alone in the frigging dark, and it would make me happy if you would share just a small slice of your life with me for once. Not to mention I've spilled my guts and told you my deepest, darkest secrets, that's why."

It was time, Kane thought—yeah, maybe it was time. "I doubt if this story will make you happy, but I'll tell you." He dived right in. No point trying to sugarcoat it.

"Six of us inserted covertly into Al Jawf to retrieve three missionaries being held in the prison there." He glanced at her. "You read the reports, didn't you?"

"Yeah, I did. But in your usual chatty way

you left out most of the details," she said dryly, slipping her hand into his. The feel of her much smaller hand in his was surprisingly comforting. Kane looked straight ahead before he continued.

"Then you know we got two of them out. They'd killed one woman before we got there," he said, still furious that they'd arrived twenty minutes too late to save her from unspeakable horrors.

"It was a bloodbath before we finally got them out. They begged us to retrieve the other woman's body. But the tangos had taken her off, tortured her in another part of the jail, and there'd been chaos breaking in to retrieve them, then getting out again—we refused to take the time."

Outnumbered twenty to one, each member of the team had a hole in him somewhere—in most cases, several holes. They were collectively bleeding like stuffed pigs.

Adrenaline high, Kane had barely felt it. He and his guys had been deaf to the women's pleas. Their friend was dead. And if the eight of them didn't get out of there immediately, so would they be. The two middle-aged women were barely hanging on themselves. They'd been in those cells for three weeks before anyone knew where they were. They'd been beaten, starved, and then tortured.

"We held off the tangos and got away by a fucking hair. The extraction team was waiting in the jungle, helo blades already spinning when we got there. Everyone was onboard. I was last man in, when one of the women told me the third woman, *girl,* was her daughter . . . a child—" Kane scrapped back his hair in remembered frustration.

AJ squeezed his fingers. "Of course you had to go back," she said softly.

"I didn't have to take the whole team in. They were ready to lift off for Christ sake!"

"They would've gone with you, anyway," AJ assured him with utmost confidence.

"No, they were all injured, the chances of finding the child were slim to none—the tangos knew we were there. The whole situation had gone tits up. No way should we have gone back in."

"But you did."

They'd all jumped out of the helo—big, shit-eating grins on their dumb faces—and followed him back in. "Yeah, we did. Because even though I ordered them to stay onboard and leave with the women, they all knew I expected them to follow me into battle." He paused to swallow back his rage. "They *trusted* me. Trusted that I knew what the fuck I was doing. Trusted that I would get them back home in one piece . . . Mind if I gloss over the details here?"

She squeezed his hand. "Sure."

"Never found the kid. But the tangos found us. Took us back to that rat-infested hellhole where we'd retrieved the women."

Kane pulled his hand out of AJ's and stuffed both fists in his pockets. Right now he couldn't bear to be touched; his skin crawled with the memories. "We were separately interrogated for weeks. Their methods were . . . creative." A shudder shook his body. Ah, Jesus . . .

He saw AJ lift her hand to touch his arm, then think better of it and drop it to her side as they trudged forward. The night was now filled with the screams of his team, the sight of them out in the stinking, muddy courtyard, bare-assed naked as they were whipped and beaten . . . and eventually shot. One by one.

And then they'd come for him. With whips and knives and small, hot metal pincers . . .

But by then he'd wished he'd died with the men, his own men, whom he'd killed. And nothing they did to him was worse than looking out into that courtyard every day for two months and seeing the bloody bodies of his men lying there.

There wasn't a night he didn't close his eyes and see them. Smell their decomposing bodies. Feel the agony they'd gone through because they'd trusted him to keep them safe. Yeah, he'd done a fine fucking job.

"Why are you punishing yourself for something you couldn't possibly have prevented?" AJ asked quietly. "You *all* had to go in and try to retrieve the child. *You had to try.*"

"I should've gone in alone."

"And been killed?"

"And been killed if necessary, yes."

She narrowed her eyes and glared at him. "So you had to do your job, but your equally well-trained, experienced team members were supposed to fly off with the women?"

AJ stopped walking and grabbed his sleeve. She punched him in the arm. Hard. "You arrogant, elitist son of a bitch. Who made you God? All six of you were there to do your jobs. All six of you knew the risks. All six of you had brains and reasoning power, for God's sake. How *dare* you think that they died because of you. They died fighting for what all T-FLAC operatives fight for. Freedom. Democracy. Liberty—all the rest of it." She punched him again. "You are such an . . . ass!"

Kane spun around in the sand to stare down

at her. She was, quite literally, hopping mad. "It was my—"

She slugged him in the stomach. "Get over yourself, would you?" She reached up and grabbed his ears between her fingers.

Christ, was she going to head-butt him?

Eyes glittering fiercely in the moonlight, AJ pulled his head down. "You did your job. They did theirs." Her fingers lost their grip on his ears, thank God, and slid through his hair as she lifted her face. "Let it go. Just let it go, so they can rest in peace." She brushed her mouth against his.

"You're still my hero, Kane Wright." And she kissed him until he couldn't recall how the conversation had started in the first place.

Distances were deceptive in the desert, the clear atmosphere made objects appear closer than they really were. And there were precious few objects out there. Just dunes of various shapes and sizes. Multiplying the visual estimation of the distance by three gave Kane a pretty accurate idea of how far away they were. Perhaps four miles. They'd walk another hour.

Which was good. He still felt raw after purging himself to AJ. He felt as though he'd just run a marathon, only to realize the finish line was a mile behind him. Wrung out emotionally, he rubbed his thumb over the back of AJ's hand which he held between them.

She looked up. "Okay?"

"Yeah." He nearly was, thanks to her aggressive treatment of the patient. The shrinks hadn't said anything different than AJ had. But their method of delivery was not quite as—confrontational as AJ's. He bit back a smile. "Ready for a break?"

She stumbled and pulled herself upright. "Getting there."

He'd insist they rest again when they reached their goal. AJ was sensible, but still new enough to want a pissing contest every time a decision had to be made. She wouldn't stop until he called it.

His calf muscles pulled and ached from striding in the soft sand, but the air had cooled to chilly, which felt good on his slightly sweat-dampened skin. Moonlight, as bright as day, shone on the sand ahead of them. The silence was absolute. No breeze, animals, or insects, just the soft huff and puff of their breath and the occasional squeak of their booted feet on the sand.

"Hang tough, Abominable Jabberwocky," he said quietly, almost unwilling to shatter the otherworldly stillness. "Almost there."

"With you, chief."

As they approached the first of three close-together dunes, AJ was ready for a break. Everything ached. "We made it." AJ hadn't been entirely sure she would, though she would have forced herself to belly crawl if she'd had to to keep up with Kane.

She was so tired, all her muscles aching, that she was ready to collapse. The only thing that prevented her from falling against that moonlit, so comfy-looking dune was the fact that beside her, Kane Wright was still upright and had a spring in his step. Damn him.

Was he an android or someth— What the hell was that sme—

"Smell that?" he asked unnecessarily.

"Yes." She slapped a palm over her nose. The stench was unmistakable. And pungently more noticeable after hours of smelling nothing but fresh air and sand. "Uh-oh."

A man's legs were sprawled from behind the biggest dune. Moonlight glittered down on him, but there was no disguising death. They continued walking. The smell got stronger.

AJ blinked and squinted to make out the details in the moonlight.

Oh, God. It was a bloodbath.

It was hard to tell where one mutilated body stopped and the next started. The corpses were joined in death by the blood-soaked sand between their bodies.

"Now, here's a way to break the monotony." Kane stepped closer, skirting the area.

"Yeah," AJ said dryly, wrinkling her nose at the sweet, rank reek of decomposing flesh. The desert sun had already baked the bodies. "A clump of corpses certainly does that, all right."

She breathed through her mouth as they moved closer to the dead men sprawled awkwardly in bloody sand. Bile rose in the back of her throat at the carnage. There was no point checking to see if any of them were still alive. They weren't.

"They were on foot," she observed, looking in the direction of the prints the men had left behind. She pointed at the sign of camel tracks veering in from the right. "That's the direction of their assassins. They came in right behind them."

"Probably the same guys who tried for us." Kane crouched to search the pockets of the man closest to him. "Looks like this happened several hours after Raazaq passed here. See how their footsteps are layered over the ones made by his camels?"

"They were doing what we're doing. In reverse. Following him out."

"Yeah. Sorry bastards were stopped before

they could reach hel—Christ." He sucked in a gulp of air. "Check this out."

AJ took the small leather folder from him. Her eyebrows shot up. "Her Majesty's Secret Service?"

Kane went to the next man. He closed the guy's eyes before reaching into the top pocket of his shirt. "So's this guy."

The hair on the back of AJ's neck stood up. One of the Royals must be nearby. It seemed highly unlikely, though.

"On vacation?" she thought out loud. "Here?" It didn't make any sense whatsoever that these guys were out here. None. "Look at this," she said, the back of her neck prickling again while her stomach did a slow slide toward real panic. "This one's U.S. Secret Service."

"Jesus," Kane muttered. "This guy's DSS. Try that one."

She looked at him, wide-eyed. "Diplomatic Secret Service?" She quickly searched the next man's pockets. Opened his wallet. A wife and two blond children smiled for the camera. God. She searched for I.D.

"*French* Secret Service." AJ's palms felt damp as she added his I.D. to the others she held. "British Royalty. American . . . What? Senator? The President? And French diplomats, their president? God, Kane."

"Yeah. The shit just took a decidedly hard hit to the proverbial fan," Kane said, his gaze sweeping over the men who'd died trying to protect their charges. "And now we know the reason Raazaq's out here in the middle of nowhere."

"But what is he up to? *What?*" AJ slowly stood, shifting her gaze to Kane's. "Worse, are we too late to stop whatever it is he's doing?"

Chapter Eighteen

There was no way—and God only knew, no time—to bury the bodies. Kane pocketed the dead men's I.D.s and gave them a mental salute. He hated to leave them all lying here in the open, but there was no choice. They'd have to be retrieved later. If the desert hadn't already buried them. Chances were good that within a couple of days, the constantly shifting sands of the desert would bury the bodies and leave no sign behind. And maybe, Kane thought, that was only right. To lie where they'd fallen. It was the most any professional warrior could hope for.

With regret, AJ and Kane left the scene of carnage and started off across the desert again.

"They must've tried to walk out. With communications blocked, they'd have had no other options," AJ speculated.

"And they got stopped before they could get help."

"Violently." She shuddered at the images burned into her brain of the eviscerated bodies lying in a pale wash of moonlight. "Whoever did that enjoyed their work. A lot."

"Raazaq's people, for sure," Kane said through gritted teeth. "And you were right about the discovery of the pyramid. They're headed in the right direction, and it's the only structure within three hundred miles. Gotta be."

"Who were those guys here to protect? That's the burning question."

"Somebody big. Maybe several somebodies." Kane picked up the pace to just this side of a jog. Clearly, he felt the same hair-raising urgency AJ did. And while it was great to know her instincts were good, it scared the hell out of her knowing they were correct and that Kane felt the same way.

All the training in the world hadn't prepared her for this. And every intuition, both learned and gut, told her to hurry. Hurry. *Hurry.*

"There could be a Secret Service convention at the newly discovered pyramid," AJ offered half in jest. While her feet could only move so fast, her insides seemed to want to race ahead. Her stomach whirled and churned and her brain jumped into overdrive. She wanted to be in the middle of the action. Neutralize Raazaq. Do *something*, damn it.

"Unlikely. Let's hit this systematically." Kane

swigged from his bottle, not slowing a step. "What do we have?"

"A known, class-one terrorist in possession of a highly contagious viral agent."

"Headed south."

"South," AJ added, "directly toward a newly discovered dig."

"Which was suddenly taken off the public's radar."

"Right." AJ uncapped her bottle and took a slug. The water tasted like nectar from the gods, even lukewarm and plastic-flavored.

"Let's say dignitaries, accompanied by their bodyguards and various branches of their own country's secret services, from all over the world, were invited to come and see this amazing find," AJ mused. "And stay where? Other than the pyramid and dig, which presumably has tents or something, there's nothing else out here." She considered it. "I can't quite see the Queen of England sleeping in a tent or on a sarcophagus, can you?"

Kane snorted a laugh. "It's a little known fact that Liz likes nothing better than a nice toasty s'more around a campfire."

AJ paused a second and then gave him a small smile. "Yeah, now that I think about it, I can picture that. Queen Lizzie. With her little empty, patent-leather purse clutched on her stomach, and wearing a pretty, blue-flowered hat to match her pretty blue suit, holding a marshmallow on a coat hanger over a fire. Possible." She smiled. "But not likely."

"No." Kane didn't smile. "Not likely. Let's say we have half a dozen dignitaries from around the world. Staying somewhere close by. To see the pyramid. To have a vacation. To do whatever. Communications are mysteriously shut down. What's the first thing that would happen from inside?"

"They would know PDQ that their communications were down. And that it had little or nothing to do with the khamsin?"

Kane nodded. "They're in possession of too many high-tech, high-powered communications devices. Something would work, even if satellite communications were knocked out. Hell, yeah. They know something's up by now. They'd want to talk to someone outside. If they still couldn't make some sort of communication, they'd walk out."

He glanced at her. Teacher to student. "What would happen from outside?"

"If outside didn't hear from *inside* at regular intervals, they'd send in air power." AJ chewed on her lower lip. "And if that didn't work, they'd send in teams. SEALs, Rangers, Recon—not to mention specialized units from the other countries." She narrowed her gaze on him. "They'd mobilize immediately. Everyone would activate their own emergency plans. Satellite pictures also down, do you think?"

"Christ, I don't know." He squinted off into the distance as if he could see their goal already. "Considering everything else, more than likely."

"Jesus," she muttered. "This is huge. As we speak, there must be aircraft poised for take off all over the world. . . ."

"T-FLAC, the Secret Service, the Mosad, and various other countries' elite services would have been on red alert the second the systems went down," Kane agreed grimly, giving AJ a faint, very faint, sense of security that there were hundreds, probably thousands of people ready to back them up the second they could. "They'll have pinpointed the location by the area blocked."

Heck, they were all probably marching on that pyramid right now, coming in from every corner of the desert.

Kane swiped at the sweat on his face with his bandanna. "They'd know immediately such a blanket blackout wasn't caused by the winds. For the last twelve hours or so they've been doing anything and everything in an attempt to get to where their people are. Nobody's going to care at this point who gets in first. They'll all have the same objective."

"Except nothing can fly overhead." AJ shot a look at the night sky as if hoping somehow to see a flotilla of Blackhawk helicopters racing in. "Not for hundreds of miles. No vehicle can breach the block. Hell, even our wristwatches are inoperable. Doesn't matter how much they want to be wherever their people are. They won't be able to . . . They're walking in. Like we're doing, or if they can muster that many, riding camels in."

"Right."

AJ glanced over her left shoulder, almost expecting to see troops marching up over the last rise. Cavalry to the rescue. A moment passed, then two. She'd really *love* to see some help coming up that rise. No such luck. Their two sets of footprints looked pretty damn lonely and frail stretching out behind them for miles.

"We're going at a pretty good clip," Kane said. "Maybe three, three and a half miles an hour. Let's say they can march in full battle gear at something similar. . . . They're at least six to eight hours behind us."

AJ grimaced. "Guess we shouldn't wait for them, then, huh?"

★ ★ ★

"What if we don't get there in time?" AJ demanded. Her voice sounded croaky and thick. They were rapidly getting more and more exhausted. The sun was up again and unrelenting. Dazzles of heat inspired little white dots floating in formation in front of her eyes and she had to blink to make them disappear. While they still had adequate water, thank God, their supply of sunscreen was running out.

The bad news was, despite the claims on the sunscreen tube, their sweat was washing off the cream. The good news was, they could still sweat. Not sweating meant heatstroke. As the body dried out, the blood became more viscous in turn, not circulating around the body adequately. Heatstroke could kill. It would be an agonizing death.

Not on Kane's watch.

"We will." Kane's voice was grim as he surreptitiously checked AJ's features for any sign of excessive fatigue, or distress. She was distressed, all right. But she was maintaining. He couldn't ask for more. Fuck, he was maintaining, himself.

"Even your strong will can't make us get there any faster," AJ said flatly. She turned to glare at him. "Stop staring at me, would you, please? If I need a break, feel sick, or otherwise require your assistance, believe me, I'll let you know. We're both equally tired, equally hot, equally footsore, and equally edgy. You don't have to check me every eight seconds, okay?"

"Thirty."

"Every thirty seconds, then."

"Yes, ma'am."

"We won't be walking forever, camel boy," AJ groused, and then under her breath, "Just frigging feels like it."

"Walking in the sand's supposed to be great for your legs, though," Kane teased, hoping for a smile.

"You've already got great legs," AJ snapped.

"Not mine, yours," he said, and finally earned the smile.

"Oh. Have I mentioned," she asked, "that heat makes me crabby?"

"Should have said something," he said. "I'd have turned on the air conditioner."

"Oh, God. Don't toy with me, camel boy."

His lips quirked, and his eyes gleamed as he looked at her. "You're doin' great, Abernathy Jawonda."

"Yeah, great. I feel so damn *useless*," she said, frustrated.

"We're doing the best we can. And right now we're the only game in town."

"Oh, no pressure."

"Relax."

"Relax? Worse-case scenario: all the world's leaders gathered in one place. Couldn't be a better setup for a terrorist. Especially someone like Raazaq. Jesus God, Kane. What if we don't get there in time?"

"If we don't get there in time, we don't get there in time. We'll deal with it then. That slimey son of a bitch is confident no one is going anywhere," he said flatly. "He'll drag this out. Terrorize the principals. Freak out the security people. *Then* he'll move. Raazaq is a control freak. He plans. He waits."

AJ nodded, remembering everything she'd ever read on the man. "His M.O. is playing cat and mouse."

"Right," Kane said flatly. "Supersize the cat, and blind the mice. That's Raazaq. And no one has any idea what the hell he's doing. But you can bet whatever he's up to, he's going to be out of the line of fire, and safe."

"Which would mean he wants to watch the fun from afar and he's sent someone else in to do his dirty work," AJ suggested with dread, trying to wrap her brain around the ramifications of numerous important world leaders being leveled by a deadly virus at the same time. In fact, they could all be lying somewhere right now, dead and dying while Raazaq was off on his next reign of terror.

"No. Raazaq'll be there." Kane was sure of it. "Right there. Certainly within visual contact himself. He was in a neighboring building when that girls' school was bombed," Kane said, voice grim.

"He watched that explosion." AJ's voice went soft, thoughtful. "He watched the fire department and EMTs scramble. He watched the hysterical, weeping families gather, and he watched those children's bodies being taken away in small black bags. Raazaq is hands-on. That's what makes him so damn terrifying. He enjoys his work, and he particularly revels in the up-close-and-personal misery and pain of others. This setup is a Raazaq wet dream. Wiping out presidents and kings and queens? No, he'll want to do this one himself. Properly protected, of course, and with an immediate means of escape.

"He could intend to kill everyone to create world chaos," she speculated, digging a protein bar out of her backpack, then thought better of it and tossed it back. She wasn't hungry enough to force down something that unappealing. Somehow she didn't imagine there was anything close to real chocolate in it.

"Or," she continued, "he could be holding the viral agent over them as leverage for blackmail."

"Which could possibly mean he has some form of communication with the outside world."

"Except he wouldn't be stupid enough to let anyone trace or track him. Damn it."

For the next three hours they kept their speculations to themselves. AJ was now moving by rote. Putting one heavy, hot foot in front of the other. Trying not to come up with every worse-case scenario, but finding her mind could be pretty damn creative when there was nothing to look at but sand, and sand, and—

Trees?

Cool, green, shade-giving . . . trees.

She blinked. "Man, does that mirage look real, or what?"

"No mirage. That's the real deal."

"Oh, God," she said on a moan, "don't toy with me."

"Water, Cooper. Real water. With trees."

"Are T-FLAC agents allowed to weep with joy?"

"In certain cases," he assured her, "oh, yeah."

There was an enormous sand dune between them and those treetops, but now that they had a tangible goal, their footsteps quickened and they scrambled up the slope like mountain goats.

They crested the rise, and there it was,

spread out below them. A lumpy sea of green.
A thousand shades of wonderful, glorious
green, green, green. Even AJ's eyes sighed in
relief.

An oasis. Verdant, lush, staggeringly beautiful after endless miles of pale sand, it shimmered dreamlike in the early-morning light.
Towering date palms, sycamores, acacias, and
carobs spread for miles before them. And even
more gorgeous than the green was the water
that fed all that lush vegetation.

Two wide, blue pools of still water glittered,
and made every corpuscle in AJ's body cry out
for a long, deep taste.

"Look at that." AJ pointed. As if Kane could
possibly miss the two enormous structures
peaking over the treetops. Illuminated by the
brilliant sunlight and crystal-clear blue sky.

On the right, a pale stone replica of a pyramid towered half a dozen stories above the
treetops. On the left, the real deal, pyramid-
wise. Pale marble, glossy as the day it was built
two thousand years ago.

Hallelujah. They'd arrived.

AJ inhaled deeply. For the first time in what
seemed like a lifetime, the simple act of inhal-
ing didn't burn the membrane inside her nose.
And the smell. The glorious smell. Water, vegetation, the faint fragrance of cooking.

The air smelled green, fresh, and life-giving.

Resisting running down the other side of the dune like a kid at the beach to fall nose-first into something cool and fertile, AJ pointed to a lazy curl spiraling into the sky. "Look. Smoke."

"No. I think that's steam. Must be a hot spring. Now, that looks interesting." He indicated a long rectangle of cleared trees off to their left.

Since they were looking down across the treetops, they couldn't actually see what the clearing was for, but it seemed pretty obvious to AJ, and her heart did an excited little flip. "What's the bet that's an airstrip?"

"Apparently the only way in and out." Kane scanned the treetops narrow-eyed. There appeared to be no roads entering the massive oasis.

Unfortunately, there was no sign of any troops, either.

No sign of life. No sound of human habitation. Still . . . "He's here." Just a feeling, but its effect was so strong, it was as powerful as a stare from an unknown source, raising the hairs on the back of her neck.

"Hell, yes, he's here," Kane agreed. "This discovery is new, fresh, important. You can bet there's someone, several someones, damn important down there." He pointed. "That looks like it might be a hotel."

"Yeah. My guess, too." AJ swiped her arm over her sweaty face. "They expect a lot of tourists, apparently."

"Let's go. We're going to drag our butts in the front door and act surprised when we bump into him. Car broke down. Didn't think it was too far to the next village. Walked—et cetera, et cetera."

AJ raised a brow. "He'll think we're morons, or be really suspicious."

"And you care . . . why?"

"Good point."

Just seeing the various shades of green made her feel cooler. Hell, her legs felt lighter, too, as they slid and stumbled their way down the dune in a cascade of rose-tinted sand. They weren't attempting to hide, which made it a lot easier to move. Until they reached the oasis, they were out in front of God and everyone as they slithered their way down the dune.

When they finally reached the bottom and level ground, they moved toward the tree-surrounded water like zombies.

"Amazing anything can grow out here, isn't it?" AJ asked in awe as they approached the tree line.

"Given water, plants will thrive anywhere.

Did you notice there's no cultivation? No crops?"

"Those over there look like olive trees."

"Yeah, and look how old they are. Probably planted thousands of years ago for whichever pharaoh was buri—Company," he said under his breath.

She'd seen them. The three men stepped from the shadows. Wearing Western dress, they were well accessorized. Locked and loaded.

"Hope these are the good guys," AJ said sotto voce.

Kane stopped, and AJ followed suit. They lowered their weapons as the men approached. As they did so, several more men came in from the sides and flanked them. A total of fifteen heavily armed men. Perfect. Just freaking perfect.

"Hands up." The tall man in the lead said flatly, motioning them with the business end of an M16. He had military-short, white-blond hair, a sunburned, craggy face, and a neck like a prizefighter. "Keep your hands where we can see them at all times." The guy scowled. "Now, who the fuck are you, and what have you done to our communication systems?"

Kane let his hands drop, but kept them in plain sight. He quickly I.D.ed himself and AJ as T-FLAC operatives. The man talking to him

I.D.ed himself as Barry Walsh, head of the Secret Service. Once he'd studied their I.D.s for what seemed like forever, Walsh handed them back.

They shook hands. Nice and polite. "Jesus." Kane looked behind the men, expecting to see the President of the United States strolling from among the date palms. "The President is here?"

"And Mrs.," Walsh said grimly. He motioned his men to stand down. "We have a situation here. Hope to hell you two came in some sort of vehicle. Nothing around here is operable."

"We walked in," Kane told him. "Can we get to cover before we talk?"

"Yeah. This way."

Walsh's men surrounded them, and they all merged into the shade of the trees.

"The U.N. is having a hush-hush world peace summit at the new resort." Walsh motioned behind him.

"First time in history this many world leaders have gathered in one place at the same time. Frankly, we—" he glanced around as if checking to make sure no one could overhear him, "—all the security personnel—were flat-out against it. Too many things to go wrong, the isolation, the fact that the only approach is by air. Having all the eggs in one convenient basket—Fuck. Was whoever thought this up smoking crack, or what?"

Kane nodded in sympathy. He'd dealt with the big shots before and wasn't surprised. "And nobody listened to you."

"They listened," Walsh admitted, "but *our* reasons for saying no were *their* reasons for thinking it was a swell idea." He grimaced. "We've all had our own people out here for months, testing security, et cetera. The hotel's clean. Every leader has their own people. Top of the line. The best in the business. Everything was set. Coordinated to a hair. Nothing was going to go wrong. Nothing." He shoved one hand over his hair and muttered a curse.

"Everything went like silk. Until the khamsin blew in. Everything electrical, mechanical—shit, anything with a fucking moving part—shut off. Blackout. We're not sure yet why it's out, but everything still is." He narrowed his gaze on Kane. "So, I talked. Spill it. What do you know? Why are you here?"

"Fazur Raazaq," Kane told Walsh and his men flatly.

One of Barry's guys straightened as if he'd been shot. He leaned down and whispered something that Kane couldn't catch, but it had Barry's eyes narrowing farther. As word spread back to the other guys, they crowded closer, some of them keeping a wary eye out on the surrounding desert, but most of them moving close enough to hear Kane's news.

"Bloody hell." A man sat down beside Barry. "Ian Graham, M15," he said, jerking Kane and AJ a quick nod. "How could Fazur Raazaq possibly have access to something with this level of classification? He'd have to have moles all over the bloody world to find out about this gathering."

"You can bet the bank that information will be revealed in time. But the breach of security isn't our problem," Kane reminded the men. "Deactivating Raazaq is."

"He's in possession of that virus stolen from the Russians last week," AJ said tautly. "And he's here now, so that must mean he's planning to release the viral agent in the hotel. Either to use the world leaders as leverage, or to kill them in one quick stroke."

"Fuck that for a joke!" Walsh snapped. "He isn't touching the President!"

"Or the Prime Minister," Graham said flatly. "We'll protect our people no matter what. But there've been no overt threats as yet. We all simply seem to be trapped here."

Walsh scowled. "We sent several teams on foot to get reinforcements. You must've passed at least one."

"They didn't make it," Kane informed him. He filled them in on the group they'd come across earlier.

"Fuck—Excuse me, ma'am. What the *hell* is going on?"

"First things first." Kane took charge. "How many of your people have desert survival training?"

"Not enough," Ian admitted.

"Then we need to give another batch some intense training, ASAP," Kane said. "Someone has to meet the troops and give them whatever we have. Which at this point is precisely nothing. You can bet that as we speak every SEAL, Ranger, Spec Ops person in the free world is on their way in. They couldn't be that far behind us."

"Without a doubt," Walsh said with some satisfaction. "But Raazaq isn't going to hold off whatever he's planning until help arrives. He's going to do whatever it is he's going to do before he can be stopped. He's a wily little bastard. Seems to have planned this to a T."

Kane nodded tightly. "Bastards screw up all the time. We'll flush him out. But I'd feel one hell of a lot better having Hazmat, medics, and transportation standing by."

"Wouldn't we all," Barry said dryly. "Shall we get some caterers in here while we're at it?"

Kane smiled tightly. "Point taken. Nobody's coming. Not for a while yet, anyway. So we do what we can."

"Agreed."

"I'll go with the team heading back into the desert." AJ stepped forward.

The fact that she was a woman didn't seem to faze Walsh. "Good id—"

"No," Kane told her. "You have to be here. Raazaq will respond to your presence."

"Then you have to g—"

"I'll be here with you. Who do you trust?" he asked Walsh.

"Brody, Todd, Dixon."

Ian spoke up, too. "I can send Doyle, Smythe, and Tennyson."

AJ smiled. "The poet?"

Ian smiled back. "He's a poet, all right. And his muse is an M16."

"Is he prepared for the desert?" Kane wanted to know.

"No one is prepared for the desert, mate. But they'd better make it."

Walsh stood up. "Covert or overt for your arrival?"

"We've met Raazaq. And unless we keep AJ hidden for the duration, he'll know she's here. We'll go overt and draw him out."

They started walking toward the hotel. It

was blessedly cool beneath the thick foliage of the date palms, and thick grasses and weeds grew with lush profusion.

"Tell us who's here."

"The President and First Lady. The P.M. of England, the Queen, too, no less. One of the Saudi princes. Queen Sofia of Spain—"

"Jesus."

"Exactly."

Raazaq was definitely here. Kane described him. But Graham told them there were over five hundred people in residence at the hotel. As soon as they'd realized that nothing electrical worked, that no vehicle or plane operated, each security team had confined their people to their quarters. Unaware of where the danger was coming from had kept the teams on high, red alert.

Food tasters. No air-conditioning, which was making tempers flare. "You wanna tell the President he can't go outside?"

"Perhaps out is where he should be," AJ said, with a frown.

"We considered it. Can't keep them secure outside. In is better," Walsh said. "But I gotta tell you, everyone is getting stir-crazy."

Graham sent one of his men for food and water for them while they formulated a plan.

Walsh and a few of his men were the only ones with weapons.

As soon as Raazaq and his key people had arrived, the guests had been thrown into chaos as his soldiers searched every room, every bit of luggage, and stripped everyone of their firearms. No exceptions. Even the cutlery had been purged of knives. The slightest reluctance to give up their weapons had been grounds for immediate death. The body count was high. Over two hundred security personnel had given their lives in an attempt at fighting back. But eventually everyone had given up their weapons. They were hopelessly outnumbered.

Until Kane and AJ had told them who it was, Walsh and his men had speculated that this was a hostage situation.

Now they were all on the same page.

Kane quickly distributed the weapons he and AJ carried, not enough for everyone, but better than nothing. With something akin to pain, she watched one of the men pick up her Dragunov. "It pulls a bit to the left," she told him, handing him the clips.

"I'll take good care of it, ma'am. And I'll make sure you get it back when this is over."

"Thanks." She gave him a smile that made the man turn red and had his eyes glazing, then turned to Kane. "Do we have—?"

He patted the duffel. "Got it covered. Let's go over the plan one more time."

It made sense for them to arrive as though they were unaware of anything wrong. Their vehicle had broken down, they'd walked—all true. Raazaq might be tempted to make contact with AJ. If not, he'd be aware of her presence and keep hidden, making his discovery more difficult.

Graham's man returned with bread and cheese and a gallon jug of fresh water. They all ate while discussing the feasibility of Kane and AJ entering through the front door or the back.

According to Walsh, most of the people in residence at the hotel were the extensive household and security staff of the heads of state attending.

"We have 216 special-forces personnel. Broken into teams. Four teams of six left at thirty-minute intervals to walk out. Another group of blokes are tinkering with planes and vehicles. Christ, I'd get my people out on a bloody donkey if I could find one." Ian glared at the surrounding desert.

"Will your people recognize Raazaq?" Kane asked the men.

"Hell," Walsh frowned, "I've seen a dozen grainy photographs of him over the years, but

I'd never recognize him in the flesh. He could be anyone in there."

"AJ and I can both finger him. We'll walk in the front door. AJ'll flush him out. She's our best bet. Sharpshooter A-1."

"Is that so?" Walsh checked her out.

Kane grabbed another couple of sandwiches, handed one absently to AJ, then took a bite of his own. "All we have to do is make contact. In the meantime I want everyone alerted to the upgrade in danger. We have to move them out of the hotel and environs—"

"Take everyone out into that?" Ian interrupted him and waved an arm at the desert that could kill so mercilessly. "Are you mad, man? I'm not dragging Her Majesty across the bloody Western Desert. Can you imagine? Can't leave her here, can't get her out. Isn't a bloody thing that moves. Two chaps have already died. Their pacemakers froze up and they dropped like rocks."

Kane swallowed the dry sandwich and chased it with two long glugs of warm water. "What's the status with the hotel staff?"

"Contained in the basement, poor chaps. Bloody hot down there."

"The hotel's chief of security is cooperating fully, and keeping the panic down as best he can."

"Where can we meet later?" Kane asked the two men.

"I'll have to find you."

"Right." Who knew where any of them would be later.

They separated—the men, in teams of two, melted back between the trees.

A ransom could net Raazaq a fortune. Some of the countries would pay. But none of them, particularly the U.S., was going to tolerate whatever that bastard had planned after this. Whatever *this* was.

"Someone spent a fortune on this place," AJ commented. "Look at it."

They started walking down the palm-lined driveway. The resort hotel was an exact replica of the pyramid slightly behind it. Blinding white stone, gold leaf on the pillars and capitals. Fountains and lush gardens.

Birdsong filled the air, and splashing water from lazily turning, decorative waterwheels provided a backdrop to their footsteps. A small flock of sheep lazily grazed on the foliage ringing the circular emerald-green lawn in the front courtyard.

There wasn't a human in sight.

"This is creepy." AJ glanced around. "Reminds me of a *Twilight Zone* episode."

"As long as you don't start singing the

theme. Here we are. Look exhausted and thirsty."

"No problem. I won't even have to stretch my acting talen—Hell's bells," AJ said drolly as four men raced from the trees, pointing an interesting assortment of weapons at them. "Here we go again."

Chapter Nineteen

It was pretty easy to distinguish the good guys from the bad guys. The bad guys were the ones with all the weapons.

One wore a suit and looked hot, annoyed, and not in the least bit happy to see them. The rest of the men, looking no happier, wore dark pants and wilted white shirts.

All of the men, except for one, were dark and swarthy. They could've been any nationality from Arabic to Italian. Wherever they were from, and whatever their affiliation, there was something about them AJ didn't like. And that was enough for her.

She and Kane wouldn't be taking any chances. Walsh and his men had no form of communication with anyone at the hotel. They called meetings by word of mouth. Bush telegraph, just like the old days. Clearly these guys, whoever they were, hadn't been told of her and Kane's arrival, nor of their identity. Until they knew all the players in this little game, AJ knew they'd have to play their cards close to the chest.

"I don't like it when you're quiet," Kane whispered from the corner of his mouth. "It means you're thinking. That generally signals trouble."

She smiled, ignored him, and walked toward the men, putting a slight sway in her hips as she tried to keep eye contact with Mr. Suit. Which was difficult because he wasn't looking at her eyes.

"You stay right where you are until we check you out," he said grimly, his attention on her boobs. Slight accent. French. Which could mean anything. AJ cataloged his appearance. Short and stocky, running to fat—fleshy lips and small eyes. His suit must've cost a pretty penny, it fit over his belly as if custom-made. Italian shoes. French tie. Not an errand boy.

"Check us out?" AJ opened her eyes wide. "Are you crazy? It's three hundred degrees out here and we just walked hundreds of miles!" She leaned in and lay one dainty hand over the suit's arm. "Honey, if I don't get something to drink—preferably with lots of ice—I think I'm gonna faint."

"*Fifty* miles," Kane corrected in a long-suffering voice, which gave AJ an indication of how he wanted this played.

"What's going on?" Kane asked the men reasonably. He looked about as aggressive as a basset hound. How he changed his entire demeanor by shifting his body and lightening the tone of his voice was something AJ was determined to study. He gave the appearance of the weakling everyone kicked sand on at the beach.

One of the men waved his weapon to indicate they be searched. Another peered down the driveway. "How did you get here?" European accent. Knew his way around the Ruger he held. Dead black eyes. Mean mouth. By the stains on his shirt, he'd been sweating for quite a while.

"Our car broke down," Kane said laconically. "We've been walking ever since, and brother, that's a damn hot, arduous walk. Can we put our hands down? I gotta tell you guys, this has been a long haul, and we're beat."

AJ kept a wary eye on a corn-fed, redheaded guy as he circled behind them. Kane gave no indication that there was anything untoward. In fact, he looked rather glazed and out of it, when seconds before AJ could've sharpened a pencil on his gaze. Damn. He was good.

The skinny redheaded guy with a painful-looking sunburned face started running his hands down AJ's torso from the back, with a hell of a lot more enthusiasm than necessary. "Hey!" She spun around and "accidentally" smacked him in the nose with her elbow. "Watch those hands!"

He rubbed his nose and gave her a wounded look. "Just searching you for weapons, ma'am." Midwestern accent. Nineteen if he was a day. He was the what-doesn't-fit-with-this-group-of-items? odd man out.

He wasn't going to find any weapons on her. Nor on Kane. Not anything he'd recognize as such, anyway. "And you thought you'd find them in my bra?" AJ turned and gave the guy in the suit a hard look. "Look, I have no idea what's going on. But we're absolutely zonked out, hot, dirty, thirsty, and I'm *way* beyond cranky. So if you don't mind, could we skip the pleasantries, check in, and discuss this over a drink?"

Suit walked down the wide steps. "Do you have a reservation?"

"Sure we do. Must be in the limo." AJ stared at him. "Didn't you hear us just say we *walked* fifty miles? We didn't even know this place existed. We spotted the oasis, and hey, lookit there, a pyramid hotel, too! How could w—"

"Calm down, honey." Kane patted her arm as if she were a small terrier.

AJ jerked her arm out of reach. "Don't 'calm

down, honey' me, you . . . you *shyster*! You told me this shoot would be top-of-the-line *everything*. Makeup, hair, wardrobe. Luxury accommodation! You. Did. Not. Tell. Me. I. Would. Have. To. Walk. Fifty damn miles! My agent is going to hear about this. My lawyer will hear about this. The . . . the photographers guild people will hear about thi—"

"Everyone in Mesopotamia can hear you loud and clear," Kane said tightly. "Look, guys," he said to the men, who'd all backed up a step when she'd started her hysterical speech, "she's a bit high-strung. Can we get out of this heat and get her a room?"

"High-strung? You moron." She turned her big, wide eyes on the suit again and played to a rapt audience. "This guy got us stuck out there. In all that nothing. Now I want the biggest, best suite in the place," AJ said crisply to a tall skinny guy on the periphery of the group, who hadn't said a word for the duration, but was looking at her as if she were his last meal. She gave him a sweet smile and sighed inwardly as he almost fell down the steps in response. The near-tumble at least forced him to close his mouth.

"Send up a chilled bottle of Cristal, would you, sugar?" She turned to glare at Kane. Her tone hardened. "And my tab's on *you*. Since you refused to bring my suitcases with us, you may also find me something decent to wear."

"Where do you thi—"

"Just do it." AJ pushed through the men and made her way up the wide, white marble steps to the twenty-foot-high front doors, which stood open, Kane beside her. The doors were intricately carved with hieroglyphics and painted dramatically in gold, turquoise, and black, flanked on either side by thirty-foot palm trees in white marble planters taller than she was.

Inside was marginally cooler than outside. But not by much. No air-conditioning moved the still air. The three-story-high lobby was exquisitely decorated, although the colors were muted, as there were no lights on. But enough sunlight streamed through the doors to illuminate the turquoise and black carpets that stretched for what seemed like miles. At regular intervals along the white marble walls, forty-foot-high gilded, gem-encrusted replicas of sarcophagi lined the walls.

No expense seemed to have been spared in the building and decorating of the luxury hotel. It had clearly been built for presidents and kings and industry giants.

Or as a trap.

They all crossed the gargantuan entry and

headed toward the registration desk. There wasn't a soul in sight. "Where is everyone?" she demanded, turning in a slow circle to stare at the men who'd followed her inside.

"You can't stay here," Mr. Suit told her. "The hotel isn't officially open yet."

"Oh, well," AJ said sweetly. "I'll just stay at the Holiday Inn next door, then."

"Miss . . ."

"Are there beds in the rooms?" AJ demanded.

"Yes—"

"Showers all working?"

"Yes—"

"And room service?"

He looked annoyed. "To a certain extent—"

"Then this hotel's open, honey, and we'll stay."

"We have a situation here, ma'am."

"We most certainly do." She waved both hands at her own attire. "And its going to get worse if I don't have a room in the next ten seconds."

The suit sighed and must have decided it would be easier to get her out of the lobby. "Only rooms available are on the fifth floor," he said, disgusted.

"Lead the way."

"The lift doesn't work."

Kane gave a long-suffering sigh. "Figures."

★ ★ ★

Two men were posted on each floor, just inside each exit door to the stairs. No way to lock any of the doors without electricity. The guards appeared to belong to whichever dignitary was on that particular floor. Kane wasn't ready to confront any of them. They were just doing their jobs. Probably as confused as everyone else in the hotel.

Let Walsh deal with the logistics of who was supposed to be where. He and AJ had to find and neutralize Raazaq.

After their twelve-hour hike, AJ wasn't quite as sparky by the time they got up five flights of stairs.

He pushed open the door to 506, and stood back, motioning with a flourish. *"Entre vous, mademoiselle."*

Bugs? she signed after walking in and glancing around.

Kane shrugged, signing back, *Probably not. Don't chance it.*

"I'm going to take a shower." AJ wiggled her eyebrows. "Find me some food and clothes."

"Right, Your Highness." He indicated he was going to search the suite first.

She signed, *Want me to help?*

The large room would be easy to sweep, and

Kane seriously doubted it was bugged. He shook his head.

After a brief hesitation, she went into the bathroom. A few seconds later he heard water running. Kane went to the ten-foot-high windows overlooking the back of the hotel. There was an Olympic-size covered swimming pool below, surrounded by empty loungers and lush vegetation.

Armed men, at irregular intervals, patrolled the area.

Clearly Raazaq wasn't afraid anyone would cause problems, otherwise his men wouldn't have let them come up without an escort. Arrogant bastard was that sure of himself.

There were over two hundred trained security personnel in the hotel. The best in the world for their particular duties. Yet Raazaq had neutralized them.

As Kane had suspected, the room didn't appear to be bugged. No need. It was clear Raazaq had effectively terrorized the guests, keeping them prisoners in their suites and unaware of what was going to happen next.

No one was going anywhere for the duration. After removing the television set, Kane dragged and shoved the unbelievably heavy Louis XIV armoire across the doorway—not much of a deterrent, but better than nothing.

Next he rummaged through the backpacks they'd tossed on the coffee table, and removed the various indistinguishable components of two weapons. He quickly assembled two good-size handguns, and lay them where they could be reached in a hurry.

Raazaq was waiting for something. What, Kane had no idea, but as long as everyone remained in their suites, he was reasonably sure they had a bit of time to clean up and scout around.

Raazaq must believe the next move was his. By now the terrorist knew AJ was in residence. Perhaps he'd call for her. Perhaps.

Kane didn't like the idea of AJ meeting with Raazaq one bit, and the thought pissed him off.

But AJ was an operative. Being in Raazaq's presence was her reason for being here. Yet now that Kane knew her—damn it, *cared* about her—the thought that she'd be in danger was abhorrent to him. A powerful rush of protectiveness swamped him. He frowned as he stripped off his rank clothing on the way to the bathroom.

They were going to have to deal with this. After the mission.

He walked naked into the bathroom, and could tell by the way AJ avoided the stream of water from the gold showerhead as she lathered up that the water was cold. Too cold. He snapped open the clear shower door. He'd warm her up in a hurry.

Her smile slammed into his gut.

"Live with it," he growled, stepping through the chill curtain of water to get to her.

"Live with what?" She looked up, blinking water from her lashes.

"Need a hand?"

Her lightly tanned skin glowed, slick and shimmering, her fiery hair was darkened and clung to her wet back and shoulders as if painted there. She held out her hand and drew him closer. "I'd rather have a bit of warm water. Live with what?"

He reached for her with his other hand, swinging her body flush against him. Her skin felt cool and slippery. "Let's see if I can make you forget about warm water and questions, huh?"

He brought his mouth down on hers. She tasted soapy. Hot. Not cold at all. He bunched up her hair in one fist and tugged her head back, kissing the arched curve of her throat, the curve between neck and shoulder. He nipped at her earlobe with his teeth, made her squirm and moan when he ran the tip of his tongue along the swirls of her ear.

He wanted to devour her. To absorb her.

Her body fit his like the missing piece of a puzzle. She curled one long, silky smooth leg around his thigh, rubbing herself against the painful ache of his erection, her arms about his neck as she returned the fury of his passion with her own.

He couldn't get close enough, and pushed her back, hard enough to elicit a little *"oomph"* of surprise, and sandwiched her between himself and the black and white mosaic wall. The hard tips of her nipples rubbed erotically against his chest as their bodies slipped and slid together. He saw her through a silvered sheet as cool water streamed over their heads.

Lorelei. Venus on the half shell. A Titian masterpiece come to life. Kane tangled his hands in her wet hair.

Her foot rubbed a maddeningly erotic pattern on his backside as she tried to pull him into her wet heat. She was determined, and she was strong. But he was more so. While their time together might be short, he wanted to give meaning to their lovemaking. He wanted to imprint himself on her. To claim and be claimed. Hell, to stamp his ownership.

Christ. When had he become so medieval?

Her long, slender fingers dug into his hair for purchase as he ravished her mouth, his body flattening hers against the wall.

"God," Kane said, lifting his head, coming up for air, breathing in the fragrance of her. "You feel so damn . . . good." His mouth captured hers again. Starving. To hell with it. Air was highly overrated.

Still lip-locked, he ran his hands through the wet and slippery tangle of her long hair, down the pure curve of her arched throat. Then paused there, fingertips on the rapid pulse at the base of her throat—alive, vibrant.

His.

He skimmed his hands across the soft swells of her breasts, then slipped one arm around her waist. Wet skin slid across wet skin. She whimpered with need as he pinched the hard point of her nipple between his fingers, his mouth hungrily devouring hers until they were both breathless and panting.

Pulling him hard against her with the strong muscles in her legs, AJ ran her palms down his chest. A little nail, and he almost came out of his skin. She bit his lower lip as she worked her hand between their bodies to cup his balls.

AJ took him in her hand. The hair at his groin was dark, crisp as it brushed against her hand. He was hard as marble, enormous in her grasp.

Kane smiled. A rare and lascivious smile that creased his lean, one-week-past-a-shave cheeks, and made his eyes look black and dangerous. "Little thing like you, darlin?" he purred in a credible Texas accent. "Think you can take it?"

She shifted her weight, and with a little jump, curled both legs about his lean waist, crossing and locking her ankles over his butt. "Try me," she whispered, her voice thick with desire.

He pressed her against the wall, braced his hands under her behind, and slid home. "Do you like that?"

"Hmmm." She'd never had a lover who talked during sex before. It made her hotter to know he cared, in the moment at least, what she liked and how she liked it. "Harder."

"Like this?"

"Harder . . . Mor—Yes. Yes. *Yes!*"

He was squishing her against the wall, his chest just as hard as the mosaic at her back. She was close, so close to the precipice . . . she felt hot, shivery, feverish. Even her hair follicles participated.

His stroke was steady and rapid, matching her heartbeats. Faster.

Faster.

Faster.

"Okay?" he asked in a low, tight voice.

She closed her eyes, concentrating on the

slow, inextricable climb. "Pretty. Damn. Fabulous. You?"

He chuckled, and the sensation of his pleasure shimmered through her, joining forces with all the other sensations to merge into an overwhelming whole.

He kissed her again. Deep, carnal, a mirror image of what their bodies were doing. Her muscles went taut, her back arched, and she cried out his name in the overwhelming force of her pleasure. Her release came like a supernova.

When it finally faded after several minutes she was surprised to find them still upright, the water continuing to cascade over them. Kane was still hard inside her.

He nuzzled her throat with his open mouth, and she found the skin there now even more sensitive to his touch. She wanted to purr.

"How was that for madam?" he asked, nibbling along her jaw.

"Satisfactory," she said in a snooty tone as she toyed with the swirls of hair on his chest. "A little more practice and madam thinks you'd make a fine—"

"Fuck!" Kane grabbed AJ's upper arms, disengaged, and spun her around, slamming her hard against the back wall behind him.

Not just hard, *violently*.

Her feet slipped and she staggered, off balance on the wet floor, as her brain tried to make sense of the lightning change from lover to attacker. Still in a sexual haze, she blinked, trying to bring him into focus while at the same time trying to find her footing on the slick floor. "Jesus God, Kane. What the hell do yo—"

The half-closed bathroom door slammed open, bouncing off the marble wall. Once. Twice.

This time AJ didn't have to fake a shriek. It burst from her lungs involuntarily as four men exploded into the bathroom.

She tried to assimilate the images through the runnels on the glass, attempting to view the entire picture from her position half hidden by Kane's large body. The shadowy man in front wavered as he raised his weapon in slo-mo.

"Nooooo—"

The glass walls of the shower stall imploded in a spray of glass, water, and bright red blood.

Chapter Twenty

Two men dragged AJ, buck-naked and dripping wet, kicking and screaming bloody murder, down the hallway. Another two followed closely behind.

She didn't give a good damn about the being naked part. She didn't even care about the four gorillas "escorting" her down the palatial corridor. How could she care about any of this when all she kept seeing, over and over, *and over again,* was blood.

Kane's blood.

She closed her eyes and saw it again, blossoming in the air like some grotesque, red feather fan. And oh, God, despite her violent struggles she could feel the hot iciness of blood running down her arms. Dribbling down her bare legs. She felt it slick on her hands. And between her toes. On her skin.

Oh, God, *Kane.*

AJ gave herself a mental shake. She recognized she was in shock. And she was scared.

Really scared. And angry. But she'd better snap the hell out of it. All of it. *Now.*

Didn't matter that she was naked as the day she was born, an armed goon on each arm, the two behind her getting a butt's-eye view to China as she heaved and struggled in their hold.

Get a grip, she told herself firmly. *Just. Get. A. Damn. Grip.*

Think calmly and rationally.

Acting hysterical was one thing, *being* hysterical another.

What would Kane do?

His eyes wouldn't be filling with tears of rage, that was for damn sure. He'd already be trying to figure out a plan to get to her. *He* wouldn't be remembering, he'd be thinking. Fine. She'd think. She'd plan. Then she'd kill these bastards and find Kane.

She tried to wipe her face on her bare shoulder. One of the men jerked her along so hard she almost bit herself. She let out an infuriated shriek and kicked out. Ineffectual with bare feet. Not to mention it screwed with her balance, and if they hadn't been holding her up she would have fallen.

The man laughed, which instead of pissing her off, calmed her as effectively as a slap.

The hallway was dimly lit. Emergency lighting only. And sweltering hot, yet she shivered as she stopped struggling. The only effect it had on her captors was that their grip on her tightened—in preparation, she supposed, for her to bolt.

But she didn't make a move. Wasn't time yet. When it was, she'd have to make it count. Eventually they'd let her go, and when they did, she'd have to focus and be ready to take action.

Was Kane alive? Would she live long enough herself to know?

If they didn't show up to meet Walsh later, would he come looking for them? In time? She dared not even think about the cavalry getting there to save the day. When she thought about it, she wanted to laugh at the irony.

She *was* the cavalry.

If Kane wasn't dead—please, God, Kane wasn't dead—then he was seriously injured. Walsh and his people were on the outside. Reinforcements weren't coming. Not yet, anyway.

As they marched her along, AJ checked for hiding places, for exits, for anything she might use as a weapon.

A half-round table held a huge urn of fresh, slightly wilted flowers and palm fronds. The metal urn was at least four feet high and probably weighed upwards of two hundred pounds. Unless she could get one of the guys to stand still directly beneath it, it wasn't going to do her much good. A discreetly placed wall fire extinguisher had been removed. But the standing ashtray container looked nice and solid. . . .

They crossed a marble floor and the elevator banks. Two easy chairs, a sarcophagus, more heavy urns, more wilted flowers. Her bare feet hit carpet again. Clearly they were heading way the hell and gone to the other end of the building. Who else was on this floor? Just them and Raazaq's people?

Despite the intentional racket she'd made, and she'd shrieked and fought like a madwoman, no one had popped their heads out of a door to see what was going on.

So much for chivalry.

To hell with curiosity.

She was on her own.

At the end of the interminably long corridor, the apes pushed open the double doors to an opulent suite and shoved her inside.

Fazur Raazaq.

No surprise.

Her guards strong-armed her across the boldly patterned carpet to stand in front of their boss, who lounged on one of the leather sofas like a sultan. There were five other men, including the redheaded kid, in the room, staring at her like they'd never seen a naked woman covered in blood before, bringing the total *them* count to nine.

Ten—including Raazaq—to one.

Not easy, but do-able, AJ thought, her brain going a mile a minute. She'd done that training exercise with fifteen guys. Managed to take out nine of them before they killed her. She'd take this much more seriously.

The men wore what appeared to be the uniform du jour. Black pants, white shirt, sweat, and a Ruger in a brown leather shoulder holster.

She was *way* underdressed.

Lifting her chin and ignoring his men, AJ gave Raazaq a narrowed-eyed glare. "Hello, Fazur," she said coolly. "This is a surprise. But I really don't think we know each other well enough for me to be standing in front of you naked."

She did nothing to cover herself. There was no point. They'd all seen everything there was to see. Not that they weren't still looking, God only knew. As a distraction to the enemy, being dragged in naked was pretty effective. They should include nudity in the T-FLAC handbook.

She stood relaxed, hands at her sides. Like

the Emperor, AJ pretended she was fully clothed and armed. She had to pretend very hard.

While none of the men made any overt move—after all, their boss was sitting right there—six out of nine men were looking at her as though she was the last steak on a starving planet. The thought sent a shudder of revulsion through her.

She couldn't have been more vulnerable if she'd tried.

The redheaded kid who'd felt her up earlier stood at half-assed attention beside the sofa where Raazaq lounged. Scarlet-faced, but unable to avert his gaze from her boobs, he stepped behind the sofa. Blushing even harder when he caught her glancing at him. AJ didn't bother making eye contact with the others, but she kept them in her peripheral vision.

Raazaq's suite was about forty by sixty, filled with fine furniture and authentic-looking knickknacks. Behind the grouping of three white leather sofas and various coffee and side tables, a teak dining room table, seating for at least twelve, stood in front of a bank of windows facing the front of the hotel.

There were dozens of objects AJ could use as weapons, if given half a chance. However, she was more interested in the weapons Raazaq's men carried.

Raazaq snapped his fingers twice to get her attention. Both arms spread on the back of the sofa where he sat, he watched her from opaque, black eyes when AJ brought him back into focus. He wore a black suit, despite the sweltering heat in the room, and a white shirt and old school tie.

He was the only man in the room not sweating.

"What are you doing here, Miss Cooper?" Raazaq's tone was hard and uncompromising. He wasn't trying to charm her now.

"Why don't you ask your trained gorillas? They *dragged* me here," she snapped. "How dare you send these Neanderthals to break into my room? They killed Kane! Do you know that? They *killed* him. In cold blood." *Fear into anger. Fear into anger.* "They shot him right in front of me! And to add insult to injury, they *abducted* me!" Her voice rose. "How *dare* you!"

Raazaq rose from his relaxed position on the sofa, nodded to the two men holding her. They instantly released her. She didn't step back, but oh, God, she wanted to. She looked the monster straight in the eye as he circled the coffee table and came to stand in front of her. The acrid-sweet smell of his cologne made her eyes smart. And the glitter of emptiness in his made her bones want to shrink. It took everything in her to stand still and not attempt to cover herself.

"I repeat," Raazaq said flatly, "what are you and your boss doing here, Miss Cooper?"

AJ rubbed her upper arms where his men's fingers had dug into her flesh and gave the terrorist a cold and haughty look. "I refuse to have a conversation with you while I'm standing here with no clothes on."

"I repeat—"

"And *I* repeat—"

Raazaq backhanded her across the face. AJ gasped involuntarily as her head whipped to one side. Pain blasted through her brain as stars burst in front of her eyes. She was fortunate he hadn't used his fist. Hand to her stinging cheek, AJ staggered from the force of the blow.

Son of a bitch.

Outrage poured through her and AJ came within a heartbeat of head-butting the little bastard, then beating the crap out of him. *Stay in character, losing your temper now could lose you the war.* Damn it, if Kane was alive, then she was going to do whatever she had to to get to him.

But first she'd do the job she'd been dispatched to Egypt to accomplish.

She lifted her head and touched her hot cheek. "Do you have any idea how much my face is worth?"

"Answer the question."

"Our car broke down," she told him, keeping eye contact. "We walked."

"Did you follow me here?"

AJ rolled her eyes and gave a mocking laugh. "My God, you're conceited. We only shared one dinner together, Fazur. I don't usually risk my life to see a man a second time. I don't have to. Men walk across blazing deserts for *me*, honey. Not the other way around. So get over yourself. And while you're doing that, get me something to wear."

His black eyes ran slowly down the length of her. The small hairs on the back of AJ's neck prickled and her heart thudded in slow, heavy beats that made her feel as though each one were her last.

"Is any of that your blood?" he asked, his tone cool. He was standing too close for comfort. AJ could feel the heat of his body, and smell his breath. Sen-Sen. His dark eyes glittered almost feverishly.

AJ thought of the little girls Raazaq had killed last month. Of the hundreds and thousands of people whose lives he'd irreparably altered by his acts of terror over the years. And now the son of a bitch had something bigger, more terrifying planned.

Not this time. She was here to stop him, and stop him she would. Taking him down was going to be her pleasure.

"No. I just explained that to you," she said flatly. "It's Kane's. Your men shot him, remember? My God, I knew when I took this assignment that I was coming to a somewhat violent area of the world, but I never imagined I would witness a killing."

She studied him closely and noted the tiny smallpox scar right between his thick black brows. A good place to aim for, AJ decided.

"Yes, they shot him. Would you like to know why?"

"I'll guess because you told them to."

"I did. You really believe the man you work for was a photographer?"

"Of course he is. I've been standing in front of his camera for weeks. His photos are published in oodles of magazines. Surely even you have seen his work. I can't believe you had him murdered." She blinked, hoping she appeared shocked. In reality, she was battling the sting of impending tears. "What do you think he is?"

"Black ops."

"Black . . . ops? You mean, like a spy?" She rolled her eyes. "Oh, please. All you have to do is open a *National Geographic* for the answer to that. My God, you *are* paranoid, aren't you? Here's a news flash, Romeo. The second I can, I'm going to report you to the local authorities and have you locked up, where you belong."

He laughed lightly. It was a charming laugh. For a psychopath. "My dear Miss Cooper, I *am* the authorities. In less than four hours I will rule the world. I'm putting *myself* where I belong."

A psycho with a mission. "W-what do you mean?"

"Do you know who is in the hotel right now?"

Other than my President and the Queen of England? "Who?"

Raazaq rattled off the terrifyingly long list. "They are attending a secret peace summit here." He shrugged. "Or so they believe. Right now I hold their fate in my hands." He cupped his long-fingered hands together, and smiled.

The smile froze AJ's marrow. Christ. "Psycho" didn't even come close to describing this guy.

She forced a short laugh. "Right. Rule the world Monday, pick up dry cleaning Tuesday. . . ." She shook her head mockingly. "If you're gonna rule the world, think you could find me a towel first?"

She wished he'd step back at least a pace. He was right inside her comfort zone, and being naked and on display was starting to fray her nerves. "Unless you plan to haul the Queen and the President up here naked as well? Somehow I can't imagine Her Majesty into kink."

Raazaq studied her narrowed-eyed. Clearly he was damn proud of his plan and wanted her to be suitably impressed. "My hotel is spectacular enough to house presidents and queens, is it not? They were all delighted to accept the invitation to see my spectacular pyramid and resolve world peace at the same time. The fools." He laughed slyly. "I am a master puppeteer, manipulating people's lives with a flick of my hand. Did you not wonder why your car broke down?"

She shrugged. "I don't care why."

"Ah, but you should care. Because it is merely a sample of what I have at my disposal." Raazaq smiled that meaningless smile again. "With a push of a button, low level energy bursts were scattered throughout the region, bringing everything to a standstill."

When she didn't respond with awe and wonder, he sighed. "We are now as my people were centuries ago. And only I can bring the modern world back. I have many electrical engineers, scientists, and technology specialists at my behest. I wanted them to create a jamming device. One claimed it could not be done. I had his tongue cut out and fed it to him in large chunks until he choked to death." Raazaq paused long enough to blow out a dismissive breath.

"The others began working diligently to create such a device. I now have the ability to shut down anything electrical, mechanical . . . anything with moving parts. I did just that at precisely eighteen minutes past two Sunday morning."

"So you rule the world by stopping time with your little freeze ray. How lovely for you." She cocked her head and tapped her bare toes against the carpet impatiently. "A new toy. Has anyone ever suggested you get some counseling? Honestly, why would you want to stop cars from moving? You *like* walking in the desert? I want to wash and get some clothes on. Then I'm going to the authorities. I'm an American. You can't hold me here."

He frowned. Slightly. His forehead didn't so much as twitch. Vain son of a bitch must've had Botox.

"Don't you want to know *why* I wield such power?" he asked arrogantly.

"If I say yes, will it get me the hell out of

here?" *Hell, yes, I want to know. Brag away. Tell me so I can strategize and figure out how to stop you.* "I'm sure you're just dying to tell me."

"Are you aware that Russia is years ahead of your puny U.S. in chemical warfare agents? No, I see that you aren't. The arms-control treaties were nothing but a joke. For twenty-five years, thirty thousand scientists, engineers, and technicians—the top scientific talent in what was then the Soviet Union and Eastern Europe—created qualitatively new families of chemical and biological agents. Agents that are different from, and considerably more sophisticated than, mere nerve agents."

"If you say so. Kinda hard to believe that a country whose people can barely find work, or the money to feed their families, is wasting time and funds to make chemicals."

"To be sold to the highest bidder. That kind of money goes a long way to alleviate hunger. I couldn't let twenty-five years of excellent research by the world's most eminent scientists go to waste." He smirked, and AJ noticed the pulse in his throat throbbed harder.

He was getting more and more excited. More careless?

"My people appropriated one of the Soviets' most creative and inventive chemical agents en route to Iraq last week. It was easily done.

Easily transported." He gave a little hum of pleasure. The kind of sound AJ made when a particularly delectable piece of chocolate melted on her tongue.

"Such a small quantity," he murmured with satisfaction. "With such large rewards."

"W—" AJ suddenly found her mouth bone dry, and she had to pause to moisten her tongue. Even her spit had dried up. They'd suspected this, of course they had. But *seeing* and *hearing* this madman talk about releasing—

"What are you going to do with it? Killing the President and everyone else won't put you in charge. Every country represented here will have someone else to step directly into their shoes. In fact, I wouldn't be surprised if the Vice President is already in office and sending people here to kick your butt back to hell."

"Oh, they're coming," he said, unconcerned. "I expected and look forward to that. But by the time the troops arrive, my job will be done, and I'll reap the benefits from far, far away."

Which meant that his jamming device must be somewhere close by. Raazaq wasn't going to *walk* out of here. "So you're blackmailing all these countries *not* to kill their leaders? You really do need counseling."

"No, my dear Miss Cooper. I'm offering, for a very large sum of money, to sell them the antidote. It doesn't matter when help arrives. Half the people infected will die. A quarter will be so physically and mentally impaired that they'll wish they'd died, and the last quarter can walk away free and clear. Of course, they won't be aware that while they haven't been stricken, they will be carriers. Their body fluids will transmit the biological agent for perpetuity."

AJ felt the blood drain from her head. "Have you dispensed the agent already?" She realized that sounded more like a T-FLAC comment than a fashion model question. "I mean, I'm not in any danger, am I?"

He smiled. A lighthearted, open smile that made bile rise in the back of AJ's throat. "Possibly yes. Possibly no. Perhaps I'm enjoying the moment and prolonging my pleasure? Good things come to those who wait, they say. Are you wondering which group you'll fall into? Killing you at this moment would spoil that surprise, now, wouldn't it? No, I think you'll just have to wait and see which way the lottery will spin for you. Just like everyone else." He looked her up and down. "Or I can keep you safe, my dear."

"At what price?" AJ asked flatly. "No thanks."

His flat black eyes narrowed as he took a step

closer and lifted her chin with his open palm. "Who are you, Miss Cooper?"

"What do you mean who am I?" She frowned and tried to evade his hand. He grabbed her jaw and held her firmly. "I'm AJ Cooper. American citizen. You're scaring the hell out of me. *Stop it.*"

"Do you work for the American government, AJ Cooper?" His hand tightened and she heard the bones in her jaw pop.

"No," she said tightly, feeling a curl of panic wrap around the nerves in her stomach. "I most certainly do not."

He dropped his hand, but AJ still felt every one of his fingers on her skin. He walked back to his spot on the sofa and sat down. "Take her to the washroom, Halil," he instructed the redheaded kid, who was still purple as a beet and practically salivating, reminding AJ that she was still standing there naked in front of all these men.

She was suddenly so cold in the tropical temperature of the room that she'd started to shiver. "I don't need anyone coming with me. And I demand to call the American consulate."

AJ had visually measured the distance between herself and each man, weighing her odds of taking one down, grabbing his holstered weapon, and firing before one of the others got her first.

The odds were not in her favor.

Raazaq turned his head slightly as the red-headed Halil came around to grip her upper arm. "Go with her. Umit," he said to one of the other men standing nearby, "obtain suitable clothing for Miss Cooper from one of our female guests on the first floor."

He walked across the room to look out of the window. "Duman, Husad, go and check to be sure Mr. Wright is dead, then report back to me . . . at the other location. You. You. And you. Stay here. Don't let her leave the suite, unless I send someone for her."

"Yes, Kadir." The two men he was sending off to check on Kane all but bowed as they backed out of the room.

"You're leaving?" AJ asked, mind jumping.

As Raazaq strolled past her he ran his nail hard across her nipple. That little bit of cruelty was senseless, and so typical of the man. AJ bit her tongue and gave him a cold stare.

"I will send someone for you, my dear. I believe you are deserving of a front-row seat." He glanced back at the boy, Halil, who stood waiting. "Get her cleaned up. And watch her closely. If her boss isn't dead, we'll use her as bait and smoke him out."

Leaving the others behind, he followed the two goons from the suite.

"Ma'am?" The kid indicated the door to the bedroom.

"What's your real name?" AJ asked the young man as he followed her into a spacious, marble-lined bathroom. They'd had to enter through a bedroom and travel down a short hallway lined with mirrored closets to get to the bathroom, giving her jittery nerves a few moments to regroup.

There was only the one way in. And unless she were an anorexic midget she wasn't going to get through the only window in the room.

Well, hell. Wasn't this *inconvenient?*

A brief glance at herself showed a pale-faced woman with a wild, unruly mane of half-dried, curly red hair, bruised-looking eyes, and a naked body liberally splattered with blood.

Surprisingly, there wasn't as much as she'd thought. AJ grabbed a large, soft towel off the shelf and wrapped it around her body. Covered, she grabbed up a washcloth from the pretty ribboned display of toiletries on a gold-leafed tray and twisted on the gold hot-water faucet. The entire bathroom was mirrored.

She glanced at the boy in the reflection over the sink area as she wet and lathered the cloth.

"My name is Halil." He leaned a bony shoul-

der against the frame of the closed door and removed a big, very, *very* nice Ruger from an
underarm holster and held it loosely in his right
hand.

He'd shoot her if she made a move, AJ
thought, but he'd be sorry.

Of course, at this distance, and with that
much firepower, she'd be very dead, no matter
how apologetic he was.

"Your mother didn't name you Halil. What
is that, anyway? Egyptian?" AJ applied the
scalding-hot cloth to her face first.

"Turkish. Halil means 'dear friend,' " the
boy said proudly. "Kadir gave me my name."

"Who's Kadir?"

"You call him Fazur Raazaq."

"What does it mean? Why do you call him
that?"

"It's Turkish, and his birth name. It means
'strong, powerful.' Which is what he is." Hero
worship shone brightly in the kid's eyes.

"He calls you 'dear friend,' huh?" AJ said
conversationally. Turkish? Had they been
tracking Fazur Raazaq in Egypt for all these
years when they should've been looking else-
where? No wonder no one had ever been able
to find his bolt-hole! Shit. She had to tell Ka—
"Do you have parents back home?"

AJ turned her back, parted the covering

towel, and washed her torso. Rubbing at a particularly nasty blotch on her belly button, sickened to see Kane's blood on places that mere hours ago he'd been kissing and caressing.

"They are dead to me. I believe in Kadir's cause. *İnşallah,* we will crush the infidels."

"Uh-huh." AJ shot a glance at the tall, lanky kid who should be taking his girlfriend out for a burger and a movie instead of being here, in the middle of what was a world incident of terrifying proportions. "God does not will you to kill, Bobby."

"My name isn't Bobby."

Great. Skip right over the "kill" part, pal. "Then Ricky."

"Brian," he said with a small, crooked smile. Oh, God. He was so young. "But now I am Halil."

It was a hell of a long way from mid-America and baseball games to working for, and believing in, one of the world's most feared terrorists. AJ tried to remind herself that she was here for bigger problems than rescuing Opie and getting him back to Mayberry.

"Could you go out and see if they've found me any clothes yet?" She was damn sick and tired of being naked. *Really* tired of it. There were things to find, and a man to kill. She'd prefer doing it fully clothed. *And, sorry, pal, but I have to have that nice big gun of yours.*

"Sorry, ma'am. I was instructed to stay with you."

"But I have to use the toilet," AJ protested, looking suitably girlish and horrified.

He blushed harder. "I'll close my eyes," he offered.

"You'll hear me."

"No, ma'am." He turned to face the door. "I'll just stand here with my back turned and hum under my breath. Will that be all right?"

AJ sighed. Barring him leaving the room, standing with his back to her while he concentrated on humming was just fine and dandy with her. "Okay, but don't peek. Promise me."

"No, ma'am. Yes, ma'am. Go ahead." He started humming. Loudly.

Really, it was almost too easy to knock him out. AJ padded across the cold floor and raised both clenched hands. She struck the back of his neck. Textbook perfect. Halil/Brian dropped like a stone. "Sorry, Opie. A girl's gotta do what a girl's gotta do."

It wasn't quite as easy to roll and strip him, but with a fair amount of muscle, AJ managed to divest the kid of his shoes, pants, and shirt. She left him on the floor wearing his underwear, and quickly tied both his hands and feet, using his own socks. Before dressing, God only knew she wanted to give his clothing a chance to cool before she put them on, she grabbed a washcloth and the ribbon tying the toiletries in a pretty bow, and gagged him.

Heart pounding, not with fear but with anticipation, she dressed quickly. They were about the same height and the pants and shirt fit, the high-topped boots, sans socks, were a little big, but tying the laces tightly made them work.

Now, to get out of here. Through the bathroom, the bedroom, and take care of Raazaq's men.

Hell, piece of cake.

CHAPTER TWENTY-ONE

Kane observed them entering the suite from his position perched high on top of the armoire.

He was ready to get the jump on them. Literally.

He recognized them from earlier. Weapons drawn, expressions grim. They headed for the bathroom, where presumably they were to check his corpse.

Life was full of little disappointments.

He'd been leaving the suite when he'd spotted them coming down the corridor. As much blood as he'd lost, he wasn't enthusiastic about trying to take them out without weapons-fire alerting the others. Not until he had a second to shore up his wounds.

But with no other choice, he'd slipped back inside and scaled the biggest, highest piece of furniture. Which just happened to be the armoire they'd shoved aside to come in earlier.

He held his weapon in his left hand. Being ambidextrous was an advantage, as they'd caught his upper arm when they'd shot him. The bullet was through-and-through, taking a chunk of muscle from his right arm, and another healthy chunk from under his arm and at his back. It hurt like a son-of-a-bitch. He'd dressed, started a half-assed job of taking care of the wound, then run out of time.

The damn thing still bled copiously, soaking his nice clean shirt and incapacitating his right hand. He'd deal with it later.

His muscles bunched for the leap as they walked right below him. He pressed his left hand, the hand holding his weapon, over his wound so the blood didn't drip down on the white carpet and give away his position above them. Time to fly down and deliver a little justice of his own.

He checked himself as one started whispering to the other. They spoke Turkish.

Well, well.

They were discussing AJ's breasts. Which would thrill her to no end, Kane was sure. Good news: AJ was alive. Bad news: She was with Raazaq. Which should have been more good news. Hell.

The goons walked into the bathroom. Kane observed their inspection of the blood-splattered stall as glass crunched under their feet.

The bathroom wasn't that big—within seconds they tore out of there like their asses were on fire, and charged across the wide expanse of the sitting room. They were going to be in deep shit for leaving him behind in the first place. Kadir, whoever the hell *Kadir* was, was going to chop them into tiny pieces and have his grandmother serve them up in a casserole.

Fatty, Kane thought dispassionately as he took out the one on the left with a bullet to the brain, saving him from the stew pot. Hell. He was up here to avoid just such a noisy come-and-get-me confrontation. Blood from his multiple wounds made the butt of the gun slick in his hand as he shifted slightly to get the other man in the site. The gun slid out of his blood-covered fingers as if it had been greased, and went sailing across the room.

He launched himself off the armoire a split second later. The target goon was still looking around, puzzled, when Kane dropped from the sky and ruined his day.

The force of hitting him from that height took both men down to the blood-splattered carpet. The guy's weapon discharged as it spun from his hand as a result of the violent contact.

Kane hooked his elbow around the guy's bull neck from behind him, and twisted sharply. The man bellowed. He had muscles in his thick neck made of rubber, but Kane was working at it. The guy bucked, Kane held on, delivering a series of hook punches to the man's head, locking his legs around the guy's torso like he was riding one of his brother's bulls.

Raazaq's man was big, fast, and well trained. But Kane was bigger, faster, pumped full of rage and adrenaline, and already feeling like Superman on speed.

Forgetting the pain, he hooked his right elbow around the man's throat, keeping their bodies close together so the other man couldn't maneuver out of his hold. He clasped his hands together around the man's neck, and pulled the cutting edge of his useless right wrist upward with a jerk of his left hand, using the guy's own body as a block.

The man croaked and struggled, like an alligator thrashing in a sack.

Kane pulled his wrists in, hard against the guy's throat. The man gurgled, bucking and straining to break free. Kane controlled him with his legs tight around his back, and wrists around his throat. The guy wasn't at quite the right angle to have his neck broken, but Kane was working on it.

Kane drew the guy's head back where he wanted it with his left hand, then drove his right hand into his throat.

The man gagged. But he wasn't going down.

With a wild burst of strength, he surged to his feet like a breaching whale, taking Kane with him.

They both staggered to regain their balance, circling, feinting. Kane's weapon was right below the sofa across the room. Fat guy's was close to the body of his partner, eight feet away.

Kane didn't mind a bit of hand-to-hand when time warranted it. But he felt the urgency and need for speed right now. "Come on, you ugly bastard," he taunted in Turkish, "get the lead out. I have things to do and a lady to find."

The other man came at him with an uppercut to the jaw. Kane dropped his elbows into the oncoming punch, following up the movement with a left hook to the man's face, followed by a right. The guy roared, face red. Head down, he attempted, rather stupidly, Kane thought dispassionately, a head-butt.

Kane used the man's momentum to grab him by the back of the head, brought his knee up in a sharp and quick slam, and heard the man's nose crunch from the blow. He released his victim and let the guy slump to the floor.

His own pain hadn't kicked in yet. Adrenaline was a terrific analgesic, but he'd better rebandage himself before he bled to death. Then he needed to go rescue AJ.

He heard slow applause and spun around to see her leaning against the doorjamb. "Very nice," she said, strolling into the room and stepping over Goon Number One. "Messy, but very well executed. You have to teach me that ride-'em-cowboy move sometime."

Her voice was steady, but Kane noticed the rapid pulse at the base of her throat, and the way her pale-green eyes glittered. She wore Raazaq's uniform of black pants and white shirt, and somebody's combat boots. Interesting.

Her hand came up as if to reach for him, but after an infinitesimal hesitation, she tucked it into her pants pocket instead.

He didn't touch her. He wanted to too much. "You okay?"

"I'm not the one with the hole in me." Her smile was a bit lopsided. "You're bleeding on the carpet."

He ran a quick visual scan to be sure she was in one piece. "Raazaq have you?"

"Not biblically, that's for sure. I was taken to him, but he left the suite to go downstairs in preparation for meeting his guest. I managed to knock out the kid they sent into the bathroom with me and grabbed these." She plucked at the shirt and pants.

Kane raised a brow. "And he left you with one kid?"

"Nah. There were four of them. I took them out."

"But not Raazaq."

She bristled. "No," she said flatly. "I didn't take out Raazaq. Again."

"I wasn't criticizing you." Kane stepped over Goon Two, and picked up the guy's Ruger. AJ opened her mouth to speak, but he held up a hand. "Let's get into the stairwell before you fill me in. Appropriate the rest of their weapons before we split."

She nodded, crossed the room, gathered the weapons, and picked up her backpack. "Grab that one's shirt." She pointed to the other attacker. "He doesn't smell quite as bad as this one. Hang tight, I'll be right back." She disappeared into a bedroom, and came back with a pillowcase in her hand. She put it up to her mouth and ripped at it with hands and teeth. Apparently to tear bandages.

"Let's go." She took up her own weapon, which was still where Kane had left it by the bathroom door earlier. Shrugged on the pack, checked the other weapons, tucked them into her waistband, and crossed the room to look out the window. "Oh, shit, shit, shit. They're going."

He had a pretty good idea, but didn't ask who and to where. Not yet. Not until they were clear.

By the time she reached him, her breathing was normal, her pulse steady. "Ready to rock. I'll take care of that arm when we're secure. Stem the blood flow so we don't leave them a trail to follow."

"Yes, ma'am," he said tongue in cheek. She'd kept her cool, but he'd seen the horror shine in her eyes for a brief second when she'd seen the blood all over him. His estimation of her grit went up several more notches. He wasn't that fond of looking at blood himself.

All things considered, he'd like it a hell of a lot less if the blood were AJ's. He stepped cautiously out the door. The wide, dimly lit hallway was clear. For the moment.

Kane motioned AJ to stay behind him as he started out. They had six hundred feet to traverse to reach the stairs. Six hundred feet of nothing but shallow doorways to take protection in if Raazaq and his guards returned.

They ran toward the stairwell like bats out of hell. "Go. Go. Go."

They shoved open the door, and raced down three flights of stairs before Kane pulled her into a shallow doorway out of sight from above. "Give."

"Take off your shirt," she instructed briskly as she finished tearing the pillowcase into strips, wrapping his arm efficiently as she talked. "According to a deathbed confession, the biochemical agent is in a black leather briefcase. That's the only intel I have.

"Jesus God, Kane. You're a frigging sieve! Crap. Here, hold this. Tighter. Yeah, like that." She gnawed on another strip with her teeth, then tied it to the strip in his hand and slid her arms around his chest to wrap his torso. Her still-damp hair smelled of soap as she brushed his chest with her head.

"Whatever he's going to do," she said as she worried her lower lip with her teeth and inspected the gash on his underarm, "it's happening now. He's forcing everyone to gather inside the pyramid immediately. If they haven't evacuated the hotel in exactly one hour, he's promised to detonate explosives and bring the hotel down."

"Same deathbed confession?"

"Different guy. I always confirm my info from at least two sources." She grinned, then leaned back to inspect her handiwork.

"There," she said dryly. "That'll do you until you're rushed in for emergency surgery. The front courtyard is already packed with people."

"The sun's straight up and no one's watch

works, so that hour's timing is going to be iffy, to say the least," Kane said grimly.

"Nobody's stupid enough to go into a confined space." But they were caught between a rock and a hard place. "They'll evacuate the hotel, and get far enough away from the building, in case he does follow through with that threat," he speculated. "But they sure as hell won't go inside that pyramid. Won't happen." The other alternative was Raazaq spraying the biochemical over the conveniently gathered crowd outside. "Airborne dispersal?"

"Yes. He has the container stolen from that Russian shipment. And it's bad, Kane, *really* bad."

"Did he say what it was? Any clue? Damn it, I wish to hell we had contact with the outside world. By now they must know what he got hold of, and will be bringing the antigen with them."

AJ rubbed her upper arms and shivered. "No one will make it if he pulls this off. They'll—shit, *we'll* either die from it, carry it in our bloodstream, or be afflicted with God only knows what hideous symptoms." She shoved away from the wall. "Come on, we have to find that briefcase."

"*I'll* find the briefcase," Kane told her grimly. "You neutralize Raazaq."

Raazaq's plan was simple. He'd gathered everyone onto the front lawn of the hotel, where there was no overhead covering. It was early afternoon, and the hot, bright sun shone down relentlessly from a cloudless blue sky. Armed soldiers had systematically gone through the hotel and forced everyone out at gunpoint. Those that had refused had been summarily shot.

Now that everyone was evacuated, Raazaq appeared to be in no hurry for them to move the several hundred yards to the pyramid.

Which either meant he was arrogant enough to believe he had time before the troops arrived, or he was planning to disperse the chemical right here into the crowd.

And they all knew it.

The circular area was large enough to hold everyone and leave a hundred-and-fifty-foot swath around the circumference for Raazaq's people to patrol. Several hundred heavily armed men encircled the crowd, herding strays like cattle into containment. The tension in the air was palpable. Every time a group tried to move off to the side beneath the dubious, but better than nothing, protection of the trees, they were shoved back into the courtyard by Raazaq's elite guards.

More than two dozen men and women, se-

curity people, lay dead on the ground. Shot
when they'd attempted to take down one of the
armed men or tried to make a run for it.

Unarmed security teams kept small, tight
circles around their principals. But everyone
knew the gesture was useless.

Kane had ferreted out Walsh and given him
an update. Walsh had better news; one of his
men had returned from the desert to report
that a battalion of men was approximately ten
clicks away. Judging distance was iffy, but even
fifteen clicks away was better than Cincinnati.

The rest of Walsh's team had proceeded on
to meet the troops and fill them in on the status of the situation.

After conferring for a few more minutes,
Walsh melted back into the trees, and Kane
scanned the area for Raazaq, but he was
nowhere in sight. He spotted AJ on the far side
of the crowd.

She'd appropriated a baseball cap from somewhere, which she now wore, hair scrunched up
beneath it, as she prowled the perimeter of the
milling and silent crowd, with Raazaq's people.
If she kept her face down and didn't make eye
contact, she'd pass as one of them. If a man
didn't know every inch of her luscious body.

From his vantage point on the steps leading
down to the enormous circular courtyard,

Kane tried to pick out the President and First Lady next. No matter what his feelings were for AJ, he had to trust her to do her job. Watching her every move was counterproductive.

He scanned the crowd. While the First Family was as exposed as the rest of the masses, their security people had done an excellent job blending them in with everyone else. If Raazaq was planning a strategic strike, he'd be hard-pressed to find individual targets. It was impossible to tell who was a key player and who was a bodyguard.

The white marble pyramid towered over the distant treetops and glinted milk-pale in the sunlight. Clearly the threat to get out of the hotel and gather inside the other structure had been a ruse to clear the hotel.

This was where Raazaq wanted everyone. Outside. In the open. Out in the hot sun. Perspiring. A perfect conductor for a viral agent to be rapidly absorbed through the skin.

Kane stiffened. "Jesus. The pyramid!"

He did a controlled speed walk down the steps and started for the perimeter. Running now would cause panic and confusion. But Christ, he needed to run.

He caught up with AJ on the far side of the

clearing near the tree line and grabbed her upper arm. "Come with me."

She gave him a wide-eyed, startled look as
she matched her long stride to his. "What's
happened?"

"Nothing. Yet."

"Then where are we g—"

"Raazaq is in the pyramid. It's the only place
that he and his key people will be safe from the
viral agent. They can't leave the area any more
than we can."

Weapons drawn, they slipped into the
wooded area between the hotel and pyramid.
"Then why did he want everyone to go inside?" AJ checked the clip in each of the
Rugers as she speed walked. Kane knew she'd
checked them several times already. But this
was show time. She wasn't going to chance
anything going wrong now.

As soon as they lost sight of crowd, they
started running. A winding path lined with
grasses meandered between the dense shade
trees up a slight rise. It was marginally cooler in
the shade, but not much.

"Son of a bitch doesn't *want* them inside the
pyramid," Kane told her, not releasing her hand
as they ran. "He knew nobody would follow
that order. He counted on it. He wants them
out in the open. Sweating. Unprotected."

"They're out there like lambs to slaughter— Jesus God, Kane." Her feet hesitated, but Kane yanked her along with him, keeping her moving. "We have to go back. Warn the—"

"Walsh is working on it, if they haven't figured it out by now themselves. We have our jobs, he has his."

They ran the long mile silently, until they finally reached the shadow of the pyramid. The path widened slightly, leading them to a low, narrow doorway overhung with shrubs and long grasses—clearly intentionally left that way for atmosphere, as the rest of the path had been cleared for foot traffic.

AJ looked up, and up. The pyramid was huge, at least five stories high. The twenty-ton blocks of white stone were smooth, and tightly interlocked, and rose in a direct line into the heavens, stark creamy-white against the blue of the sky.

The pyramid itself was a work of art, priceless in its antiquity, a testament to man's creativity. It had stood here for over two thousand years. Or had it? Was it, too, part of Raazaq's devious plan?

Either way, AJ wondered if it would survive today.

She used both hands to cup her weapon and stepped into the opening.

The temperature immediately dropped twenty degrees. There was enough light streaming in from the outside to show their way down a flight of rough-hewn steps descending at an angle of approximately twenty-five degrees. The ceiling sloped thirty feet above them as they raced silently down the stairs, their feet almost silent on the hard stone. A metal handrail and small recessed lights led the way down, disappearing into what looked like a black hole.

It got progressively darker as they left behind sunlight and fresh air and came to the bottom of the stairs, into a small chamber. Discreet spotlights illuminated unblemished walls of hieroglyphics. Clearly there was a generator or other power source here. Something not affected like everything outside this building.

The room smelled faintly musty, but there was also the pungent stink of sweat, and the sharp, acrid-sweet smell of Raazaq's cologne.

He's here, AJ signed. She indicated across the chamber to the ascending staircase.

Kane nodded, pointed to their boots. They undid laces and tugged off their footwear. At this point they needed every element of surprise open to them. Barefoot was quieter. AJ tucked their boots and socks out of sight behind a labeled display of baskets and small bottles.

They started up the stairs. Past the mammoth stone that was marked to indicate it had been moved to reveal the ascending passage at the time of discovery.

AJ's heart raced as her feet padded up the cool steps. At the top of these stairs, or in the next chamber, was Fazur Raazaq. She was going to do her job and rid the world of a monster.

She halted when Kane grabbed the back of her shirt, then quickly spun around. *What?* she demanded with raised eyebrows.

You go back, he signed, *get people to safety. I'll finish here.*

She froze, stunned, one foot on the next step. She stared at him. He signed again. *Go back. I'll finish.*

He didn't trust her to do the job. Or do the job right.

Jesus God. The knowledge struck a blow to her heart. Ego. Struck a blow to her *ego.* After all they had been through . . . all they'd shared . . . *No way in hell!* AJ mouthed silently, shrugging off his restraining hand and spinning to race up the stairs.

Time was running out, she could practically hear the sand pouring out of an old-fashioned hourglass. *And he wanted her to go back?*

She felt his hand on her again, and angrily

shrugged it off. He grabbed her arm and spun her around and she tumbled several steps down to stand just above him.

Let me go, you dumb-ass, she mouthed, fury whipping through her blood like a forest fire. *What the hell do you think you're doing?* She pushed at his shoulders. The stairwell was only a yard wide, the stone on either side of them dark with damp. The smell of Raazaq's cologne surrounded them.

They were eye to eye.

AJ shoved again, but this time Kane grabbed her face in both hands.

And kissed her.

The act shocked AJ so much, she almost screamed out loud in sheer surprise. What the hell was he thinking? The kiss was over almost before it had begun. Puzzled by the rage and desperation in the ill-timed kiss, she braced her hands on his chest.

"Wha—"

Be careful, he mouthed as he brushed his finger down her cheek. His hands were warm. Her skin, cold. AJ paused there for half a heartbeat, then nodded and took off up the stairs. She could hear the faint shush of Kane's bare feet running lightly behind her.

They emerged silently into a larger room at the top of the stairs. The Queen's Chamber, AJ would bet. It was lavishly decorated with hieroglyphs embossed and painted in vibrant colors, highlighted with gold. Across the marble floor lay a gold sarcophagus. The lighting here was soft and almost dreamy. Artificial palm trees, replete with dates, swept up to the unblemished limestone-gabled ceiling.

AJ pointed to one of three side corridors. Touched the tip of her nose and pointed ahead. *Follow his smell.*

Kane nodded.

The first corridor smelled flat and faintly musty. The second, blocked by a long-ago rockfall that had yet to be excavated. The third corridor—like the story of Goldilocks and the Three Bears—was just right.

Raazaq's cologne. Bingo.

It felt to AJ as though slow, *agonizingly slow,* hours had passed since she and Kane had entered the pyramid. But logic told her they'd taken less then ten minutes to sprint through the staircases and rooms to get to this point.

Now the question was, were they in time to stop a madman?

CHAPTER TWENTY-TWO

There was a metal door at the top of the stairs. Titanium by the look of it. The dull surface gleamed in the glow of the small, recessed lights on either side. Hardly part of the original decor. Someone had done some serious remodeling.

Weapon locked and loaded, AJ looked at Kane with raised brows. How the hell were they going to get inside undetected?

He indicated she cover him, crouched down, ran his fingers carefully around the paper-thin crack. A crack so fine, not a glimmer of light from the room beyond shone through. He ran his hands around, all the way around. Twice.

No handle, no keypad. No way in. Other than the faint sound of AJ's breath, Kane couldn't hear a damn thing. If Raazaq was inside the King's Chamber, then the room, the door, the fucking pyramid, were soundproof.

Christ. So near and yet so far. Nothing short of a nuclear blast was going to open that door.

May I? AJ mouthed politely, leaning over his crouched position. She rapped sharply on the door with her fist.

Kane rose to his feet. If it made her feel better to at-tempt . . . it—

The door slid slowly open.

Hot damn.

He shot her a quick glance. *Ready?*

A nod. Gleaming green eyes.

Weapons at the ready, they stepped into the room.

"Welcome, I've been waiting for you." Raazaq's voice was muffled inside the heavy white biohazard suit he wore.

Kane counted six other people suited up. No one seemed particularly concerned with their presence. But then, if he were the one holding a high-tech-looking laser gun, he would be pretty unconcerned, too.

"Shit," AJ whispered beside him.

That about covered it.

Bright white sterile walls, chrome, steel, computers blipping, monitors flashing. The King's Chamber had been converted into a lab.

"Impressive, *evet?*" Raazaq motioned several of the men forward to divest Kane and AJ of their weapons.

"Yeah, it is," Kane said dryly. On the wall above a bank of TV monitors, red numbers on three small digital clocks ticked away the count-down. One read nine minutes, two seconds. The next read zero. The third, four minutes, eighteen seconds. "Too bad we don't have time to admire your handiwork."

His eyes on Kane, Raazaq said to AJ, "So I was right, Miss Cooper. Your friend is *not* what he seemed. And clearly I underestimated *you*. Now, please to give your guns to my men, both of you. Any small spark at this point and you would go . . . *pouf*."

"But then, so would you," Kane pointed out, shaking his head no as two men approached them to relieve them of their weapons. The men hesitated, looking to Raazaq for direction.

Kane felt a slight brush of air against his back as the door closed silently behind them.

Four minutes, fourteen seconds.

If the clocks indicated what Kane believed they indicated, one batch of the virus had already been dispersed. They had four minutes and . . . eleven seconds . . . to stop the next one.

"Hand over your weapons or I will shoot the girl." Raazaq took one of the futuristic weapons from his men. It looked small and deadly in his gloved hands. Kane had never seen anything like it. He had no idea what the weapon could do, and he didn't particularly want to find out.

"Go for it," he said coldly, not looking back at AJ to see her reaction to his offer. He shifted his feet slightly to stand in front of her. "You'll be doing me a favor."

"Excuse me," she said indignantly, stepping forward and around him to give him a hard punch to his good shoulder. "Don't *I* get a vote?"

He pushed her back, flat of his hand to the middle of her forehead. Not lightly. *Get behind me, damn it.* "Lady, you've been a thorn in my side, and a pain in my ass, for days. I'd shoot you myself if I didn't object to wasting the bullet." He moved away from her, crossing the room while Raazaq's men grinned from behind their faceplates.

Four minutes, eight seconds.

"You low-life, unchivalrous bastard!" AJ shrieked. The baseball cap flew off her head, strands of red hair trailed behind her like a flaming banner as she charged him.

Fully entertained now, Raazaq's men started to laugh.

Kane sidestepped at the last minute. AJ kept going, hit Raazaq full force with the hurtling weight of her body, and took him to the floor in a tangle of arms and legs so perfect, so classic, Kane almost applauded. Damn, she was good.

He didn't wait to see who was where. He left Raazaq to AJ. There were a few other problems for him to deal with.

Three minutes, forty-nine seconds.

AJ thumped her butt down hard on Raazaq's chest, pressed her knees into his shoulders, and placed her feet on top of his flailing hands to subdue him. She pressed the barrel of the Sig over the faceplate, directly in line with the smallpox scar in the middle of his forehead. He bucked. She pressed down harder with her knees, leaning her entire weight into it. While he tried to twist and buck his way from beneath her, AJ used one hand to fumble for the fastenings on the helmet protecting Raazaq's brain from her bullet.

One of the men raced over, grabbed her with an arm about the throat, and tried to yank her up and off. AJ shot out her arm, slamming the heel of her hand up into his balls. Bio-hazard suit or not, the guy felt it. He gave a high-pitched scream, fell to the floor, rolled around in a fetal ball, clutching himself, and screamed like a girl.

Three minutes, thirty seconds.

"Now, where were we?" AJ rode Raazaq's bucking body like a barrel racer as she struggled to remove his head-covering one-handed while maintaining her balance.

Encumbered by the bulky biohazard suit, he couldn't maneuver as quickly or as efficiently as she could, but he sure as hell tried. Bucking and squirming, he screamed for his men to get the crazy bitch off him. AJ finally managed to fumble the helmet off, and flung it aside.

She pressed the barrel of the Sig hard between his eyes. "Let me get rid of this ugly scar for you."

She averted her head—

"Nooo!"

—and pulled the trigger.

Two minutes, eleven seconds.

Covered in his blood, AJ jumped off Raazaq's lifeless body and raced to assist Kane, stepping over the guy on the floor who was sobbing and screaming, still clutching his balls.

Kane was doing fine on his own. Three men lay dead, a fourth looked like he was trying to crawl into a monitor headfirst, a fifth was circling Kane, and number six slumped against the closed door, either dead or unconscious.

One minute, fifty-two seconds.

AJ raced to the bank of monitors and panels of flashing lights across the room. What to do? What the hell to do? Crap, she'd never been very good with computers. She stared at the rows of buttons. Some lit, some not.

Looked up at the digital clocks on the wall.

One minute, thirty-eight seconds.

She fired into the console, then stood, feet braced, arms extended, and emptied the entire clip into the beeping, flashing mass of confusion.

The room went completely dark.

In seconds, flames exploded from a hundred different places as wires shorted and connections broke.

"Haul ass, Aphrodite Jacintha," Kane shouted from the door. "This place is gonna blow!"

AJ spun around to stare at him. "What did you say?"

"I said, haul ass! Come on!"

She looked over her shoulder. By the fire's light, she saw the timer had stopped at one minute, eleven seconds.

Had it worked?

Please, God. *Had it worked?*

AJ didn't stay to find out. Spinning on her heel, she charged across the room, jumped a couple of bodies, and raced to-ward Kane.

He jerked open the door, grabbed her hand, and pulled her after him, slamming the heavy door behind them. They raced down the stone steps together in the pitch dark. A shout and shot from behind them were cut off by an agonized shriek. Smoke billowed overhead through the now-open door. The noxious cloud chased them down the stairwell, thick and cloying. It whirled in their passing and whipped along just a breath behind them. They heard the *snap-crackle-pop* as the flames grew and fed on Raazaq's state-of-the-art lab.

"*Go! Go! GO!*" Kane shouted, hauling AJ behind him, his fingers like an iron clamp around hers.

God, it was dark, the air almost too thick to breathe. They both hacked and coughed as they raced through the blackness. Raced for their lives.

They skidded around a sharp corner. *Slam!* AJ's shoulder bounced hard into an invisible wall; without a pause she pushed off it and kept going.

Through the Queen's Chamber, down the corridor, down another flight of stairs, the fire hot on their backs now. Hot air pushing at them. Flames licking at the ceiling. Sucking up oxygen. Hard to breathe. Harder to see.

Fifty-two seconds, she counted off in her head. Fifty-one.

Down the stairs, along another corridor. Down the next flight. AJ's breath wheezed from her burning lungs.

Faster. Faster. Faster.

The fire raced them to the oxygen outside.

The powerful stench of burnt hair, fried electrical components, incinerated plastics stung her nostrils.

Tears streamed down her cheeks. Couldn't see anything, anyway. Throat raw. The only sane thing, Kane's hand, strong and sure gripping hers as they flew across the stone floor.

The stairs trembled and shook beneath their bare feet.

Kane was practically pulling her arm out of the socket, but AJ wasn't about to complain. She was running flat-out, but he was still faster.

He missed a step, tripped down several of them, had to hop, skip, and jump to regain his balance, then righted himself and continued on. "Faster, damn it!" he yelled. "Faster!"

A square of sunlight. The exit. Straight ahead.

Thank God.

Kane hauled her the last few feet, then pushed her outside ahead of him just as an ominous creaking groan rent the air.

"Move it!" He shoved her hard. "*Go. Go. Go.*"

AJ staggered, then turned back to grab his arm. "What the hell are you doing? *Come on.*"

"I'll be right behind you."

"No." AJ grabbed his hand in both of hers. "Togethe—Oh, God. Your ankle?"

Is broken. "It's fine. Move it, Cooper. Just fucking move it!"

AJ grabbed his arm and slung it around her neck, hand dangling over her shoulders. She held on to his fingers tightly. "I don't go anywhere without you."

Leaning heavily on her, because he had no choice, Kane ran in an agonizing hobble, skip. "Stubborn woman."

"Obstinate man." The grip she had on his hand was so tight, it cut off his circulation. Jesus. What a woman.

Down the path. Winding—shadow, sunlight, shadow, sunlight. Dancing black spots. White-hot pain. Fear like he'd never known before. *AJ. Jesus, AJ. Got to get her to safety.* He ran faster. Shadow, sunlight, shadow, sunlight.

He stumbled badly. She held him up.

"You can do it. You can. Just a little bit farther. Almost there." AJ kept up a panting litany as they stumbled and fumbled their way as fast as they could.

Christ. Not fast enough.

Billows of black smoke filled the air. He felt enormous heat on his back.

It was going to blow. The whole damn thing was going to blow.

"Faster," he croaked. "Faster, for Christ sake!" Sweat popped out on his forehead and black spots danced in his vision. He staggered as the white-hot pain lanced from his ankle directly to spear his brain. His knees buckled. He almost dragged AJ to the ground with his dead weight, but she grit her teeth and pushed him upright again.

He tried to unhook his arm.

Her short nails dug into his hand and she hitched her shoulder. "I'm . . . not . . . done . . . with . . . you . . . yet!" she panted, dragging him along willy-nilly. "Come on, Wright, you lily-livered sissy-pants! Suck it up and move your ass, damn it!"

They burst through the trees at the bottom of the hill.

Into chaos.

People were screaming, crying, running around like chickens with their heads cut off as they panicked after the fact. The crowd was in full-blown survival mode as security personnel raced their people back into the hotel and out of the way of falling debris.

"Just a little farther. You can do it, you can do it." AJ panted, all but carrying him. Kane outweighed her by at least eighty pounds. He wondered if AJ was even aware of just how much of his weight she was bearing as they stumbled across the lawn.

Raazaq's men were fleeing for safety just as fast as everyone else.

They were a hundred yards from the front doors when the ground moved beneath their feet.

Kane flung himself at AJ, taking her down to the buckling lawn, where he covered her body with his own and pressed her flat. There was a sudden, expectant silence—

Then all hell broke loose.

Sand shifted as it had for centuries. As if driven by an earthquake, the ground bucked and twitched with the explosion. The white marble pyramid imploded in a mile-high white mushroom cloud. Flames and thick black smoke licked at the sky for hundreds of feet.

Kane buried his face in AJ's neck, covering her head with his arms as best he could.

It was over quickly. He waited several minutes before he looked up.

"You're squishing me!" AJ wiggled beneath him.

"Stay where you are." Kane flinched when he moved. The leg hurt like a son of a bitch.

"What? Did something get you?" She squirmed more aggressively. "Damn it, Kane, I should be the one on top, protecting you. You're the one who's hurt!"

Kane shifted off her back, and started laughing.

The sound of aircraft filled the air. Panting, drenched with blood and sweat, they rolled over, looked up.

The cavalry had arrived.

"Is that the prettiest sight you've ever seen?" AJ gasped, staring up at the Harrier jet fighters followed by Blackhawk helicopters coming in to land.

It was a good sight—hell, even a *great* sight. "No."

She rolled her head to look at him. "No?"

"No. *You're* the prettiest thing I've ever seen. Your face after we made love on that voyeur camel was incredible. You sitting on Raazaq's chest was pretty damn spectacular. Hell, watching you eat an orange fired my jets. *Those* are the prettiest sights I've ever seen." He grinned, lacing his fingers with hers and bringing their joined hands to his lips.

"In fact," he said, kissing her fingers, "*any* view with you in it is the prettiest sight I've ever seen."

Her eyes brimmed with tears.

Oh, crap. "That's a bad thing?"

AJ flung herself on top of him. "No, you crazy, wonderful man, that's a *wonderful* thing. I love you. I love you. I love you."

"Thank God," he said with heartfelt relief. "I was afraid I was going to have to take you off somewhere and hold you prisoner until you admitted it."

"It wouldn't've taken long," she said, nibbling a path from his chin to his lips. "You fulfilled the gypsy curse."

"The gyp—I guessed your name?" He tried to look surprised. "No way. Which one was it?"

"Never mind. Hurry up and kiss me, would you?"

Kane threaded his fingers through her hair. "With pleasure, Aphrodite Jacintha, with pleasure." He pulled her head down and crushed his mouth to hers.

She punched him even while she was fully engaged in kissing him back.

"Hey, Coop? If Wright's bothering you that badly, get off him," a laughing voice suggested. "Geez, you two, do you know how much trouble your disappearance caused?"

"Go 'way, Hawk," AJ muttered, not looking up. "I have this man in custody."

"Well, yeah. We can see that. But you might want to take a quick look around before you interrogate him further."

AJ lifted her head. "Oh, crap," she whispered, meeting Kane's amused gaze.

They were surrounded.

Killian, McBride, Tariq, Christof, Wondwesen, and Hawk circled them. Between their legs, AJ observed uniformed military personnel pouring onto the scene. She was suddenly aware of the noise. Aircraft, vehicle engines, men shouting. It was pandemonium. People and camels raced about, vehicles drove across the lawns and flower beds. A jeep swung down from the sky, suspended by a military-green parachute, to land a few feet away. Then another. And another. The sky was filled with the noise of approaching aircraft and the ground with the roar of four-wheel-drive vehicles.

Ari Tariq reached out a hand to help her up. "Jesus," he said, looking her up and down, then swung around to check out Kane. "Which one of you is bleeding like a stuck pig?"

"Neither." Kane grinned, allowing McBride to haul him to his one good foot, where he stood balancing precariously. "AJ took out Raazaq. It was a beautiful sight to behold."

"Excellent. We'll hang on your every word over a brew later," Tariq said. "In the meantime, you two have a line of people waiting to talk to you. Coop, you go ahead. They're waiting for you in the dining room. We'll send this one in after he's patched up."

"Who's waiting?" AJ hugged her success to

her. The guys were treating her like one of them. She'd completed her mission—and Kane Wright, by damn, *loved* her.

"Justice Department, Secret Service, and our people—Other odds and ends."

AJ pushed her hands through her hair and tried to clean herself up. Impossible. If nothing else, she was still covered with Raazaq's blood. She grimaced.

Christof pulled his gray T-shirt over his head. "Here," he said, blushing. "It was clean this morning. Take a moment to wash up and ditch those clothes before you go in, if you want."

"Bless you." She took the blond giant's shirt. Her gaze flickered to the team. "His ankle's probably broken, and he's got a hole that needs stitches, somewhere other than his hard head. Take good care of him, please, you guys."

"You gonna marry that girl?" Hawk asked conversationally as the men watched her walking away with unqualified appreciation.

"The minute I can walk down the aisle," Kane assured him. He closed his eyes. "Is she inside?"

"Yeah, wh—" Killian asked, and turned just in time to break Kane's fall as he passed out. "Aw, shit!"

"Wuss," Wondwesen said affectionately,

helping support the fallen man. "Let's get him to the field hospital so they can patch up his owie before his Amazon sees him like this."

"Man, that is one lady I wouldn't want to mess with," Killian said, getting a hold of Kane's shoulders.

"Yeah," McBride said with a wide grin. "Join the crowd."

"What the—" Kane said, opening his eyes. He blinked AJ into focus.

"You fainted," she said cheerfully from her seat on the edge of his bed. Her face was scrubbed clean, her eyes sparkled, and she appeared to be wearing nothing more than another man's shirt.

"I did *not* faint."

"Yes," she said, stroking his face with cool hands, "you did."

"Lost consciousness," he corrected, surreptitiously looking her over for damage. "Where are we?"

"In the hotel. They gave us a nice fresh suite to stay in for the next week or so."

"Quarantine?"

"Yep. As far as they could ascertain, only one vial of the virus was released. And they're hoping that it was inert without the other agents being released to mix with it. But they don't know for sure. So no one leaves until the twelve-day incubation period is over. We're here for the duration."

There'd been grumbles and groans about that. But not many. People were too glad to be alive. And most of them were still scared, so they weren't going to protest too much. Besides, here they had a pool of the world's finest virologists and viral specialists. The best medical personnel, the best antidotes, the best physicians.

From the President of the United States down to the most junior busboy, everyone, without exception, was under quarantine.

She brushed Kane's hair out of his eyes. "How do you feel?"

"Like I have a whopping big cast on my leg."

She grinned. "Good, you won't be able to run."

Kane hooked his palm behind her head. "I'm not going anywhere." He brought her face down to his and kissed her. "I love you, AJ," he said against her lips. "I love you more than I ever dreamed it was possible to love."

"Good," she said briskly, sitting up. "Because I have a proposition for you."

"A proposition? Not a proposal?"

"I'll handle one, you handle the other."

"Yes, ma'am."

"There's an opening for operatives to work as a couple. Did you know that?"

"There is?" he asked, straight-faced. Jesus. This woman was going to lead him a merry dance; she was going to give him prematurely gray hair and a life filled with joy. He couldn't wait.

"Yes. There is. So I was thinking—"

"Angina?"

"What?"

Kane laughed, grabbed her, and held her tight against his body, then kissed her long and hard and deep, since it was the only way he could think of to shut her the hell up.

When he finally let her up for air, he looked down into her eyes—something he planned on doing every day for the rest of his damn life— and said, "So? You gonna marry me, or what?"

"Oh," her smile was radiant, "*now* it's my turn to talk?"

"One-word answer."

"Yes."

Kane grinned and pulled her back into his arms, where she belonged. "That's the one."